LIGHTNING MEN

THOMAS MULLEN

ABACUS

First published in the United States in 2017 by Atria,
an imprint of Simon & Schuster, Inc
First published in Great Britain in 2017 by Little, Brown
This paperback edition published in 2018 by Abacus

1 3 5 7 9 10 8 6 4 2

Copyright © Thomas Mullen 2017

The moral right of the author has been asserted.

A CIP catalogue record for this book
is available from the British Library.

ISBN 978-0-349-14310-1

Printed and bound in Great Britain by
Clays Ltd, St Ives plc

Papers used by Abacus are from well-managed forests
and other responsible sources.

Abacus
An imprint of
Little, Brown Book Group
Carmelite House
50 Victoria Embankment
London EC4Y 0DZ

An Hachette UK Company
www.hachette.co.uk

www.littlebrown.co.uk

Thomas Mullen's *The Last Town on Earth* was named Best Debut Novel of 2006 by *USA Today*, and he was also awarded the James Fenimore Cooper Prize for excellence in historical fiction for *The Many Deaths of the Firefly Brothers* and *The Revisionists*. His works have been named to Year's Best lists by *The Chicago Tribune* and *USA Today*, among others. His stories and essays have been published in *Grantland*, *Paste*, and the *Huffington Post*, and his *Atlanta Magazine* true crime story about a novelist/con man won the City and Regional Magazine Award for Best Feature. He lives in Atlanta with his wife and sons.

ALSO BY THOMAS MULLEN

The Last Town on Earth

The Many Deaths of the Firefly Brothers

The Revisionists

Darktown

For Susan Golomb and Rich Green

It is like writing history with lightning.
> President Woodrow Wilson, admiringly,
> after watching the Ku Klux Klan
> propaganda film *The Birth of a Nation*

Any candid observer of American racial history must
acknowledge that racism is highly adaptable.
> Michelle Alexander, *The New Jim Crow*

The tunnel is long and dark, and though his feet are moving it feels like he is being pulled by some other force, and then the tunnel recedes and he is alone before the vastness of the Georgia sky. To his right in a lavender glow swirl wisps of indigo cloud that surely will dissolve once the sun rises. To his left is darkness. He feels poised there, on the edge of night and day, on the cusp of summer and fall, because the morning is so much cooler than he'd expected. The shirt he's wearing is not sufficient, but at least it is his shirt, he remembers it from so long ago, and the reason it's too thin is because it was summer back when he was arrested, his clothes exchanged for a prison uniform. So long ago now. He stands there, shivering, taking in how tall the sky feels, how tiny he is, and it is just so amazing to be standing here alone that tears well in his eyes.

He walks slowly, because he does not want to limp on his first walk as a free man even though his right knee aches as it has for the last two years, since the fall at the bridge. He knows that his right shoulder carries higher than his left by a good inch or two, a result of the chain gang, swinging an ax until his very body was transformed.

He'd forgotten how it feels to walk in the outside world without hearing his wrists and ankles jingle. It is as though sound has been removed from his body, like some prophet has cast out the demon.

His old shirt fits loose around his slop-thinned waist but tight in the arms. He has crushed rocks and laid asphalt, he has built roads and repaired bridges, dug ditches and laid sewage pipes. He even assembled coops for poultry, not unaware of the irony that he was a prisoner building a prison for lesser creatures. He once killed a four-foot copperhead coiled beneath fallen leaves two autumns ago—or maybe it was three;

time moves in a haze now—by bringing the head of his shovel upon the beast's endless neck. He had later wondered at his own reflexes, thinking perhaps it would have been smarter to let the snake bite him, let it inject that poison into his veins so that in a few hours all this misery would pass. There had been days and nights he wished he'd done so. But now he feels differently, because those days and nights have fled and he has survived to see this breathtaking dawn.

The pants he's pretty sure aren't his. They fit his torso well enough, but they're three inches too short. They must have belonged to some other Negro prisoner, maybe someone who won't be out for years, so Jeremiah walks with the fall air chilling his ankles.

He hears birds calling even though the nearest tree is hundreds of yards away. He doesn't see any birds in the sky yet, though it's brighter now, the east a dark blue and the lavender shifting over to the cloudless west. The sun has peeked over the flat earth and Jeremiah has acquired a shadow, it is long indeed and with each step he takes, that giant shadow makes a mightier stride.

There had been a time when he'd thought he was through with God. He learned not to ask the Lord for release, not to ask for concrete and specific things—a visit from his beloved, or at least a letter—and instead to ask for the intangible. Calmness. Patience. The ability to make it to the next tomorrow. Walking slowly now, he thanks the Lord he'd briefly given up on, the Lord who'd not given up on him, the Lord who had seemed to inflict far too much wrong upon Jeremiah, so much wrong that it seemed beyond any mistake, beyond any difficult and inscrutable lesson, beyond anything but outright malice. Was God evil? Jeremiah had wondered in those first weeks in prison. That questioning has passed. He cannot help himself from saying, "Thank you, Jesus," saying it loud enough that someone would have heard him if he were not so alone.

He's walking faster now, the shock of the world's vastness fading only a bit, the unsettling aloneness, the lack of other people attached to him at either side, and though he does not know what he's walking toward, he knows he needs to get there, faster, his shadow keeping pace.

He's not even a quarter way down the wide dirt drive, the soles of his old shoes making faint impressions in the dawn-damp earth, when he turns around and gives the prison one last look. The limestone gleams white in the sharp-angled rays of the morning sun, American and Georgian flags hanging limp atop their poles. The prison is silent from out here, no buzzers or alarms or cries, no movement, indeed he's the only thing that seems alive, until a sudden twitch draws his eyes to a formerly motionless silhouette above. One of the guards with a rifle, looking down on him.

"Nigger, you'd best move a lot faster'n that!"

Jeremiah cannot help but increase his pace despite the shame of it, despite knowing that he is free and that the guard no longer owns him. He feels like an escapee, though he does not know what he is escaping into.

Georgia State Prison sits on the outskirts of Reidsville, or perhaps in the center of Reidsville, Jeremiah isn't sure, or maybe the problem is that Reidsville is the sort of place with no center, only outskirts, and anyhow Jeremiah had never before been outside Atlanta so he has no clue where he is.

The warden who'd handed him his old clothes and some notarized papers along with seventy-five cents had given Jeremiah directions to the train station, but Jeremiah has already forgotten them. It was so hard to listen to minor things like turn here, straight there, bear left, when the enormity of his release hung so close. He had told the warden that he was going to the train station because his family was going to pick him up from there, which was a lie, because his mother and sister fled Georgia sometime in '46 and there is no one here for him.

No, not quite no one. There is his girl, and though she stopped sending him letters years ago, the memory of her touch and her laugh were about the only things that kept him going. He's dreamed of her so many times he wonders if his imagination and longing have transfigured her in his mind, if she actually doesn't look or sound at all like he remembers. Yet the thought of her powers him forward.

The warden of course had not returned his watch, so he doesn't know how long he's been walking. Long enough to wish he'd been given a canteen.

The newly paved road is shaded by two rows of mighty oaks. On either side lies farmland, peanuts and corn and even some cotton. He passes meager shacks, roofs leaning and windows nonexistent. He smells honeysuckle and ragweed and he's wiped the dust from his nose with his shirtsleeve, as even a kerchief is beyond his means right now, nothing in his pocket but the seventy-five cents. He doesn't rightly know if he'd had those seventy-five cents when he'd been arrested or if they're some state-sanctioned allowance.

October and the red wasps are out, hovering over flowers and darting across the road. He remembers how the wasps always seemed to get in the way this time of year, but now he doesn't mind them, yet another aspect of life he'd almost forgotten about.

Then he hears, faintly but distinctly, a siren.

He walks faster, his heart announcing itself to every part of his body. Hands shaking, feet nearly tripping, fingers scratching at imaginary bugs on his cheeks and chest and neck. The sirens grow louder. Why is he scared? Those sirens couldn't possibly be for him. It sounds like at least three different vehicles echoing across the plains. He tells himself it's a caravan to or from the prison, but the panic won't abate.

The sirens fade, to the point that he's not sure if he hears them anymore or if perhaps he'd only imagined them. Perhaps he will be hearing them in his sleep, intermittently, forever.

He knows the prison is on the Negro side of town, so when he sees a small clapboard structure in the distance and smells biscuits, he thanks Jesus again, trusting that this is an establishment he's allowed to enter.

Two cars are parked in front. A sign over the door informs him not of the name of the establishment but the fact that God watches over the premises, which is either a blessing or a warning to potential thieves. Inside it appears to be part café, part grocery. Four aisles on the right are lined with goods, and to the left sit three small tables and a counter. A thin old Negro woman, sixty if she's a day, and the first female he's seen in months, observes him warily through thick eyeglasses, her hair pulled back in a severe bun, stacks of cigarette boxes on either side of her shiny metal register.

He smiles and for the first time in he can't remember, he talks to a free stranger. Not sure if his "Good morning" sounds dated in some way, if his smile or his very manner is off. How do strangers in 1950 say hello? he wonders.

Five minutes later he has sopped up every last bit of gravy with his biscuit and has ordered a second. It is beyond delicious. And the coffee, good Lord, it's doing such things to his heart and mind that he'd not thought possible. He is a blank slate, and every taste is imprinting itself on him like a new language, a new sense entirely.

I am not a fully formed thing, Lord. I am clay. I am not cast into the mold I have been consigned into. I can still be anything. He prayed this repeatedly over the years, so many times, both a promise and a plea.

He is standing to leave now, tired of the woman's long and suspicious looks his way, as if she is waiting for him to do some wrong. As if he's just dying to break another law. In truth, he was disappointed to realize when he paid that he'd figured the math wrong and he has but a dime left. He'd like to buy some smokes but those are beyond his reach, and how is he going to afford a ticket to Atlanta?

The door opens and a bell chimes and in walks a Negro man, his hair white and Brylcreemed back in waves from his shiny forehead.

"Ay there, Marcie, how you doing?"

"Fair to middlin'. Gonna be a beautiful day, Reverend."

Overhearing strangers is so odd, that and the glances the reverend has cast his way, unless Jeremiah's imagining it, which maybe he is. His instincts tell him he needs to leave. He walks toward the door, trying to give the reverend plenty of space, afraid of any accidental contact, wary of tripping others' alarms.

Outside it seems three hours warmer. The sun is awake now and has amassed its power. He should have asked them how much farther it was to the station, but he'd been afraid. Afraid of what? He doesn't know.

Then the door opens behind him and he hears the reverend's voice. "Good morning!"

Jeremiah turns. The reverend is walking toward him, a bag in one hand. He is a tall fellow and his frame bears evidence of more than just reading the Good Book. To the preacher's left is what must be his blue Ford pickup, as it hadn't been there earlier.

"Good morning, Reverend," Jeremiah replies.

The reverend takes in the too-short pant legs, notes the hair in need of a trim. Jeremiah wears a beard as well, not because he prefers it but because his weekly trip to the prison barber for a shave is normally scheduled for a few hours from now.

"A good day to be alive, isn't it?" the preacher asks.

"Yes, it is, Reverend."

Crows call in the trees above, blaming each other for misdeeds.

"How long has it been for you?"

"Five years. And one month. And six days."

"Ah yes, no one knows arithmetic quite like a man in prison." The reverend pauses, perhaps trying to determine what crime Jeremiah must have committed to receive such a term.

"Where are you headed?"

"Atlanta. Somehow. Train, I suppose."

"Nearest station is in Statesboro."

Another town he's never heard of. "Okay." He points down the road. "That way?"

"More or less. But it's about thirty miles from the ground you're standing on. What's your name?"

"Jeremiah."

"You know the Good Book?"

"Yes, sir."

"Jeremiah was a prophet. He foretold God's covenant with Israel. That they were the chosen people and would be saved."

"*For I know the thoughts that I think toward you, saith the Lord, thoughts of peace, and not of evil.*"

The reverend smiles, reassessing him. "You do know it."

"Wouldn't lie to a preacher, sir."

"It's one of my favorite chapters." Silence for a beat. "But there was an if. Just like there is in modern times, there's always an if. The if was, God would save them *if* they worshipped Him and only Him, not any false gods. We sin, but there's always forgiveness. Like a parent's unconditional love. But with God, there is that one condition: that we worship him."

Jeremiah is surprised to find himself being taught a lesson after five years and one month and six days of ostensibly being taught a lesson, but this happens to be one with which he agrees.

"Yes, sir."

"There was a fire this morning," the reverend says. "White folks' house burned down, don't ask me how. You're a lucky man."

"How's that?" Lucky is something that Jeremiah surely hasn't felt in a good while.

"One of three things occurs when they release a Negro from that jail, son. One is that the prisoner has family or friends arrive to pick him up. Two is that, if his people don't have a vehicle, the prison takes him by bus to the train station, where his people meet him. And three, if he doesn't have any people to meet him at all, they let the prisoner walk. They give him seventy-five cents, am I right? And about an hour or two after he's done walked away and maybe spent that money on a pack of cigarettes or some food, the local Reidsville police arrest him for vagrancy."

"I got out legit. I didn't bust out."

"That don't matter."

"I've got these here papers," and Jeremiah reaches into his pocket, only to stop pulling when he sees the way the preacher is shaking his head and laughing.

"Don't matter, son. That's how they do. I seen it happen too many times. That house caught fire this morning, all the police headed over to help the volunteer firemen. Which means that whoever was supposed to arrest you had greater things to deal with."

The preacher pauses to let this sink in.

"I was you? I'd get down and pray to God tonight and thank Him for setting that fire, and ask that He didn't kill anyone to do it, because if He did then you've got those deaths on your soul as thanks for your freedom today."

Jeremiah thinks about this. It seems exactly the sort of randomly violent act God would commit, to confuse and test us. He had heard that the local cops did such things, of course, and he had met many prisoners who claimed to have been released and then re-jailed in shockingly quick time, but he'd not considered that such a fate could befall him.

"I didn't ask Him to kill no one for me."

"I'm not saying He did, son. I'm just saying the dice were cast in an unusual way this morning, and you're the beneficiary of a strange roll indeed. And it's gonna cost me half a tank of gas to drive sixty miles round trip and two dollars to buy you a ticket to Atlanta, but that's what I'm gonna do, because if the Lord sees fit to set a fire to keep you out of jail, the least I can do is make a small sacrifice on your behalf. Get on in."

"Thank you, sir."

"Thank Him, like I said."

A siren interrupts their exchange. Jeremiah turns his head and the land here is so flat that he can see, far behind them, a squad car racing their way. He looks at his Good Samaritan and sees that the preacher's air of casual wisdom has been replaced by something less secure.

"I'll . . . I'll go my separate way," and Jeremiah starts to leave.

"No. You stay here." Still, the reverend sounds nervous as he watches the road. The squad car will be upon them in seconds.

"I don't want to cause you no harm."

"Just hold tight."

Jeremiah's hands are shaking. Why would they be after him again? Why do they act this way? *I don't understand this world.* Not *this world* meaning the outside as opposed to prison, but *this world* meaning everything. Given all that has befallen him, he knows that some basic ability to make sense of events and rules and cause and effect is essentially broken in him. The world operates according to a perverse logic he is doomed not to fathom.

The squad car slows down and pulls into the lot. Gravel crunches as it parks beside the pickup.

Please, Lord, not now please not this I have tried to be faithful and good and I must find my girl and we will grow old and worship You together please please I will be Your servant I ask only for this please.

The preacher gives Jeremiah the briefest of looks, not even turning to face him, and he says, "I'm sorry, son."

"Hey there, Odell," the officer says as he exits the car and walks up to the preacher. Whitish-yellow face, like freshly whipped butter, and the butter's starting to melt because his skin is shiny, Jeremiah can see the glisten even though the officer's wide-brimmed hat blocks out the morning light. His tan uniform shirt is damp in the armpits and he sounds tired.

"Good morning, Officer," the reverend says.

"Who that you got with you?"

Jeremiah looks away, avoiding eye contact. "Jeremiah Tanner, Officer, sir."

"Just got out, huh? What you doing with him, Odell?"

The reverend, too, stares straight ahead. "I was just offering a ride to someone. Didn't mean no trouble by it."

"Hell," the cop says, just like a basic exhalation, as if unaware it's not a polite word to use around a man of God. "What a morning."

"Those people okay?" the reverend asks.

"What people?"

"The fire. I can smell it on you."

Jeremiah can, too, the cop carrying with him a miasma of burned wood, a scent familiar from winter fireplaces but different, too, something else mixed in, bitter and sharp.

"It was awful. Awful."

Please, Lord, please spare me please.

Seconds pass and that appears to be all the officer can speak of the matter. He stands there with one hand against the roof of the pickup, and at first Jeremiah had taken this for a proprietary mannerism (*I own this pickup and the two of you both*) but with each passing second it seems different.

"Are you all right?" the reverend asks.

Please, Lord, please do not let this man take me.

Jeremiah is still afraid to look directly at the officer but he's watching from the corner of his eye and it seems like the officer takes one of his hands, the one not holding on to the truck, and drags it up his own body as if trying to make sure it's all there, and it lingers over his heart. Then the cop falls.

"Officer Dave?!" the reverend calls in alarm. The officer lands on his side, a wholly unnatural and strange position, one arm pinned beneath him and the other hand still gripping his chest as if trying to find a handle there, something to switch it back on. The reverend gently rolls the officer onto his back.

More wrinkles have gathered on Officer Dave's forehead than Jeremiah has ever seen on a white person. The cop seems to be holding his breath, his face red, his entire body clenched like the fist that can't find a handle for his heart.

"Officer Dave, can you speak?" The reverend is panicked and only later will Jeremiah wonder if he's seen this sort of thing before, because surely preachers visit many a deathbed but how many times do they see the hand of God strike so clearly and violently?

The officer lifts his head a bit off the ground, like he's trying so hard to reply that his entire body moves even if his tongue won't, and then his head hits the ground and he unclenches.

"Oh Lord! Oh Lord!" The preacher is as still as the cop for a moment, and then he reaches for the white man's wrists, checking for a pulse. "You hang on there, Officer Dave, you hang on!" From here Jeremiah can't see the preacher's face as he intones with the sudden clarity of his profession, "Lord Jesus, please spare this man. Please let him see his family again, Lord."

Jeremiah wonders if the reverend knows that the Lord has received wildly conflicting prayers from this very spot, within seconds.

Did You do this, Lord? Did I?

The reverend stands, looking first at the squad car and then at Jeremiah and then back at the fallen man. "We gotta . . . We gotta get him to a hospital. Help me get him in!"

Getting Officer Dave into the pickup is difficult, as they are both wary—or Jeremiah certainly is, at least—of touching a white man, especially a defenseless one. They carefully lift him from either side, almost like pallbearers, and part carry, part drag him, his shoes etching long trails in the gravel. They manage to sit him in the passenger seat, and after Jeremiah closes the door, the cop's head leans onto the glass, looking uncomfortable and perhaps dead already, but the reverend insists he's alive yet.

Jeremiah picks up the man's hat, which had fallen off, and he holds it in his lap as he hops into the back of the truck. The sun shines hot on Jeremiah's skin as the reverend hits the gas and they speed off, leaving the squad car and grocery behind like a tiny island of civilization in the midst of God's wilderness. The wind is too loud as they speed along and Jeremiah is left with his thoughts, his shockingly answered prayers, his profound confusion.

Did You light a fire for me and kill innocents, Lord? Have You struck down this man as well? For what have You marked me? What is in store?

He stares at the cop's hat, upside down in his hands now, sees the sweat stain and feels the dampness there, and he holds it to his nose and breathes in, taking the scent of the woodsmoke and holding it in his chest.

They reach a town and the reverend drives through a stop sign while honking his horn. The truck pulls into a circular drive beside a white building that back in Atlanta would have been considered small but here it's the county hospital.

A thin white man in a blue smock is waving his arms in the universal symbol of *do not proceed* which Jeremiah knows so well from his time working the rail yards but the reverend proceeds nonetheless, pulling up right in front of this outraged white man.

"We don't take coloreds here!"

"I got a white man that's sick! A policeman!"

The white doctor or orderly looks through the window now, and though Officer Dave's mussed and sweaty hair against the window hardly looks official, he can see the uniform shirt and the badge and now the white man realizes this is a serious matter. He looks back at the reverend, then at Jeremiah in back, as if searching for weapons or signs of blood.

"What happened?"

"We were talking and he just up and keeled over! Don't know if it's his heart or heat exhaustion from the fire or what, but he needs help!"

The white man tells them to wait there, and they do, at least until he's disappeared into the building.

"Get out," the reverend says as he opens his door. Jeremiah climbs out of the pickup, and the reverend reaches into his pocket and hands Jeremiah a five. "That's plenty for a ticket to Atlanta." Then another five. "And that's insurance against the Atlanta police using your empty pockets as an excuse to get you for vagrancy."

"Thank you, sir. Thank you very much."

"You'd best get away from here now. Gonna be crawling with cops in a minute."

"What about *you*?"

"I'll manage. Now walk down that way to the corner and you catch the bus to Statesboro. Bus don't come soon, might want to hide someplace. I'll do what I can for you."

"Thank you."

The preacher grabs Jeremiah's shoulder now, holding him for a second, seeming to want a last, good hard look at this man for whom the Lord has made such a startling intervention. He says, "May the Lord bless you and keep you safe," and Jeremiah nods, then walks away.

The Lord sends the bus in mere seconds. It is nearly empty and Jeremiah sits alone in the back, the wind through an open window warm in his face.

He rides for what feels like an hour. Finally the bus passes through the ghostly beauty of live oaks dripping with Spanish moss—so foreign from Atlanta, like another world—and then past the one stoplight en route to a small train station flanked by palmetto trees. Three colored people stand outside in the colored waiting "room," a mere platform with a roof but no walls. The white waiting room is indoors.

As he boards the train, stepping onto the front colored car that smells like soot, he ponders the reverend's words about his namesake prophet's warnings. He marvels at the morning's events, wondering if he has the strength to endure whatever the Lord might throw at him next. Why would Jeremiah, who already loves God, need to be tested like this? And if Jeremiah truly does love God, why does he always think the Lord so cruel, so manipulative, so hurtful? Is this really love, or something worse? If Jeremiah is undeserving of all the ills that befell him these last five years, is he also undeserving of being spared at the expense of Officer Dave and the white people in the burned house? How would the preacher figure that kind of *arithmetic*?

Jeremiah sits by the train car's window and feels the world pull out from beneath him, first with a weary immensity and then with more speed and power until he is near weightless, hurtling north toward the city from which he'd been exiled.

1

Officer Lucius Boggs looked at other men differently now. He had always been fairly comfortable about his own appearance, his five feet and ten inches, thin and healthy, neither the fastest nor the strongest but falling somewhere in the middle. He had thought of himself as normal, an overgrown kid who eventually realized he was a man. But since taking this job, his perspective had changed. He came to realize that he was looked at differently by those who were taller—and many men were. In those first weeks, his snug uniform shirt only advertised the fact that his frame was not rippling with muscle, that he was not as intimidating as many of the men he encountered on the streets. So he'd added to his workout routine, spending two hours at the YMCA most days, the heavy bag and the speed bag, jumping rope, lifting barbells, and then, after showering, descending a flight of stairs to the Y's basement, which served as the precinct for the Negro officers. As a result of those months of commitment, he'd added a good fifteen pounds of muscle and had moved up a shirt size, but he still felt very much in debt to the billy club on his belt and the pistol in his holster. Whenever he met a man, he made note of the fellow's height, he glanced at the fellow's chest and the reach of his arms, making calculations. This felt mercenary and superficial, yet it was the sort of vital note-taking that, Sergeant McInnis had drilled into him, may well save his life, or his partner's. *Always know what you're up against and what you're dealing with, and how you'll get out of it if it turns ugly,* McInnis was fond of saying. And the world had a habit of turning ugly.

So the man who was crossing the street tonight, Boggs quickly surmised, was around five six, and the way his lightweight jacket hugged his frame made him appear slight of build. The jacket was buttoned and there were several places he might have been carrying a weapon. He lit a cigarette using a silver Zippo, which meant he might have been a veteran, and thus familiar with firearms, and he used his left thumb on its wheel, which meant he was a southpaw.

These were the sorts of things Boggs thought about now when he saw strangers.

Boggs and his partner, Tommy Smith, were walking their beat on Jackson Street, a few blocks south of Auburn Avenue. Less than a minute after the man crossed the street, a block ahead of them, they smelled it: he wasn't smoking tobacco.

"Interesting," Smith said. The man turned a corner, and before they could think of pursuing him, they saw a car turn onto Jackson, headlights off. It pulled out of their view, behind a two-story building that had once held a Pentecostal church but had been vacant for a year. For a moment they faintly heard voices, but no door opening or closing. Then the car reappeared, its headlights on this time, going back the way it had come.

"You approach, I'll smoke him out," Smith whispered.

They split up, Smith silently creeping toward the far side of the building, then hiding around the back alley corner. From the near side, Boggs stepped carefully until he'd reached the alley behind the boarded-up church. He saw a man leaning against the alley wall, an apple crate on the ground beside him.

"Evening," Boggs said, and he'd barely asked, "You have someplace to be?" before the man's eyes lit up and he darted away in the opposite direction. Where Smith was waiting.

Smith stepped into the alley and tackled the man, whose momentum carried him straight into the ground, hard. Smith had him cuffed in seconds, then stood him up, pressed him against a wall, and patted him down for weapons, finding none.

"Whoa, hey, this is a big misunderstanding!"

In the apple crate Boggs found mason jars of white lightning and a King James Bible.

"Looks like you've been misunderstanding the law about corn liquor," Boggs said.

Even so many years after Prohibition, Atlanta remained strict about alcohol, granting liquor licenses only to a few establishments. Selling moonshine did not bring in the big bucks it once did, but bootleggers still found customers, ranging from pool halls and clubs that lacked licenses to individuals who preferred the strong stuff to watered-down beer.

"Look, I'm sorry, I ain't never even done this before," the bootlegger insisted.

"Sure, and it's our amazing luck to catch you the first time," Smith said. He removed the man's cash-stuffed wallet from his pocket, turned him around, and pushed his shoulders down. "Sit."

An ID card proclaimed his name Forrester, Woodrow W., Neg. Short and a bit hefty, he seemed terrified by his plight, his sweaty forehead glistening in the beams of the officers' flashlights. This alley, like so much of their beat, was not graced with streetlights. Boggs and Smith replaced their flashlight batteries weekly.

"No, really! A buddy a mine usually does this, and I kept my distance, but he got sick and said he needed this stuff sold pronto or he'd be hard up. He only does this 'cause he got four kids to feed, and I got three myself."

"That's a pity," Smith said. "Those kids ain't gonna be fed with you in jail, are they?"

Boggs picked up a jar and swirled it around before he unscrewed the lid and took a sniff, not even needing to bring his nose close to pick up the tang. He opened the Bible, which was hollowed out from Judges to John, the hole filled with about twenty pre-rolled marijuana joints.

"Come on, now, y'all weren't hired to be giving other colored men such a hard time. I'm just trying to get by."

"You're *getting by* by poisoning our community with this junk," Boggs said.

"Just this one time! It was a mistake, I own up. I plead guilty right here, right now. But, come on, it's just the one time, and I can't be going to no jail. I got me a real job, too."

"Doing what?" Smith asked.

"I cook at the phone factory's cafeteria."

Smith tsk-tsked. "They ain't gonna keep no man with a criminal record."

"Come on, now. You can keep all of that money, too. Take the shine, or pour it all down the drain, whatever you want. Just don't give me no record."

Flicking his flashlight off, Smith crouched in front of Forrester. "Number one, you do not bribe us." He pointed at his own face. "This look white to you? Y'all may bribe the white cops to look the other way, but you don't do that with us. Got it?"

"Yessir."

The fact that he'd even tried to bribe them, Boggs thought, argued for Forrester's honesty: if he'd been selling reefer and moonshine before, he would know the ropes, know not to make such an offer to the city's Negro officers.

Of course, there may have been another explanation. Perhaps this fellow was in fact a regular dealer and had learned that some Negro officers *could* be bribed. Boggs had never taken a cent, and he was certain Smith hadn't, either. But from what they'd learned over their two-plus years on the force, it seemed half of the white officers took bribes, so how long would the Negro officers resist? The son of a preacher, Boggs was all too familiar with the fallibility of men, even men with power. Especially men with power.

"Number two," Smith said, still crouched in front of Forrester, "I'm a hardworking fisherman and I ain't about to cut loose a catch. Only way I'd even *think* about doing something like that is if I knew I was about to catch a bigger fish. You follow?"

Judging from Forrester's furrowed brow, he did not.

"We take you in," Boggs translated, "unless you know someone bigger we can take."

"Oh, come on, now, I told you I'm new at this. I don't know no big fish."

"Then I do feel sorry for you." Smith grabbed Forrester by the collar and pulled him up. "Because it's the minnows like you, without any information to sell, who get fried first."

Boggs asked, "What about that friend of yours? He know anything?"

Forrester's head moved about as if trying to spy some escape route, but he said nothing.

The nearest call box to request a wagon was two blocks away. Smith pushed Forrester from behind, not too hard but enough to make a condemned man start moving to his sad destiny. They'd only taken a few steps when he blurted out, "I know when the deliveries come!"

Boggs, who had been in front, turned around. He put a hand on Forrester's chest to stop him. "First you've never done this before, and now you know when the deliveries come?"

"Like I said, I cook at the Phelps phone factory. Clean up, too. There from before lunch to midnight, three days a week, and sometimes their deliveries ain't food."

Boggs looked over the cook's shoulder into his partner's eyes. Smith, who always seemed more skilled at spotting lies—possibly because he himself was the more experienced liar, Boggs wondered—looked interested.

"Go on," Smith said.

"Look, I keep my nose clean, you know, but a few times I been out there throwing trash away and then all of a sudden a truck come up and two fellas jump out and a couple more pop out and they be moving some crates into different cars, like, and then the truck pulls out straightaway. Barely there a minute. And I think to myself, okay, whatever it is they're delivering is something they're awful anxious to be rid of. But, you know, I don't ask no questions, not being the type to get involved in no nonsense like—"

"When does it happen?"

"Eleven thirty. On Wednesdays."

In other words, in thirty minutes.

At half past eleven, Boggs was leaning against the brick wall of the Phelps factory, two blocks south of the tracks, an industrial corridor of Cabbagetown where trucks pulling in or out would not be viewed as suspicious. He was hidden from the street's view by a parked truck emblazoned with a painting of a smiling white woman who held a receiver to her ear. This close up, her eyes seemed to glare at him in anger despite that smile on her face.

Smith stood a block away, around the corner of an alley, viewing the street. Trains had been whistling all night. On the way here they'd walked through a tunnel under the train tracks, the smell of coal hanging thick in the dry air, and even at that hour they could see the glow of welders' torches as men repaired busted tracks and train cars at the nearby rail yards. They'd skirted the haunted graveyards of Oakland Cemetery, which held legions of Confederate dead, among many others. And they'd passed through the wood-shavings-scented air of the Pencil Factory, where a young girl had been murdered decades ago, a sensational crime for which a Jewish man was later lynched. To the west loomed the dark downtown office towers and scaffoldings that rose like skeletal haunts above half-constructed new buildings.

Staking out a suspected transfer point for reefer and shine was beyond their typical duties. They would need to bend the truth with McInnis, make like they'd simply stumbled into the delivery. Had they done things by the book, they immediately would have reported what their informant told them, then they would have gone about their typical nightly duties, hoping the Department would send some vice detectives to stake out the area. But they knew that wouldn't happen. No white officers would have felt the need to stake out a drop in what they still referred to as "Darktown."

Boggs and Smith had known for a while that, if they wanted to stop the flow of drugs and moonshine into their community, they would have to do it themselves. Yet they were denied many of the powers white cops took for granted. They still could not drive squad cars or patrol outside of the Negro neighborhoods that constituted their beat. Even so, that geographic restriction left them with more than enough turf to patrol, and then some: more than a third of Atlantans were Negro, yet they were crowded into only a fifth of the land.

And only ten Negro officers patrolled those thousands of souls.

They still could not wear their uniforms to or from work, and therefore had to change in the basement of the Butler Street Y, their extremely insufficient, mildewed, rodent-infested home base. They still heard the white cops refer to other Negroes as "niggers." They still felt that their hold on their jobs was very tenuous indeed. They lived with the fear the other shoe would drop, that one of the Negro officers would make some horrible mistake, or more likely some horrible mistake would be invented by the white cops and pinned on them, and then Mayor Hartsfield or his successor would have the necessary ammunition to end this odd experiment, at which point Boggs and his fellows would be back to their old jobs, as insurance salesmen and elementary school teachers, butchers and janitors.

Boggs heard the sound of a heavy truck approaching.

He peered over the fender of the telephone factory truck he was hiding behind and saw a green canvas-topped six-wheeler pull into the lot. It looked like an old military vehicle that had been sold at auction after the war. The passenger door read Cherokee Flooring and listed an address in Dalton, ninety miles north. The door opened and out jumped a stocky Negro, tweed newsboy cap pulled low. The engine still running.

"Let's go, let's go," someone said. Boggs heard what he thought were two sets of feet, then more, coming from various directions. The rev of an engine and now another vehicle was pulling into the lot. He crept forward until he was leaning just past the front edge of the Phelps truck. In addition to the passenger he'd spotted, two other men, both Negroes, were standing at the back of the flooring truck. The second new vehicle was a green Dodge pickup, idling at the back of the flooring truck. Two other men, both white, joined them, everyone hurriedly unloading crates from the flooring truck into the Dodge.

Two white men. Still, Boggs had expected this. Most moonshine was made far outside city limits, in the North Georgia mountains or across state lines in the Carolinas and Tennessee. They'd been hearing rumors that moonshiners were planting marijuana as well, to make up for the fact that shine didn't bring them what it once did. Pretty much all of those mountain folk were white, driving down from their Smoky Mountain hollers.

Atlanta's Negro officers were not allowed to arrest white people. They were barely even supposed to *interact* with white people. But Boggs and Smith were tiring of their powerlessness.

Boggs crept until he was nearly at the back of the truck, loosening the billy club from his belt. He heard what sounded like the clinking of full glass containers. He heard someone say "let's go" again and could hear crates landing heavily.

Just as a man was emerging from the truck, Boggs stepped behind its rear and swung his club into the back of his skull. The man dropped.

Boggs found himself staring into the eyes of the next part of the assembly line, a white man in a black derby hat and wrinkled gray jacket, struggling under the weight of two stacked crates, his eyes wide at the sight of a Negro in a policeman's uniform.

"Police! Put that down and put your hands up!"

After a frozen second, the man tipped the crates forward. Boggs leaped back as glass exploded all around him, heavy jars landing on his feet, shards and alcohol everywhere.

"Police! Everyone down!" Smith yelled, emerging from his hiding spot on the other end of the lot.

Boggs saw a dirty, clay-caked boot stepping out of the rear of the flooring truck, and then the rest of the body appeared, but what Boggs's eyes fixed upon was the shotgun and he pretty much didn't see the rest.

He dove down to his right, back to where he'd been hiding before. A deafening boom. Chunks of brick and mortar showered down on him and sprayed across the lot.

The shotgun exploded again. Then three smaller-caliber shots, hopefully Smith's gun.

For only the second time in the line of duty, Boggs drew his sidearm, thumbing back the hammer. Back on his feet, he ran to the front of the truck, stepping around it quickly, his gun held in firing position with both hands, his feet square beneath him, trying to adopt the practiced pose as perfectly as he could in such imperfect conditions.

He didn't see anyone at whom to point the gun. He could see his partner sprinting toward him, running with his gun pointed as well, and then the scene before him seemed to break apart. The Dodge and the flooring truck both pulled out of the lot. Their engines sounded like they were being taxed to their limits, wheels skidding in the pool of moonshine and then gaining traction, squealing as they raced away.

Another boom as someone fired the shotgun from the rear of the truck. Boggs ducked, heard glass breaking, wood splitting.

He called out to see if his partner was all right but the only reply he received was the sound of Smith's shoes tapping a sprint as he raced down the street. The two trucks were headed in opposite directions. Smith was chasing the Dodge, so Boggs ran into the street behind the flooring truck, which was already forty yards away and fast disappearing. He glanced at its tags but it was too dark.

He imagined himself firing at the truck. He could see it like in one of the gangster pictures, Cagney firing and hitting one of the back wheels, the tire popping or maybe the wheel springing loose from its axle. Then the entire truck would lean hard to the left, and the driver would panic, try to right it, but that wouldn't be possible at such a speed, and the entire vehicle would topple over as if in slow motion. Then the explosion, or at the very least a vast crumpling upon itself. The driver would be killed and Boggs would lose his badge for recklessly firing at a fleeing vehicle, would perhaps be indicted for manslaughter, and the city of Atlanta would have one less Negro officer. Which would be a great excuse for letting the other nine go as well.

He holstered his unfired gun as the truck disappeared from view.

He sprinted a block to the nearest call box. Panting, he had to repeat himself for Dispatch, describing the vehicles and explaining the directions in which they were headed. Late on a weeknight, the roads clear, catching one or the other should have been possible, even likely, but he knew this would go nowhere. He could expect no hot pursuit or roadblocks and certainly no arrests. The moonshiners might as well be in the mountains already.

As Boggs called it in, Smith returned from his futile chase, surveying the lot. Smashed bottles, a black Ford that had been parked there riddled with bullets, its windshield shattered, gun smoke lingering in the dry air. Lying in the center of the lot was the white man Boggs had knocked out. He was breathing and his pulse was strong, but Smith could already predict McInnis's reaction. He cuffed the man's pale wrists.

Then he saw the other body.

It was lying three feet from the phone truck Boggs had been hiding behind. A Negro, though Smith could only base this on his hands and jaw, as most of the skin atop his head had been blown off, at least on the side that was pointing up. He'd fallen mostly on his back, slightly on his left side. He wore work boots, jeans, and a tan flannel shirt flecked with dark red.

"You shot him?" Boggs asked, returning out of breath from the call box.

"No. Did you?"

"I didn't fire a round. You sure you didn't hit him?"

"I was over there." Smith pointed to their right. "I fired three shots, up this way. This fella was shot from where you and I are standing now, facing that wall. Unless . . ."

Smith turned around and crossed the street, Boggs following. He walked into the tunnel that cut beneath the train tracks, shined his flashlight. He saw a small puddle of what smelled like fresh tobacco juice. Then he turned around again and faced the factory, imagining a rifle in his hands, squinting to take aim.

"Thought I heard a rifle," he said. "They had a lookout here. When we popped up, he started firing at us. Must've hit his own man." He looked at Boggs. "That's some kind of luck, for the dead man and for us."

Minutes later, the adrenaline rush was making Boggs feel like his feet weren't quite touching the ground. He kept seeing the shotgun pointed at him. Since swearing his oath, he had been punched, kicked, hit, bit, sliced, driven into, and even kidnapped, but this was the first time a weapon had been fired at him.

Sitting on the ground and conscious again, hands cuffed behind him, was the man Boggs had bludgeoned. The fact that Boggs had knocked out a white man was altogether too much to comprehend right then.

Officers Dewey Edmunds and Champ Jennings, who had heard the shots from six blocks away, were the first to arrive. They took in the scene. Shards of glass and chunks of the brick wall lay scattered across the lot. Moonshine had mixed with mortar dust to form a viscous alcoholic sludge.

Smith explained what they'd just missed.

"Good fucking Lord, boys!" Dewey holstered his weapon and started laughing. "Should we all just hand in our badges now, or wait 'til the sergeant gets here to make it official?"

"We'll be all right," Boggs insisted, his ears still ringing.

Dewey and Champ made for an odd if affable pair. Champ, the biggest of the Negro officers, eschewed a billy club in favor of the handle of what had been his lucky ax. Raised in a small Negro community in

South Georgia, he tended to see the good in people. Dewey, the shortest officer in the city but an indomitable former boxer, believed that anything a civilian said was most likely a lie.

Dewey whistled and shook his head at all the exploded glass. "I'm getting drunk just *smelling* this shit. Don't nobody light no cigarettes 'round here, got it?"

Champ had actually been reaching for one, and he tried to surreptitiously slide it back into his pocket. He hoped they hadn't noticed.

Dewey shook his head at four abandoned crates, two that had been left on the ground and two that had apparently fallen out of one of the fleeing trucks. "No wonder my phone bill's so expensive," he said. "They be charging me to cover their costs on running this shit."

"You think the phone company's really running shine, or the runners just use this spot?" Champ asked. His family hadn't moved to Atlanta until he was twelve, and he spoke with a thick country accent that endeared him to the few people who weren't terrified by his size.

"I don't know. Call an operator and see if she sounds drunk."

"Nah, white lady operators don't touch this stuff."

"Boy, what are you talking about? You think white ladies don't drink? You think their shit don't smell?"

Champ folded his arms. "What I mean is, all this here is for Negroes and you know it."

"Damn right," Smith said.

"Your turn," Sergeant McInnis said to Boggs, after speaking to Smith for a few moments on the other end of the lot. Boggs didn't care for the approach, dividing them to hear their separate answers and see if they were congruent. That was how they spoke to subjects.

The words *kind* or *friendly* did not spring to mind when thinking of their white sergeant. McInnis had seemed extremely uncomfortable in their presence back when they started, and they'd wondered how long it would be until he quit, outraged at having been appointed the colored officers' keeper. Yet McInnis had won Boggs's respect over the last two years. He had stuck up for his Negro charges during a few disputes with white officers, and he seemed to be taking to his role and the outsider status it lent him within the Department. Perhaps he'd simply learned to accept an untenable situation, because by now it was clear his superiors would not be transferring him elsewhere, and he was stuck as the lone white cop at the Butler Street precinct.

"You fired no shots?"

"No, sir."

"Give me your sidearm."

Boggs obeyed. McInnis checked the chamber, smelled the barrel, felt its coolness. The lack of trust stung. McInnis handed his weapon back.

"Where did you catch the dealer?"

"Jackson Street, behind that old holiness church."

"Which means you passed two call boxes on the way here." McInnis had very dark hair and equally dark, thin eyebrows. He was squinting despite the fact that it was hardly bright out, as if he had a migraine.

"I'm sorry, sir. We were rushing, to get here in time."

"You nearly rushed into your grave. Arresting a dealer in an alley is one thing, but you show up at a drop and you can expect to be outgunned. I'm not surprised *Smith* came out guns blazing, but I thought you were smarter."

"Yes—"

"Vice will be here in five minutes and for all I know we just scotched a sting they've been working on. Hell, the man you knocked out could be an informant. And the dead man—Smith, you'd best hope he was shot with a different-caliber weapon than you're carrying."

"Sergeant," Smith said, "there is no way I shot that man."

"Maybe *I* believe you, but how do you think the cops in Homicide are going to feel?" He switched his gaze between them. "Not only did Smith kill a man, but Boggs knocked out a *white* man."

From there McInnis found plenty of other issues to vent about, everything from Smith now needing to fill out a Weapon Discharge Report to dealing with the imminent arrival of an *Atlanta Daily Times* reporter; the city's only Negro daily was always hungry for examples of its colored heroes in action. His voice rising, he ended with, "Not to mention the fact that we're in a white goddamn neighborhood."

Yes and no, Boggs thought. The factory was a few blocks beyond their official beat, but the color line was blurring here; postwar crowding was pushing Negroes into areas formerly considered whites-only.

Boggs and the others weren't given new maps to reflect changing demographics; they'd merely been given cryptic advice from McInnis about "staying in your area."

Boggs glanced at the arrested white man, whose head hung low, as if asleep. Would the white cops confront Boggs for having hit a white man, even one who was committing a crime? It was absurd to think it, which probably meant it was so.

"Are they going to question Mr. Phelps?" Smith asked. Champ and Dewey stood by the abandoned crates, inventorying the jars of moonshine and bales of dried marijuana buried beneath larger bales of pine straw.

"Who?" McInnis asked.

Boggs motioned to the sign ten feet away from them, "Phelps Telephone, Connecting You To The Future!"

"The owner," Boggs said. "Maybe he knows something about it."

"No, I do not think the detectives are going to accuse one of the richest men in Atlanta of selling moonshine and marijuana. Though I do expect they'll let him know his wall got shot up and his lot's been turned into a crime scene."

"Rich folks don't break laws?" Smith asked.

McInnis folded his arms. "I'm not saying it would shock me if a fellow like that was in on it. But he wouldn't be stupid enough to use his legitimate business as the staging area. And the larger point is, it's not ours to worry about."

Smith had read the tags of the fleeing Dodge, but odds were it was a stolen car, or at least stolen tags. He motioned to the man they'd arrested. "Can we question him now?"

"No. You cannot. Detectives will do that."

Smith opened his mouth to say something, then closed it. Then opened it again. "Sergeant, just a few questions. Please. He's right there."

"As you very well know, that is not your job, Officer Smith." He pointed at the two squad cars pulling up, lights flashing and sirens blaring, white cops inside. "It's theirs."

2

The first time Denny Rakestraw had seen Terminal Station, he'd thought it was a castle.

His German-born mother had been fond of reading him folktales and adventures of warring dukes and counts, Visigoths and Romans. Perhaps his predilection for violence had started with his first wooden knight's sword, with which he had accidentally broken his mother's favorite rocking chair, whose right arm had not been able to withstand one of his mighty swings. He'd been four or five, yet his parents had held on to that one-armed rocking chair for years, as if to commemorate their son's destructive ways.

He still recalled his first trip to the train station, tagging along with his parents to pick up some visiting aunt or uncle or great-someone. Definitely castlelike, with its two turretlike spires surveying the city from some seven flights up, its wide expanse covering a full city block, and the black smoke emanating behind it as if witches' cauldrons were boiling or perhaps peasants were burning their belongings to hinder the advance of rampaging marauders. Rake's eyes had been wide with excitement. His parents had expected the lad to be thrilled at the sight of so many trains, but when they took him inside and he saw no knights, no dragons, not a single mace or coat of arms, he'd been crushed. His parents had misconstrued his tears as panic at the crowd: people everywhere, Georgians from outside the city taking the day train in for an afternoon of shopping at Rich's, Northerners on layover enjoying lunch before boarding the train to Florida, resplendently dressed matrons holding the suited arms of important Washington husbands as they prepared for the bacchanalias of New Orleans, and, even then, bedraggled Negro families making their way to the fabled colored-friendly jobs in places like Chicago, Milwaukee, New York. All this sundry humanity, but no knights.

Rake still thought of this sometimes when he drove past Terminal Station, especially after dark. It no longer loomed above downtown the way it once had, as the skyscrapers had caught up, but it still felt magical, a portal to other worlds.

His squad car's lights were flashing as he pulled directly in front of the station, gliding past the line of taxicabs and ignoring the complaints of taxi drivers upset that he'd claimed the best spot. His partner, Parker Hillis, radioed to Dispatch that they had arrived.

Half past eight in the evening. A few hours after one of the frequent, spectacularly beautiful fall afternoons that made Rake certain God was a Southerner. They hurried out of their squad car but didn't run, ever mindful of looking in control, never panicked.

Inside, the marble-floored lobby was crowded enough to make a four-year-old cry. The announcer was noting that the 9:10 to Chattanooga was en route and due to appear on platform six as Rake and Parker dodged hurrying passengers who did not seem as concerned about bumping into police officers as they should have, because they had trains to catch, appointments to make, vacations to commence, trysts to consummate, children to give large teddy bears to as apologies for their absence. No one had time to make eye contact.

"I'll deal with the Negroes," Rake told Parker as they moved against the current, toward the double doors beneath the sign Waiting Room. "You focus on the white folks."

The brightly lit waiting room contained two dozen rows of worn but well-maintained wooden pews. Luggage sat in piles, kids slept on parents' shoulders, and the commotion was at the far end of the room.

"Thank God you're here!" A man in a green Terminal Station uniform and cap intercepted the officers. "I was just about ready to take the law into my own hands."

"That's never a good idea, sir."

"Well, I don't mean me personally. But I been working here ten years and I never seen a nigger with the gumption to pull this kind of—"

"Excuse me, sir," Rake cut him off not because he saw the Negroes but because he saw the crowd that was blocking his view of the Negroes.

Most of them had their backs to Rake, but a few stood profile and were talking to each other, some shaking their heads, most of them looking very angry indeed. As he often did, he was walking into trouble.

"Police! Back away, please!" Rake didn't want to sound so loud as to alarm anyone but he needed to raise his voice to be heard. The crowd parted for the two officers and as Rake walked forward he saw a Negro man sitting in one of the wooden chairs that lined the perimeter of the room. So at least he hadn't been quite brazen enough to sit in one of the pews, where he would have been harder to remove. Yet it was plenty brazen. He sat there motionless, shoulders slightly slumped, almost as if he had thought no one would notice him, though he could not have been more visible here if he'd been in a spotlight, or on fire.

He wore a brown tweed jacket and blue trousers, with a light-yellow shirt and green tie. His porkpie hat lent him the air of some of those jazz musicians Rake had seen pictures of, the ones who didn't want to look like formal bandleaders so much as idiosyncratic professors of some new and yet-to-be-explained subject. Beside him was who Rake assumed to be his wife, with straightened hair and a bright red coat that would have been attention-getting even if her skin hadn't been drawing all the attention she needed.

On her lap sat a wide-eyed Negro boy who looked too old to be sitting like that but too young to be hearing what he was hearing.

The Negro saw Rake coming, then looked straight ahead again as if he could will this away. Parker held up his hands and told the gathered crowd to go sit down. Everyone in the room was watching.

Rake stood directly in front of the Negro. "Sir, the colored waiting room is on the other side of the building."

"I know where it is." A Northern accent, of course. His voice was shaking and it sounded almost like his teeth were gritted, but not quite. Rake had been a cop for two and a half years and he was well accustomed to speaking with people who were under stress. He had conversed with people who used voices they had never before employed, had consoled women who screamed in registers they'd never wanted to reach. People sounded all kinds of weird when talking to cops.

"Sir," and the *sir* was deliberate, and perhaps enough to further anger some of the witnesses if they could overhear, which Rake hoped they couldn't if Parker was doing his job, "this waiting room is for whites only. You need to go to the colored waiting room."

"We went there when our train was delayed. But it is filthy, as I told the station attendant." Hell, maybe he *was* a professor, his diction was so formal. "So we moved here."

This close and Rake could see that the Negro also wore a black cardigan sweater beneath his jacket, a Northerner dressed far too warmly for a Southern autumn. That was hardly the only reason, Rake suspected, that sweat streaked the man's cheeks.

Rake looked at the wife, who turned her eyes away, either respecting Southern decorum or just scared. More like terrified. The two were a bit portly, dark-skinned, and the lad on her lap was wearing short pants that showed off calves that hadn't yet lost their baby fat. The kid was amazingly still. She had been holding him with both arms, but now one of her hands reached over and touched her husband's elbow.

"Jonathan, please."

Rake waited a beat, hoping the wife's voice would do what the cop's couldn't. But still the Negro stared straight ahead.

"Get the damned niggers out of there!" someone shouted. Rake felt his body tense. He'd thought Parker was disarming that side of things, but apparently some of the angriest ones hadn't been able to resist tossing a verbal grenade. More would come soon, or worse. Rake glanced briefly at the crowd, could see Parker talking to a trio of men in work clothes, local boys perhaps awaiting the next train to Norcross or Marietta, men who were about ready to see that justice was served if these cops weren't up to it.

"Sir," Rake said, harder than before. "You cannot stay here."

"There was trash on the floor of the restroom," the Negro said. "And it smelled of vomit. My little boy was in there with me. No one should have to put up with that."

Rake hated this. Everything about it. The faces staring at him from all sides now, the hostility he could taste in the air like fires lit from fallen leaves. Hated the confines he had to impose on this man.

But also: hated the Negro's superior tone, the Northern sense of horror at seeing what goes on down here in Dixie, the distaste for this foreign land and its customs.

"Sir, I can talk to the station manager about cleaning the colored section. But you need to head over there right now."

"My family and I have as much right to wait here as any of these people do."

"Not in the state of Georgia, you don't." Rake stood a bit to the man's side, but still the man stared straight ahead. "What's your name, sir?"

"Jonathan O'Higgins."

The fact that this Negro had an Irish surname only seemed to add to the absurdity, the mixed-up madness of life in America, Atlanta, Rake's beat.

"Mr. O'Higgins, where are you from?"

"Philadelphia. We're en route to New Orleans for a speaking engagement. I'm a scientist. That may shock you. But I'm a human being and I won't be held in that chattel pen of a waiting room."

Rake saw the wife's fingers tighten around her husband's elbow.

O'Higgins was taking it too far. Rake didn't like this situation either, but that didn't give the Negro the right to take a condescending tone.

"That doesn't shock me at all, sir. But someone with such impressive credentials should realize that there are penalties for breaking the law."

Someone from the crowd called out that it was time for "you cops to haul that nigger to jail."

"It's my job to enforce the laws of the city of Atlanta. And our laws are different from the ones you're used to up in Philadelphia. I don't expect you to like them. But they're the law, and I do expect you to obey them. If you do not, you'll spend the night in something that looks a lot more like a chattel pen than that waiting room does."

"Jonathan," the man's wife said. "Enough."

Rake counted to five in his head. He hated that the Negro was putting him in this position. *You are so lucky that I am the white cop who took this call.* His first partner, Dunlow, would have knocked the Negro unconscious by now. So would dozens of other cops.

"It will give me no pleasure to arrest you, but if you don't comply with my orders, that's what I'll do. You will spend the night in jail, possibly longer. I don't know what will happen to your family."

At that, the kid started crying. He was about the same age as Denny

Jr. and it was amazing how similar crying can be. Rake felt an inner hand clench something in his chest. He saw the wife tugging on her husband's arm even as she looked at her son and shushed him, and with that O'Higgins said, quietly, and to his wife but not to this white cop, "Let's go."

Rake backed up as the family stood, the boy still in his mother's arms, head buried in the crook of her neck. O'Higgins picked up his two large suitcases. Rake heard "about time" and other grumbling, and he walked a few steps behind them, partly to ensure that they would follow through and partly to discourage onlookers from throwing anything.

He followed them halfway through the lobby, where a white-haired Negro janitor mopped a recent spill.

"Night in jail would teach him a lesson," admonished the station agent, who Rake hadn't realized was trailing him.

"While we're telling each other how to do their jobs, how 'bout you make sure the colored bathroom gets cleaned?"

The station agent scowled. "The colored bathroom? First, I gotta go clean the seats they were sitting on before white people sit there."

"Is it just me, or is stuff like this happening more often?" Parker asked as they returned to their squad car.

"I haven't kept track," Rake said. He had noticed the same thing, in fact, but he was loath to engage in conversations like this. His first partner had been a violent bigot. Parker, in contrast, was someone he'd known all his life; they'd grown up together, and, after the war (where Rake served as an advance scout in France and then Germany), both had joined the force in '48. They'd been partnered two years now, and Rake trusted him. Still, such conversations always made him uncomfortable.

He would have felt far worse had he known what his brother-in-law, Dale, was doing at that exact moment.

3

The gibbous moon hung low in the black sky, intermittently veiled and then revealed again by the passing gossamer clouds, as if winking its approval as Dale drove north. They had left their urban neighborhood thirty minutes earlier and now all around them was country, the trees dense in patches and blocking out the night. It was a wonder they could go so far in so little time.

There were five of them, three in Dale's coughing Buick and two trailing in a Ford pickup. In shotgun sat Mott, an old buddy who had joined Dale in many a scrap, though most had occurred back when they had a lot less mileage on them. Before wives and kids and boredom.

In the back sat their friend Irons, who could bench three-fifty and was rumored to have once worn a necklace of Jap ears, each of which he'd cut off himself. Dale had never been in a position to acquire such wild jewelry, having been ruled out for military service due to something funny about his heart, which he insisted the doctors had misdiagnosed, and in fact he'd tried enlisting not only with the army but also the navy and coast guard, hoping one of their physicians wouldn't have such sensitive hearing or follow the rules regarding military checkups quite so strictly, but no luck, the pencil pushers had all ruled him out. Dale found it hard to imagine, actually cutting someone's ear off. According to Irons, those ears had come off Japs who were already dead, which made it slightly more possible to imagine, but still. Damn. That was serious stuff, and Dale was thrilled to have the fellow in his backseat, honored, even. Irons was someone Dale wanted to learn from, and the fact that they were out together like this was Big.

They'd met at Sweetwater Mill a couple of years back but Irons had been let go—Dale heard a rumor Irons had gotten in a tussle with a coworker. He hadn't heard the story from Irons, and in fact Irons was a difficult fellow to get to know. One of the things Irons was good at, which was further evidence of his overall impressiveness: being silent. Dale himself found it difficult to keep his mouth shut, especially during stressful moments, or after he'd done or said something wrong. Irons, on the other hand, was a master at *not saying anything at all*. His size helped. It said things words could not. Made words unnecessary. Dale wasn't big like Irons, wasn't a war hero like Irons, and he possessed instead a nervous energy, constantly folding or unfolding his arms, cracking his knuckles, making stupid jokes. Such habits pretty much ensured that people were *not* intimidated by Dale. Which he further resented. Which reinforced his need to make stupid comments again, and so the cycle spun.

Tonight, though. Tonight would be something. Dale had received the call that afternoon: his target would be in position by ten, and likely drunk, thus particularly easy to terrorize. Hopefully he would not be so inebriated as to not comprehend what they were doing to him, not remember it the next day. Dale would do his part to ensure the man remembered, and Irons would certainly help.

Irons had done this sort of thing before. Dale was almost positive. He'd heard stories. With the kinds of details one couldn't make up. Some of which, honestly, he didn't like dwelling on, yet he found himself thinking about them when he lay in bed at night, trying to fall asleep.

Which was why he was out here in the sticks, taking a stand, doing some good. Being a man of action. Someone his kids could look up to. Even though he would be wearing a hood, would get no credit. He would be the silent savior of his community.

He felt his nerves the farther he drove his fellow Klansmen north, so he joked with Mott and the still-silent Irons, talked about baseball and the news. The defending champion Yankees were up on the Phillies in the World Series. Dale didn't care much for either team; mainly he was thankful the Phillies had unseated the Dodgers as NL champs, so people didn't have to endure another year of Jackie Goddamn Robinson playing on baseball's grandest stage.

"Doesn't really matter that the Dodgers didn't make it," Dale admitted. "Gonna be even more niggers in the league next year."

"Not necessarily."

"Dam's done broken, they're flooding in."

"Ye of little faith." Mott shook his head. He'd always been a calming influence in Dale's life, talking him out of rages, gently reining in some of Dale's more outlandish plans. He was glad to have Mott along tonight, even if this was a proper occasion for rage and big plans.

There was so much bad news in the world right then, which they discussed as they drove north. Joe McCarthy was hammering away at his list of radicals in the US government, and a new book about the recent trial of red spy Alger Hiss implied that Communists had infiltrated every nook of the US government. It felt like they were in a strange, almost drugged moment in which America was going to get pulled into another world war. Truman had lost China, Mao topping Chiang-Kai-However-You-Say-It, and we were in Korea now, with Mao threatening to get involved, too, if our troops crossed the 38th parallel. Even in Indochina, Communist troops were gaining momentum against the French. America was damn encircled in Reds, seemed like.

Mott, shining a flashlight on the map that lay across his lap, told Dale to turn off the road. Dale's contact had told them a nearby park would be a convenient place for them to don their robes and hoods. Dale drove down a narrow dirt path beneath low-hanging oak boughs gone spectral in the darkness.

From out of the Ford came Iggy and Pantleg. Iggy was another friend from way back—he'd grown up in Hanford Park along with Dale and Mott, lived a mere three blocks from where he'd been raised. His parents lived in the same house where his lifetime of height intervals was marked on the pantry molding, yet now they had the privilege of living *five doors down* from a family of Negroes. Iggy was as anxious about doing something as Dale was. Pantleg was a relative stranger to Dale, some friend of Iggy's from the rock quarry where they worked. They were both of average height, stocky, and toughened by their arduous labor. As Iggy exited the Ford he grinned mischievously, his mussed blond hair adding to the look of a kid out to cause trouble. A kid holding a fifth of bourbon.

"All right!" he shouted. "Beautiful night to be out amongst God's creatures!"

A hearty swig and he passed it to Mott, who passed it to Dale without partaking. Mott had become a teetotaler, which was a shame. One of his kids had nearly died of measles a few years back, during which time Mott had made a deal with the Lord never to touch a drop again if He spared Mott's boy. He was a man of his word.

Dale could see that Iggy and Pantleg, in contrast, had gotten quite the head start on drinking, could smell it from their pores, so he took a double snort himself.

Mott opened the trunk and they started donning their robes, shaking lint from the hoods.

"Gonna be fun!" Iggy said, louder than Dale would have liked. They were just a mile away from their destination, the only sound the cicadas that were still another week or two from going silent for the season. Iggy was crazed, the way Dale remembered him when they played football together, driving himself into a fury beforehand. It made Dale's blood pump faster, and he smiled to himself as he held the hood in his hand, felt the power in it. The eyeholes black and staring back at him, waiting to be filled.

Iggy said, "Great night to be out and busting some niggers!"

Dale stopped. "Wait, Iggy," he said. "I thought you knew. The fella we're going after, he's a white man."

A hearty swig and he passed it to Mott, who passed it to Dale without

There were days Dale didn't remember, so many days they probably constituted years if he strung them all together. Those days were gone from his memory not because he'd blacked out—though he was no stranger to alcohol—but because they were meaningless. Not in some highfalutin intellectual way, but meaningless in that not a damn thing seemed to happen. He woke, he ate, he went to work at the textile mill. He inhaled lint and exhaled lint; he saw some lint mixed with the snot when he blew his nose into his kerchief. Then he went home and did the domestic thing with the kids and wife until he fell asleep. So many days like that, unimportant, not remotely memorable. And then one day *something actually happens* and you realize you've been chosen and it's a day you'll always remember and things click, fall into place, whatever phrase you want to call it but let's just say the day seems to goddamn *glow*.

That day had come a week ago. As he'd left the mill after a late meeting, he'd been struck by the darkness, evening falling sooner now. Streetlamps illuminated the small front lots of the people unfortunate enough to live across the street from the mill. Dale himself couldn't even smell lint anymore, the scent of it was burned permanently inside his nostrils, his skull. Sue Ellen claimed to like the smell of it on him, and he chose to believe her. He probably had enough of it bound to his insides, you could knit a sweater with it. Or at least a sock. The string intertwined with his muscles and tendons, his body literally becoming his work.

A green Plymouth approached, parking on the street a few feet away. The driver emerged, a gray fedora casting his face in shadow. A bit short, he wore a blue blazer and brown pants and shoes that clacked as he stepped toward Dale.

"I have a friend in Rockdale," the fellow said, extending a hand, his left.

The unexpected Kluxer code took Dale a second.

"I've been meaning to ask about him," he replied, extending his left so they could clasp hands and make the Kluxer shake, fingers loose and only their palms touching. Dale had loved this sort of thing ever since he'd first joined, the passwords and secret handshakes his father had taught him, the spycraft of it. Real life could be so goddamn boring otherwise.

Dale had been initiated at sixteen amid the fiery ceremony at Stone Mountain, he'd paid his Klecktoken membership fee, he studied the rules set forth in the *Kloran*, and he was on time with his dues every year, so he'd always chafed at the fact that they hadn't promoted him up the ranks. He'd always thought he was a natural for the Klavalier Klub, the secret police of the Klan, the ones who take military action when needed. Yet it seemed to him that the local Klavern was far more interested in talking about business and crafting overly complex ways to financially punish businesses that were too friendly to Negroes; it wasn't as engaged as it should have been in Klan basics: Breaking bones. Cutting skin. Keeping the Negro hospital busy.

Ten minutes later they were sitting at Yancey's, a bar Dale knew quite well on account of its proximity to both work and home. The stranger, who introduced himself as Jimmy Whitehouse, had led Dale to the back room, where four small tables hugged the walls and the music from a lone banjo player up front wasn't distracting.

Jimmy Whitehouse ordered a Coca-Cola. Some of the older Kluxers were like that, alas. So Dale, for perhaps the first time in his life at a bar, did the same.

"I'm from up in Coventry," Whitehouse said. He looked to be fifty, and when he removed his fedora he revealed a clean dome upon which two tufts of hair clung near the ears. Damn but Dale wished he had a beer and not this stupid Coca-Cola. "You're probably wondering why I'm talking to you and not one of the ranking members of your Klavern. Truth is, I wanted to be sure I could find someone who could be trusted. What I'm in need of is a small group that's willing to take risks for what's important."

"Then you're talking to the right fellow." Which would have been an excellent time to punctuate things with a sip of beer. He felt like an actor with the wrong props.

Whitehouse removed a kerchief from his pocket and blew into it. When he finished, he put it away, but he'd failed to remove a large bat that dangled from the cave of his left nostril. It was distracting, but Dale elected not to say anything about it.

"Glad to hear it. I was sent to you in particular—by whom, it isn't important. There's a matter that needs to be dealt with, but for various reasons it can't be done by the Coventry Klavern. We feel it should be done the proper way, one hand washing the other."

"Of course." Dale had no clue what Whitehouse meant, but he didn't want to look stupid. And that booger was distracting, vibrating as Whitehouse breathed. Dale rubbed at his own nose as a hint, but Whitehouse didn't catch it.

"So I'll just say it straight, and you can turn me down if you want to. But the fellow who needs to be punished is a white man."

Dale wondered if he'd misheard.

"He's the son of a friend of mine, in fact. They're both in the brotherhood, but they ain't what I'd consider active members. Anyway, my friend's son married a good woman, but he's been out drinking and running with loose women. He works in banking and insurance, and he is without scruple—he's cheated several families, getting them to sign documents they don't understand for policies that don't exist. Why the law doesn't get after him for it, I can't say. Bottom line, we feel that if he's scared off his path now, there might be time to save him yet."

"So this . . . This job doesn't have anything to do with what's happening here in Hanford Park?"

Whitehouse frowned. The goddamn booger was still dangling there. "No. Like I said, one hand washing the other."

Dale knew he wasn't doing a good job hiding his disappointment. He had assumed this meeting was to lay plans for the Negroes who, over the last few weeks, had moved into Dale's neighborhood of Hanford Park, on the western edge of Atlanta. Two years ago, when, like now, Negroes had dared encroach on Hanford Park, Dale had tried to enlist the aid of his cop brother-in-law, Rake, but had been given the cold shoulder. Someone else had taken care of things, thank goodness, burning a Negro's house down. Two years later, the problem had returned. So Dale had assumed this meeting was to address *his* Negro problem, yet they were talking about beating up someone way out in Coventry. A *white* someone. What the hell kind of Klavern was this?

"I believe in the creed," Whitehouse said. "I like to go roust the niggers as much as the next man, but you need to understand your history. The Kluxers are about more than the color of skin. We are the moral authority. Back in the day, we rousted drinkers, we rousted adulterers, we rousted those who tried to profit inappropriately from the churches. Like Jesus throwing out the moneylenders. Of course we rousted the niggers—that's one of the fundamental basics of maintaining an orderly society. But so is the sanctity of marriage. So is a man's obligation to his family and community. So is the right to capitalism and a fair profit. No wonder the Communists are gaining left and right—we have not been keeping our house in order."

"You're right," Dale said, so swayed by the man's words that it almost felt as if he had a buzz going. Better still, the force of Whitehouse's speech had finally dislodged the booger, sent it fluttering onto the table and almost landing on Whitehouse's folded hands.

"This job, it's about more than this one fellow I'm sending you after. It's about reminding everyone that we still are that moral authority. That we have a larger role. After the state cops came down so hard on us, everyone wanted to disavow us." A few years ago, the Georgia Bureau of Investigation had indicted some local Klan leaders. "All those years of FDR and his Jew Deal made everyone crazy! So the Klaverns quieted down, people stopped supporting us, and next thing you know there're darkies wearing police badges! Well, I say it's time to stop that tide."

Dale had been nodding constantly for a solid minute now. He never would have believed this scenario had it been sketched out to him that morning, but the way Whitehouse put it had the air of gospel truth. Something needed to be done, and this was the way to start it.

He understood now the "one hand washing the other" bit. What Whitehouse said reminded Dale of things forgotten, stories from his father and uncle, that in fact the Kluxers had once rousted not just coloreds and Jews and Communists and labor agitators but other non-leftist white folks, too, philanderers, those who brought dishonor to their communities. (The idea of beating a fellow simply because he had a taste for alcohol seemed a bit much—surely Dale had misheard Whitehouse?—but that explained the Coca-Cola.) Often, it was best for the local Klavern to ask Kluxers from a far-removed area to step in and do the job. That way a man wouldn't have to beat his own neighbor. One hand washed the other. One hand lifted the phone to call for aid and the other hand grabbed a whip and a gun. I take care of your problem, and you'll take care of mine.

If Dale helped him with this sinful white man up in Coventry, Whitehouse was saying, then the Coventry Klavern would in turn put an end to the Negro disruption in Hanford Park. And that was a bargain worth making.

A week later in the Coventry woods, Iggy was holding his hood, his robe billowing in the light breeze. "What in the hell are you talking about, Dale?"

Dale felt his heart sink. "Our target, he's a white man," he explained. "An adulterer and a cheat and a fellow that needs—"

"*What?* Jesus Christ, are you deranged?" Beside Iggy, Pantleg, too, was shaking his head in horror, the moonlight reflecting off his balding pate.

Dale had not personally recruited all of them, only Mott and Irons. Both of whom initially had been bewildered by the concept of beating up a white man neither of them knew, but they'd warmed to the idea when Dale explained how this was just advance payment on an entire legion of countrified Kluxers coming down to Hanford Park to drive the coloreds out. Dale had left Mott to recruit two more. He now turned to his best buddy. "Mott, you said you'd told 'em."

"Aw, I may have left a few things out."

"A *white* man?" Iggy practically spat. "This some kinda joke?"

"No, it's not a joke," Dale said. "It's us stepping up and doing our duty." He tried to sound calm as he made the sales pitch the way Whitehouse had, but Dale was no orator, and he did not have this crowd on his side.

Iggy said, "You made us drive all the way out here for nothing, goddammit."

"Not nothing," Pantleg said, "we passed some colored shacks a few minutes back."

"Yeah, that's right." Iggy perked up immediately.

"No, fellas," Dale tried to regain control, "we need to stick to our mission here and not get distracted."

"Shut the fuck up, Dale," Iggy snapped.

"Come on, now," Mott chided him. "We're supposed to be in this together."

"Screw that. We got our own mission." Iggy proceeded to tell the others that they had skirted past a Negro part of town, that he had observed a couple of youngish males wandering to their tiny house, maybe a mile from here. "Should be easy pickings."

Dale said, "Listen, I gave a man my word, and the way I was raised, a man's word counts for something." He could feel this long-awaited evening slipping away from him. "I know it ain't usual what we gotta do tonight, but the time has come for men to step up and do what they need to do. You still with me, Mott?"

"Course I'm with you," Mott said, loyal and steadfast as ever. But he added, "Maybe we can get after those niggers when we're done with our job?"

"Sure, if there's anything left."

Iggy laughed, then took another pull on the fifth. "Y'all are damned crazy." Then he looked at Irons as Mott and Dale pulled on their robes. "What about you, big man?"

All eyes on Irons. Despite his intimidating size, he seemed uncomfortable with the attention. He finally said, "I come here with them, I'll leave with them."

Thank the Lord, Dale thought. The mission would have been impossible with only two.

"That enough to change your mind, Iggy?" Dale asked.

"Fuck no. Only white ass I'll kick is yours, you keep pushing that damnfool line."

Dale felt his face redden and he could see Pantleg smile just before the son of a bitch pulled the hood over his head. Dale's fists were at his sides and he was not one to stand for being insulted, particularly around others, but he told himself to cool it. He had a Colt .38 revolver in his pocket and a bit of bourbon in his veins and he knew if he let himself take too much offense at Iggy's ravings then this evening would go sour very quickly.

"Come on," Dale said as he, Mott, and Irons walked back to their car. "Let's get to it."

The isolated Lean-To roadhouse looked like an old hunting cabin the owner had built an addition onto. One story, a long porch, the old roof slightly aslant. The wooded driveway leading to it was surprisingly steep, giving the building a vista in three directions, piney woods receding into the dark. Dale had spotted three other cars parked on the grass before him, which was more than he'd been told to expect.

Dale killed his lights as Mott asked, perhaps hopefully, "This a whorehouse, too?"

"I don't know." Dale rolled down his window to listen for music or revelry but couldn't hear anything. They were parked a good fifty yards away.

"I see three cars. Who-all else is in there? Friends of his?"

"Whitehouse said our man would definitely come out last, other than the fella that owns the place. And he told me the owner won't mind what we're doing at all. So that only leaves one unexplained car."

A light rain started falling, barely more than a mist. They sat for a while, mostly in silence, and Dale felt his enthusiasm for the job dampening. He hadn't realized he'd signed up for a stakeout.

The Lean-To's door finally opened. One light above the door lit a bowl of the lawn in front of it, though not enough to reveal where Dale had parked. Dale could see this man was not their target, too young, looked barely twenty-one. He walked over to a long Chevy and got in.

"Duck down," Dale said, feeling juvenile about it as he lowered his head beneath the dash. Seconds later he saw the light from the exiting Plymouth illuminate the top of his seat, then heard the gravel crunch as the car passed them and drove down the steep drive.

Another ten minutes later, that double snort of bourbon was feeling like a bad idea indeed. Dale had been fired up before, but now he was about ready to lean his head on the wheel and sleep. Christ, what was he doing here? Then the door opened again.

"That him?" Mott asked.

"I can't tell," Dale said angrily, drizzle on the windshield obscuring his view. Turning the car on to run the wipers would startle their target, so he simply said, "Let's go," and pulled on his hood. He opened his door and walked quickly, the others following.

Through his eyeholes he saw, stumbling toward a parked DeSoto, a man who matched Whitehouse's description of "twenty-nine, tall, thin, light brown hair that he obviously pays a great deal of attention to, and likely wearing a hat that costs half as much as a decent used car."

Just to be sure, Dale called out the man's name, "Martin Letcher?"

The man looked up. Appeared to have difficulty finding their forms in the dark. Then appeared to doubt his own vision. Then made a panicked burst toward the DeSoto, dropping his keys as Dale and the others ran toward him full speed.

Torches—this would have been better with torches. In the old days they would have been on horseback. Jumping out of a parked car in a gravel lot hardly had the same grandeur as tearing across a field astride stallions, a fiery torch in one hand and a pistol in the other, but this would have to do.

Unable to find his dropped keys, Letcher ran. He wasn't none too fast. Most surprising was the speed of Irons—he'd been a few steps behind Dale yet he was the one who sprang upon Letcher, driving him into the earth in an expert tackle. Dale was shocked such a big fellow could be so quick.

"You got the wrong man!" The first time, the ground muffled Letcher's cry, so he turned his head and screamed again, "You got the wrong man! I got no problem with you fellows!"

Irons rolled Letcher underneath him, so as to see his eyes.

"You're Martin Letcher, ain't you?" Dale called out, trying to establish some control while Irons did all the fun stuff.

"Yeah, but I'm in the brotherhood! Jesus, you got the wrong man!"

He sounded terrified, and that was before he'd been hit a single time. Irons commenced to strike him square in the face, then again, then again. It turned out Irons was quiet even when engaged in furious acts of violence. Not a sound, not even a grunt as he swung.

Finally Dale had to grab the big man's hand and get him to stop. At this rate Letcher would be unconscious before they could tie him to the tree and break out the strap. Per Klan regulations, Dale had brought a four-inch-wide by three-foot-long leather strap, nailed to a round wooden handle for easy gripping. He'd never used it in his life.

"We need him awake for the next part," Dale said, motioning to the strap, the rope in Mott's hands. Then he looked down and saw that he was already too late. Letcher was oblivious to all around him, his eyes shut, the skin from temple to jaw pink and pulverized. No way in hell would he wake anytime soon.

"Christ, Irons, you didn't leave nothing," Mott said.

"We can still do it," Irons said, standing up slowly, the hood and robe accentuating his size. Dale, puny beside him, realized he had unleashed something he would not be able to restrain.

"There's no sense tying him up if he won't even know what happened," Dale said. This was a right royal mess. They'd gotten the beating part done, had goddamn excelled at it, but without the target knowing why they were doing this, the ultimate meaning would elude them. It was reduced to savagery, randomness. Letcher would wake up with no clue why he'd been attacked. That righteous something that had filled Dale's chest dissipated, leaving him cold and empty.

Then they heard the Lean-To's door open, only the lights had turned off and they couldn't see who'd opened it. They could only hear the voice, *her* voice, and it was pure rage: "Stay the hell away from him!"

So many things that Dale had not expected. Clouds were fleeing suddenly, because the moon was back in view and he could see—just a bit, the moonlight not strong but enough—and the figure by the building was in a pose that struck true fear in his gut, even before he heard the boom of her rifle.

After the boom, Irons backed up a couple steps, weirdly, spastic. Then it was like his legs gave out, and the immense man crumpled. Then a second boom, and Dale flinched even more than he had the first time, because he understood what was happening now. He didn't think he'd been hit yet by the rifle the woman was holding, but Mott screamed in pain.

She was hollering at them to stay away. Dale finally remembered that he had a .38 in his pocket. It was like the inner gears of his brain had gotten jammed, sabotaged by something, but finally he was reaching for the gun and his joints were the opposite of jammed, they were moving too fast, so fast he nearly dropped the gun but he managed to cock the hammer and fire twice.

"Run!" Mott screamed, racing down the hill toward their car.

Dale looked down and got just enough of a view of Irons to know he should not be looking there, that he'd see that image in his nightmares for a good while, perhaps forever. Red everywhere, the man's skull no longer oval, not remotely geometric at all.

Dale fired a third time, running backward while he did so, and then the sole of his boot caught a particularly wet patch and he slipped, landing on his ass. His hood askew, he couldn't see a damn thing, so he tore it off, turning to run toward the car, firing behind himself blindly.

Inside the car, Mott held his left shoulder tight. Dale began to ask if he was all right but Mott screamed at him to turn on the goddamn car.

Another rifle blast and Dale heard an impact. He backed out as fast as the car could go, which was actually quite fast, and hit a tree. "Fuck!"

"Drive, goddammit!"

Some shifting and he managed to turn around and then came another blast and this time he felt something toward the rear of the car. He floored the gas and they were back on the main road seconds later when what looked like a ten-point buck leapt across the lanes, within mere feet of the car. It was gone as soon as it had come, like some apparition from Dale's addled mind, such a vision that it would have seemed an ominous portent if not for the fact that the damn thing was a few minutes late, all the bad had already happened, and Dale hadn't the faintest idea what he'd do next.

4

Boggs would one day remember that season as the time all the trees fell. The newspapers would find elaborate ways of explaining the phenomenon, something to do with the unusually dry spring and summer starving the root systems of stately white oaks and sweetgums and Shumards, leaving them brittle as matchsticks. And then the hard rains and gusts of the late-summer storms, gales that would continue to swoop in despite the turning of the season to autumn as if so full of fury and rage they would not heed any calendar, tearing across the Georgia piedmont with such suddenness that tornados spun in their wake. No twisters touched down in Atlanta, thank goodness, but the winds and the sudden downpours combined with the dry roots, many of them so ancient that their time had come regardless of such meteorological irregularities, and down the trees came.

Late one night a red oak that had been planted in the eighteenth century, making it possibly older than this nation itself, fell across the length of Auburn Avenue, crushing the top two floors of a brick building and wiping out the fortunately empty offices of two accountants and an attorney. Then there was the magnolia that lost a massive limb, the rest of the tree just fine but that one thick bough plummeting onto the wrought iron fence of the elderly Camilla Drummond, widow to one of the first Negro bankers in Atlanta. The impact of the fall knocked over several candles that she was still fond of using in lieu of electric lights, igniting a blaze that the too-late white firefighters were unable to extinguish. She escaped in time, but passed a week later, of a heart attack, as if she realized the Grim Reaper had her in his sights and she was unwilling to fight him. The next month a hickory crushed eight fortunately empty cars on Houston Street.

For Boggs, it got to the point that, when he was on duty walking the streets off Auburn Avenue—the wealthiest Negro street in the world, according to some magazine reporter, a fact proudly repeated by civic boosters—if he heard too loud a sound, one of his first assumptions was that somewhere a tree had fallen.

But what he heard now was altogether different, and more painful: a woman's piercing scream, an arrowhead lodged inside him. Each time she paused for breath it was like pulling the prongs out, hurting worse because he knew it would come back, and it did, louder than before.

Boggs and Smith made eye contact for a moment as they listened, then ran toward the building from whence the scream came. Smith pounded on the door and started to call out "Police" before it swung clean, and he hurried inside, Boggs a step behind.

The hallway was poorly lit and narrow, the walls marked with water stains. Three doors led to different apartments, as the old house had been partitioned into separate quarters.

A barefoot girl walked down the steps from the second floor. Eyes wide. Maybe seven years old, pigtails and a long dress. Somewhere above them the woman was still screaming.

"Who's yelling?" Smith asked her.

The girl's voice was so soft they barely heard her. "They say some-one's dead."

Two right hands fell onto the handles of holstered guns. "Where?"

The girl pointed up the stairs. They ran past her, Boggs telling her to stay down here.

The stairs led to a tiny landing, the beginning of what had once been a hallway, only a wall had been dropped into it and now three more doors led to three more apartments.

The screamer was using words now, "OH MY GOD OH MY GOD OH MY GOD!"

They drew their weapons and opened what they thought was the correct door, which wasn't locked. Then into a clean kitchenette, the old wooden floor creaking beneath them. One wall was decorated with a child's pencil drawings. Then a short hallway and into a small bedroom, two beds squeezed in a corner, and on one sat a young boy. On the other bed a lump, covered in sheets. A body?

Smith stepped into the room and leveled his gun at the lump, keeping its fatal gaze clear of the boy on the other bed. The boy was maybe three, Boggs guessed, and he didn't move even as these two armed men entered his bedroom.

Boggs pulled at the sheets. The lump was a little girl, about the same size as the boy, perhaps his twin, huddled into the fetal position, eyes red and cheeks covered in tears. She was shaking but otherwise she didn't seem to notice them.

Smith pointed his gun up at the ceiling.

The screams grew louder, coming from the next room.

There was no closet or anyplace anyone could possibly have hidden in this tiny room, so they left the kids and walked into the hall and into another small bedroom, and there on the floor, on her knees, was the screaming woman. Her hair had been in a bun but strands had come loose, ragged, her fingers had been pulling at it and there was blood on the shoulders of her dress, from her hands, which were holding someone, what used to be someone, now just a body, his face bloody. The wall to the side of the bed and one of the pillows were a deep, deep scarlet, the darkest red it can be without being black.

She paused for another breath and she turned to face them. At the sight of their guns she pulled her hands away from the body, but then she grabbed it again when she realized the body would have fallen onto the floor if she had fully released him, so she held him awkwardly, poised between the need to display her open palms to the police and her fear of what would happen if she ever let the man go again.

Boggs stepped forward, scanning the bed for a weapon. Had she shot him accidentally, was there a fight? That tended to happen. Had he killed himself, and had the weapon fallen nearby, and she could grab it and do Lord knew what with it given her current state? He didn't see one.

He would later rethink this moment and recall that there had been no smell of cordite, and he noticed right then that there was little mess, no immediate signs of struggle, though there would be time later to look for clues, piece together a narrative.

"Ma'am, are you hurt?" he asked, putting his pistol back in its holster. "Have you been shot?" He gestured toward her bloody shoulder.

Now her voice was a broken, small, staggered cry, the same words as before but infinitely smaller, "Oh my God . . ."

Smith left to check the rest of the apartment again, make sure no attacker lingered, no weapon at hand, no injured children. Which would leave Boggs to begin the arduous and nearly impossible task of returning her to earth, bringing her soul back down, getting her to breathe and please Jesus don't scream again, and explain to him what happened, what if anything she'd seen, and they were so very sorry for her loss.

Even sorrier than usual.

Because Boggs saw the photograph on her dresser, a portrait of the couple, the woman in what might have been a green dress with ruffles at the shoulders, the man in a plain suit and fat tie, and his eyes were familiar, familiar but different, because the man was smiling in the photo. But Boggs had no recollection of him smiling before. Who was he? It took a second, then he remembered the alley, and the moonshine and marijuana, and even the man's presidential name from his ID: Woodrow W. Forrester. It was the fellow who'd been so panicked about feeding his babies and who had told them about the moonshine and marijuana drop, insisting this was not the sort of thing he would normally do, but he had to help his friend, and here he was dead less than twenty-four hours later.

After a Negro doctor had given Mrs. Forrester a mild sedative, they questioned her about her husband, whom she described as a good father, loving husband, regular worshipper at Wheat Street Baptist, the very church behind which they'd busted him.

"Was he much of a drinker?" Smith asked. Boggs tended to let his partner do more of the talking when they questioned women. Ladies just seemed to love the fellow.

"Never. Never touched the stuff. He's not that type."

Despite the denial, she didn't seem to be wearing The Armor. The Armor was what Boggs called the facade victims' families typically wore when they needed to protect themselves or the memory of their loved ones. Folks who wore The Armor sometimes had secrets to hide; even with the initial shock of a murder, The Armor was firmly in place as they parried the officers' attempts to learn more about the deceased.

They wore The Armor to keep the cops from learning how this loving father was in fact a womanizer whose lothario ways had gotten him in trouble with other husbands in the neighborhood, or this charming young son in fact had a habit of breaking into homes, or this grieving widow was herself a cunning bookie. Yet sometimes The Armor was worn by the innocent, who had nothing to hide but their dignity, and they were so deeply offended to be questioned by these employees of the corrupt City of Atlanta, these paid enforcers of Jim Crow, that they refused to play along. So when Boggs came up against The Armor, when his questions were deflected by those steely looks, he told himself not to hate the wearer, tried to remember that they may be innocent and hurt, and that The Armor was strictly protective. Yet he hated it every time he saw it.

Mrs. Forrester's lack of The Armor was striking. She felt no need to protect her husband from questions that struck her as ridiculous.

"Do you know where he was last night?" Smith asked.

"Bowling. With his best friend, Lou Crimmons. They in a league down at Al's Lanes."

They both wondered whether this Lou Crimmons could be the regular dealer he'd told them he'd been covering for.

"Your husband bowl often?" Smith asked.

"Oh yeah, twice a week. Says it keeps him sane. I don't mind—it's better than other things a man could be up to at night."

They left her apartment with a list of his friends and acquaintances but little else. She had no idea why someone would hurt her husband, let alone walk into his home and shoot him dead. The children, thank goodness, had been out when it happened and hadn't seen anything.

As Boggs and Smith stepped outside, they lit cigarettes to deal with the stress of interviewing a new widow.

At last night's shoot-out, the Negro who'd been killed, by a stray bullet from his own lookout across the street, was named Wilbur Hayes. He'd done time for bootlegging back in the thirties, as well as more recent stints for assault and battery. And the white man Boggs had knocked out was Hank Loring, who lived in Reynoldstown, south of the tracks and not far from Sweet Auburn. At roll call today, McInnis had informed them that Loring had already posted bond. This seemed rather hasty; McInnis had assured them Vice was pursuing the case, questioning both Loring's and Hayes's known associates to find out more about the trade, but Boggs and Smith didn't buy it. From what they could gather, white officers were far more concerned with Boggs's hubris: word was spreading through the Department that Boggs had knocked out a white man. The fact that reefer was being trucked into the Negro community seemed of lesser import.

Boggs and Smith were met at the corner by Champ Jennings and Dewey Edmunds, who had been canvassing the neighborhood. No one claimed to have seen anyone unusual enter or exit the Forresters' building. No one even claimed to have heard any shots.

"Shooter used a pillow," Boggs told them. "There was one in the bedroom with a hole blown through it, and burn marks."

"So it was some'n knew him well enough to get real close," Champ said.

"Or he knocked him out first. I didn't notice a bruise, but the autopsy will say."

"Ol' lady in 2B across the street," Dewey said, "she claims she didn't see nothing, but I don't care for the way she said it. Seemed real scared."

"She's hiding something?" Smith asked.

"She had a whole lotta crosses on the walls," Dewey said, "so I laid in about Jesus wanting us to profess the truth and whatnot. She still said she couldn't help, but she thought long and hard about it first."

Champ rolled his eyes. "He invented a Bible verse, and she called him on it."

"Goddammit, I ain't no preacher's son like Boggs," Dewey snapped. "I was paraphrasing the Lord, all right? Paraphrasing."

"There was no 'Letter to the Sicilians' in the Bible," Champ said. "And if you'd let *me* talk more, I woulda got it out of her. Ol' ladies love me."

"I do not care to hear a thing more about what you do with old ladies."

Boggs tried to ignore them, looking up at the apartment building they were discussing. He saw a sliver of light through parted curtains in one of the second-floor windows, and no sooner had he noticed it than the light vanished, the curtains closing.

"She's skittish, that's for sure," Boggs said.

"Let's see how she sleeps tonight," Dewey said. "Let the guilt settle on her, then talk to her again."

"Let *me* talk to her again," Champ said.

"Fine," Dewey said. "Bring your Bible and some love potions. Rub her shoulders real good while you question her. Maybe her bunions, too."

"There's something else," Smith said. He explained to Champ and Dewey the connection between Forrester and the previous night's drop.

Dewey whistled. "So someone took him out for ratting about the drop."

"And I gotta tell y'all," Champ added, "when the white cops showed up last night? They moved me and Dewey away from those crates right quick. Like they didn't want us to get too close a look at what was in there."

Perhaps those white cops had been offended by the presence of Negro officers. Or perhaps they'd been taking protection money from the smugglers, and they were outraged that Negro officers were interfering. One of the white officers had even wanted to arrest *Smith* for Hayes's murder, backing off only when McInnis stood up for his officer. Until the autopsy was complete and they knew what caliber bullet had killed Hayes, white cops would believe Smith was to blame.

"You ask me?" Dewey said. "The ol' broad is smart to be keeping her mouth shut."

5

That same evening, Rake's night off, he sat at the kitchen table, worrying about his brother-in-law. Cassie was showering, after putting the kids to bed, but Dale had just called, telling Rake he urgently needed to talk in person.

Rake feared that the reason for Dale's urgent request to talk came down to one of three things: to borrow money, to confess to something, or to invite Rake to do the kind of thing that would later require its own confession.

Rake dearly loved his sister, Sue Ellen, and it pained him that she'd paired with someone like Dale, the very manifestation of lowered expectations. Just smart enough to get himself out of the various troubles he was getting himself into. Just lazy enough to skirt by at the mill where he passed time until the next paycheck, much of which he spent at bars. Just loyal enough that he had not, as far as Rake knew, cheated on Sue Ellen, which was both good and bad, because if he ever *did* cheat on her then Rake would beat him senseless, which would be fun, and which might also persuade her to leave him, which would be spectacular. But then the two little ones would be fatherless. So Rake's most realistic hope for Dale was that he might continue to be *just enough* to not make Sue Ellen too miserable and not drive Rake too crazy with his moronic schemes.

Rake rose from the table when he heard the wheels of Dale's car crush twigs in the driveway. He looked out the window and noted the way his brother-in-law walked, hands deep in jeans pockets, shoulders hunched as if quite a bit colder than he should have been.

A brief handshake, a terse conversation about the health of the kids. "So, uh, yeah, you're probably wondering what it is I wanted to talk about," Dale said as he sat on the couch. Rake didn't reply, just waited as he sat opposite Dale in one of the chairs. Since earning his badge, he'd learned the importance of providing empty verbal space for suspects and witnesses to fill with facts and suspicions, clues and admissions.

"Look, you know I'm not a fellow who likes asking for help on anything." Dale was looking away. Elbows on knees, tension compressing him. "But I got myself in a scrape, and, uh, I'm okay but one of us didn't come out too well. Not too well at all."

He started scratching at some invisible guilt near his right eyebrow, until finally Rake had to prod him, calmly, with "Why don't you just tell me what happened."

Dale recounted the sordid events of his "night ride" in Coventry. The more Dale said, the warmer Rake felt, sweat at the base of his back despite the crisp fall air blowing through open windows.

"The thing about it is," Dale said, "I've been looking into the newspapers, and I ain't seen much. The *Constitution* had a couple lines about a local man being shot up in Coventry, but that was it. It gave Irons's name but didn't say anything about it really, didn't mention the Kluxer attire he was wearing."

Rake seethed. His mind focusing on *Kluxer attire, gunshots, dead man.* "Jesus Christ! What were you . . . ?" and he shook his head. "Why in the hell are you telling me this?"

"The man that asked me to do the job, Whitehouse, he's up and vanished. I never had his number to start with, but when I called the operator to try and track him down, it's like he don't exist. My buddy Mott, he's okay, his shoulder wasn't hurt too bad and he just told the hospital he'd been cleaning his gun after having a drink and it went off. My taillight got shot off and my fender got dented, but I got 'em both fixed already."

"Dale. I don't give a damn about your fender. You just confessed, to a police officer, that you were party to a killing."

"But *I* didn't kill him, it was the lady who—"

"And you didn't go to the local police, you didn't tell anyone, you just ran off?"

"What else was I supposed to do?"

Rake let a few seconds pass, each of them filled with the infinite other options Dale could have chosen. "You had a hood and cloak on the whole time?"

"Well, no . . . The hood fell off at one point. I was running for my life, so I had to leave it there."

"Jesus. Did it have your name or initials stitched into it, any tailoring at all?"

"Course not." Dale dared to scoff at that, mocking Rake's ignorance about Kluxer attire.

"You're sure? No merit badges for learning how to tie a knot or beat up old Negro ladies?"

"*No.* And I don't care for the way—"

"Do you have any goddamn idea how much trouble you're in?" He struggled to keep his voice down lest he wake the kids. "Someone might have seen your tags. Was it a dirt drive? If so, you left tread marks. You left shell casings. And who else knew you were going there?"

"It was just the three of us: me, Mott, and Irons. I didn't tell nobody." His squirrelly tone implied otherwise.

"That's really all? You're sure?"

"*Yes,* that's all."

Rake ran his fingers through his hair, which, sadly, was thinning before his thirtieth birthday. With this job and this family, he would surely be bald in a few years.

"Goddamn it. You stupid son of a bitch."

He was furious not just at Dale but at himself for not having slapped some sense into Dale before something like this happened. His best opportunity had been two years ago, after a cookout one night, when Dale had tried to recruit Rake to do "something" about a Negro family that had moved to their neighborhood. Dale had been on his third or eighth beer at the time, and the "something" had not been discussed in detail, mainly because Rake had dodged it, trying to end the conversation as quickly as he could but also delicately enough to avoid offending his brother-in-law. It was damned challenging to maintain pleasant family relations when one of your relatives proposed such things. A couple weeks after that conversation, the Negro's house was torched, but the arsonists were both teenagers, not linked to Dale. Fortunately the Negro homeowners had been away that night. They soon sold the lot and moved elsewhere.

Two years later, Negroes had again breached the Beacon Street border into Hanford Park, so history was repeating itself. Or perhaps this time history had a new twist in store.

"Look, Denny," and Dale stood, perhaps to establish some authority as the senior of the two. "I understand you're upset and that's why I'm not gonna take much offense at how you're talking to me, but—"

"Sit back down."

"No, I don't care to be lectured to and looked down on."

"Dale, if you're up at my level it makes it a lot more likely that I'm going to swing at you, so, for your own protection, sit the hell down."

Dale looked into Rake's eyes for a few charged seconds. Whatever pride he'd tucked away to come here had insisted on emerging again, but now he appreciated the soundness of Rake's advice. He sank onto the couch.

Rake asked, "What in the hell were you even doing up there?"

"I told you, I *thought* I was helping out their Klavern so they'd help mine. Jesus, Denny, you can't be blind to what's happening: we got three families of coloreds here in our own neighborhood and I've heard tell there are more looking to buy. Kluxers need to step up the way we used to, only too many are scared by what happened a few years ago."

What had happened a few years ago was that the state Bureau of Investigation had helped prosecute a number of high-ranking Klansmen on the heels of some particularly severe beatings that made headlines (the beatings of white labor unionists had especially incensed people). That old-school violence no longer seemed to be appreciated by the kinds of folks who spoke fondly of a New South, and the state legislature even passed an anti-mask ordinance, discouraging the kinds of Klan rallies that had once been commonplace. Most Klaverns were reluctant to raise hell at the moment, for fear of spies and more indictments.

Yet from what Rake understood, the Klan was still alive and well, if quiet. He had learned since taking his oath that a shocking number of Atlanta's finest wore the white robes. Some joined out of family tradition, some did so simply because they felt it was required to get promoted on the force. And many joined because it gave them license to conduct the sorts of activities that were now frowned upon when wearing a badge. When the law became too constraining, a cop could trade one uniform for another. And the reform-minded governor who'd launched that GBI sting proved to be a one-termer, so the winds were shifting again.

"Either Whitehouse is hiding out because of how wrong things went, and he doesn't want to get blamed," Dale said, "or maybe he wasn't who he said he was. I tried getting his number from the operator, but there isn't a single Whitehouse in Coventry or the dozen other towns I tried."

"Is it like the Klan to use aliases like that?"

"Not usually."

"So you and some pals drove out of town to beat up a complete stranger you don't know from Adam, a white man, at that. And you did so at the word of another man you don't know from Adam, who may have been lying about who he was."

"I realize it sounds odd after the fact."

Rake could call the Coventry police and find out what they knew, read the report, see if the woman had been charged or was the shooting ruled self-defense. Was the fellow they'd beat up in the hospital somewhere? The fact that Dale's abandoned Klan hood hadn't been mentioned in the newspapers was not surprising, but it set Rake's mind working. Had the responding officer hidden it when he'd found it, to protect the Klan's reputation? If so, was it just to keep the Klan out of the papers, or was it because the local police had been involved somehow?

"Tell me more about Mott and Irons. I want their phone numbers, occupations, addresses, family, churches." He found a pad and paper. "Did any officers drop by to check out your buddy's story at the hospital?"

"No. He just told the doctors that his gun misfired."

"And you're sure the fellow you beat up isn't dead?"

"Well, no, but I've been checking the papers. It's not like I was going to call the hospital and ask. And again, for the record, I never laid a hand on him. It was all Irons."

"Oh, sure, you just stood there egging him on with your gun. Speaking of which, get rid of that gun. Forever. You left shell casings on the ground and bullets in the side of the building probably."

Rake asked about Whitehouse, what he looked like, what car he drove, what they discussed, funny turns of phrase, anything at all that might help. Dale had nothing. Or next to nothing: "He had, well, he had an awful lot of nose hair."

Rake stared. "He had a lot of nose hair. Great, Dale, thanks, I'll put out an APB for a man with a lot of nose hair. How hairy was his back?"

"I'm just trying to help."

Rake quizzed him about Irons, then let out a deep breath and marveled at the enormity of this problem he'd been handed.

"I know I fucked up, Denny." His voice small and thin, almost breaking. "I can barely afford the mortgage on our place—I didn't get no GI Bill loan like you did, and when I didn't get named foreman last year . . . We're barely scraping by, all right? I can't have this neighborhood turn into Darktown."

Rake waited for Dale to put himself back together.

"Tell absolutely no one about this conversation." Though he greatly distrusted Dale as a keeper of secrets. "Not even Sue Ellen. If anyone talks to you about that night, whether it's your buddy Mott or a relative of the dead man or God forbid another cop, tell me immediately."

"I will. Absolutely."

"Jesus Christ. I cannot believe I have to help a group of Kluxers."

"We prefer 'Klansmen.'"

"I prefer 'goddamn idiots.'"

Dale took his medicine in silence this time.

"Understand this: whatever blackmail you pulled on Sue Ellen to con her into marrying you is the single smartest move you've ever made. Because if not for that, I would drag your ass into jail right now. For criminal assault at the very least, accessory to murder as a bonus. But I don't want my nephews to deal with that, let alone my sister. So I'm going to *try* to help you out of this. But if you do anything remotely that stupid again, if you even float the idea of messing with the new Negroes in Hanford Park, then Brooks and Dale Jr. *will* grow up without you, one way or another. Understand?"

Dale stood and walked to the door. "Take your shots, Denny. A man's down in front of you, so stomp on him all you like. Enjoy it."

"I don't *enjoy* putting my job at risk to help you. I need you to be smart in the meantime."

"Yeah, well, Sue Ellen's probably looking for me, so I need to get back." And without so much as a thank-you, Dale closed the door gently behind him.

6

Dinner with Lucius's family had always been a stressful experience for Julie.

The Boggs patriarch lived in a large bungalow, complete with a second-story addition, just a few blocks down Auburn Avenue from the Irwin Street Baptist Church that, legend had it, he'd built from near nothingness into what it was today, one of the largest churches in Atlanta. The house had always seemed perfect to her, or at least unattainable: its well-shined floor, the artwork on the walls, the furniture that wasn't worn or in disrepair or covered in bedsheets. The sheer lack of problems, the absence of the sort of blemishes she was so very used to tolerating. As a maid, Julie had worked in such houses, but she'd never been entertained in one, never seen one owned by colored folk.

The family even had their own maid, a silent older lady named Roberta, who did the cleaning and most of the cooking for Mrs. Boggs— Julie hadn't even realized that was possible, had assumed some law forbade it. The flat look on Roberta's face when she served the family their dinners was one Julie knew all too well, and she wished there'd been some way to commiserate with her, some secret wink or signal, yet the one time they'd made eye contact Julie had seen an iciness there that made her tongue stick to the roof of her mouth.

Her first dinner here, at a surprisingly formal Sunday dinner a year ago, Reverend Boggs had asked her if she'd understood his earlier sermon or if it had been difficult for one who hadn't been raised on the Good Book, what with all those superstitions and African rituals that persisted along the Georgia coast where she was from.

"I enjoyed it quite a bit, sir," she'd responded. "My family came to Atlanta when I was six, so I don't recall much of those times."

"I'm sure they've brought enough of that with them, though," he'd replied. "Voodoo dolls and snakes and whatnot."

"They're remarkably modern, actually," Lucius had interjected. "They even have indoor plumbing."

Lucius had meant that, she knew, as a shot at his father's condescension, yet the reverend had happily taken it as a shot at her family, laughing at her perceived backwardness while the others all smiled uncomfortably.

She felt very aware of her ebony skin, noticing the lightness of Lucius's mother and sister-in-law. They no doubt accentuated it with the kinds of skin-bleaching creams and lotions Julie couldn't afford. She wasn't the darkest person she knew, but damn close.

The conversation that first afternoon had been a verbal minefield, as Lucius's parents prodded her this way and that, trying to make something explode. *It's too bad that darling child of yours couldn't make it today, we were hoping to meet him.* And, *Is your father still searching for work, or has he landed something stable? Do let us know if he needs any leads, as we could probably help line something up.* Even their favors dripping with insincerity. They had made a show of asking Lucius, as if Julie wasn't sitting right there, how certain lady friends of his were doing, girls with names like Leila and Marion and *Geneviève*. Those lacey, embroidered names reminders to Julie that the privileged Boggs son was an eligible bachelor indeed, with scores of women to choose from. The parents seemed to think—or were desperate to pretend—that Julie was a mere friend, someone he was tolerating in a Good Samaritan kind of way, tending to her and her four-year-old son until he decided his good work was finished and then he could move on to marry a Geneviève. So Julie was pleased by the way he deflected their questions (*I don't know, I haven't seen her, I'm really not sure*).

She'd hated every minute of that first dinner, and she couldn't imagine how the initial conversations between father and son had sounded, Lucius telling the upright minster about the fallen woman he wanted to bring into their sacred house.

The intermittent dinners had become slightly less awkward over time, but she had a feeling tonight's would be the worst yet. She could only imagine how the reverend and his wife would respond to the big announcement.

One year after that first visit, she was back in their immaculate dining room, which had hosted so many important Negro business leaders and academics, and even a few important white folks whose names she didn't know (Reverend Boggs dropped names the way hungry men dropped crumbs, littering the floor with them while he ate). Her four-year-old, Sage, sat in a chair across from Lucius's nephew and niece, as if he belonged at this table, too. Because he did, or at least would, as soon as Lucius worked up the nerve to tell them.

She was lost in thought, fretting over when and how Lucius would say it. Failing to pay attention was dangerous with this crowd, as the conversation could veer anywhere so quickly. They seemed to be talking about relatives of Lucius's partner, Tommy Smith—his sister and her husband had recently bought a house in a white neighborhood.

"It's risky," Reginald said.

"Are you saying they made a mistake?" Reverend Boggs asked.

"Not necessarily. But buying in a white neighborhood, you know what could happen."

"I don't think it will this time. I think the white community understands." Housing for Negroes was scarce, after so many years of rural sharecroppers leaving their hoes behind and moving to the city in search of a better life.

"They do?" Reginald seemed to hold back a laugh. "Have they changed that much in two years, when the Calvins' place was burned down?"

"I pray that they have."

"Well, when you have to request divine intervention, that means it's a risk." Lucius's elder brother was a manager at Atlanta Life Insurance, one of the largest Negro-owned businesses in the country. Lucius had briefly worked there after the war, he'd told Julie, but he wasn't a numbers man and hadn't taken to the work. "We wouldn't even offer them fire insurance if they asked for it. They're on their own."

"How's work going, Reginald?" Boggs asked.

"Good. We just closed a strong quarter. More folks seem to be getting work. It's not as good as during the war, but it's better than it's been."

"Well, I'm glad some coffers are growing these days," Mrs. Boggs said dryly.

Lucius took the bait and asked, "How's the Fall Fund coming, Father?"

"It's coming along," the reverend replied. "I'm still hoping to get enough to expand the church's footprint, but we'll have to see what the Lord has in store."

Although Sweet Auburn was still the cultural and commercial capital of Negro Atlanta, over the last few years it had become more fashionable for well-off Negroes to move to the West Side, on the other side of downtown, near Morehouse and the other universities. This was putting a drain on Irwin Street Baptist, apparently.

"Wheat Street just added another wing," Mrs. Boggs said. "And now they're installing air-conditioning in the entire church."

"I don't need to hear about Wheat Street at my own dinner table, thank you," the reverend snapped. "Let's change the subject, please."

Lucius normally had great tact, but Julie had noticed those graces tended to fail him around his father. And so, right when it seemed the old man was at his crankiest, Lucius said, "There's something that we wanted to share with you tonight."

His nervousness no doubt tipped them off, and the use of *we* put it in lights. She saw the looks in their eyes, and noticed that the reverend leaned back in his chair as if hoping to escape the reach of an incoming blow. She could only look at so many of those forced-polite expressions before she cast her eyes down at the table. Lucius took one of her hands in his and stood, so Julie did the same, which made her feel even yet more vulnerable. Without further preamble he said, "The other night I asked Julie if she'd be my wife, and I'm happy to announce that she accepted."

She smiled, uncomfortably, trying to keep the smile there even during the silence that followed, the silence that could not possibly have been as long as it felt.

"Congratulations! That's wonderful." The voice that finally rang out was William's, God bless him. Only twenty, the youngest of the Boggs sons had missed, either out of sheer goodness or youthful naïveté, the deep displeasure in his father's eyes.

Reginald stood up, smiling now, and hugged Lucius. Then pecked his future sister-in-law on the cheek. "Congratulations."

Reginald's wife, Florence, was right behind him, hugging Julie extra tight. Then she explained the situation to her confused children: "Little Sage is going to be your cousin now," and the oldest one, the boy, nodded slowly, trying to puzzle this out.

Mrs. Boggs did not dispense any hugs, as she'd chosen that moment to walk into the kitchen and discuss dessert with Roberta.

The reverend cleared his throat, turned to William, and asked him how his classes at Morehouse were going. Lucius held Julie's hand again and she could feel how sweaty his palm was as they stood there, listening to the youngest Boggs man, who seemed uncomfortable at taking the spotlight from them but would not disobey his father. William started talking about his courses in public speaking and theology, and eventually Julie and Lucius sat back down.

Later, in the sitting room, Julie sat with Florence as the eldest Boggs grandchild showed off what he'd learned in piano lessons, which wasn't much at all.

"He's very talented," Julie said, charitably, as the child played a series of notes that had never been intended to go together. Florence's younger two and Sage were watching with almost fearful expressions, as if the piano were a torture device that would be applied to them next.

"Thank you. We started him on it when he was four."

Was that a dig at Sage, who was the same age and had never touched a key before?

"They're real good kids," Julie said.

"I'm worried about them, though. Can you believe it with the schools going down to three hours? This is crazy." Due to severe overcrowding and lack of funding, Atlanta's few Negro schools were now operating on a rotation system, with children in class only three hours before they were dismissed and the next group came in. "How are they supposed to learn like that? I had to give up my own teaching job, because every third hour I need to bring one kid in or the other out. The NAACP is suing to make the city give our schools equal funds, but I'm not holding my breath."

"It's a shame." Talk of politics worried Julie, as there were so many more players and acronyms that she didn't know, and the Boggs family's alliances weren't always clear.

Then Florence scooted a bit closer to her on the sofa. She said in a low voice, "Girl, they didn't treat me much better at first. You'll wear them down eventually."

Julie smiled, amazed at how badly she'd needed to hear that.

"The reverend and Felicia are very proud, is all," Florence confided. "Sometimes, the ones who are proud of how far they've made it are the quickest to disapprove of others making that same climb."

On the porch, Lucius and Reginald were smoking cigars in the dry autumn air. Smoking, like Reginald's fondness for bourbon, was anathema to their clerical father, but Reginald seemed to revel in his objections. Lucius himself was prohibited by police code from touching alcohol, so his taste for tobacco had only grown since he'd taken his oath.

"A man needs at least *some* vice, am I right?" Reginald smiled. "And now that you're officially giving up women, you'll have to move up to the good cigars."

"Not on my salary."

"How's work going?"

Lucius was never sure how to describe it to his friends and relatives. On the one hand, he was hailed as a hero to be one of the first Negro officers. They were role models, authority figures, Jackie Robinson with sidearms. On the other hand, white officers mocked and insulted and sometimes nearly killed them, laughing as they gunned their squad cars' engines toward any Negro officers they saw crossing the street. The people they arrested hardly treated them better. No one being busted on possession of narcotics or assault or theft ever paused from his ranting to thank the officers for taking this important step for Negro rights.

"It's okay," Lucius said. "Just had a little incident with some moonshiners. White cops didn't love how we handled it."

Just before dinner, he'd received a call from Smith: Lou Crimmons, the man Woodrow Forrester's widow had said was his best friend, had been killed that morning. Mere hours after Forrester's murder. According to witness reports, Crimmons had been shot three times while walking down Hilliard Street at half past noon. Witnesses claimed a man wearing a hat tipped low and a bandanna over his mouth had pulled up, shot Crimmons, then jumped out to take something from the dead man's coat before driving off. As these things went, the witnesses disagreed on everything else: the car (a black Ford or a dark blue Buick convertible with the top up), the shooter's appearance (thick glasses versus no glasses, brown leather jacket versus gray coat), his hat (brown fedora? black derby?), his skin color (dark brown or medium toned). Oh, and the car's tag numbers? No one had noticed them.

Boggs and Smith were nearly certain now that Crimmons was the man Forrester had spoken of, the friend who usually sold jars and joints but had taken sick, asking Forrester to sell in his place. Then Forrester gets caught by Boggs and Smith, and in exchange for his freedom he tells them about the upcoming shipment, which they disrupt half an hour later, and the next day Forrester is killed. Another day later, the man he'd been subbing for is killed, too.

"We should have interviewed Crimmons," Smith had said to Boggs. "Shouldn't have left it to the white cops."

In truth, they had no say in the matter. They only worked the 6 p.m. to 2 a.m. shift, so they were the ones finding bodies or evidence of break-ins, and then they'd file their reports and clock out. McInnis never would have allowed them to interview friends and acquaintances of murder victims; that job was left to white detectives. No matter how well Boggs and Smith did their jobs, they felt sabotaged by white officers, who could arrest an innocent Negro they didn't like, brutalize witnesses, and present skewed evidence to white juries.

Three bodies in three days was a particularly bad run, but hardly unprecedented. Boggs had seen quite a few bloodbaths where liquor got to flowing and tempers raged. He had arrived at cramped apartments after husbands or brothers or old friends had finally done what they'd long threatened to do, then turned the weapon on themselves, unwilling to live in a world whose lines could so easily be crossed. Affairs interrupted, old scores settled, blood feuds magnified. Pride became even yet more important when people had little else, and it must be defended at all costs. The costs were huge.

When Boggs had taken this job, he had seen himself as a standard-bearer for his people, but sometimes he felt more like a pallbearer. It was all he could do to keep going, trying to do what he believed was the Lord's work, despite his persistent doubts.

＊

At least Smith got one piece of good news when he'd called: according to McInnis, the bullet that killed Wilbur Hayes, the black smuggler at the telephone factory, was a .30-30, likely fired from a Winchester rifle. So Smith was officially off the hook. But only *officially*. Unofficially, McInnis warned, Smith should assume that most of the white cops would still think he'd shot Hayes and stashed a rifle somewhere. He should consider himself watched.

As if he didn't already.

＊

Reverend Boggs, waving his hand disgustedly at the smoke, joined them on the porch, followed by William. "I've told you not to do that here, Reginald."

"It's a special occasion."

Lucius never understood how Reginald could charm his way out of his father's disfavor, whereas Lucius always struggled for some modicum of acceptance. *Well, Father, I've grown tired of trying to win your approval. You're the one who has to accept something for a change.*

As Reginald asked William about his classes, Lucius found himself beside his father.

"I won't lie and say I'm pleased with your choice," the reverend said. "I was disappointed you didn't follow me to the pulpit, but ultimately it was the right thing, since you certainly haven't chosen a preacher's wife."

Lucius decided that letting his father's slights pass would be better than escalating the matter. He didn't want the night of the announcement to be remembered for a screaming match. He said, "I'm sure William will find a woman more worthy of your approval."

"Look, Lucius, there are marrying women and other women. Can't you tell which she is? You've had your fun, but it's time to move on."

Lucius did move on—off the porch and into the house, where, seething, he told Julie it was time to go.

＊

"At least he didn't threaten to disown you," Julie told him a few minutes later. They were two blocks from her house now, Sage asleep in his arms, the boy's head digging into his shoulder.

"You look good carrying him," Julie smiled. "It's nice, him having a daddy."

"I might not look so good by the time we make it to your house. Ten blocks is pushing it, even for a strapping lad like myself."

The walk to her house was mostly south, toward the tracks, and these last few blocks were the worst of it. Not much to look at by day—shotgun shacks and crumbling bungalows and two-story brick buildings that had been subdivided into more apartments than one would think possible—and by night the sheer darkness and shadowed outlines of those slouched buildings and the whispered and laughing voices that came seemingly without source caused in Lucius a distinct sense of alarm that his beloved lived here. He wished he could rush the engagement and marry her next week, not just because he was dying to have her but also because the thought of her living out here was constantly on his mind. The more he'd fallen for her, the more menacing the neighborhood seemed to become. This wasn't just a place he visited. A piece of himself lived here now, and it wasn't safe.

They passed three men sitting on a crumbling porch. Coins dropped onto piles and he smelled that at least one of their cigarettes was in fact marijuana. They were laughing as they gambled, paying no heed to the passing family.

Lucius stopped. He hardly looked intimidating with a child on his shoulder, and no uniform, but still he used his deeper cop register and said, "Take that inside, gentlemen."

He paused only a moment, then resumed his walk. They muttered behind him, too quiet to make anything out.

"You don't have to do that," Julie said.

"I do." *You are a cop twenty-four hours a day,* McInnis always told them.

In fact, there was a reason Boggs was particularly bothered about today's murder of Forrester's friend, Crimmons. The address of the shooting was only two blocks from Julie's house, and it happened in broad daylight. He wondered if little Sage had heard the shots.

They reached her house, a cramped bungalow that, divided in half by a too-thin wall, her family shared with another. He offered to carry Sage inside and lay him in the tiny bed that sat beside hers, but she said her mother was likely indecent at this hour. She never wanted him in her house, he'd noticed.

"Lunch on Tuesday?" he asked after he gently transferred Sage into her arms, impressed at how effortlessly she carried him despite her smaller frame. Girl was stronger than she looked.

"I hope so; I need to check."

Between his working six nights a week and her cleaning and serving for white people in a different part of town, her short lunch break was the only time they could meet, other than his one day off. Even then, he needed to borrow his father's car, pick her up, and dash to a deli in Sweet Auburn. They spent most of that time driving.

He kissed her good night and waited until she'd closed and locked the door.

Free of Sage's forty pounds, he pinwheeled his right arm and stretched his neck from one side to the other. He could again hear the stoned gamblers laughing, and he felt his blood rise.

Not in this neighborhood. Not anymore.

His decision made, he started walking toward them. Then he stopped when he saw, on the corner across the street, a solitary figure standing like a sentry.

Solitary in more ways than one. Bartholomew Kressler, one of Sweet Auburn's stranger characters, was a madman of perhaps forty-five who insisted that he was a white man whose soul had been trapped in a Negro's body. He had no occupation anyone knew of yet he was always finely dressed, pince-nez and all, though his clothes frequently needed mending after he got into fights with other Negroes, whom he uniformly insulted, asking who they thought they were to share the sidewalk with him, don't you inferior beings have any manners? He had twice been arrested for sitting in the front of a bus and refusing to move despite the driver's protests, as he claimed to be white, insisted his unseen whiteness gave him the prerogative to park his behind wherever he chose. Lucius had arrested him for public drunkenness twice.

Boggs crossed the street. "What brings you here, Bartholomew?"

"That's *Mr. Kressler* to you, boy." He spoke as formally as Boggs's old Morehouse professors, and today he was wearing a white-on-blue windowpane blazer over gray slacks that could have used laundering.

"Easy there. I'm in no mood."

"Of course not. Because you're looking for the big nigger."

"Excuse me?"

"The biggest one there is." He watched Boggs for a moment, then his shoulders sagged and he wore a chagrined look. "Really, you are such a dim race. Do I have to spell it out for you?"

"Spell *what*?"

"Thunder Malley. You and your partner were looking for him yesterday on Hilliard Street, but you couldn't find him."

Hilliard Street was where Woodrow Forrester had lived. "You were there?"

"I was . . . in the alley across the street, pondering Kant's theory of freedom. While I stood there, I saw you and your partner, and those other two black cops. And about an hour before you had arrived, I had seen something else. At five, perhaps five thirty? Thunder Malley."

"What exactly did you see?"

"Thunder went into that building, with his little helper, the one with the reddish hair. They went in, and five minutes later they scurried off."

No wonder the old lady across the street hadn't wanted to admit what she saw. Thunder Malley, a six-six behemoth, was a loan shark and ran a protection racket. The Butler Street precinct had been watching him for years, but they had yet to turn up hard evidence, as no one dared inform on him. They hadn't thought he was involved in moonshine or drugs, but perhaps he was expanding his services.

"Mr. Kressler, sir, what did you hear?"

Bartholomew wrinkled his nose. "I would rather discuss this with white officers."

Boggs held out his right hand as if modeling a watch. With his other hand he grabbed one of Bartholomew's and held the two beside each other. Bartholomew's skin was darker. "You see that, right? You understand who you are."

"What you are referring to," an outraged Bartholomew said as he reclaimed his wrist, "is the body to which I have been confined ever since the horrible experiment. It's what I am on the *inside* that matters, and I expect the deference that is my due, boy."

Boggs told himself to take a breath and not ruin this. "Sir, I can arrange to have you speak with our white sergeant if that makes you more comfortable."

"It would, but where? In your *black* precinct?"

"He'd be happy to meet you wherever you're most comfortable, Mr. Kressler."

This is as crazy as he is, Boggs thought. They could never put this lunatic on a witness stand. But if he could provide details, that might lead to more evidence, or a witness who was actually sane.

"I suppose a conversation with your sergeant would be wise," Bartholomew said, after giving the matter considerable thought. "I can certainly empathize with the poor fellow. We're the only two white men who spend all our time in Darktown."

7

After Dale's startling admission about his night ride, Rake had waited one day before investigating. He'd wanted to wait even longer, in hope that his rage might pass so he could see things clearly, but he didn't have time to wait for it to fully pass. It likely never would. Dale was his problem and would continue to be.

So, hoping he wasn't making a terrible mistake, he called the Coventry sheriff's office, explaining that he was an Atlanta cop hoping for more information about the shooting.

He'd already confirmed what Dale had learned, that there was no one in the area named James or Jimmy or even J. Whitehouse. Not in Atlanta, Coventry, or the surrounding counties. And APD's Records Department didn't have it listed as a known alias.

A Coventry deputy forwarded his call to the surprisingly gentle-voiced Sheriff Marone.

"One of my colleagues happened to be up there yesterday and heard about it," Rake lied, "and then last night I had a drunk in the tank who mentioned something about a roadhouse beating. Made me wonder if he maybe knew more about it."

He couldn't let them realize he was calling for any but official reasons. He had, in fact, arrested a drunk last night, and the man had said nothing of the sort, but Rake didn't mind dangling the wino like this. Cops were used to chasing false leads. He gave Marone the name and address of the drunk, whom they'd released already.

"Interesting," Marone said. "You know that the man who was killed was from Atlanta, I presume?"

"Yes, sir. Walter Irons." Rake had checked Irons's police record: three priors, two for bar fights and one for assaulting a woman in front of a passing beat cop. Just another fellow who was more muscle than brains, more temper than thought, more bad luck than good.

"I've already spoken to detectives in Atlanta about him," Marone said. "We're looking into it."

"What do you know about the man Irons beat?"

"Martin Letcher's a banker, for First Regional of Coventry. As was his old man. We haven't yet determined why a group of roughnecks from Atlanta would see fit to show up at an out-of-the-way spot like that, but we will."

Rake tapped a pencil, staring out the kitchen window at their small backyard. Two cardinals alighted on the lowest branches of an oak whose trunk Rake had painstakingly cleared of ivy two summers ago, and below them Denny Jr. reenacted violent crashes with his toy trucks. They'd owned the house nearly five years, since shortly after Rake returned from the war.

"You don't think it was just a barroom brawl got out of hand?"

"Didn't have that look." Marone's tone hinted at knowledge he was not going to disclose.

"What can you tell me about Letcher?"

"Got beat half to death and nearly the other half, too. Fella that was on top of him did it with his bare hands."

"Is Letcher still in the hospital?"

"I expect he will be for several more days."

"He the kind of fellow that makes a lot of enemies?"

"I imagine most bankers have enemies, but that doesn't mean they're in the habit of being beaten like that. Coulda been angry folks who got turned down for a loan or lost their house, or Communists who hate bankers, for all I know. But his father, who's retired now, is well respected. His was one of the only banks around here that stayed open through the Depression."

"Were Letcher or the barmaid able to describe the attackers?"

"Nah, she was too far away, and all he saw were fists 'til he blacked out." So the Coventry cops weren't letting on that it was the Klan, not even to other cops. Marone was keeping that information to himself, but why?

"How's the barmaid doing?"

"Ah, she's tough as hell. Not the first fellow she had to take down like that."

"Really? First she's killed?"

"You don't need to worry about her. Or any of this. I do appreciate the call, Officer . . . Rakestraw." The pause like he was looking for Rake's name, which meant he'd written it down. *Shit.* "But I think we'll be all right on our own up here."

❧

Martin Letcher's pretty eyes were so light blue they seemed to glow, like the sunstruck surface of Caribbean waters in some vacation magazine. Many a woman had no doubt lost herself in those eyes, Rake figured, but right now they were just the merest sparkle in a face that looked destroyed.

Dark shiners still hadn't quite faded. Tape stretched across the bridge of his nose, so swollen it was hard to assess how well the doctors had reset it. Bandages covered both cheekbones, and at least two teeth were missing.

"Sorry to bother you, sir, but I'd just like to ask you a few questions."

A few hours before his shift, Rake was not in uniform, had not even displayed a badge. Hoping to make this as informal as possible. He'd made his way to the room without incident and had been fortunate to find Letcher alone. The small room held one bed and a tiny table of medical implements. Propped up on a small mountain of pillows, Letcher had been reading the newspaper. His right hand had been replaced by an enormous club of a cast, so he gripped the paper with his relatively unscathed left hand. He was barefoot and had two of the cutest little callus-free soles Rake had seen on a grown man.

"Ask away. Surprised an Atlanta cop would care, but sure, the more help the merrier. I want those sons of bitches in jail or dead."

There was nothing for Rake to sit on, so he stood, glancing for a moment out the window at the perfect autumn sky. The drive here had been postcard gorgeous, windows down all the way.

"From what I understand of the incident, sir, you weren't able to get a clear look at your attackers?"

"Course not, they had hoods on."

So the Coventry cops were going out of their way to conceal the Klan connection, but the victim had no such agenda.

"Do you have any idea why the Klan would come after you?"

"No and hell no. I'm with them all the way, a hundred percent."

"Ever wear the robes yourself?"

Letcher paused. "Most fellows know not to ask that."

Rake realized there must be some code with which Kluxers identified themselves. He'd just exposed himself as a nonmember.

"I'm just trying to find out who did this to you, sir, but if you aren't interested in my help I can be on my way."

"Okay, look: I do what I have to do to keep up appearances, you get me? But I ain't out there running around all night dressed like a fool. I got other things to occupy my attentions in the evening, if you get my drift." He grinned, the jocularity all but overshadowed by those missing teeth. "The thing of it is, many folks in the Coventry Klavern are friends of mine."

"Have those friends been able to shed any light on what happened?"

"No. That's what's so damned odd. It's like some splinter faction or something. I have friends in the right places, you hear me? My bank owns a quarter of the mortgages in this town, and a hell of a lot more besides. We do business down in Atlanta, too, matter of fact. So if the Klan had a problem with me, I'd know it."

It was a risk to come here. For all Rake knew, Letcher would tell Sheriff Marone everything they discussed, leaving Marone to wonder why this Atlanta cop was so incredibly interested in the beating. The Coventry police might then look into Rake and find their way to Dale.

"I apologize if this is talking out of turn, but what if I told you that they did what they did because of how you carry yourself? The women and drinking, that is."

"I'd say the hell with you. How's that?"

Rake smiled. "I'm not judging you. I'm saying, what if the people who did this to you were trying to teach you some lesson because they thought a small-town banker should be home with his wife at night?"

"First, I'd say you're crazy. Second, I'd say, who the hell says I'm *not* home with my wife at night? And third, or whatever the hell number we're on now, I'd say that if that's why they came after me, why didn't they goddamn say so? They didn't say anything. Not a word." Rake wasn't sure if Letcher was always this flippant and off-color or if pain medication had taken the wheel. "They just started beating the hell out of me for no reason. Feel like I've been having the world's worst hangover ever since."

"How about jealous husbands?"

"Why are you so interested in who I may or may not be screwing?"

The cussing braggadocio was not what Rake had expected from a man of Letcher's station. He rather liked the fellow.

"I'm just looking to confirm or rule out some rumors I'd heard."

"What goddamn rumors? Who you been talking to?"

"Does the name Jimmy Whitehouse mean anything to you?"

"Not a thing. And I'm getting tired of the questions."

"Just a couple more. You mentioned you do business in Atlanta. What kind?"

"Little of everything. Loans to small businesses, real estate, even own a stake in some mills down there."

"Is Sweetwater Mill one of them?"

"How you know that?"

"Lucky guess." Whoever had sent Dale to beat up Letcher was someone who knew them both. The person pulling the strings wanted to teach Letcher a lesson, and he knew Dale would eagerly do so with minimal prompting. Rake was looking for something that could connect the two men, and he'd found it. "How long have you owned it?"

"Don't own it, just bought a big stake. An investment. I felt it was undervalued after the war ended, and textiles is one industry that isn't going anywhere. People aren't gonna start walking around naked, are they? We'll always need clothes, and Georgians are damn good at making 'em, and they do it cheaper'n Northern union folk do."

Sure, Rake thought, and it helps when the Klan attacks union organizers like they did in the thirties. "During the course of buying in, did you find yourself making any enemies?"

"Look, buddy, I'm in the business of making money, not friends. I told Sheriff Marone the same thing: if he wanted a list of everybody who'd want to see me taken down a peg, it'd be a long goddamn list and I wouldn't know half the names. There are people I've never heard of probably hate my guts. That's the cross I bear. But which of them hates me enough to throw on a robe and try and kill me? Hell, that's another question entirely, and I don't know the answer yet. Do me a favor and come back when you've figured it out, all right?"

Back in Hanford Park, the birds seemed especially talkative as Rake walked Charles Dickens, the golden retriever Cassie had insisted they buy shortly after they bought the house. Rake had been less than thrilled with the idea of an additional responsibility, their two kids plenty disruptive enough, but he'd come to enjoy the excuse for long walks. He tried to determine his next move.

He'd been out only a few minutes when something caught his eye: a flyer taped below a stop sign. Printed in large block letters were the words "Zoned as a White Community." Exploding across the center of the page was a lightning bolt, just like the ones sewn onto the sleeves of SS troopers he'd seen in Europe.

He cursed under his breath, then looked behind him. Empty lawns and a clear street. He tore the flyer off the post and stuffed it in his pocket. "This isn't good, Charles Dickens."

The Columbians were back.

8

Nearing seven o'clock that night, Boggs and Smith lingered outside Kato's Gym, which had produced most of Atlanta's great Negro boxers over the last twenty years. It sat a block north of the tracks that ran along Decatur Street, near some of the seediest bars and brothels.

Winning the respect of their community was one of the most important jobs Atlanta's first Negro officers had set out for themselves. The best way to do so was to demonstrate without question that they made the neighborhoods safer. First they took the drunks off the street, the men who'd start drinking at sunrise and would be staggering across the street by noon, or passed out in doorways. They moved the craps and dice players off the sidewalks, so little kids wouldn't have to step past them on their way to school anymore. Then came the small-time madams and moonshiners, drug dealers and thieves, gamblers and extortionists who had run rampant in Sweet Auburn and the other Negro neighborhoods before '48. They had taken most of the worst offenders off the street, either catching them in the act or convincing some brave civilians to file charges against them. But they had never managed to catch the man who loomed largest, both literally and figuratively: Thunder Malley.

Story was, Malley had established himself as an enterprising acquirer of illicit goods while living in some of the labor camps that sprouted outside Savannah's shipyards and factories during the war. He and a small gang had sold smokes, moonshine, reefer, and opium to the exhausted laborers whose lives consisted of long days in factories or docks, then short nights in hastily constructed shacks lacking heat or plumbing. Once the war wound down, Malley, like so many, had hopped the trains for the greater splendor of Atlanta—he was wanted for a couple of murders, supposedly, but when Smith had placed calls to the Savannah police for more information, he was told otherwise. Murderer or not, Malley and his associates were known to demand money from small-time colored businessmen as a "cost of doing business." Malley also loaned out money at fierce rates, with fearsome penalties for delinquency. Everyone was too terrified of him to tell the cops anything on the record.

Which made Bartholomew's eyewitness account so intriguing. Talking to Boggs and then McInnis, Bartholomew had described Malley perfectly, down to his attire and the license plate of a brown Ford that turned out to be registered to one of Malley's cousins. Yet McInnis shared their lack of confidence in Bartholomew as a witness worthy of being called to the stand. If they wanted to arrest Malley, they needed more.

So Boggs and Smith stood beneath the unlit awning of a pawnshop when a man in a newsboy cap and a slim-fitting houndstooth blazer emerged from Kato's Gym, his wooden soles tapping double-time on the sidewalk.

Smith stepped out of the shadows. "Hey there, champ."

Spark Jones stopped and was very still for a moment. Boggs could sense the man's power in the way he held himself; even at rest he seemed capable of doing severe damage in the time another man would need to blink.

"Officer Smith. Why so close to my office, man?"

"I don't know which girl you're crashin' with these days."

"Well, I don't always make those decisions in advance."

Boggs envied his partner's ability to rack up informants. When the two had started working together, Boggs had made note of Smith's dropped *g*s and his propensity to cuss. He had read Smith's file and saw that he'd attended Atlanta University for two years, whereas Boggs himself had graduated from Morehouse. Boggs had assumed, then, that *he* would be the leader of this partnership, but it had taken barely a day before he realized Smith was not a man who would be led. Boggs may have been the more comfortable of the two in a formal setting, like church, or a professor's house on the West Side, or standing at a lectern before some Negro civic organization. But Smith moved effortlessly through the pool halls and gambling parlors and decrepit apartments where they spent most of their time. There, it was Boggs's proper diction that seemed off, and he found himself mimicking his partner's speaking style more.

"Let's walk until you're comfortable," Smith said. He led Jones and Boggs into an alley a block away. Once there, he said, "Got a few questions about reefer and shine. Jars and joints."

"I don't put none of that poison in me. My body is my temple."

"But you have ears and you hear things in that gym. I know some of those boys can't help talking. You have any idea where we could find Thunder Malley?"

"You serious? Thunder Malley? I thank God I'm not privy to that man's comings and goings."

Smith said, "We just want to talk to him. We've heard he trains here a lot, but funny enough, no one's seen him lately."

"All I can tell you is that I ain't seen him in, I don't know, three days."

"You hear any word that he's taken a step up from shakedowns to drugs?"

"You trying to get me killed?"

"We never had this conversation," Smith assured him. "I'm just trying to confirm what I've already heard."

Spark made a show of looking to his right and left. Then sighed. "Man, that ain't even new news. From what I can tell, he been doing that for a while."

"You know an alley bootlegger named Woodrow Forrester?"

"Why?"

"Got himself shot. Him one day, and a fellow named Lou Crimmons the next."

Spark nodded. "Yeah, they were tight."

"Part of Malley's crew?"

"I think so. Couldn't swear to it."

"Why are so many dealers dying lately?" Smith asked. "Seems like the folks moving reefer and shine are getting a whole lot more violent."

"There's a turf war, and the turf's moving every week."

"How so?" Boggs asked.

"When there were solid borders between colored areas and white areas, everybody knew their territory, right? But now we got Negroes crossing lines for houses, crossing lines for apartments, and that means crossing lines for booze and reefer. Used to be one gang handled things for colored folk only, but now those colored folk have moved into what used to be white neighborhoods. Whose turf they on now? Ain't like the boys on top pass out color-coded maps."

"Shine comes from up in the mountains," Boggs said. "And now it's looking like more reefer does, too. Those are all white folks up there. For a Negro to try running an operation here, he'd need to get those hillbillies to work with him."

"Them hillbillies ain't as bothered by the color thing as most white folks. Only color they care about is green. They want to drive their load in, get a big wad of cash, then drive out fast."

"You said turf war," Smith noted. "If Malley's on one side, who's on the other?"

"You know the name Quentin Neale? Folks call him Q?" The boxer paused, saw their blank faces. He described Neale as very light-skinned, tall, thin mustache, and far stronger than he looked. "Scary fella, new in town after he was run out of New Orleans. I hear he's butting heads with Malley. Things are about to get a whole lot messier."

"Why's that?"

"Word is, Malley has protection from white cops." They had suspected this, hoping it wasn't true. It explained why the white man Boggs had knocked out the other night had been released so quickly. "They get their cut and let Malley be. Y'all might not like that, but at least things had a certain equilibrium, you know? But now you Negro cops been arresting alley dealers and bootleggers, making it bad for Malley's business. Between that and the color lines shifting, everything's out of whack, and you got different groups fighting over turf and trying to keep their boys out of jail. You escalated things big-time the other night when you busted that drop. Made Malley look weak. I'd bet that's why he's killing his own men for ratting to you—gotta show he's still the boss and ain't afraid of you."

"Well," Smith said, "feel free to spread the word: we *are* bad for business."

Jones chuckled. "I ain't spreading a damn thing, because we never had this conversation. If you're serious about going after Thunder Malley, all I can say is I'm glad I don't have your jobs. Now, I got a girl waiting on me. 'Night, gentlemen."

With that, he took a glance out of the alley to ensure once again that no one had seen him conversing with the police, then strutted down the street.

9

Shortly after Rake had walked his first beat in '48, he had received an invitation to join the Klan. An envelope had been left in his locker—*inside* of his locked locker—with cryptic instructions to be at a certain intersection at a certain hour.

Rake's opinions on Klansmen, "the Negro question," and other related matters owed much to that most important element of Southern character: one's mama. Ingrid Rakestraw had been a child when her family emigrated from Germany to Savannah, then Atlanta. They'd arrived in the Georgia capital shortly after America's entry into the Great War, when a propaganda campaign marked "Huns" as an inhuman enemy to fear. Huns raped nuns in Belgium and beheaded French children. They were thuggish by nature but cowards who would rather sink a ship from an invisible U-boat than confront an American on a fair battlefield. Although Ingrid could learn to bake cathead biscuits instead of German poppy seed rolls, serve red velvet cake instead of stollen, and wear the latest American fashions when her parents could afford it, she could not erase her thick accent, could not defend her older brother when he was beaten, frequently, by neighborhood boys for being a rotten Heinie, and could not deflect the bricks tossed through her family's windows.

Years later, she taught her sons never to treat others that way. Like most white folks, she and Rake's father knew few Negroes, but the biggest beating Rake ever saw his father give his older brother was when Curtis and two friends had cornered and robbed a Negro boy. The word *nigger* was verboten in the house where Rake grew up. This opinion made the Rakestraws progressive on race, and it took some amount of courage to stand against the greater Southern tide—he knew that Cassie's family, for example, believed quite differently—but in Atlanta they were not completely alone in their opinion that Negroes deserved better.

So when that Klan invitation had appeared in his police locker, he'd ignored it.

He had zero desire to join what his father had always described as a ragtag group of bullies and Neanderthals. After ignoring the invitation, he had been approached by Parker; they weren't partners back then, but old friends.

Parker had gently recommended that Rake reconsider about the Klan: "You might want to put away your high-mindedness for one evening and play along. Job can be hard enough without making things even tougher on ourselves."

"Play along? With a bunch of—?"

"It ain't what you think it is. It's more like an Elks Club, with sillier uniforms. I signed on, but it's not like I've rustled any Negroes or anything."

"Well, I'm glad to hear that."

"I'm trying to help you. If there's an opening for detective and it comes down to two cops with identical marks, but only one is a Kluxer, which one you think they'll pick?"

Rake had heard that, too. A recent, much-discussed story in *Newsweek* had even claimed that a third of Atlanta cops were Kluxers. Still, he'd insisted to his friend, "That's not true."

"Oh, that's right, because you're so perfect and pure that you'll surely impress people soon enough."

Rake *did* think he would impress the right people. He *did* think he could advance without a Klan Kard. Hearing Parker speak of such things as if they were fanciful wishes made him worry that he was naïve.

Now, two years later, he had worked his way up from where he'd started: patrolling rough neighborhoods with a corrupt partner who'd tried to drag him down, too. He had solved a high-profile case, and though the Department had kept the results of that investigation secret for political reasons, Rake had sat in a room with the chief of police himself, had won his way onto an unofficial fast track for promotion. He had a better beat and was now partnered with Parker, who perhaps wasn't the most ambitious cop in the world but was a reliable fellow to have beside you when things went bad, and good company besides.

Still, Rake knew he was far from the most popular man in the Department. His awful former partner, Dunlow, had gone missing under mysterious circumstances, leaving behind a handful of loyal compatriots who viewed Rake with suspicion. Some, he gathered, suspected him of killing Dunlow, or at least being complicit in his murder. Others weren't so sure but still hated Rake, convinced he represented a dangerous new breed, one not beholden to their beloved structures and traditions, one who must be taken down before he got too big.

A few hours after Rake had driven up to question Letcher, he and Parker worked the night shift. They made an arrest for disorderly conduct; responded to a domestic altercation involving a cleaver, arriving just in time to prevent the situation from escalating to homicide, and caught two kids who'd been trying and failing to steal a new Packard.

Driving back to the station to fill out paperwork and call it a night, Rake tried to sound casual as he asked, "I need to ask you a question about the boys in the white robes. Somebody I'm trying to protect, a confidential informant," he lied, "got himself in a scrape. He claims he was recruited by a man from the Coventry Klavern who said they needed someone from an Atlanta Klavern to beat up a fellow in Coventry, some sinner who needed to be set straight. A *white* man."

Judging from Parker's perplexed expression, this was news.

"So my CI and some friends went up there, but while they were beating the fella up, someone shot and killed one of the Kluxers. Have you heard anything about it?"

"Not a thing. I'm hardly an active member with them, I just do enough to keep appearances." Rake was struck by how similar that statement was to what Letcher had said, joining only "to keep up appearances." It made him wonder how many men did that, or claimed to. How could one divide the true believers from those who went along to get along—and did it matter?

"Well, let me know if you hear anything."

"Hey, bud, I'm happy to help you most ways, but being your spy in the Klan won't be one of them. I'm not looking to get myself killed."

"I don't need a spy, I just need to find a fellow named Whitehouse."

He repeated Dale's admittedly vague description of the man, then explained what little he'd gathered about Letcher. "What I'm trying to figure out is, why would someone send fellows from one Klavern into another town to rough somebody up, then vanish?"

"It's not unusual to ask folks from another Klavern to do your dirty work. Especially if the fellow's white—that way you aren't beating up your own neighbor, who might recognize you or your car. Hell, if Letcher is part of the Coventry Klan, this could be something they all voted on when he wasn't there, 'cause he was out doing whatever it is that got him on their bad side."

"My informant says he left his hood at the scene, but that didn't make it into the papers. I think the police up there might be trying to keep the Klan clean of it."

"If I hear anything, I'll let you know," Parker said. "But don't get your hopes up. Those boys used to be big talkers, but they've gone quiet lately. They're all convinced they're being spied on."

"By whom? If so many of 'em are cops, who'd be doing the spying?"

Parker smiled. "Fellows like you."

10

"Girl, you are *huge*."

Standing at her front door, Hannah Greer put a hand on one of her expanding hips and shot Smith a look. "That ain't a polite way of putting it."

"Well, you got a whole lotta baby in there. Can you fit through all the doors in here?"

It was hard for Smith to imagine how much more his sister would change in the two months leading up to the due date. Hannah had always been rail-thin, and still was, every part of her petite as could be, with the one giant exception.

"Maybe you can eat lunch somewhere else," she said.

Hannah was his cousin, biologically, but they'd been raised thinking each other siblings. Smith hadn't been told until age sixteen that his true father had been lynched at a 1919 parade, when Smith was an infant, because he dared wear his uniform from the Great War, enraging the white people in his rural Georgia town. A few months later, after Smith's grieving mother drank an eighth of rye and walked in front of a train, his aunt and uncle took him in, raising him as their son.

"I'm kidding, you look beautiful and you know it."

He was joking to relieve some of the pressure about why he was really there. The brick on the dining room floor.

It had been thrown the previous evening. Hannah had been woken by it, but her husband, Malcolm, a bouncer at a nightclub, worked late. She had called to let Malcolm know, but not until he arrived an hour later had he seen the note someone had left behind, on their front step. Hannah had placed it on the dining room floor alongside the brick, so Smith carefully picked it up with a handkerchief. *NIGGER GO HOME* in black ink on a white sheet of paper. It had been held in place by a rock.

"You both touch the note?" Smith asked, and she nodded as he slipped it into a file folder from the briefcase he'd brought. You couldn't fingerprint bricks or rocks, but paper was another matter. Though he doubted the attackers were that stupid. "First note like this you've seen?"

"First one left here, but we've had a few in the mail."

Malcolm was at the local hardware store, buying a new window.

"Why didn't you tell me?"

"I'm telling you now."

"Do you still have them?"

"We've thrown them all in the trash." She thought for a moment. "But trash day's tomorrow, so there might be a few in the barrel if you really want to look."

"I do." He would dig out whatever he could find. He wanted to take all the notes himself, pass them on to McInnis, ask him to get them fingerprinted. He could predict the response: *This isn't your or my beat, Officer Smith. The notes must be investigated by the officers in that neighborhood.* So he told Hannah to call the police, get a cop here, and fill out a report, even though he doubted white officers would do much at all.

"How you feel about the neighbors so far?"

"We haven't had a lot of conversations. No one came by with cookies or anything."

Two other Negro families had moved onto the block south of here about a month back, and apart from some threatening mail, their moves had been uneventful, as far as Smith knew. He wondered now whether they, too, had windows shattered but had kept quiet about it, or if things were escalating.

"You have any friends nearby?"

"The ones who told us about this place are on the other side of Beacon Street," which used to be the unofficial border between the races. "I walk there a lot still, do my shopping at the grocer's, even though there's a white one that's closer. Malcolm says it'll get easier soon. But this doesn't feel easier."

Smith had noticed two For Sale signs in the neighborhood when he'd walked here from the bus stop. He was willing to bet those signs had appeared after the Greers moved in.

"What if the next thing they throw is a firebomb," she asked, "like they did to that family a couple years ago?"

"I'll talk to the white officers," he told her. He thought about Rakestraw, one of the few white cops who seemed somewhat decent.

To try cheering her up, he asked her for a quick tour of the new place. It needed plenty of work, as the previous owners hadn't been much for upkeep. But it was an actual, freestanding house, and she and Malcolm had *bought* it. Neither of their parents had been homeowners. Hannah and Tommy grew up in a rented two-bedroom apartment until Smith hit puberty and the idea of him continuing to share a room with Hannah drove their parents to rent a three-bedroom a few blocks south of Auburn. Within a few years, the old man had passed away; their mother, a seamstress, now rented a place with one of her sisters, just getting by. Smith sent her some of his pay every month.

"It's a shame Daddy couldn't see this," Hannah said. Smith nodded as they gazed for a moment at the barely furnished living room, their memories briefly filling the space.

"It's amazing, girl. And it's *yours*. No one's taking it."

When Malcolm returned, he hung the new window while Smith checked the perimeter of their house for any evidence. Finding none, he sifted through their trash in search of more hate mail. He found four letters, two of them typed and one written in block letters. The typed ones appeared to have come from different typewriters, but there was enough overlap in the phrasing to suspect the same author. Then again, the language was hardly unique. *Get your filthy nigger asses out of our neighborhood. You do not belong here. The longer you stay, the worse you'll make it on yourself.*

After installing a new window and eating lunch, Smith and Malcolm smoked on the back deck while Hannah baked dessert, all of them insisting on normalcy as they awaited the police. When they arrived (*if* they arrived), Smith planned to hang back; he knew white cops would be even less inclined to help if they learned the victims were related to one of the hated Negro officers.

"I didn't fight a war just to come home and let some crackers bully me out of my own house," Malcolm said.

"Me neither. We'll get to the bottom of it." Smith waited a moment, then changed the subject. "How are things at the club?"

"Swingin'," Malcolm said in his double bass voice. "Feck's got a good thing going over there." His hair was a bit tight, as he seemed to like it, matching his thick beard. Hannah had married him three years ago; they'd known each other in high school. According to Hannah, he'd been a more outgoing sort before the war, but his time in the Pacific had changed him. Didn't laugh as loud or as often. Smith, too, had seen more than his share of violence, having served in the 761st Tank Battalion, the famed Black Panthers, but he liked to think that his prewar personality remained intact. Maybe he was fooling himself.

For a while, Malcolm had trouble holding down steady work. Hannah's income as a maid was all that supported them for a time. Only recently had their situation stabilized, when Malcolm got the bouncer job. Then, a few months back, one of his uncles, a farmer in North Georgia, passed away and left them his land, which they sold for the down payment on this house.

Smith asked, "You ever see some folks at the club acting pretty high from something that ain't liquor?"

"Sometimes."

"You get the feeling that's becoming more common?"

Malcolm took a long drag on his cigarette. "Feck doesn't tolerate that in his place. We toss people if they get out of control, but no, I've never seen anyone smoking it in the club."

"Good. We've been tracking some folks who are bringing it into the city."

"Surprised they have you doing that. Ain't that something the white cops handle?"

"They're happy to let a few things slide so long as it's on our side of town, but we're working on changing that." Two turkey vultures tilted their wings in the perfect sky. Owning a back porch must feel fabulous. "Something else I been wondering: you fellas ever had trouble with Thunder Malley?"

Malcolm raised an eyebrow. "Why you ask?"

Boggs had told Smith about crazy Bartholomew supposedly being able to place Malley at the scene of Forrester's murder. Smith wouldn't share that with Malcolm, but he said, "I know Malley leans on businesses for protection money. We've put a stop to most folks who do that, but he's been a tough one to nail down. And now I got reason to believe he's moving into moonshine and drugs."

Malcolm thought long and hard. Smith was accustomed to people turning silent when Malley's name came up. "Man you should talk to is Feck," meaning Malcolm's boss. "I don't know if he pays for protection or not, but I know he's no fan of Malley. In fact, yeah, I've *heard* Malley's been moving drugs. Gets 'em from the mountains or something, from the same crackers who make the shine. Nothing I know for sure, just things I overhear."

"I'll talk to Feck. Been meaning to catch some music anyway."

Smith checked his watch. He'd need to leave soon to be at the precinct in time. He wondered if the cops would ever come.

"Ever hear of a fella named Quentin Neale?" he asked. "Goes by Q? Tall, light skin, from New Orleans?" Malcolm shook his head no, so Smith continued, "We're hearing him and Thunder don't much like each other. They in some kind of turf war."

"That's a vote in his favor, then."

"But it's the kind of not-liking that leads to a lot of bodies. Anyway, you hear anything about either of 'em, let me know."

Malcolm nodded and they sat wordless for a spell. The silence in this part of town was otherworldly.

"Personally, how I see it?" Malcolm said. "Fellow wants to get himself high, dull his pain, fine. Man needs to get by somehow, and it's better than taking out his aggressions on somebody else." His eyes had wandered while he shared this, but now he looked at Smith. "I suppose you paid to feel different. But I woulda thought you'd agree, *in here*," and he tapped his chest. "Live-and-let-live kinda fellow that you are."

Smith had heard this argument before, often from men he was arresting. To hear it from family was another matter, making him ponder where his true opinion laid, one not dictated by paychecks or superior officers, Jim Crow or the City of Atlanta. *In here,* his heart. But what was *in here* that hadn't been touched by someone else, either bosses or money, preachers or God?

"I like living-and-let-living. It's when folks start dying I have to pay attention."

11

A month ago, a knock after dark would not have alarmed Cassie Rake-straw. But that was before the Negroes had moved into Hanford Park.

So when she heard the knocks at eight o'clock that evening, just after putting the kids to bed, she hurried to the kitchen, retrieved her pistol from the top pantry shelf, and checked that it was loaded. Then she carefully pulled back the parlor curtains to afford a side view of her unexpected visitors, who were knocking again.

They turned out to be white. In fact, once she got a good look at them, she figured they were Bible salesmen.

She slipped the gun in her pocket and answered the door.

"Evening, ma'am. Is your husband at home?" The speaker was tall and thin, dark hair sadly raked across a head gone otherwise bare. Something about the way he wore his short-sleeved blue button-up suggested that he didn't normally dress this well. Hard to put her finger on it; the shirt just seemed to want to be on someone else.

Beside him stood his wife, no doubt, though her hair had gone mostly gray before any of his. She wore glasses and a blue dress that seemed just a touch too fine, like it was her church outfit on the wrong day. She clasped a manila folder and a small stack of paper to her breast.

"He's at work right now," Cassie said, then added without knowing why, "he's a police officer."

"Oh, wonderful," the man said. "We picked a great house to finish with tonight. Ma'am, my name is Paul Thames and this is my wife, Martha Ann."

"I'm Cassie Rakestraw. Good to meet you."

"Sorry to bother you in the evening, but this has taken longer'n expected. We're representatives of the Collective Association of Hanford

Park. CAHP for short. As I'm sure you know, ma'am, our wonderful neighborhood has been infiltrated by Negroes over the last few weeks."

"Yes, it's too bad."

"Three houses so far, which is three houses too many." He looked familiar, though Cassie couldn't recall why. "We're making a point of talking to every homeowner here in Hanford Park to do what we can to protect the neighborhood. It's a great place, idn't it?"

"We like it very much."

"I've been here since '32 and Martha Ann grew up here."

"Three generations back, in just half a mile," Martha Ann added.

"Raised three boys, one we lost in the war, God rest his soul, and one's up in Marietta and the third moved down to Florida a few years ago, but we don't hold that against him. My point is, it *has* been a great place to raise a family, and you did yourself a smart thing moving in here. But if we let the niggers keep moving in, we're all in a spot of trouble."

"So we're taking a page from the West Side's playbook," Martha Ann added.

Then Cassie remembered being at her sister-in-law's place a few months ago, when Sue Ellen's kitchen sink was backed up. She saw an image of Mr. Thames crouched down on all fours, a wrench in his hand, later making some silly joke as he cleaned grime from his fingers. He was the local plumber.

"But the West Side did wind up going colored, didn't it?" Cassie asked.

"True, it didn't work out so well for them," Thames said. "Some of their strategies were spot on, they just didn't always handle things so well."

Cassie had learned quite a bit about the West Side's changing demographics from her husband. A neighborhood association of concerned homeowners had done what it could to stave off colored encroachment. Anytime a Negro dropped by to look at houses, representatives of the association showed up in force to inform the Negroes that, contrary to what they had heard, they were not welcome here.

There had also been some beatings and a few bricks tossed through windows.

"You're right, though," Martha Ann said. "The West Side did go colored, and the prices went down and all those folks took a big hit. Now, we aren't wealthy people here, our houses are our lives and our investment, and we can't let them come and destroy that."

Her husband went on, "The Realtors and bankers, they all say the same thing: once the coloreds move in, your home value just about vanishes overnight."

Cassie didn't like thinking of this. She felt like her head had barely made it out of the fog of having her first two children so close together. How long had she been having a decent night's sleep now, a few months, tops? It was all she could do to keep the two little ones alive, protect them from electrical outlets and fend off stray dogs and block Denny Jr.'s desperate and tenacious attempts to climb every vertical structure he came across, and then cajole and beg and plead that they go to sleep at night while her husband was at work, whereupon she collapsed into bed, alone. And additional concerns: painting one of the bedrooms, planting some azaleas to spruce up the front yard, repairing the deck—all these tasks existed in some theoretical, additional mental space she did not yet possess. Even yet larger concerns, such as their ability to pay the mortgage each month, and the larger demographic forces that seemed intent on redrawing the map of so many Atlanta neighborhoods, were so far beyond her ken that just contemplating them hurt, actually physically hurt her, in the base of her neck and her shoulders. Everything this couple was telling her had the unfortunate glare of a truth she wanted to look away from, but the harder she tried the brighter it got.

She was not by nature a worrier. The tomboy only daughter following five brothers, she'd been raised to be tough and to focus her energies on whatever task lay before her rather than fretting over what might lay beyond it. She'd known Rake (Denny to her) since they were thirteen, when her gauntlet of older brothers had devised a series of tests for him, an Olympics of manliness they insisted he needed to medal in if he wanted to continue seeing their kid sister. The test had involved outracing one of them in track, outhitting another on the diamond, and shooting a Coke bottle from fifty yards away with an old family rifle. Cryptic hints had been dropped that he might also need to outbox the eldest brother, who had moved out of town to work in an iron smelter in Birmingham but was legendarily tough. Denny lost all three of the tests that first day, but kept returning every Saturday, finally outracing the one, then eventually outslugging the second. He had yet to outshoot the third when Cassie learned of the competition and, outraged to hear that her own dating rights were being so handled, calmly walked outside, took the rifle from Denny, and proceeded to shoot better than not only her future husband but all her brothers.

She had remained a better shot than Denny, until the war.

"From what we understand," Thames said, "these are mostly good Nigras. They didn't know they were buying into a white neighborhood. They were hornswoggled by some of those unscrupulous Realtors, and now they're caught in a bind that ain't of their own making."

Denny Jr., in pajamas and mussed hair, appeared at her side. "Mommy, Maggie woke up."

"Get back in bed, sweetie." He obeyed, and she told her guests, "I'm gonna need to run. I don't disagree with what you've said, I'm just not real clear on what you're asking."

Martha Ann reached into her folder and handed Cassie a mimeo-graphed map of Hanford Park. The three Negro homes were circled. Martha Ann pointed to the Rakestraw home on the map, dragging her finger to the nearest of the three circles to demonstrate how close they were.

"We feel the best way for us to defend our rights is to use simple economics," Mr. Thames said. "It's a sacrifice, and I'll confess that it's not easy for me to ask this of anyone, and that's why I bring my wife here for moral support." Another awkward smile. "But our intent is to raise enough money for CAHP that we can approach the Negroes and offer to buy those homes back from them. Then we can resell 'em to white families."

"It's worked in some other neighborhoods," Martha Ann said with an emphatic nod.

"Like I said, most of them are good Nigras and don't want to be a problem. I think they're ashamed, and even a little embarrassed to real-ize the mess they've caused. But they can't just move out, because then they're out all that money, and they'd be as financially ruined as we all stand to be if they *don't* leave."

"So our giving money might hurt," Martha Ann said, "but if we all can hurt a *little* together, and buy them out, then it'll spare us from much worse pain later. Once we've bought the places back, and resold them to white folks, we'll be made whole, or close enough."

Now Cassie could hear Maggie's cries, that annoying kind of cry that isn't panic as much as mild unhappiness that only yet another visit from Mama can solve.

"We'll accept any contribution at all," Thames said. "Some of the donations have been five dollars, and one was as high as a hundred. When we combine forces like this, we can ensure the community stays the way it should be."

She agreed with them, but she wasn't sure if Denny would. She told them she wouldn't be comfortable making a decision like this without her husband, but they could drop by again another day. That would give her some time to convince him.

They smiled their thanks and left behind some flyers and information about an upcoming meeting she'd try to attend. Then she closed and locked the door. On her way to the kids' room to check on Maggie, she first stopped at the pantry, returning the pistol to its hiding place.

12

Nearing the end of their shift, Boggs and Smith walked down Krog Street, a narrow road with ramshackle shotgun houses on one side and the tall brick wall of a recently shuttered textile mill on the other. A squad car passed them, slowly, which struck them both as odd, since this wasn't a usual cut-through.

Then another squad car approached from the opposite side, pulling over in front of them. The first car stopped at the end of the narrow road.

"Stay cool," Smith said.

Headlights shined in their faces, blinding them. Doors opened and closed, the slams loud and violent. Out stepped silhouettes unblemished by details or identifying marks of any kind. Boggs held his right hand high to try to block the light, then traded hands so that his right could be near his gun. He couldn't tell how many there were, likely four at least, maybe more.

"Well looky here, we found ourselves a couple a genuine blue-gummed Senegambians."

"They seem far from their native habitat."

"Still imitating police officers," another said. Boggs still couldn't see any of their faces. He also couldn't tell if they were holding weapons, as most of them stood behind their cars. Behind Boggs and Smith was a brick wall, a great place to gun people down if they were so inclined.

"Skin's like camouflage, ain't it? Funny thing is, they actually think it works."

"Don't you fellas have somewhere you should be?" Smith said.

"*You're* the ones who have been in the wrong place way too often lately."

"This is a polite warning," another said. Boggs wished he could see them, wished their voices weren't so similar. They sounded young, all officers, likely no sergeant among them. Messengers sent by some higher authority. "You may walk this beat, but you don't own it. There are business arrangements and social compacts you'd best not interfere with."

"We know how to do our jobs," Smith countered. "Why don't you go do yours?"

The one standing in the middle laughed, gesturing to the squad cars. "You see how easy it would be for us to take you down if we want? And we got plenty others happy to help us out. You want to stay alive and in uniform, you stick to arresting drunks and thieves, but don't you think about going no higher'n that."

"This is our territory," Boggs said. "And we won't be threatened." He wanted to let his hand go toward his holstered gun, but he couldn't tell if they already had guns on him, in which case a sudden movement would be his last.

"If you even tried to lay a hand on us," Smith said, "the chief would go through the roof and you know it. You wouldn't want to lose your meal ticket, would you? Unless there's another meal ticket you're protecting?"

"This is your only warning," one of them said. "Next time, we won't use *words* to make our point."

The silhouettes dissolved back into their vehicles. One of the cars feinted toward them, causing them to back up a step, and they heard laughter as the cars shifted back to reverse and pulled out of the alley.

After they were gone, Smith shook his head. "Spark Jones said Malley has police protection. I'd say he's right."

After two, they made it back to the station to clock out and change. Supposedly the prohibition against their wearing their uniforms home was for their protection, lest some drunk crackers ambush a lone Negro officer and do to him what had been done to Smith's soldier father a generation ago.

As soon as they walked in, McInnis walked right up to them, which wasn't his usual MO. *Lord,* Boggs thought, *what now?*

"Smith, your sister just called," McInnis said, his voice grave. "She's unhurt, but she's at the hospital. Her husband got beat up in Hanford Park."

13

They spent far too much time in Grady Hospital's colored wing. Interviewing victims and relatives, lingering in waiting rooms to see who else showed up and to gauge degrees of guilt based on the reaction to their questions. Trying to interrupt mothers' tears with queries about when she'd last seen her boy alive, trying to snap stunned widows from their fugue long enough to learn the names of best friends and worst enemies. It was both the best place to find information and the worst place to be if you cared about your soul, for they hated what they had to do there, like sticking their fingers in people's wounds.

This was Smith's first time at the hospital as kin to a victim. He didn't like this role any better.

They made their way through the crowded emergency room and then a long hallway crowded with beds that couldn't fit in rooms already filled beyond capacity. Before swinging doors marked Surgery, they found Smith's mother and sister, too agitated to sit in the empty quartet of waiting room chairs.

Smith hugged both of them in turn. His mother's eyes were puffy and her cheeks glistened, and her hair was pulled back in a light knot. Hannah was worse, shaking as he held her.

"He's in surgery," said his mother, Michelle. She seemed shell-shocked, a cold tension he'd never heard in her voice before. "A nurse came out about thirty minutes ago. She said his . . . life isn't in danger, but they needed to attend to some internal bleeding."

"What happened?" Smith asked.

"I don't know," Hannah said, her voice thick. "He was working late and I'd fallen asleep. Then I got woken up when a neighbor knocked on my door, said it looked like Malcolm was lying on the sidewalk. Didn't know how long he'd been lying there."

"Any police come by?"

His mother made a face like he'd told an off-color joke. So he asked Hannah what time Malcolm usually got off work.

"Depends on what act they have that night. Sometimes ten, sometimes two. He usually drives, but he took the bus today because I told him I . . . needed the car." Her voice broke.

"It's not your fault," Smith said. They could piece things together later, find Malcolm's work schedule, ask his boss when he left, interview the bus driver for confirmation, find out which neighbor had spotted him. "We'll find who did this. You'll need to file a police report."

"You two are here now, isn't that enough?"

"We're not on duty," Smith said. "And I'm family, so it should be someone else."

"I don't want to talk to white cops. They haven't done a thing about the brick thrown through our window, have they? For all I know, they're the ones who *did* this!"

"Tommy, let her be," his mother said. "Now isn't the time for your protocol."

Pressing Hannah may have appeared cruel, but he wanted to believe that proceeding by the book would increase their chances of seeing some modicum of justice.

Smith said, "We'll make sure the officers in your neighborhood take this seriously." He himself didn't believe that, and it wasn't his style to make empty promises. He wasn't handling himself right, the officer role not fitting so well when he wore the victim role beneath it. So he told himself to focus on the officer part. "Me and Lucius will be back in a little while. We're going to check the house."

"Right now?" his mother asked, meaning, *At night? In the dark?*

"Yes." The look of horror on their faces actually made it less frightening, to be reminded that he did things that others dared not.

Two flashlight beams, meek against the overwhelming darkness of the night, as Boggs and Smith searched the block. All they found was blood.

Getting here had not been easy; first a fifteen-minute hustle to Boggs's parents' house, where Boggs left a note on the kitchen table and borrowed his father's car, then the fifteen-minute drive across town. They barely spoke, Boggs warily watching his partner, who was livid and uncharacteristically silent.

Malcolm had been found not in front of their house but five houses south. That partly explained why Hannah hadn't been woken up by the beating, but still, they must have been quiet. Not even a confrontation, perhaps, just a sucker punch or other blow from behind, then a beating while he lay on the ground.

No sound but crickets and frogs as they moved about. It was past four now and nearly every light in every house was off, yet they still tried to find something, anything. A bottle with fingerprints, a bottle cap, a scrap of clothing, a cigarette butt. Yet they were searching the cleanest block in Atlanta.

Most of the blood had pooled in one spot, but some of it drew a jagged trail for ten feet, ending at a smaller pool. Perhaps they had dragged him, or, once they'd left him, he had tried to crawl toward his house but hadn't made it far before collapsing.

One of the neighbors surely saw something. Yet none had opened their doors to ask what was going on. Smith and Boggs were trying to be quiet, but still, someone must have known they were here, watching them through barely parted curtains.

Then headlights swallowed their flashlight beams and made them redundant.

"Took them longer than I thought it would," Smith muttered as the squad car silently pulled over.

"What are you boys doing out here?" a voice barked.

Smith stepped closer to the open window of the driver, whose face he couldn't yet make out. The "boys" only made him angrier, and he had half a mind to shine his flashlight directly in the cop's face. The other half of his mind knew that would be a terrible mistake.

"I'm Officer Smith and this is Officer Boggs." He leaned toward the window, no doubt closer than the driver wished a Negro to be. He could see the driver now, a middle-aged white cop whose thin, rough cheeks seemed to cave into his face, as if some inner tension were slowly sucking him into nothingness. Never seen him before. "A relative of mine was assaulted here a few hours ago."

The white cops got out of their car and walked over quickly. Boggs stepped close as well, to show he would not be intimidated. He and Smith both had weapons hidden away in ankle and small-of-the-back holsters. They never would have come here at night unarmed. But they knew that openly displaying firearms would have sent any white witnesses to their gun cabinets.

"This ain't your territory, and you're out of uniform besides," the one who'd been driving said. Boggs recognized him: Brian Helton, one of the cops who enjoyed goading the new Negro officers even more than most. He'd been a friend of Lionel Dunlow's, the sadistic bully who'd been Rakestraw's old partner. After Dunlow had mysteriously disappeared two years ago, Helton had been very vocal indeed about his opinion—shared by many others—that the colored officers must be responsible. So they'd all been questioned, despite McInnis's outraged objections. Boggs and Smith had confessed that they'd despised Dunlow, just like the others did, but they had lied when they'd claimed to have nothing to do with his disappearance.

"We're not on duty," Smith said. "We just came over from the hospital. Either he was attacked as he was walking home, or he was beaten somewhere else and dumped here."

"Walking home? Here?" the other cop asked. He was tall and had more padding in his shirt than he should have, his cheeks doughy and pale, the hair beneath his cap light. Everything about him made Boggs think of a biscuit. "There's your problem, then."

"How's that?" Smith asked.

"This is a white neighborhood, that's *how*," Helton answered for his young partner. "He shouldn't be here."

"He's not breaking any laws living here," Smith said, "and you know it."

"How 'bout disturbing the peace?"

"The one who got beat up was disturbing the peace?" Boggs snapped.

"How many assaults have there been in this neighborhood in the last three months?" Helton asked. "I'll tell you, since it's my beat: zero.

Now he moves in and look what happens, less than a month after him showing up."

"I think your cause and effect are a little backward," Boggs said, seething. His partner looked on the verge of attacking Helton.

"I think everything about this situation is backward. It's backward he thinks he can move here and not have trouble. It's backward the city thinks it can pin badges on the likes of you and turn you into cops."

"Doesn't look like you're much of a cop yourself," Smith said. "Man gets beat nearly to death on your watch and you don't know anything about it?"

"Who says we don't know anything about it?" the younger partner said. Which won him a quick, angry look from Helton.

"Well, let's hear what you know, then," Boggs said.

"He don't know what he's talking about," Helton said with a dismissive shake of his head. "And neither do you. Unless you want to see more violence out here tonight, you'd best get a move on, now."

"We can take care of ourselves," Boggs replied.

"Apparently Tommy's relations can't."

Smith stepped closer to Helton. Boggs grabbed Smith's left forearm to keep him from going any farther.

"What do you know about what happened?" he demanded. "First a brick through their window, which I bet you didn't even do a damned thing to look into, and now this. Who did it?"

He felt the awful possibility then: white cops might have done this to spite Smith. Cops over on this side of town could have been attacking Malcolm at the same moment that cops on the other side had been warning Smith and Boggs to lay off the drug trade.

"Well, Tommy, let's just say that we all seem to know more about some things than we're saying, don't we?"

"You're never going to give up thinking we had something to do with Dunlow, are you?" Boggs asked. "Not even after Internal Investigations told you we had nothing to do with it."

"No. I am never going to give that up."

"Can I ask what the hell y'all are talking about?" asked Biscuit.

"Ancient history," Smith said.

"In any case, take this as friendly advice," Helton said. "Hell, or unfriendly advice, I don't care. You might want to get yourselves back to your part of town right now. There appear to be some white folks who aren't as friendly as us roaming about tonight."

The cops got back into their car and drove away. Only then did Smith realize Boggs was still holding him by the forearm, as if he feared his partner would chase them down.

Ten minutes later their search still had yielded nothing when they were startled by a voice shouting, "Police! Put your hands up!"

They turned toward the street. The beam of a flashlight illuminated Boggs's chest. A figure was striding toward them, and with the glare they couldn't see anything but a fuzzy shape.

"*We're* police!" Smith shouted back. "Officers Smith and Boggs! Who are you?"

"Christ," the voice said, not an answer but a sigh of exasperation. The flashlight pointed at the street now as he did something funny with his arms. "It's Rakestraw. What are you doing here?"

They stepped onto the street, close enough to see him stashing a sidearm into the belt of his blue jeans. The realization that a gun had been trained on them hardly calmed their nerves. They'd been furious driving over here, and everything that had happened since had only made them angrier.

"Checking a crime scene," Boggs said.

"This isn't your beat."

"Yours, either," Smith said.

"I live two blocks away."

"My sister lives here." Smith pointed behind him. Then he shone his flashlight on one of the pools of blood and explained what little they knew.

"I had no idea," Rake said. "I was just walking 'cause I couldn't sleep."

"With a gun?" Boggs asked.

"Sometimes. Anyone file a report?"

"Not yet," Smith said.

They had worked with Rake, hesitantly and from a distance, on a murder two years ago. No one else knew about their temporary alliance, which would have been considered treasonous to the other white cops, and could have gotten Boggs and Smith disciplined for going beyond their bounds. They still weren't sure if Rake could be trusted.

"How long has this been Helton's beat?" Smith asked.

"About a year. I'm sorry for your relative. I hope he's all right. But I wouldn't hold your breath on a fellow like Helton looking into it."

"Or anyone else," Smith said. "Someone threw a brick through their window the other night, and no cop even took a report. And I don't recall any arson arrests after folks burned down the Calvins' place a couple years ago."

"There was an investigation, but no arrests," Rake answered, and seemed to think of something for a moment, his eyes far away.

"I'm gonna walk the block," Smith said, as if he couldn't stand being around Rakestraw this long. "See if I find anything."

Once he'd left, Boggs said to Rake, "Neighbors must have seen or heard *something*."

"I'm not knocking on doors."

"Why not?"

"It's not my beat. And the folks who live here have a right to be left alone and not bothered about things like this."

Boggs hated that answer, its skewed view of rights. He took a breath. "If you can't make it formal, you can at least ask around, casually, at the next neighborhood cookout. You live here. You must hear things Helton doesn't."

Rake hesitated, and before he could deliver another lame response, Boggs pressed, "I did you a favor once."

"We helped *each other* then."

"Then I'm just asking as one cop to another. I want to know who did this."

"This has been a hell of a week for me promising favors," Rake said, Boggs not catching his meaning. "But, yes, I'll see what I can find out for you. In return, *you* can do *me* a favor: don't come over here again. Showing your faces only makes it worse. If it isn't Helton causing trouble, it'll be someone else, and you know it."

Blame the Negro for causing trouble, Boggs thought. *Disturbing the peace.*

Footsteps, and they turned to see Smith's silhouette walking toward them. He was holding something in his hand, a sheet of paper that flapped gently with each step.

"Took this from the telephone pole at Myrtle and Spruce." As he stepped closer, the flyer's capital letters made its message especially clear: "Zoned as a White Community." Below it was a lightning bolt, blood red. "Last time I saw one of these," and he tapped the bolt with his free hand, "I was in a tank in Germany."

14

Rake didn't even try to fall back asleep after returning home. He was still burning with the shame and embarrassment he'd felt when, talking to Boggs and Smith, he'd realized his own brother-in-law may have been the assailant. It had turned his stomach, talking to Negro officers and feeling like his own family's foibles were out for all to see.

Why? He tried to puzzle this out. Unlike most of his fellow officers, Rake did not despise the Negro cops. He'd probably had more conversations with Boggs than any other white cop except for Boggs's sergeant. He was glad the city had hired them, because if they could prove themselves worthy, then the city would hire more, and soon their numbers would be enough to adequately patrol all of their own neighborhoods. Then, white cops like Rake would never have to venture into colored neighborhoods again.

Rake had told Boggs he would look into the assault mainly as a way to keep Boggs and Smith away. This was *his* family and *his* neighborhood. Having Boggs and Smith around would inflame the tensions that were already inspiring many to join that new neighborhood association Cassie had told him about. He hadn't liked the idea of the group taking donations to pressure the Negroes away, and he'd told her as much. It just felt unseemly; if the group didn't succeed in their scheme to buy out the neighbors, he'd asked Cassie, what would their next tactic be? Assault? She'd argued that the donations idea was expressly designed to avoid violence; they had chosen dollars and checklists as weapons, rather than bricks and bats. So why wouldn't Rake support them? He had grudgingly agreed, partly because he saw her point and partly because he didn't want to argue anymore. So yes, if she really wanted to contribute, he'd allow it.

That had been yesterday. And now that there *had* been an assault, he wondered if he'd been right all along. Maybe he should look into the neighborhood group as possible suspects, see who was involved.

The first thing he did that morning was walk through the neighborhood and tear down the White Community signs, of which he found four. He had torn down two others a few days ago, and some of these new ones had been affixed to the very same poles from which he'd torn the first set down. Which meant they may have been put up last night, possibly by the assailants.

The signs were the unmistakable mark of the Columbians. He couldn't believe they were back, but he knew he shouldn't be shocked anymore. The real shock had come four years ago, when he had returned from the war and discovered an identical sign in the neighborhood where he and Cassie had been renting an apartment. It wasn't the White Community that had stunned him so much as the accompanying lightning bolt.

When he'd grown up, Atlanta, like so many cities, had its share of Silver Shirts and Black Shirts and other Fascist groups, all of them blaming the hard times on the coloreds and the Communists, the Papists and Jews. Rallies were held across the city, even a march through downtown, spearheaded by men claiming that the nation's problems were due to FDR's Jew Deal and his socialistic, labor-organizing cronies. When we declared war on Hitler and Mussolini, those groups had gone quiet, but now that peace had returned, those voices had grown louder again, as if Fascism were merely a fashion that had gone out of style due to wartime scarcity, like long dresses and pleasure drives, and now it was back, at least in certain circles.

In '46 the Columbians, clad in brown Nazi-style fatigues with lightning bolts on the sleeves, encouraged their fellow white Atlantans to take up arms against the uppity Negroes who'd returned from Europe with dangerous ideas like equality. *Strong white men must stand up to keep the races separate! We must fight for the American white workingman!* Rake remembered a rally they'd held at Sweetwater Mill, where he briefly worked—and where Dale still did. He'd been disgusted by the Nazi salutes (they even greeted their leader with "Heil!") and dumbstruck to see that such things could persist after the war, and *here.* One morning he had passed a group of them in the small green space that gave Hanford Park its name, doing calisthenics and conducting quasi-military drills.

Dale had even flirted with joining them, expressing his admiration for their show of strength and bravado. Rake had just fought and won a war to rid the world of Fascism, whereas Dale's closest exposure to a battlefield had occurred at his local cinema, on account of the heart murmur that rendered him 4-F. Yet here the dust had cleared and apparently it was all right to don the enemy's uniform. So much about Rake's return to peacetime had been deeply disorienting, like he'd entered some fractured cosmos that had been improperly assembled from broken pieces.

Shortly after the war, Rake and Cassie had bought their house, thanks in large part to a GI Bill loan. That same month, a group of Columbians badly beat Negroes in another neighborhood a few miles north. The group held a rally in front of a Negro's new house, and a head Columbian made a few too many comments about overthrowing the governor and the president as part of their master plan for creating a utopian all-white nation. With that, he and two others were jailed for usurping police powers and inciting a riot. Only a few short months after they had appeared on the scene, the group vanished—or so Rake had thought.

Because who was putting up the signs in Hanford Park if not them? It was possible they were the ones who'd attacked Smith's brother-in-law. It also was possible Dale himself was guilty. Rake had warned Dale to lay off the new Negro neighbors, but betting on Dale's intelligence and good faith had never been a good idea.

There was another possibility, convoluted but troubling: Dale said he'd made his night ride to Coventry so that the Coventry Klan would return the favor. So perhaps a posse of hooded, robed goons had driven down from the sticks to beat up a Negro in Hanford Park, and the Columbian signs were just a coincidence. Perhaps every variety of hate was converging on Rake's neighborhood.

Rake took a short walk to the house of his first partner, the brutal and disappeared Lionel Dunlow. A massive oak dominated the front yard as thoroughly as Dunlow had dominated everyone around him. The small bungalow cried out for a new paint job and the lawn could have been mown; Rake recalled Dunlow complaining about his lazy sons, and it saddened him to see that they hadn't picked up the slack in his absence.

He knocked on the door. Through an open window he heard a radio program finish its report on Joe McCarthy's latest speech, then move on to the latest from the Kefauver hearings on organized crime.

The last two years had not been kind to Dunlow's widow. Her hair had gone from slightly gray to completely white, and she'd cut it severely short, as if to spite the world.

She had refused to believe Dunlow was dead for the first six months, but the Department's investigation, after weeks of fruitless searching, eventually went cold. After which reality and the need for survivor's benefits had overcome her denial. An empty casket had been buried with full police pageantry on the coldest February day of 1949.

"Officer Denny."

"How are you, Janisse?"

"Sun rises, sun sets. In between I manage to get by. You any closer to finding out what happened to him?"

This was why he'd hesitated coming here. Reliving this history was not pleasant.

"I wish I could say I was."

"Well, then. You come by for any reason other'n to make me feel bad?"

"I was hoping I could talk to your boys a minute. They around?"

"What'd Knox do this time? Or maybe I don't want to know."

"I'm sure it's nothing. I just need to cross something off a list."

She looked two miles past caring anymore. "They're around back."

The backyard, too, was overgrown, and at the very back sat Dunlow's old work shed, whose roof appeared to have collapsed recently. In front of it was a mess of possessions that the two Dunlow boys were rummaging through to see what was worth saving. Old bicycles, piles of wood planks, collections of rusty paint cans. Rake said howdy to Knox, twenty, and Buddy, eighteen. Knox wore a sleeveless T-shirt that displayed his muscular physique—he was six four, Rake guessed, and his recently shaved head confirmed the rumors that he'd enlisted for

Korea. Buddy was no slouch himself, but he was thinner and appeared almost tiny beside his brother.

"Looks like fun," Rake lied.

"Big branch landed on the shed the other night," Buddy explained. "Then it rained."

"What's new with you, Knox?"

"Enjoying my last days of freedom. I'm back at camp tomorrow, then we ship off next week."

Knox had kicked around at odd jobs the last two years. Even when his father had been alive, Knox had been the sort to get into plenty of trouble—brawls, underage drinking, once even taking a stolen car for a joyride—and had avoided jail time only because of his father's pull at headquarters. He'd still been given a couple passes after bar fights, but that wouldn't last forever.

"Good luck over there."

"Thanks. What's up?"

Both their faces echoed their father's so much it was hard to look at them.

"I was wondering if you boys could tell me where you were last night."

"Why?" Knox asked, not without aggression. He cleaned his greasy hands on a rag.

"I was here," Buddy said, "Knox was out."

Knox slugged his younger brother in the meat of the shoulder. "Shut *up*, Buddy."

Back when Rake had been visiting the family semiregularly, during the first weeks of Dunlow's disappearance, this had more or less been the dynamic: Knox truculent, ready to fight over anything, and deeply suspicious of Rake; and Buddy disarmingly honest and up-front, not at all his father's son.

"What were you out doing?" Rake asked Knox as Buddy winced and shook his arm.

"What is this about?" Knox demanded.

"Last night one of the new Negro neighbors was roughed up."

"Who cares?"

"I do. It's my job to care."

"Your job to do a lot of other things, too, not that you have."

"We didn't do anything like that," Buddy said, seeming hurt, and not just in the shoulder.

"Okay." Rake nodded, taking this slow. He'd already made note of the lack of cuts or bruises on the young men's knuckles; then again, the damage to Malcolm Greer may have been administered with a baseball bat or two-by-four, or the assailants might have worn gloves. Buddy's face was acne-scarred but otherwise unblemished, but Knox had what appeared to be mild bruising to the right of his lips. "The three of us know you boys firebombed a Negro's house two years ago. Because he'd moved into Hanford Park. Now some more Negroes move in, and one of 'em gets beat nearly to death. So it's only natural I should drop by."

"I don't even remember what he's talking about," Knox said to his brother, smirking.

Rake had let the boys go that night in '48, and he still didn't fully understand why. Perhaps he had taken pity on them, because their father had just gone missing and he sensed something terrible had happened. It made him wonder what it would be like to be raised by an arrogant and violent man like Dunlow. Perhaps Rake had let them go because he feared what would have happened, if they'd been prosecuted, to their already imploding family. And perhaps he'd done so simply because they were white and so was he.

"Just because I did you a favor once does not mean I'm inclined to do so again. Especially over something as rough as this. Would you like to see some photos of the man?"

Knox laughed. "If I want to see a beat-up nigger, I won't ask *you* to show me."

So much for expecting Knox to take this seriously. "It will make things go easier if you tell me what you were doing last night and who you were with."

"Knox, just tell him," Buddy said.

"Can it! Why should I say anything to this son of a bitch?" He turned his ire back to Rake. "Acting like you're all helpful, like all those times you stopped by before. You think we don't know? Plenty of Dad's friends say it was *you* who did him wrong. They say *you* got plenty to answer for." He looked about ready to spit in Rake's face, or throw a punch. And though he was but twenty, he would be a lot to handle.

"Who says that about me?"

"Plenty of folks. Like Uncle Brian, for one."

"Uncle Brian, you mean Officer Helton?" They weren't actually related as far as Rake knew, just "uncle" as in "one of Dad's best friends." "Don't believe everything you hear. That's my first piece of advice for a fellow about to head off to war."

Knox thought for a moment. "You were in France, right?"

"I was. Then Germany."

Knox sighed. "Look, I was with my friends Jimmy Sanders and Mel Haines and we were drinking at Mel's place, all right? We got good and drunk, which is our right."

"And what'd you do after that?"

"Fell asleep."

Three knuckleheads getting drunk was hardly an alibi that would cover them from assaulting a Negro. "How'd you get that bruise on your face?"

"I was teasing Mel about his girl not putting out and we wound up wrestling a bit."

"And you were here, Buddy, and your mother can vouch for that?"

"Yessir."

"We done?" Knox asked, flashing his greasy fingers. "I gotta wash up."

"One last thing." Rake didn't like Knox's story one bit, but he would let it go for now. He'd have to find the friends and see how their stories differed. "You know anything about those signs around the neighborhood, say White Community with a lightning bolt?"

Knox shrugged and Buddy claimed to have seen them but not know anything more.

"Any of your friends part of that group, the Columbians?"

Buddy said "No," and Knox, scoffing, said, "Hell no."

"Good. Stay away from them, and if you hear anything about 'em, let me know."

After Knox left to wash up, Rake asked Buddy, "You out of school yet?"

"I finish this year. Then I was thinking of joining the force."

"That's good." Thinking it was or it wasn't. "Third generation of Dunlows to wear the badge."

"Seems like the thing to do." And that was it, so simple. The same reason most men gave for joining up. After a pause, Buddy added, "You know, I used to think it was my fault, him running off. Thought maybe if I'd tried harder, done the things he asked more. Not been so mule-headed . . ."

"I don't know what happened to your old man, Buddy. But I am dead certain it had nothing to do with anything you did or didn't do." He pointed at the ground. "Now do your mother a favor and mow the lawn before she has to remind you again, all right?"

15

It was growing dark and Julie knew she still smelled of roast chicken, knew the scent was in her hair and on her clothes, and she'd need to hang the dress on the line in back and let the autumn air clean it for her, as she only had so many outfits and not enough time. She hated to come home smelling of richer food than that which she could provide for her own son, who'd probably supped on more of Grandma's runny soup. Her feet were tired and she was looking forward to nothing so much as sitting down when she was stopped short by the ghost at her door.

"Julie."

Her mouth hung open but she couldn't breathe.

"Julie. My Lord."

The ghost walked up to her, put its arms around her before she could stop it. Her arms hung at her sides while he embraced her, squeezed her to show that he was real, he wasn't a ghost at all, and she could feel his heart beating with what appeared to be joy and it was when he moved to put his lips on hers that her arms regained life and pushed him away.

"Stop," she said, backing up and taking the full measure of Jeremiah for the first time in five years. Thinner than before, leaner in his face, whole new angles to his cheekbones. His hair freshly cut. Smelling of shaving cream, mint, and menthol. The shirt she didn't recognize, but it was old, some hand-me-down or something he'd scavenged, or maybe five years was enough to forget about little things like clothes, and big things, too.

He had smiled when he'd approached her, but now he looked hurt. He also looked like he'd been crying earlier, his eyes red, cheeks tacky.

"It's me. I'm out. I'm free." He held up his shackleless hands, palms out, as if he were the risen Christ and she an unbelieving disciple. "I guess it's a surprise to see me. I would have written to let you know, but you stopped writing me back."

"You stopped writing *me*." Her voice small.

"I wrote you and wrote you."

Maybe he was lying or maybe her parents had intercepted his letters from prison. All she knew was that within the first few months of his incarceration, his letters had ceased, and then her family had moved after their old landlord kicked them out on account of her being in a family way, and they'd moved three times in two years before winding up here.

"Took me a while to track you down. Didn't know you'd moved. Didn't know a few other things, either. Like the boy. My son. Pretty surprised when I knocked on that door and your mama answered and I see that little fella walk up and look at me," he was smiling again, "my own little eyes staring at me from two feet up. I about passed out. Got dizzy and everything. I tried to pick him up but your mama kicked me out."

She felt her own eyes tearing up.

"You told me you lost the baby. Why'd you lie like that?"

"I was telling you what you wanted to hear." Her voice nearly a whisper.

He shook his head and she hated him for it. Did he not believe her, was he trying to rewrite their history? Perhaps he'd forgotten the time she'd told him she was pregnant, and he'd looked at her like she'd confessed to some horrible crime. She still could not forgive him for that reaction.

"I can't believe . . . ," he started. "I can't believe you would lie about that."

"I guess we both did things the other couldn't believe. Like you running with your brother's boys and getting into all that trouble. Bringing that into my life."

"Julie . . . That was a long while ago, and I made a mistake and I—"

"Look, I'm glad you're a free man, but I'm not going back to that. And I'm not going back to you. Now, I've had a long day at work—real work, honest work—and I need to rest, so you can be on your way."

She waited for him to move, but all he did was issue an empty laugh. "That's all you got for me? Five years in there and that's all you got?"

"That's all I got. You and me, we're done and gone, a long time ago."

"He's my boy."

"Not anymore. He never really was—you saw to that. Running with that crowd, which I *told* you not to do. Getting yourself mixed up in that, which I *knew* would be trouble. You had a choice between me and your brother, and you chose him."

"I chose *you*." He seemed shocked, desperate. "How can you say that?"

"You chose him first, and that's what caused all the trouble."

"I . . . I made a mistake, I know, but then I *helped* you, girl."

"You did, and I thanked you, but by then you'd done enough harm."

"I been in there five years and—"

"And five years I been out here working and raising a boy on my own. Five years I been on my knees cleaning and cooking and washing for white folks and coming here to collapse and maybe hold him awhile before I fall asleep." *Five years I've been dealing with the looks and the comments. Five years my own mama's been doing me the favor of keeping Sage all day so I can try to make enough money to feed us.* "Don't you tell me about *your* five years."

Light behind him as the front door opened, her mother's slight silhouette etched there. Julie realized she herself was shaking when she saw how still her mother was, realized she was crying when her vision began to fuzz.

"You go on now, Jeremiah," her mother said. "Parnell be home soon and he won't be any happier to see you."

Mentioning Julie's father was the wrong thing to do, for Jeremiah's chest seemed to rise at the suggestion that he might back down from another man.

"I have a right to see my boy."

"He's not yours no more! He's mine, and soon he'll be another man's, because I'm *engaged*. You never wanted to be a father, and you never will be."

"And he's a policeman," Julie's mother said. Julie didn't know where Sage was. Her mother needed to close that door, because if Sage walked out and Jeremiah approached him, Julie didn't know what she might do, scream or throw herself upon Jeremiah, and she feared she would wind up hurting Sage in the midst of such rage.

"You ain't marrying no policeman." Thinking she meant a white man.

"I am. There are colored policemen now, and Lucius is one of them. He's a good man and a strong man, and he'll be here for us in a way you never were."

"Lucius." Speaking the name into reality. Then standing there stunned a few seconds. "I'm in prison, and you're running around with a policeman. Lord God." He stepped back like he'd been struck dizzy again, the free world spinning too fast for him.

"Why'd you even come back here? Your people moved up to Chicago, on account of what you and your brother did."

"Maybe I'll get to Chicago eventually. Or maybe I'll stay here instead. Maybe I want to have something to do with that little man in there."

"That won't happen. Now leave."

"I want to see my boy."

"Don't cause no scene, Jeremiah," her mother warned. "Don't make us call the police."

"The police? Yeah, call Julie's new man. That'd be perfect. Call him out here."

"Go on," Julie all but hissed, frightened by Jeremiah's lack of concern.

"Let me say good night to him. I barely got to say hello before."

She did not want to waste another syllable on him. They stood there a long, silent moment.

Finally she walked toward the door. She had to pass him, and he reached out for her forearm and clutched it, not even tightly, but that slight contact was enough.

She could not contain the rage any longer. It tore itself out of her chest, balled her fingers into fists, animated her arms, and sent surges through her legs. He was trying to block her blows and was stumbling backward but she felt parts of him, she knew she made contact, his body would give way to hers this time, she would punish him for everything and do so *right now,* and she heard her mother screaming and then she could hear Sage crying and it was that alone that would have made her stop if not for the fact that, at the same moment, other arms were pulling her back.

Many different people yelling *Stop* and *Quit that now* and *Hey* and she couldn't move her arms. Her hair had come unpinned and been thrown wild in her face and she couldn't see well but eventually she recognized the voice of Mr. Cummings, her neighbor, and the old fellow they called Pitchfork who didn't really have a home but always seemed to be about. The two elders were holding her back while a third man she didn't even recognize had a hand at Jeremiah's chest.

"Enough, enough," Mr. Cummings said, and they released her. She gathered herself and she felt her mother's hand at her shoulder, ushering her to the house.

Sage stood in the threshold, wailing now, not stamping his feet the way he did when in the throes of a tantrum but simply planted there, terror contorting his face, his voice ringing out. Julie shook and she scooped him up, hoping he could anchor her somehow, when she knew that wasn't how it worked at all, it was she who should be doing that for him, and she'd failed at that, too, and her mother closed the door behind them.

"Go on, now," the men said to Jeremiah, whoever these men were.

This wasn't what he wanted. He'd barely held her, and hadn't even gotten a chance to tell her about the miracle, the white cop collapsing, his train north. He licked his lips and tasted blood, reached into his back pocket for a handkerchief but found none. Such were his possessions. His nose bled—girl was *strong*—and he wiped away what he could and tried to spit out the rest and he must have looked like hell.

"Go on home."

Home. Where was that? What had become of this place? Five years and now the war was over, his mother and sister were in Chicago where a winter of medieval proportions would soon set in, he suddenly had a four-year-old son, and the girl he'd been dreaming about all those nights didn't want him. He gazed at the small, subdivided house, blinds drawn. Night had slowly seeped around him while he'd been standing there, like there was a night spigot and someone had turned it on an hour ago and it had pooled at his feet and now he was submerged in it, and so was this barely recognizable city. He was drowning in night and there was nowhere for him to go.

Yet Jeremiah walked, pride stiffening his shoulders and holding him up taller than he felt. He willed his bad knee not to bother him as he walked on and the men watched him. First prison, now this: he was always walking away from things.

This would be his fourth night in Atlanta. He'd arrived three days ago and had walked from Terminal Station back to where he had once lived. The city alive around him, everywhere motion, trains unloading passengers, streams of people walking to this bus stop or that, striding through the city, Atlanta itself a vast spiderweb of different routes superimposed upon each other, and for a while Jeremiah had been the only one motionless, caught in the spiderweb, until the very spider himself, a big cop with a hand on his billy club, wandered over and told him to *get a move on, boy*, so get a move on Jeremiah did.

Emerging from the station, hearing the sounds of the trains and in the distance the freight cars and the legions of men loading and unloading the freight, he'd wondered how many of them down there he knew. That had been his job once. The Negroes had stuck to their workstations and the whites to theirs, though their jobs were mostly the same, because so many men were off at war that the managers could not afford to be choosy. Jeremiah had started when he was sixteen. The first thing he did was wonder why the white man who hired him, who was tall and broad and appeared capable of lifting an entire train car should the mood strike him, was not at war, but he didn't ask. This was *essential war work,* he would later learn, a legal term that meant they wouldn't be drafted as a result of such employment.

Only sixteen years old but there was work to be had, money to be made. He'd never been much for schooling and there was but one high school for Negroes anyway. Jobs everywhere, if not loading and unloading trains then building bombers and fighters up north of the city, building trucks and jeeps and boats, sewing new uniforms and tents and building vehicles and fortifications, so much that would later be destroyed and thus require even yet more uniforms and jets and trucks. They were making things the world would swiftly unmake, and the business of it was grand.

Buildings growing across the city, scaffolds rising and bulldozers beetling everywhere, newness so sudden that you had trouble remembering what had existed before. Maybe it had been an older building or a shack or someone's untended back plot but now a five-story frame stood there, workers like monkeys dangling in every direction. Too many people in town to fit, the job sites wanted them but the landlords didn't, the city just didn't possess the apartments and houses for them yet, so they crammed in, two families to an apartment, three, four. Everywhere clotheslines, everywhere children in the streets and on the sidewalk, everywhere cans of garbage being knocked over by dogs, raccoons, rats, cars. Jeremiah's family was lucky to have been there first, he'd been born in Atlanta, not like so many of the new folks with their country accents and strange ways. He'd been poor all his life but suddenly he owned things these country folk wanted desperately; he and his friends could buy their own cigarettes, they could sneak drinks, they or someone they knew always heard when the moonshine was coming in, when a few extra cartons of cigarettes had accidentally fallen off a train, there was money to be made, money to be made.

Until his brother got greedy, talked Jeremiah into feeling the same, and it all went to hell.

So long ago. Those days etched in his mind like when he'd shut his eyes after a light had become too bright, the shape of things scored inside his iris, only it stayed there, even after five years of closing his eyes. He'd wake in the morning and still see it there, the Atlanta he'd left behind, but the new city before him didn't match that memory. It was enough to drive a man mad.

He was walking away from her, and the little boy, the anchor he hadn't known he'd had.

Since arriving in the city, he'd sought out old friends or friends of his mother's, people who in some way might substitute for his family. He could find so few of them. Neighbors told him this person had moved to Chicago, that one to Kansas City, these to Toledo. Where on earth was Toledo, and why would one move there? All the people he'd known had been replaced by more country folk, more of those accents. The city at least smelled the same, pork chops and chitlins and pigs' feet, he smelled spilled beer when he passed the bars on Edgewood, he smelled the vomit and piss and sweat, but it was new people's sweat.

His brother was dead. His mother and sister had fled to Chicago with his mother's latest boyfriend, according to one of her letters. He knew they blamed him for his brother's death. The mere possibility of revisiting all that pain made him not want to consider the journey north, to Chicago and the unknown cold and unknown masses and the very known, very much hated pain of his family.

Some of his friends had vanished to prison—a handful he'd seen there with his own eyes—and some to the grave. How frightening to realize that, to ask after someone and be told he was dead, to have someone killed by a mere utterance like that. And so matter of fact. *He dead. Didn't you know?*

He had nowhere to go.

He was walking down Decatur Street, shoulders hunched and hands crammed into his pockets against a chill he wasn't dressed for. Two men were about to pass him when one of them stopped, his thick brows arched.

"Jeremiah? Jeremiah!"

He dimly remembered this man but could not recall his name. He couldn't even place how he knew the fellow—had they lived on the same block or played sandlot baseball or shot pool? The man introduced Jeremiah to his friend, whom he called Bucket, and Jeremiah nodded a wary hello as the Forgotten fellow smiled as if he and Jeremiah were long-lost friends.

"What happened to you, boy? Been forever."

"Been down in Reidsville. Five years."

"Oh, damn, that's right! The tobacco boys!"

Forgotten explained to Bucket that this here Jeremiah had been nailed for swiping crates of smokes off the trains and reselling them during wartime. Frame job, just something the cops needed to pin on Negroes, that's how they do.

Forgotten insisted they go into the bar and have a drink. Jeremiah was a free man and this stood for some celebrating. While in prison he had promised himself he'd never touch the stuff again. But this was the first time since his release that someone seemed happy to see him, and because he was hungry he figured drinks might lead to food. So he joined them, even though he felt uncomfortable around Forgotten, as if the man himself were some sin Jeremiah had committed and not atoned for. There was just something unnatural about not remembering someone who seemed to know you so well.

Soon he was half drunk on half-beer. People trickled in, some faces he remembered but not their names. Faces he had not thought of in years, and to be reminded of them made him smile, grinning like an idiot just to hear people say his name, *Jeremiah it's good to see you, boy,* and he began to feel alive again.

"Where you living?" Forgotten asked.

"I, uh, I don't have a place yet." He had slept the night before in the hallway of an apartment building where some of his friends had once lived. Hadn't meant to sleep there, but after knocking on the door and finding no answer, and after slumping against the wall and sitting down to plan his next steps, exhaustion had taken him. "I just want to find a job."

Forgotten laughed. "They ain't going to hire no Negro with a record! You unemployable, Pure-boy."

Pure-boy, what some of the men in his brother's crowd had called him. Because he dared discuss the Bible with them, because he had resisted drinking and smoking reefer for so long, or what had *felt* like so long. Perhaps it had only been a few months. How sad, he realized. His willpower had held out for what had felt like an almost biblical amount of time, but that was just the blink of an eye to God. Yet they'd continued to call him Pure-boy.

"I'm a hard worker."

"You are your record, Pure-boy. Ain't no one gonna hire a colored man who robbed from his last boss."

He needed to believe that Forgotten was wrong. Surely someone would be impressed by his willingness to push himself, the sheer physical endurance he'd displayed on the chain gang.

"There's the other kind of work, you know what I mean," Forgotten said. "Only kind you'll ever make any money off."

"I'm not interested. I'm meant for better things. I believe that."

"That right?"

"I'm not a fully formed thing. I'm the Lord's clay. He has plans for me."

Bucket had been half eavesdropping, half checking out women as he'd leaned against the bar beside Forgotten, and he chimed in, "Yeah, you got yourself a real messiah quality. First I saw you, I was gonna ask you when you were gonna do your next miracle."

Bucket and Forgotten burst out laughing. Jeremiah felt the channels in his mind thicken, anger and fear and embarrassment. There *had* been a miracle already, that officer in Reidsville, and these two saw fit to mock him?

"You can't understand," he said. "Your minds are messed up with this poison."

They laughed harder, asking him what about the poison *he* was drinking, and by the way, when was he going to pay for his drinks?

Jeremiah reached into his pocket and removed some of the very little money he had left from what the preacher had given him. He placed it on the bar and thanked the men for their company and took his leave, realizing he still hadn't eaten and that once the buzz faded his stomach would commence tormenting him.

Outside it was even yet colder. Why had he spoken that way? Maybe they might have put him up for the night if he hadn't said anything. He would need to find another hallway, and quick. Back before his sentence, police would jail or beat Negroes who were out at this hour unless they carried something from an employer excusing them. He imagined that was still the case.

He passed the mouth of an alley and something hit him in the cheek. His body swayed and before he could fall completely he took two more blows, one of them dead on the nose.

The world reset itself at an incorrect angle and he was staring at the side of the building, diagonal across his vision, and a figure stepped in front of him. It reached into his pockets. There was a second one, reaching for his ankles, removing his shoes. He was kicked until he rolled onto his back, the better for frisking his front pockets, where he'd kept his scant money.

"Thank you, Country," one of them said, and only later would he understand it as an insult to the rural Negroes moving into town, as they didn't realize he was from here, that he was Atlantan through and through, that his blood and his family's blood had been spilled here long ago, but none of that toil led to something better, it wasn't like farming, where your sacrifice bore fruit, it was just hurt, and right then he hurt about as bad as he could, until one of them lifted a boot and the hurt stopped.

16

Eight o'clock, the city dark as Smith walked with Dewey Edmunds—McInnis liked to switch their partners some nights to ensure they all knew and trusted one another. Dewey was the shortest cop at the Butler Street precinct, officially five five (the cutoff established for Negro officers), but everyone assumed he'd been on his tiptoes when measured. The fact that he also might have been the strongest cop dissuaded people from commenting on his height.

"How's your brother-in-law?" Dewey asked.

"Bad. But he's conscious again."

"He remember anything?"

"No." Smith had visited Malcolm in the hospital that morning, mere hours after the attack. Hannah had been sitting with him, and after Smith had sat with her for barely ten minutes, Malcolm had opened his eyes for the first time. Well, one of his eyes. The other was so dark purple he wouldn't be opening it for days. His head heavily bandaged, casts covered his left arm and right foot, which hung from the ceiling like he was a human pendulum. Simply looking at him had hurt, Smith feeling a tingle in his lower abdomen like the first time he rode in a plane, that awful awareness of how fragile we are.

Malcolm had stayed awake just long enough to say he didn't know what had happened. He dimly remembered being hit in the head, but that was all. No faces, not even any voices. He hadn't even recalled for certain when he'd gotten off the bus or how far home he'd walked, if he'd been attacked where they'd found him or if he'd been dumped there, couldn't even remember how late he'd worked beforehand.

Despite the brick through their window and plenty of dirty looks from white neighbors, Hannah had told Smith that she and Malcolm hadn't endured any confrontations worth mentioning. Until the very afternoon of Malcolm's assault, only a few hours beforehand. A white man, she told Smith, had come by with his wife, claiming to represent some neighborhood group. They offered to buy the Greers' house back for three thousand dollars and even showed them an envelope full of cash, right there. They had actually pressed it into Malcolm's hands, Hannah said. The white folks hadn't liked it when the Greers refused; they said they'd thought the Greers were "good Nigras" but they were being proven wrong. Hannah hadn't gotten the couple's names, but Smith took down their description.

Then there were the letters. As far as Smith knew, the white officer who had responded to Hannah's call about the brick hadn't learned anything, or even tried. Smith would have to drop by her house again soon, see if any more letters had come that day.

Nurses had interrupted the conversation before Smith could get much more out of Malcolm. Hopefully his memory would clear soon. Smith needed to find these men who had so broken his brother-in-law, men who would probably be successful in their task after all, because if Malcolm was laid out very long, and if he couldn't work and earn money to pay his mortgage, they'd lose that house one way or another.

Smith and Dewey called in to Dispatch every hour on the hour to report their whereabouts and get updates from McInnis. When they checked in at eleven that night, McInnis relayed a "call for service" at an apartment two blocks away, a scared neighbor reporting the sounds of a struggle between a man and a woman.

They hated such calls. Either the woman was indeed being beaten but would turn into a doe-eyed defender of her abusive lover in their presence, or she'd stay silent and scared while the man launched into the kind of rage that only occurs when other men dare show up in his home and tell him how to behave.

This time, they heard shouting before they even knocked on the door. It was coming from within a beauty parlor on Edgewood, just down the road from some of the rowdier nightclubs and bars. The sign on the glass read Closed, but an inner light cast shadows.

"Police, open up," Dewey said as he banged on the glass. Smith stepped back, checking the street for loiterers.

After a second knock, a young woman opened the door. She smiled and said, "I'm sorry, we're closed." She seemed out of breath.

"I'm not here for my hair, ma'am," Dewey said. "I'm here because your neighbors heard screaming, and so did I. Everything all right?"

"I guess I got a little loud there, having a disagreement with my business partner."

Smith stood behind Dewey, hands at his belt.

"Mind if we come in and talk to your partner?" Dewey asked, edging forward as if he'd already received his answer.

"No, really, I'm fine, I need to be shutting down now and heading out myself."

But her voice was strained, and she didn't look at all pleased as she made eye contact with Smith, who entered a step behind Dewey.

Before them the vinyl cushions of six metal swivel chairs shined in the light of a small desktop lamp twenty feet away. The room otherwise empty.

"Everybody out," Smith announced to the emptiness. He saw a door behind the desk, marked Restroom. Five feet beyond that was another door, unmarked.

"She's just in the bathroom," the woman explained.

"Ma'am," Dewey said, "we got a report there was yelling between a man and woman. That man in the bathroom by any chance?"

A toilet flushed.

"That's just my partner, Lucy," she said.

"Where's that other door go?" Smith asked.

"Storage room. Ain't nobody in there," she said, answering a question he hadn't asked.

The bathroom door began opening. Smith's hand drifted onto the handle of his gun.

"Step out slowly!" he commanded.

He was fixated on that bathroom door, and the light from within that fell slantwise across the dark room, and the elongated shadow that appeared for but a second until the person (a woman indeed) shut off the bathroom light. "Whoa," she said when she saw her unexpected guests.

"Open that other door," Dewey commanded.

The woman who'd answered the door obeyed. It was dark in the storage room. Dewey couldn't see anything other than the near side of a shelf, full of small containers of hair supplies and cosmetics.

"Turn on the light," he told her. She stepped inside and reached for the string dangling there, but when she pulled, the *click* failed to illuminate anything.

"It's out, I guess," she said, so Dewey reached for his flashlight, not trusting this at all, and when he turned it on he saw a man's belt buckle—much higher up than it would normally be—and the buckle came closer as the man took a mighty stride forward. Smith, in the main room, had been keeping his eye on the second woman, but when he sensed movement from the storage room, he turned, and out of the darkened space like some trick of a conjurer emerged one of the biggest men he would ever see.

And one of the fastest. Dewey was still trying to remove something from his belt as Thunder Malley lifted him off his feet. Then Malley took another step into the room and tossed Dewey through the glass window onto the sidewalk outside.

Smith was so stunned by the feat he stood there an extra second, marveling at the display, how a grown man could be thrown aside like a toy, and the shards of glass still falling from the windowpane onto the tiled floor inside and the cement outside. Then one of the women set upon him, hitting him with what he would later realize was a hair iron, knocking off his hat and sending sparks through his skull, and then the woman from the bathroom was on him, too, hands around his neck and nails slicing through his arm. Smith tried to knock them away as he saw Thunder Malley moving toward him.

On the sidewalk, Dewey blinked a few times to figure out why his bedroom ceiling was full of stars. The screaming from inside brought him back.

He rolled over, cutting his chest and right forearm on shards of glass. Gradually he raised himself, in stages, knees wobbly at first, his head no higher than his heart, and he exhaled extra slow, like he'd been taught to do after taking a solid punch, and then he lifted his shoulders and looked at his foe.

As a boxer and running back at Morehouse, Dewey had won a reputation as a competitor who would not be brought down easily. He'd heard his fellow officers joke about how maybe he had been wearing high heels the day he'd been measured for the job, and they probably wouldn't believe the truth, that when the old white man from the city government at the police interview had marked his height as five four, Dewey had said, *No, sir, I believe you're mistaken, it's five five,* and he'd said it in such a way that the white man had eyed him for a cold second or two, probably never having heard a Negro address him that way, and instead of snapping at Dewey, the white man had said, *I suppose I may have mismeasured.* Either intimidated by Dewey's stare or just figuring, okay, little fellow, if you really want to be out on the street, you go right ahead and take your chances and it surely won't be on *my* conscience.

The fuzzy objects in Dewey's vision resolved themselves and he saw Smith completely ensnared in women's elbows and hair like some epic Greek statue come to life. Then he saw Thunder Malley grab Smith by the neck and slug him twice in the face. Barbers' scissors resting in glasses ten feet away shook from the force. The women's interlocked limbs held Smith up for an extra second before realizing he was unconscious. Then they let him drop.

Dewey ignored the front door in favor of the gaping hole he'd made in the window. And perhaps a gun at that point would have been advisable. But McInnis had given them strict rules of engagement regarding firearms. The very reason the Negro officers had been hired was because of community outrage over years of police brutality, endless beatings, and more-than-occasional shootings. It wouldn't do if the Negro officers were as trigger-happy as their white counterparts.

Another way of looking at it: the lives of Negro officers weren't worth much, so the Department would appreciate them relying on their billy clubs, thanks, and only unholster their guns if they saw a subject reach for one first.

So it was a billy club that Dewey removed as he jumped down from the windowsill.

"Thunder Malley, you're under arrest."

Malley took one stride toward him, halving the distance. Lord God he was big. At the moment his foot came down, supporting his generous center of gravity, Dewey swung the billy club into the side of Thunder's knee.

The big man screamed in a way he perhaps never had before. Tendons tore and the knee buckled. He reached for it with his hands, cradling it with those massive fingers, and even down on his knee, he had maybe an inch on Dewey. The women standing over the fallen Smith were frozen in place as if realizing they needed to precisely record this historic event.

Dewey drove the club butt-first into Thunder's solar plexus. Thunder doubled over, his head nearly butting Dewey aside.

But when Dewey moved in for a final blow over the back of Thunder's head, something hot seared his forearm. He pulled back, his fingers instinctively releasing the club, and saw one of the women before him, gripping a straight razor. The only reason none of his blood was on it was because she'd cut him so fast.

She swung again, this time for his chest, and he backed away fast enough for it to miss him, though not entirely—he'd later see that she'd torn a perfectly diagonal stripe across his uniform shirt.

Without enough time for him to even debate the ethics of hitting a woman, which he'd never done in his life, he stepped forward and threw a jab at her nose and she was down.

Behind her was the other woman, whom he pointed at. "Don't even th—"

Then his head was thrown to his right a few inches, his neck reluctantly following. He crashed into a chair, leaned on it, and it swiveled around, which was good, because otherwise he would have hit the ground again, but was also bad, because after he finished a full revolution he was facing Thunder, who had just hit him with a right hook and whose fist was already moving back toward Dewey's face.

The second punch was just as hard. Maybe harder, aided by the fact that the chair swung Dewey square into it. This time he stumbled back and crashed into the hairdresser's table, the back of his head shattering a mirror.

The only thing more terrifying than seeing Thunder Malley readying to throw a punch was seeing *two* Thunder Malleys readying to throw a punch. But that's what Dewey saw, his brain addled by the blows.

He moved away in time, then told himself to remember his footwork, all those old lessons and drills coming back to him. He nearly stepped on Smith and the fallen woman—he didn't usually have obstacles like that in the ring. The other woman had backed up, giving the men some space.

Dewey squinted and the two Malleys resolved back into one. His billy club still dangled from his wrist strap but he decided to go with the skills that had brought him this far, sticking the club into his belt and holding his fists in position.

"You're making a mistake," he said to Thunder.

Who laughed. "You're the one making the mistake, little man. You in the wrong weight class."

Malley threw another right, which Dewey dodged again.

"And what you gonna do, throw me in jail for a night? Last time you put one of my boys away, he was out by morning. Y'all can't touch me."

Even aiming a punch at Malley's head was out of the question, he was so much taller. But the big son of a bitch wasn't used to fighting, Dewey could see. He usually didn't need to, only needed to stare hard at someone. He clearly didn't like using his left hand, and he was limping on his injured leg, so Dewey cheated to that side.

He could feel blood trickling warmly down his forearm.

Malley's reach was damn near double Dewey's. So when Malley threw another right and Dewey slipped under it, he moved as fast as he ever had to get inside and unleash a 1-2-3 combination to the same spot he'd billy-clubbed earlier.

Malley groaned, and Dewey backed the hell out of there before Malley could wrap his massive arms around him. Malley punched again, but off balance, unable to catch up with his faster opponent, and he seemed shaky, the knee giving him trouble.

Again Malley threw a right, but Dewey ducked, his lack of size an advantage now. Malley's fist found nothing but air and he swayed like a heavy bag mid-workout. Dewey delivered another three punches and could smell a ham sandwich Malley had eaten for lunch.

Now Malley was the one staggering backward into a mirror.

Dewey took his club back out and swung it into Malley's knee again. The big man screamed and fell onto his other knee, one hand planted on the ground to keep him up.

Malley's head now in striking distance, Dewey jabbed him twice with his left, breaking his nose. Then a roundhouse right, made awkward by the trailing billy club but still true enough to make that big head roll on its neck as if trying to escape the body that had gotten it into so much trouble.

Yet the head rolled back again, still tethered by the thickest neck Dewey had ever squared up against. He saw big Thunder Malley's eyes go white, eyeballs rolling so high that Dewey knew to step back to give the Goliath room to fall. He landed flat, right next to Smith, whose body actually bounced from the force.

The impact roused Smith. He opened his eyes and found himself staring, from two inches away, at Malley's knocked-out face.

"Thunder," he said, slowly. "Damn. You're under arrest."

Twenty minutes later a crowd had gathered outside the salon, kept back by McInnis and six other officers, two of them colored and four of them white cops who had heard on their car radios that an officer was down and that Thunder Malley was actually being arrested. They couldn't resist seeing this for themselves. The whites cops stood there like guests at a party who wouldn't dream of helping with the dishes but were happy to be entertained.

Smith felt lightheaded but had refused to let an ambulance take him away, not that one would have made its way to this part of town all that quickly. They were still waiting for the wagon that would drive Malley and his two accomplices to jail—it was still unclear whether the women were in fact accomplices or victims of his extortion, but their stories were changing so fast that the officers decided a jail cell might be the perfect truth serum.

Malley lay facedown on the salon floor, conscious but handcuffed and under strict orders to not so much as roll over. Dewey stood beside him, uniform shirt torn in the back from when he'd destroyed the glass window and torn in front from the razor. He wasn't bleeding as badly as he by all rights should have been; the slash in his arm wasn't deep, patched up with a first aid kit from McInnis's squad car. He could use a few aspirin but didn't feel any worse than he had many other times in the ring. Champ Jennings stood beside Officer Sherman Bayle, both of them smiling as they asked Dewey to retell it for a fourth time.

Finally the wagon that would ferry Malley away appeared, lights flashing and horn honking to part the crowd. As it neared the curb, McInnis leaned toward the open passenger window.

"Not here. Park five blocks that way."

"What?" the driver asked. "Dispatch said he's in there."

"I said I want you to move this wagon and park it five blocks east. And if that's too complicated, maybe you can try driving a garbage truck instead."

"Yes, sir."

The driver shifted into reverse and turned around. As he drove away, Smith said, "I don't understand, Sergeant."

"Just watch."

McInnis stepped into the parlor. "All right, Thunder, your chariot awaits."

Dewey tugged on the cuffs, pulling Malley to his knees, and then the juggernaut stood, McInnis and Bayle making brief eye contact to acknowledge the awesomeness of the man's size.

"I can walk him out," Champ said, assuming the task should be his since he was the only one who came close to being Malley's physical equal.

"No," McInnis said. "This is Edmunds and Smith's collar. You two stay here with the ladies and see if they change their tune once he's out of earshot."

Malley was too proud to keep his head down, even with the flashes from the camera held out by a photographer for the Negro *Atlanta Daily Times,* who stood beside reporter Jeremy Toon at the front of the crowd, Toon scribbling furiously in his notebook. Malley's pride suited McInnis just fine, as it made it even easier for the witnesses to see the eyes of Thunder Malley, confirming it was really him. Dewey trudged a step behind the big man, one hand at the chain of his cuffs and another at what would normally be called the small of his back, except nothing about Malley was small. Two paces behind walked Smith, head still woozy but posture military perfect, eyes forward, resisting the temptation to scan the crowd's reaction.

He could hear it, though. Comments and whistles and murmurs as they walked past the bars and nightclubs, the sounds of windows opening so heads could poke out, porch boards creaking as second-floor onlookers peered at the sight. He heard a few people cheer, and as they made it a third and then a fourth block he even heard some laughter, as jokes at the expense of the great Thunder Malley could now be issued without fear of violent bodily harm. Smith wobbled at one point but he managed to right himself. It felt like the longest walk of his life, yet with every step and every gasp from the crowd he realized it was perhaps his most important. Even more people were in the street now, a borderline carnival breaking out as they watched the spectacle of Smith and the shortest police officer in the city of Atlanta marching their legendary subject down Edgewood.

"Y'all are crazy," Malley muttered under his breath. "You got nothing on me. I got friends who ain't gonna like this."

"We got you for assaulting two officers, at the very least," Dewey said. "You want to tell me the names of those friends of yours, so I can go after them next?"

No reply.

The wagon's driver stood beside the opened back door and observed, "That there is one big nigger," earning daggers from the eyes of Dewey but not Smith, whose eyes were still too foggy to issue a mean stare. Dewey pushed down on Malley's shoulders until the big man was safely inside, then slammed the door.

"What's the charge, and where are they taking him?" Toon asked.

Smith looked at the reporter and said, "We're taking him to jail, where he belongs. And he ain't coming back, people." He stepped away from Toon and moved his dizzy eyes about the crowd, partly so he could address everyone and partly because he was still having trouble focusing on anything. "If that man's leaned on any of you, if you been too afraid to say anything about it before, the time has *come*. Come to the Butler Street precinct and we'll take down your report. Or call us and we'll come to you." He pointed to the wagon, which was now pulling away. "That man don't own you anymore, understand? You don't have to live in his shadow, or anybody else's." Then he nodded and walked back to the scene of the crime, ignoring Toon's questions.

"Well done, gentlemen," McInnis told Dewey and Smith when they returned to the salon. The crowd was still watching, too amazed to leave just yet. McInnis's eyes lingered on his bruised and bloodied officers. "You sure you don't want an ambulance?"

Dewey said, "I'm good," and Smith agreed, "I'm sure, sir."

"Good," McInnis said. "That would kill the mood."

17

It appeared to be a vacant lot unless you looked real close. The land sloped steeply down from the road, weeds and scrub grass giving way to layers of Virginia creeper and kudzu, those leafy vines blanketing the ground entirely, and then farther down—almost invisible from the road—hid a ramshackle structure that only a very unfortunate soul might consider as living quarters. Perhaps it had been a large storage shed for one of the adjoining properties, back before the land had been parceled into smaller lots, or even the cover for a moonshine still before this narrow road was paved. No more than thirty feet long and with a slanted roof barely eight feet off the ground, it sat so close to the creek that Rake figured a hard rain might flood it. The odds of it having indoor plumbing were approximately zero.

With no mailbox or number affixed to its unpainted door, it was barely an official address, but this is where two sources had told Rake he could find Delmar Coyle, former and perhaps present Columbian. Also former prisoner, released from Reidsville a month ago.

Grant Park, a thickly wooded neighborhood southeast of downtown, boasted a swimming lake and stately Victorians in its northern half. This address, however, was in the less desirable southern edge, where petty crimes were more common. Untended vegetation grew far into this narrow, dead-end street; ahead was a small clearing for cars to turn around in, complete with recent tread marks. It did not seem an auspicious place to plot a revolution, Rake figured, but then again Coyle had plenty of solitude to hatch his next harebrained scheme.

Rake had spoken to Knox Dunlow's two friends, whom Knox claimed to be drinking with that night. They both backed Knox's story, though it was possible they were lying and had all decided to beat up

Malcolm Greer once liquored up. Or, it was possible Knox had finished drinking with them, driven home, seen Greer walking down the street, and had decided to pull over and teach the Negro a lesson himself. Rake certainly found that credible, though he had no evidence, and other cops would be extremely reluctant to charge Dunlow's son with anything. Plus Knox was about to leave for Korea.

Rake had read the report on Malcolm Greer's assault—taken without any testimony from the then unconscious victim—and he noticed it hadn't mentioned that the victim was related to Officer Smith. No evidence was noted, nor was there any record of an investigation beyond that first night. The cops in charge of the area clearly weren't doing a thing.

For all he knew, they were the ones who had attacked Malcolm.

Rake loved living in Hanford Park, where men could change their car's oil in their driveways while listening to the Bulldogs game, or just fall asleep on the back patio, which he did the morning after many a late shift. He wouldn't have wanted to police such a dull area, where the chief complaints were the occasional break-in or gripes about a noisy neighborhood party or that fellow who mows his lawn before eight on a Sunday. Recent events were making him reconsider that assessment. His desire to learn what had happened was about more than just paying back a debt to a colored cop he barely knew. And it was about far more than his strong and oft-regretted favoring of underdogs. It was about the fear that his own power, that of his badge, would fade if they did nothing about the crime.

He walked out of the car and descended the slope to Coyle's place, pant legs instantly damp from the dew that clung to the vines even in the afternoon. Red oaks towered overhead; the yard probably got no more than an hour of sunlight when the boughs were full.

A dog started barking. Rake's right hand migrated to his holster in case something should come charging.

He was ten feet from the door when it opened. The snout of some tawny mutt appeared, a hand gripping its collar. "Hush, Max."

The dog downshifted to a growl. His owner had a military haircut and bony features, his sleeveless T-shirt revealing ropy arms veined with tension as he held the mutt back. Blue eyes beneath a furrowed brow.

"Delmar Coyle?" Rake asked.

"That's me, and I done my time already. What's this about?"

"Just wanted to ask you a few questions. Without canine interference."

Coyle pushed the dog back as he stepped outside and closed the door behind him. Rake couldn't get a look inside. The building had two small windows on this side but they were both so filthy they may as well have been painted black.

"Enjoying the free life?" Rake asked.

"I am, matter of fact." No longer crouching, he was tall, with an inch or two on Rake, but much thinner. Perhaps he was only malnourished and made lean from the labor camp, but with his wary eyes and sharp chin it gave him the look of a hardscrabble survivor after some great disaster. "Man was meant to be free. Not tied down in a prison or anyplace else."

"You weren't in jail very long, though, were you? Conspiring to overthrow the government doesn't carry the kind of sentence it used to."

Coyle folded his arms, restraining himself physically as well as emotionally. "I served my time."

"Is this your official address, Mr. Coyle?"

"What's official mean? I'm not allowed to vote in your elections anymore, so it's not like you need to send me a registration card. And I ain't making money to pay taxes on, either."

"Well, I wouldn't want to have to arrest you on vagrancy charges," Rake said.

"My family owns this land. Look it up. And I ain't a vagrant. I have money."

"How do you earn it?"

"I have supporters."

"Supporters? Like you're running for office?"

"I have supporters."

"You were onstage at that rally at the Sweetwater Mill a few years back, weren't you?"

"Can't say for sure. We did a lot of rallies then."

"I recognize you. I was working there at the time."

"And now you're a gorilla in a cop suit. How 'bout that."

"Watch your mouth."

"I have a right to say what I want on my property. And you still haven't said why you're bothering me."

Rake removed the lightning bolt sign from his back pocket and unfolded it in front of Coyle. "This look familiar to you?" It was covered in black dust from the fingerprinting lab—they'd turned up one set of prints, not Coyle's.

"Seen signs like 'em, a few years ago."

"You put any of these up recently?"

"I ain't saying I did. But there's no law about posting signs."

Actually, there were all sorts of such laws, but Rake wasn't interested in thumbing through the bill-posting regulations to determine whether the display of that specific leaflet on that particular street pole was allowed or not.

Four years ago, Coyle and his gang had committed several assaults and bombed Negro homes on the transitioning West Side. Now he was free, and it was happening again.

Rake said, "It's funny; if you put this sign up in Germany right now, you'd be arrested."

"But here in the States we have freedom of speech. You can call that funny if you want."

"Where were you the night of the seventh around eleven, twelve o'clock?"

"Here. Asleep."

"Anyone able to swear to that?"

"I'm not married, if that's what you're asking. What's this about?"

"A Negro was beaten nearly to death, right by one of those signs."

"Good."

Rake stared him down just enough to let on he didn't appreciate that, but not so much as to let Coyle think he could knock Rake off stride. "You enjoyed prison that much?"

"I hated it. Most folks in there are dumber'n posts. Don't know the first thing about politics or history. And I'm in no rush to get back there, which is why I have nothing to do with what happened to that nigger, whoever he was. Just because he got beat up where one of those signs was doesn't mean I had anything to do with it. If he got beat up on the same block as where somebody was flying an American flag, would you arrest a veteran for it?"

"I *am* a veteran, and I'm going to give you one day to take down every one of these signs, wherever you and your little buddies put them. Exactly twenty-four hours from this moment. And then, if I ever see one of them again, I will stuff it down your throat myself."

Coyle's reaction to the threat was an ironic smile. "Yes, sir, Officer, sir."

Rake stepped closer. "You think this is funny?"

"No, I think abuse of power is profoundly serious."

Rake knew he needed to cool it. But he wouldn't back down to this moron. "You have a fondness for the Nazis?"

"They know what they want and how to get it."

The present tense in that sentence was as galling as its sentiment. "Maybe you didn't see all the bulletins while you were over here shirking duty, but they lost the war. So I don't think they were terribly good at getting anything, other than killed."

"You know what's really terrible about it?" Coyle asked, stepping to his side, slowly, to give himself some room. "It was the damned Reds that beat 'em. Everybody over here likes to make like it was our dough-boys and capitalist power that brought them down, but that ain't so. It was the Red Army driving them back, making them put most of their resources on the Eastern Front, making it easy for us to take Normandy and go from there. Everybody here feels good about it, but they're kidding themselves. All along, *we* had been warning people that it was the Communists who were the ones to worry about, not the Nazis, and they went and proved us right. Our government *had* agreed with us, until Pearl Harbor confused 'em. If the damn Japs hadn't done that, we would've let Hitler take Europe and wipe out the Reds and the Jews. Then we wouldn't have the Reds taking over like they are now."

"I don't recall there being anything 'easy' about Normandy, but maybe that's how it seemed from over here. Watching the movie reels between John Wayne pictures."

Fluent in German, Rake had served first in army intelligence, trans-lating missives they intercepted from the Nazis, and then as an advance scout. He hadn't landed on D-Day but had come over soon after, then had been dropped behind Nazi lines in France, stealthily moving his way across the ravaged landscape. More than a year later, he'd been one of the first to see the Dachau concentration camp. For two months it had been his job to arrange tours of that unique circle of hell, marching German civilians through the gas chambers and showing them the skulls, forcing them to acknowledge what had been occurring on their watch, under orders of the leaders they had put in office. Like pushing a house-training puppy's snout in its own shit, showing them their sins, ensuring there could be no denials. *You were wrong and we are right.*

He tried to contain his rage as he addressed this man for whom the Nazis remained role models, "You sure seem to possess quite the military knowledge for someone who wasn't there."

"I know how to read. Words on the page and between the lines."

"Mind if I take a peek inside and see what sorts of things you're reading?"

"Yes, I do. That's my home and what I read is my private affair. Get a warrant. For God's sake, I haven't been out but a month and I'm not harming anyone. Why don't you spend more time cracking down on the niggers tearing the city apart? It's all over the papers, murders and rapes. Instead of patrolling the dangerous areas, you're out here bothering me."

"Tough talk from a fellow who doesn't have an alibi for that night."

A tan Chevy sedan rolled down the street, slowly, as if it had been planning to pull over and park but now saw the squad car and realized its plan was unwise. The driver started a three-point turn on the grass of the dead end.

Rake walked toward it, holding out a hand. The car stopped.

"Turn off your engine. If you're here to talk to Mr. Coyle, please, don't let me stop you."

The driver and the passenger looked at each other. They had the same buzz cuts as Coyle, the driver's blond and the passenger's brown. The passenger nodded, and the driver cut the ignition. Rake rested his hands on his belt, one of them on the handle of his gun, as he invited them to come out slowly. Coyle walked over as well.

"Well, howdy, boys," Rake said. "Is this an official gathering of the master race?"

"We don't want no trouble," the blond said. He looked barely eighteen, if that, and his passenger a few years older. Neither was as thin as Coyle, and Rake sensed in them a calm kind of wariness, like they were not unaccustomed to risky environments.

"Can I see your ID?"

"I do something wrong, Officer?"

"I just like to know to whom I'm speaking."

Back in the "house," the dog started barking again.

The driver's ID said he was Neville Connors, twenty-two years old last month, with an address nearer to tony Inman Park than Rake would have figured of someone who spent time with trash like Coyle. The passenger claimed not to have his wallet on him but volunteered his name as Joey Boyd Green.

"You out here to plan the next bonfire with Delmar, get out your hoods and whatnot?"

"Fuck the Klan," Joey snapped. "They call us goons, but they're just a bunch of pussy business owners who don't have the gumption to do what needs to be done."

"And what's that?"

"Tear it all down," Neville said, "so we can build it all up."

"Democracy is weak," Joey said. "It'll collapse on itself, and when it does, we'll be ready to set society right. We'll be ascendant."

"That's a mighty big word."

"It means we will rise."

"I know what it fucking means."

"Joey B., shut the hell up," Coyle said.

"No, please," Rake said. "I'd love to hear more about this revolution. I want to make sure I'm on the right side when it comes."

"We don't want any trouble with the law," Coyle said. "And all they were doing was coming to say hi to me. That's not illegal in this country, yet."

"No, but beating up Negroes is." Rake asked them where they'd been the night Greer had been assaulted; Neville claimed to have been asleep after a long day working at Sweetwater Mill—where Dale worked, interestingly—and Joey said he'd pulled an overnight job working road repair downtown. Then Rake repeated his warning about the lightning bolt signs.

"Guess I'd feel more comfortable about things," Neville said slowly, "if I knew the police were helping keep vermin out of white neighborhoods."

"We enforce the law," Rake said. "We're plenty busy these days without having to keep our eye on kids who fill their heads with nonsense from the wrong side of the war."

"We're not kids," Neville said.

"Well, you certainly sound short of full-grown men when you spout fairy tales like this one just was," and he motioned to Joey Boyd. "Next time you feel like falling in love with a second Lost Cause, ask Delmar how he enjoyed prison. And stay the hell out of Hanford Park."

The sound of Max barking was finally drowned out by the squad car's engine. Rake circled around the end of the road, his wheels slow in the mud as the three young Columbians stood still like deranged yard ornament statues, watching him leave.

18

The celebratory feeling that coursed through the Butler Street precinct after the arrest of Thunder Malley proved short-lived.

Less than twenty-four hours after the arrest, at their 6 p.m. roll call, McInnis stood before them stone-faced and announced, "Thunder Malley died in custody early this morning."

Ten men were punched in the gut.

"He was being transferred to a cell when he broke out of an officer's control and began strangling him. Another officer shot him, twice." McInnis held in one hand the limp pages of the report he was now recapping, his language equally bloodless. He dropped it on the nearest desk, Smith's. "You can take turns reading it. I know it feels like it cancels out a lot of hard work from all of you." He glanced at the bruises on Smith's face, the tight expression on Dewey's lips. "These things happen. Let's get out there and have a solid night and watch each other's backs."

With that, they were dismissed. Yet they stood in place, except for Smith, who grabbed the report and read it, which didn't take long. Next Boggs read it, then the others, as McInnis walked toward the large map of their beats that was adorned with thumbtacks denoting crimes and persons of interest. As if he'd just conveyed an utterly trivial message.

These things happen.

Smith cursed under his breath after reading it. Dewey picked up a mug and swung his arm toward the wall, magically creating hundreds of pieces of porcelain. Smith didn't even mind that it was his mug, he was so enraged by the news. Boggs couldn't believe it, but he could. Every time they tried to make real progress, it blew up in their faces. He tried to walk a moral path, yet it was littered with the bodies of his good deeds—and too many other bodies.

"This is a joke, Sergeant," Smith said.

"I don't like it, either," McInnis claimed.

"We're supposed to just accept this?"

"As opposed to what?" McInnis waited a long moment, the silence making his point. "You're not allowed to resign, in case any of you are considering it." A bad time for a joke. They had already lost three officers to resignations since '48; each had offered different reasons, but they knew the truth, that it crushed the soul to accept the contradictions of their job day after day, to be both authority figures and second-class citizens.

"White cops are undermining us in our own neighborhoods," Boggs said. "We've heard they were protecting Malley's operation. They liked taking a cut from the big man, but once he was put in a spot where he could possibly inform on them, they knew how to shut him up."

"I'm hearing a lot of speculation. And no names. Do you have any?"

Silence. Smith recalled how Malley had taunted them that night, warning that they were making a mistake, that he had "friends" who would have him out of jail by morning. He'd been right, but not in the way he'd meant.

"It's one thing to accuse a white officer of taking kickbacks," McInnis pointed out. "It's quite another to accuse one of murder."

Hopefully McInnis was only pretending to be obtuse. He couldn't be under any illusions as to the purity of their fellows on the force: before their time, he had been involved in a sting that resulted in a number of officers being fired for running an illegal gambling ring. The Department-wide animosity it earned him was likely the reason he was exiled here to the Butler Street Y. Ever since, he'd become hesitant to engage in battles he couldn't win.

"They're undercutting us at every turn, Sergeant," Dewey said.

"We can't do our jobs," Boggs added, "if white cops are backing the people we're trying to put away." And then killing them when the Negro cops got too close.

Smith threw up his hands. "It's like expecting us to be firemen while white cops play with matches."

"I'm perfectly aware of the challenges here," McInnis said. "But I don't hear anyone offering solutions; I just hear complaints about reality. Dealing with reality is our job."

Was he telling them they needed to gather evidence implicating whichever white officers were involved in drugs? But they were expressly not allowed to conduct investigations, especially into the activities of white cops. Boggs felt his chest tighten at this contradiction.

"We've heard that Malley had a rivalry with someone named Quentin Neale, or Q," Boggs explained. "We don't know much about him, we think he's new in town, but he might be running drugs and shine, too. Maybe the white cops who'd been working with Thunder decided they wanted to back Neale instead."

Smith shook his head. "No, they just wanted to silence Malley. So they did."

Boggs looked up and said to McInnis, "There's one more thing. We didn't get their names, but two squad cars of white cops threatened me and Smith to lay off drug cases a couple of nights ago."

"When was this?" It was difficult to gauge McInnis's reaction to anything, but he finally seemed concerned.

Boggs and Smith explained the brief encounter, which they hadn't even shared with their fellow officers. They hadn't seen the point, as they hadn't thought any good would come of it, and the story only made them seem impotent. Even now Boggs felt shame in relaying it.

"Did you get the squad car numbers?"

Boggs recited them.

McInnis folded his arms and nodded, thinking. "I'll poke around at headquarters and see what I can find. In the meantime, it's three past six and I don't have a single officer on the streets. Go put out the fires, gentlemen."

19

Raising two little ones was proving to be more of a trial than Cassie had anticipated. Yes, their needs were endless, but she'd expected that. What made the experience harder was that she pretty much only spent time with children and other women. As the youngest daughter with four brothers, she'd long realized that she preferred the company of males. Her humor tended to be coarse, her sense of decorum negligible. The other housewives of Hanford Park wanted to gossip—about who had awful taste in decorating, about who might actually be Jewish, about who might be having an affair with her child's football coach, about the principal's wife's drinking problem. Cassie would have preferred if the housewives themselves had drinking problems; that would have made them more entertaining. Instead, she was subjected to endless teas, as though they all aspired to some higher class, followed by chatty afternoons in the park. She'd rather chase Denny Jr. and Maggie around the yard, get her knees dirty, sweat a little, but the other mothers only wanted to sit down and chitter away.

The sudden encroachment of Negroes into Hanford Park, terrible though it was, finally gave her something to *do*.

Which was why she found herself sitting in the cafeteria of the small elementary school that her children would be attending in a few years. The adorably cute, tiny dining tables had been laid on their sides and leaned against the far wall, making room for a dozen rows of munchkin-sized wooden chairs on which sat, knees bent high like Brobdingnagians, forty adult residents of Hanford Park. They faced a small podium that stood in front of two windows that would have offered a view of the grassy field and swing sets if not for the fact that it was night, safely post-bedtime for the many parents who comprised a good portion of the Collective Association of Hanford Park.

Denny was at work, as he almost always was in the evening, so she sat next to her sister- and brother-in-law, Sue Ellen and Dale. She'd told Denny she'd be going and he hadn't objected. Then she'd told him she planned to donate to the neighborhood fund. He hadn't liked that, and they'd argued again. *This is our home,* she'd said, *and this is a peaceable solution. Why not support it?* He'd finally capitulated, but she wasn't sure if he'd merely done so to end the conversation.

On the walls around them was a brightly colored phantasmagoria of children's drawings, third-graders' yellow self-portraits and first-graders' verdant landscapes and kindergartners' blobby scribbles like Rorschach tests only they could explain. Cassie's own little artists wouldn't get a chance to decorate this school if the neighborhood association didn't do its job.

The meeting was called to order by Don Gilmore, a fiftyish, white-haired fellow who owned a hardware store. He favored plaid shirts and corduroys. The first few minutes passed tediously as he thanked the various women who'd provided baked goods for the meeting and the men who'd hung signs to spread word about tonight.

"To go over financials real quick, first of all thank you to everyone who has contributed to the fund. We've spoken to two of the Negro households so far and plan to meet with the third soon. We don't yet have a sale, I'm sorry to say. I think they're hesitant to sell at too much of a loss, but if we can come close to raising what they all paid, I'm sure we can convince them. What's the latest number, Paul?"

In the front row sat Thames, the plumber, who apparently served as CAHP treasurer. He replied from his seat that they were up to four and a half thousand dollars, with one half of households contributing.

"Now, that's just what I'm talking about," Gilmore said. "It's great we have that much, and there's still half the neighborhood that hasn't contributed yet. If you haven't, please do your part, folks. The more contributors we get, the less each household needs to give. Now, I'm just a humble carpenter but I get simple math like that."

Cassie looked around the audience and saw only one of the police officers she knew who lived in Hanford Park. Like Denny, most of them worked nights.

She raised her hand and stood. "In addition to giving money, I was wondering what else people could be doing to help. Like you said, we can't wait too long, and I'm not someone who thinks we can just talk away problems."

"You're my kind of lady," Gilmore said. "There are definitely some steps we all can take. First of all, be extra visible; it's a great time of year for it, but really, make a point of taking walks and being out in your front yards, gardening and whatnot. And I'm not just saying that because we sell gardening equipment at my shop." An awkward laugh. "Although we do. And we got a sale going. Point is, be out there and keep your eyes open. If you see any Negroes driving down your street, make note of it: the kind of car, the license plate, time of day. If they appear to be with a Realtor of some sort, then *definitely* make note of that. We have allies on real estate boards and we know lawyers, so we can make life difficult for them.

"Second, if any Realtor should come knocking on your door asking you to sell, tell 'em *no.* Be real clear about that." Applause, first a bit and then the whole room. "No matter how strong some of us are, we cannot preserve Hanford Park if even a sizable minority of folks choose this as the time to move out. So even if you were considering selling for unrelated reasons, like you're older and want a smaller place, I beseech you, folks: just wait a little while longer, because if you list your property now—even if you have no intention of selling to Negroes—you could still be taken advantage of. These realty folks have done all kinds of dirty tricks—they might make you think you're selling to a nice white couple, and a white man even signs the papers at the closing, but then on moving day who should show up but some Negroes. So hold off. We need to hold each other accountable—sometimes all it takes is one more house."

A man toward the back raised his hand and asked, "If we *do* see Negroes looking around, what should we say to them?"

"I would politely inform them that this is *not* a transitional neighborhood. They've most likely been told it is, which is why they're looking here. We need to let them know in no uncertain terms that they've been misinformed, and that they should do their shopping elsewhere." Applause. Gilmore added, "But we want to avoid confrontation. Assume good intentions, clear up their misunderstandings, and ask them to leave."

Dale muttered under his breath, "Gimme a break."

"I expect most of you have heard this by now," Gilmore said, "but there was an incident here a couple of nights ago. One of the Negroes in Hanford Park was roughed up. We don't—"

He was cut off by applause. First just one pair of hands, then several. Dale was especially quick to join in, Cassie noticed, but she and Sue Ellen held back.

Gilmore held out his hands. "Now, now." He grinned awkwardly. "I don't condone that, and that's not what this association is about. I helped form this group so we could resolve things without violence, all right?" A few murmurs of assent, a few grumbles. "We all know there are different ways this can go, but I believe we can save our neighborhood without having incidents like that. I don't know who roughed the Negro up, and I hope that person isn't in this room and isn't a part of CAHP."

Dale made a scoffing sound, quietly. Sue Ellen hushed him.

Gilmore continued, "It shows how important it is that we get to work, because a few more events like that could backfire. If people start thinking violence can break out at any time, that ruffians rule our streets, then we all lose."

When the meeting ended, Cassie waded through the crowd and approached Thames.

"Excuse me, Mr. Thames? Cassie Rakestraw. You were by a few nights ago and my husband wasn't in. Please add this to the till." She handed him forty dollars.

"Thank you so much," the plumber said, he and his wife smiling.

When Cassie stepped back, Sue Ellen and Dale were right behind her. Her sister-in-law said quietly, "We should give, too, Dale."

"Aw, thing is, I left my wallet at home." He patted his pockets sheepishly. "We'll get 'em next time."

20

Three knocks, the third extra hard. He could hear *shushing* from inside.

"Get outta here!" Mrs. Cannon said through the door.

"Please open up, ma'am. I just want to talk to you."

Silence. Then a small, hidden sound. Its very smallness was what made it so noticeable, the pitch of it, how unlike everything else in the environment: different from the sounds of engines driving past, from the occasional honks, even from the birds calling out above. *My son.*

"Don't be coming here, Jeremiah! My husband owns a gun."

"I'm not here for no trouble, I just want to *talk*. Please, Mrs. Cannon."

He counted, one, two, three, and at about five the door opened.

"What do you want?" demanded Julie's mother. She was very short, almost a dwarf. Lord only knew how she had produced a beauty like Julie. They did have the same eyes, though, long and narrow and capable of seeing through you, into you, wherever you didn't want them to see.

"You tossed all my letters, didn't you?"

"What are you talking about?"

"She said I never wrote her. I wrote her *every week*. Letter after letter. She sent me a few in the beginning, then they stopped."

"Don't ask me to explain how that girl makes her decisions."

"She thought I stopped writing her because *you* were throwing out my letters before she could see 'em. You wanted me gone from her life."

"You *were* gone from her life. You were in jail, boy."

"I know where I was. I know very well where I was."

"You got Julie in a fix and then you got yourself into even more trouble, and that's that. She's moved on to better things."

"I was expecting more of an apology."

"From me? *Please*. Find your people up in Chicago, Jeremiah. They can help you, but we can't. Julie has herself a real man now and she ain't wasting no time on you."

He saw movement behind her. She noticed the track of his eyes and she tried to block his view, but he spotted the boy down the hallway, in overalls and a white T-shirt. Lamplight framed his face perfectly, an almost Christ-like aura around his hair.

"Hey, there, son." Jeremiah smiled without meaning to. "Do you know who I am?"

"Don't you talk to him!"

This was why Jeremiah was still alive. This was why he had been spared. This was why his time in prison had finally ended and he was breathing again in this strange world.

"Come on out and say hello."

"I said, don't you talk to him!" She tried to close the door, but he stuck his foot in it. The shoe was an old and half-rotten one he'd found in a garbage barrel, and her surprising strength nearly broke his foot. He leaned a shoulder into the door and forced it back open. As he stepped into the room he saw her fall, the squat body and its surrounding robe billowing out, a wooden table toppling, a dish shattering on the floor.

She screamed at him to leave, her scream less loud than he'd expected, pain cutting it down. The boy was running away.

"No, come back, boy!" He'd frightened the kid, and he didn't want that and didn't want the old lady on the floor, either, even though she deserved it, just punishment for how she'd come between him and Julie. Not even jail would have been enough to break that love, he knew, but the old lady had thwarted them, had probably even thrown some Gullah hex on him. The kid was running, turning a corner in the hallway, and a door slammed.

"Come on, boy, I didn't mean to hurt her!"

He stepped around Mrs. Cannon, who was cursing him now in her ancient tongue, surely setting pagan spirits upon him, and he arrived at the narrow door the kid had slammed. He didn't even know the boy's name! The kid was so many worlds away from Jeremiah, yet also so close, just this thin door between them. It was locked.

"Jeremiah, you leave that boy be!"

He rattled the knob. "Come on, boy, I just want to talk to you. Daddy wants to meet you."

He could hear the boy crying now, screaming for his grammy.

Faster than he would have thought, Mrs. Cannon was on her feet and upon him, hitting him with an umbrella. He knocked it away after a few blows. She winced, gripping one of her wrists.

"I'm calling the police! You get out of here!"

He transferred his rage to the door now, pounding on it again and again and not relenting even after he felt the door give and heard the soft crunch of old wood tearing from its hinges.

The little boy inside was still crying and screaming.

Lord, what am I doing? What have I done? And what would you have me do?

He paused for a moment, overcome. The old lady was screaming for help. He screamed, too, for the child to come out, explaining that he was his father, that he must be obedient, and Jeremiah was still in the midst of this torrent of parental advice when one of his hands was pulled behind his back.

Another arm across his chest and someone was hitting him, jabbing him hard in the back of the ribs. The air went out of him and he tried to get away but even as his feet moved some other force was guiding him, manipulating him, and then he was across the room and into the side of a couch, whose arm came just a crucial inch below his privates but still he hit against it so hard that he doubled over and collapsed on it, someone very heavy pinning him down.

He heard the click and felt metal around his wrists. In a way, he had felt not completely dressed without it these last few days.

The man wouldn't stop yelling, so Champ Jennings pressed his head down a bit to muffle his voice with pillows.

"I said *can it.*"

"Ma'am, do you know this man?" Dewey Edmunds asked. This was always the first or second question asked in such a dispute, sometimes following, "Are you all right?"

She didn't answer the question, instead running to the door that Jeremiah had been pounding on.

"Who's in there?" Dewey asked. He was still holding his club, though he didn't expect he'd need it again on this fellow.

"My grandbaby!" the old lady replied. She knocked on the door, trying to soothe the terrified child, coaxing him to open up, explaining that he was safe now.

"That's my son!" the man screamed after managing to lift his head off the pillow enough.

Dewey and Champ exchanged glances. "Is that true, ma'am?" Dewey asked.

"He's no good! He a thief and a crook and he just now got outta jail! We don't want nothing to do with him!"

They had been only a block away when they'd heard the screaming, and as they'd run down the street they'd seen the door wide open, the old lady on the floor. These calls were never pleasant, and this one was becoming as complicated as the rest.

"Ma'am, is this the boy's father?"

Even with the pillow again muffling Jeremiah's mouth, he was clearly screaming, "Yes!"

"He a murderer! He not welcome in this house!"

Champ reached into the man's pockets. "Got any ID, buddy?"

He did, one that had been issued mere days ago, probably when he'd been released from prison. Jeremiah Tanner, twenty-four, his address listed simply as the "City of Atlanta," as if prison officials thought Negroes were animals who wandered rootless through the streets.

The kid was still screaming on the other side of the bathroom door and Dewey, father of two, couldn't think with it. Calls involving children were the worst. After only a year on the job, he felt himself hardening, a certain stoicism creeping into his psyche, but when the kid screamed Dewey heard his own boys. He desperately needed it to stop.

The bathroom door had been torn from its hinges, so he gently moved it aside and laid it against the wall. A little boy in overalls stood by the toilet, his cheeks and the crotch of his pants wet. Dewey crouched down on one knee.

"Son, my name is Officer Dewey Edmunds. Everything is all right now, so you can come out. I'll let you look at my shiny badge."

"Are you . . . ?" the kid sniffled as he tried to speak. He looked about four or five. "Ar-Are you Lucius's friend?"

Dewey wondered whether he'd heard the kid right. He looked at the old lady, who shifted her eyes to the floor. "Yes. Yes, I'm friends with Officer Lucius Boggs. How do you know him?"

"He's gonna be my daddy."

The man on the sofa's "No!" would have been far louder had Champ not pressed him into the cushions again.

Dewey looked at the old lady, who met his eyes this time and nodded. Some odd mixture of shame and pride, pleading and defiance. Then he stepped back and looked at Champ, the two of them realizing this was not a typical domestic incident after all.

∽

Julie's courtship with Lucius had been founded on lies.

She knew Lucius had once had another fiancée, a proper lady named Cecilia. Daughter to one of the wealthiest Negroes in Atlanta, who owned five barbershops across town, the proceeds of which he'd used to amass an empire of apartment buildings. Lucius wasn't one to divulge much, but Julie learned that he and his former love had courted for well over a year, in the mannered way of the Negro elite: attending church services together, sitting stiffly beside each other—no hand-holding, she assumed—while listening to his father's sermons. Attending church socials, visiting each other's homes for tea, always with witnesses. She hated herself for imagining it, Lucius in his finest clothes sitting in a plush chair opposite Cecilia, no doubt a high-yellow octoroon in a pretty ruffled dress, maybe chiffon, perched on a fine sofa beside her matronly mother, whose husband had managed to buy them a grand home with sitting room and a piano. The kind of house Julie herself worked in. But things hadn't worked out, the dainty Cecilia deciding she couldn't handle the stress of being a policeman's wife.

Which was when Julie met Lucius, two years ago now. She'd been working at a congressman's, and Lucius had been investigating the death of another maid. After the chaos that followed, Julie found herself out of a job, so Lucius stepped in with some leads on other white families who needed help. At first she'd been angry at him for costing her a good job, poking his nose into other folks' business, but the fact that he'd taken the time to drum up names of future employers spoke well of him. That was Lucius for you: so noble and dignified he'd see his duties to the end, cleaning a mess others would have walked away from. The fact that he wanted to bed her certainly didn't hurt.

Maybe that was crass, but she'd known it from the start. Those churchgoing boys were the worst about darting their eyes at the supposedly sinful parts of your body. Like he'd never seen a good-looking woman before. She'd known men who were far more forward, and at first it bothered her that he was so *proper*.

After she'd found another job, he'd stopped by to check on her. "I just wanted to make sure you'd gotten on your feet again," was how he'd put it when he surprised her one fall day.

By which he meant, *I just want to get you off your feet.*

"I'm doing just fine, no thanks to you."

He raised an eyebrow. "I helped you find that job, didn't I?"

"After you cost me that last one."

"You wouldn't have wanted to stay there, trust me."

"I'm sure you're the kind of fellow who's *used* to people trusting him," she said, and he didn't contradict her. "Is there any other reason you came by?"

Her directness seemed to throw him. "Well, yes. Matter of fact, I was wondering if you'd like to join me for lunch sometime."

"Why, so you can question me about some other crime?"

"No, this would be a crime-free conversation."

"You allowed to do that?" She was stringing him along, enjoying how desperate and unmoored he looked. So different from the polished, upright veneer he'd worn before. "Me being a former witness and all? That don't break no police ethics laws or nothing?"

"I'm confident the city of Atlanta would have no issue whatsoever with me taking you out to Etta's Spot sometime."

They'd shared only three dates over the first few months. On their first date, he'd asked her which church she worshipped at, and he'd seemed just short of horrified when she mentioned her family didn't strictly belong to any.

Lucius had invited her to come to his father's church, said she could sit with him, but she declined, intimidated by the idea of sharing an aisle with his extended family. Instead, they started making the occasional Sunday lunch date, and she later learned that the only reason he'd been able to get away from his family and the ritual of after-services socials was because he'd lied to them about being needed at the precinct. Surely he knew that, in a community as small as Sweet Auburn, word would spread that the son of Reverend Boggs was out with some common gal on Sunday afternoons.

A screwball matinee at the Royal, peach ice cream at Trellin's, but no candlelit restaurants and certainly no smoky dance clubs where they might lose themselves. All the while, she kept Sage hidden, never mentioning that she had a child. She made it a point to be outside the house waiting for Lucius when he arrived; she'd told her mother she was seeing a proper man now and her mother had understood, taking Sage on errands beforehand.

Then one day when she knew her mother had taken Sage out, she couldn't resist inviting Lucius in, beckoning him with the promise of some pecan pie she'd baked—the restaurant where they'd just eaten had unaccountably been out of his favorite dessert, so she knew he wanted it. She knew he wanted a lot more.

The curtains drawn in the dark parlor, she'd deliberately not turned on the light lest it reveal some child's book or toy, not that Sage had many. This was the first time Lucius had set foot in her apartment. After each date he had insisted on walking her home, ever the gentleman, but she had always invented an excuse why he shouldn't: her father was sick, or her mother was upset with her and would take it out on Lucius if she laid eyes on him. Once in the small kitchen, she hit the lights.

She had only removed the pie tin, releasing the aroma of brown sugar and buttered crust, when she felt how close he was standing. She turned around and he kissed her, hurriedly, as if afraid she would try to escape. Which was the furthest thing from her mind. He wasn't such a great kisser, truth be told, so rushed, almost panicked, though he'd get better in time.

It was the kind of kissing that involved hands, that required hands, those fingers acting out in larger scale what his tongue was trying to say. She rubbed at his chest, she kissed his neck and loosened his tie so she could get at that delicious spot in his clavicle, and he took that as an invitation to work the buttons of her blouse, and maybe she'd intended that invitation, it was funny how one action caused another, not always deliberately planned but welcome nonetheless, and Lord it had been awhile since she'd done this, far too long.

It was late afternoon and light poured in through the alley-side window above the sink. Lucius had some trouble with the buttons and she helped him, then moved on to his, and then he was *really* rushing, which she minded and didn't mind, because who knew when her parents and Sage might return, and who knew when she might see him again, who knew how long this would last until he came to his senses and returned to the next pale and delicate Cecilia. One thing Julie did not feel right then was delicate as he hitched up her skirt and worked at her panties and she tore off the tourniquet of his belt. He was strong, lifting her up to get them started, and though she was not new to this she'd never done it standing up before, or really she wasn't standing so much as leaning and being supported, but he was standing, quite tall and stiff until he wasn't, as it didn't last all that long but had been fun while it lasted.

Fun while it lasted being the epitaph of their relationship, because they had barely finished when she heard the front door opening.

His eyes bulged and she laughed at his panic. Quickly with the buttoning and fastening now, and she had to grab a dish rag and use it between her legs before stuffing it in the trash can, hurriedly washing her hands as Lucius wiped at the sweat on his forehead.

She heard Sage's voice before she heard her mother's.

She couldn't look at Lucius right then. She stared at the entryway to the kitchenette and called out, "We're back here."

She'd known it was inevitable but had somehow kidded herself into thinking he might respond differently.

Little Sage barreled into the room as he always did, smiling, even though she saw blood on his left eyebrow.

"Mama, Mama, I fell!" Voiced with enthusiasm, as if this were a great accomplishment.

Then she was on her knees fussing with him. She wasn't deliberately avoiding Lucius's gaze, she told herself. Then her mother entered and it fell on Julie to make the awkward introductions.

"Lucius, this is my mother, Glenda. And Sage, I'd like you to meet Officer Boggs."

Now her eyes could not shift fast enough, looking at Sage as she applied a small bandage to his brow, back at Lucius and the shock in his eyes, one of his hands actually at his breast as if trying to keep his heart inside, then back at her mother. Her mother's face showed both guilt, for not keeping Sage away again, but also relief. The truth was out and the inevitable could occur.

Sage was in the middle of a convoluted story that involved him pretending to be a fighter pilot and misjudging his landing and she told him to hush, they had a guest.

The preacher's son managed to say, "Hello, ma'am," not abandoning etiquette even as everything was falling apart.

Julie saw her son and her mother the way he probably did then. She'd been working in white folks' homes long enough now, had gained that new perspective, and she saw her boy's bare feet, her mother's old housedress. Somehow Lucius had managed to see past the garbage sometimes found on their street, the cracks in the front of the bungalow, the shifty men shooting craps outside, but never again. She would have loved him on the spot if he'd managed to see beyond those bare, dirty feet and instead notice Sage's impossibly beautiful round eyes, ignore the ill-fitting clothes and instead be charmed by his gentle nature, but surely that was too much to wish for.

Her mother took Sage's hand and told him, in Gullah, to use the bathroom. Julie had not made a secret of her ancestry, but still she felt ashamed to hear those syllables in front of Lucius.

"You have a son?" he asked once they were alone, his eyes already moving from shock to hurt. Anger would be next. "Is this some kind of joke?"

"It's not a joke. It's my life."

"You just somehow failed to mention this before?"

"Why mention it before? So you could look at me the way you're looking at me now?"

"How I'm looking . . ." He searched for words. "I can't believe you *lied* to me."

"I never lied. You never asked."

"Is this funny to you? You think you're being clever?"

"I haven't done anything you haven't. You're hiding *your* family from *me*. I'm betting the other girls you've seen, they woulda met your parents by now, right? You wouldn't be taking them to random spots where you know your relatives won't be 'cause they're busy churchifying."

"That's not . . . true." But the fact that he could barely get that word out proved otherwise.

"We've both been hiding things, so don't pretend no different. At least *I'm* being honest."

He gave a hostile laugh. "You're honest about your dishonesty. That's wonderful."

"I don't need to explain myself to you." She stepped back and put a hand on the pie dish. Mockingly sweet, she asked, "Do you still want some pie, or maybe you've already had what you wanted and now you can go?"

He shook his head. "*I'm* not the one in the wrong here."

"In the wrong?" The more horrified he looked, the angrier she grew. "In the wrong? That's where I live, Lucius! Welcome to The Wrong! That's how some of us live, believe it or not!" She stepped forward and swung, hitting him in the chest with the flat of her hand. He stumbled back, and as she pulled her hand back a second time he yelled at her to stop, and she froze there in that pose while he backed up again.

Another step and he opened the door.

She was alone and crying hard when the toilet flushed and Sage walked in asking for some dessert.

It had taken him three whole weeks to return. Early March and she was in the front yard planting lilies—leftovers from her employer, who had bought too many. Her knees were damp through her long skirt when she leaned back and saw him. Late on another Sunday afternoon, he wore his finest once again—a gray plaid sport coat over black pants and shoes that winked at her—having wandered here after thanking God for His many blessings.

"What do you want?" she said, standing up and brushing dirt from her hands.

"I wanted to see how you were."

"I'm fine—why wouldn't I be? You think I've fallen apart without you?"

Sage was inside. She had tried to talk him into planting with her, but his earlier obsession with digging and shovels had been mysteriously replaced with an equal passion for sweeping and mopping, which he was happily doing while her mother prepared a stew.

"I wanted to say I was sorry," he said. "For reacting the way I did."

She wielded silence like a weapon.

"I was surprised. I think I had a right to be."

More silence. Each seemed afraid of what the other might say or do, and equally if not more afraid of what they themselves would say or do.

"When were you planning to tell me?"

"I don't know. You talked a lot about how much you love playing with your niece and nephew. I thought maybe you wouldn't be so against the idea once you found out."

"Nieces and nephews are different from . . . adopting someone."

That word, so hoped for as to be forbidden, was strangely thrilling to hear spoken aloud. As if by acknowledging that the word even existed, he opened the door to the possibility.

"I'm sorry I didn't say it sooner. But I knew you'd be done with me."

He motioned to the three wooden steps. "Mind if I sit?"

"Those fine britches will mind it. Steps are dirty."

He sat down anyway. As someone who laundered and folded clothes so many hours a day, the sight of such slacks on a step like that offended her, though she was glad he wasn't running away this time.

"Where's the father?" he asked.

"Very far away. He ran off once it happened."

"Do you know where to?"

"Chicago. But I don't care."

"He wasn't that important to you?"

She didn't care for the implication. "He was, once. But he made some bad choices. Him leaving was good in a way. I haven't heard from him in years. I certainly don't want to."

She sat beside him. They were quiet for a while. She'd noticed this about him, that he could be so calm, that he didn't feel that nervous or boastful need to fill all available space with himself the way other men did.

"So is he named Sage because he's wise or because he adds flavor to life?"

"Because it's easy to yell," she laughed.

"I didn't really get a chance to meet him last time. Is he here?"

"Wouldn't be nowhere else. Hold on."

A minute later she'd coaxed the boy outside, though this time she made sure he was wearing shoes first. He was still holding his little broom, which her mother had woven herself.

"Hi there," Lucius said, standing now.

"Say hello, Sage."

"Hello."

"What do you have there?"

"My broom."

"You like to sweep?"

"I *love* to sweep." To demonstrate, he began sweeping the front walkway.

"He's real cute," Lucius told her. "Has your smile."

She realized she was hugging her own arms then, aching over how tantalizingly close Lucius seemed, and how far away he was at risk of becoming.

He would tell her weeks later that, when he had first seen Sage in her kitchen, seconds after he'd been inside of her, he had felt in a way that he was looking at his future. The preacher's son had already moved on to guilt for what he had done, and he'd seen in Sage a personification of his lust, the natural result, as if Sage were his own boy and time had merely sped up. He would tell her this, admitting it made no sense, but he said it had been God's way of talking to him, explaining that actions have consequences, and even more importantly they have reasons, which aren't always understandable at the time. She would listen to this explanation from him, thinking it odd, as if she and her son were mere vessels for the Lord's cosmic conversation with him, but if it's how he made his peace with things, she could accept it.

Sage seemed so lost in sweeping that he seemed to have forgotten the adults behind him.

Lucius said, "Maybe next Sunday we could take him to that new

Disney movie, *Cinderella*." About a poor girl turned into a princess, she'd heard.

"Don't say sweet things you don't mean. Don't be stringing no girl along."

"I'm not stringing you along. But . . . Do you have any other secrets I should know about?"

Which would have been the time to answer honestly, to correct what she'd said about Jeremiah being in Chicago, but that had been at least partially true, hadn't it, as Jeremiah's people had fled there after his trial? Right then she'd felt surrounded by the many kinds of pain that truth can inflict, yet she felt like she had—miraculously, briefly—been spared that pain, and she was too scared to allow it any closer.

So she'd grinned, sly, knowing what it could do to him. "None I feel like telling you about right now."

That had been more than a year ago.

And tonight, the very rare evening when she was not at home but had been out at a friend's house, getting a rare glimpse of what it was like to not already have children, playing bid whist with girls she'd known for years, a call from a neighbor came, saying there was a ruckus at her house and she needed to hurry back home.

She hadn't even entered the house yet when she saw through the open door the two Negro policemen talking to her mother, a notebook on one of their laps, and Sage holding a small shiny badge in his hands, and her heart sank as she realized that the time for telling Lucius those other secrets had come.

21

"My brothers," the Grand Wizard intoned, "we must discuss an urgent matter."

Dale's view through his new hood was not clear, and as he wasn't the tallest man in this Klavern he could only occasionally view through the spires of his brothers' pointy hoods the head of the purple-garbed Grand Wizard.

Dale had come to the basement of this Congregationalist church with profoundly mixed emotions. Per Rake's instructions, he had not talked to anyone about what happened in Coventry. He hadn't overheard any talk about the murder, other than some of Irons's former coworkers expressing their shock at his death. No one from the Klavern had approached him, but that made him even more nervous, especially now.

"A matter that may actually divide us good Christian men," the Grand Wizard continued from the stage. He sure had a way of dragging things out, taking long pauses for effect.

This was the local Klavern's first gathering in months. Dale recalled when they had met monthly, but after the Georgia Bureau had cracked down on some of the more reckless branches, a chill had set in. A meeting was supposed to have occurred last month but was called off, either due to illness or schedules, which had struck him as both laughable and infuriating: this was war, so who gave a damn if some important poo-bah had a sore throat or someone's wife had a birthday that night? What a sad outfit the Klan had become—and here in Atlanta, where it all started, the imperial City of the Invisible Empire!

This was the reason he'd been so eager to take that night ride in Coventry, even against a white man under odd circumstances. Something needed to be *done,* goddammit, and it was finally happening: this meeting was overseen by the Grand Wizard himself, overseer of the entire KKK in Georgia. This meeting wasn't a full Klonkave with Klansmen from all over the state, but still, Dale was glad the Grand Wizard was finally taking the events in Hanford Park seriously.

The Grand Wizard stood alone on the Sacred Altar, and positioned around him at their proper stations were several officers in their resplendent satin finery: the red-caped Night Hawk (security), the blue-robed Kludd (chaplain), the golden Klaliff (vice president). The crimson-bedecked Kladd, or conductor, a building contractor who lived only a mile from Dale, had called the session to order but now deferred to the Grand Wizard.

"A matter that may in fact expose a rift between us, one that we must address lest it widen into a chasm that destroys us."

Oh no. Dale felt in his gut what was coming.

"Some of you have already heard, but for those of you who haven't"—and here he paused yet again, longer than he needed to, so long Dale felt even more certain that this was an elaborate production to expose him, to force him to come forward—"last week there was an unsanctioned ride in Coventry."

Unsanctioned. His fears were right: Whitehouse was not really with the Klan at all; he'd set Dale up, but why? Or perhaps he *was* with the Klan but was doing things his own way, forming some splinter group that had tired of the larger organization's dithering, in which case Dale needed to keep quiet lest he become a casualty in this unexpected civil war.

The penalty for betraying the Klan, he'd always been taught, was death at the hands of another brother. He'd been trying to *help* all along, but everything had gotten so mixed up.

"The target was a good, Christian, white man of Anglo-Saxon heritage. Yet three men wearing the holy uniform attacked him, and very nearly killed him. Before they could finish the job, a bystander stepped forward and fired at the Klansmen, killing one of them."

In addition to fear, Dale felt anger, a sense of unjust persecution. If his beating of Letcher had led another Klavern to beat up the black man in Hanford Park, *one hand washing the other,* then the men in this

Klavern should be happy about what he'd done. They clearly weren't. That argued that the two attacks might not be related after all.

He had persuaded Mott not to come tonight, the reason being that shoulder injury. Mott had needed five stitches and sported a thick bandage on his shoulder, but he'd been sure to wear dark shirts every day and had done his best to act normal, complaining about a pulled muscle whenever someone noticed him holding it funny. Hopefully no one would connect his bum shoulder to the night Irons was killed.

"The Klansman who was killed, my Christian brothers, was one of our own. Walter Irons." Clearly Irons's death was news to some. Dale heard some muttering, but from too far away, plus the hoods did muffle quite a bit. "I would be lying to you all if I told you that I knew Brother Irons well. But he did not deserve to die, did not deserve to be laid low like that, and certainly not while wearing the holy uniform."

Yet another pause. Dale felt a tremendous need to pass gas but he didn't dare, as if the sound and certainly the smell would mark him as the very offender the Grand Wizard was trying to identify. He needed to go to the bathroom, frankly, needed to curl into a ball and be gone from all this, and he wasn't sure if he could make it.

"Brother Irons leaves behind no wife or child, and for that I am thankful, but he does have family back in Alabama that grieves him."

It was torture not being able to look at anyone. He wanted to see Iggy's and Pantleg's expressions, read what they were thinking. Were they on the verge of ratting him out? Were they frightened themselves, afraid they'd be in trouble by association, even though they didn't actually take part in that beating?

He hadn't told Rake about them. He'd made it sound like only he, Irons, and Mott had been involved. Why? Well, partly it was true—Iggy and Pantleg had split off before they dealt with Letcher. The rest was shame: they had mocked his plan, insulted his manhood, threatened him, even. He didn't want Rake to know he wasn't fully respected by his peers, so he hadn't mentioned them. Yet he'd sensed even then in Rake's living room that the omission was a serious tactical mistake, and he feared it would be his undoing.

"The person they attacked is a man named Martin Letcher, a banker and a gentleman of good standing in his community. Why Brother Irons and his two fellow riders were in Coventry that evening is unclear. But because a man has been killed, and under such circumstances, this is a weighty matter that threatens our very organization. I can only assume that Brother Irons's two fellow riders are from our Klavern as well. Standing here before me right now. Brothers, I ask that you step forward and explain yourselves."

The longest silence of Dale's life. It stretched before him like the agonizing walk before a firing squad, a plank over roiling seas. He told himself to be still, to not turn his head—until he realized that others were turning their heads, in hopes of seeing someone step forward, so he turned his head, too, mimicking their innocence.

Please, blessed Lord, let Iggy and Pantleg stay quiet, too.

"My brothers, even if those who took part in that ride are not in attendance today, I ask this: if any of you know anything at all about what transpired, any evidence or even hearsay, the time has come to step forward. Not only is one of our brothers' reputation at stake, but so is the great cause to which we have dedicated ourselves! So is the blood that has been spilled by generations to protect our families and our homes, to strengthen us against our enemies, to unify us against our foes!" He had switched into an altogether different register. Dale's fear made a corresponding leap to sheer terror, and even as his heart raced he was certain everyone else's did as well, that the Grand Wizard's rallying cry was stirring them, the congregation restless. He was doomed. "We must not allow them to divide us, my brothers! We must be strong like our fathers, strong like their fathers, strong like our founders who defended the Southern way of life!"

Dale's unseen compatriots were calling back in the affirmative, some yelling, "Step forward!" to rouse whichever of them was afraid to do so. Dale could feel himself shaking, terrified the others could see it, the entire room vibrating from all the yelling.

He could see it now, Iggy stepping forward, or Pantleg, removing their hoods and declaring that Dale had led them astray.

Lord, they would tear him apart.

Then it subsided. The hollers and rebel yells and commands and even the voices in Dale's head, the better angel of his nature that seemed to be telling him, *Go on and be done with it, be a man*—even that damned annoying angel shut up, and the room grew silent.

He had nearly lost control of his bowels. He smelled something rank and feared perhaps he'd passed gas after all, but no one was saying anything, no sound in the room.

After a long stretch of silence, the Grand Wizard intoned, "Very well. Perhaps the other riders were from another Klavern. But if there is treachery in our midst, we will smoke it out."

Afterward, Dale was one of the last to exit—not wanting to appear too rushed, he had made a point of chatting with his fellows in the later, hoodless portion of the night's proceedings. He sorely wished alcohol were part of the Klavern ritual, but he accepted their line of thinking that it was a poison of the Irish and Italians and other low folk, even if he happened to enjoy the stuff immensely.

He had made brief eye contact with both Iggy and Pantleg but had elected not to speak to them, afraid any wrong move might inspire them to reconsider their silence.

And he was greatly annoyed by what had *not* transpired tonight. The Klavern had discussed the Hanford Park Negroes but had made no plans for a night ride. What was the point of their coming together if they weren't going to do anything? The Grand Wizard had hinted that plans were in the works, so why not share them? What the hell was the point of being in a Klavern if you couldn't run the niggers out of your own backyard?

He was nearly out the door when he heard the Kladd say, "Dale, may I have a word with you?"

It felt like being invited into your boss's office after some failure, if your boss was someone who could have you killed.

Their hoods were off now, and Dale nodded to the Kladd. Who was more commonly known as Andy, and going bald, his remaining hair drenched in sweat.

"Dale, meet the Grand Wizard. This is Dale Simpkins, a friend of mine."

It occurred to Dale that he wasn't entirely sure what to call the

Grand Wizard, whether "George" was too familiar or "Grand Wizard Ansley" too stilted. "Mr. Ansley" sounded too subordinate, though at that moment Dale did indeed feel small. He elected not to call him by name at all, simply saying that it was a pleasure as they shared the ritual handshake. Without his hood, the Grand Wizard's face nearly matched the Kladd's robes, ruddy from the yelling.

"Dale," Andy said, "I know Brother Irons didn't have many friends, but he did work with you at the mill, correct?"

"Sure. But he got fired awhile back."

"Do you have any idea why he might have gone up to Coventry on that ride?"

"I don't. I mean, I'd heard he'd been killed up there but hadn't known 'til tonight that it was from a *ride*. I mean, wow, that sure is strange."

"It is," the Grand Wizard said, his voice cold, and hoarse from his earlier performance.

"He was a big man," Andy noted, looking at his superior but seemingly speaking to Dale, "but he'd never struck me as the sort to do something so headstrong. I fear he may have been led astray by someone else. One of the other two riders."

"Could be," Dale said. *Please, God, let this conversation be over.* He looked at Andy because he feared the Grand Wizard, feared lying to so powerful a man. "I can't rightly say."

Grand Wizard and Kladd exchanged glances. Just then they were joined by a third man, with short gray hair and a hard stare.

"Dale, this is Brother Brian Helton. He's a policeman. He's also part of the Klokann."

Dale shook hands with Helton, who looked familiar. The Klokann was the investigative wing of the Klan, rumored to be staffed only by police officers and detectives.

"If you do hear anything at all," Andy said to Dale, "please let us know."

"I will, you can count on it." He could feel all of them studying him, Helton especially. Was Helton investigating what had happened that night? Had he walked over just so he could get a closer eye on Dale? "You know, my brother-in-law's a cop, too. Maybe I could ask him?"

Helton offered a cold smile. "I know who your brother-in-law is. He turned down an invitation to join us."

"Yeah, he's not a real social kind of fellow."

"He's dug his grave," the Grand Wizard said. He put a hand on Dale's shoulder and squeezed it, a bit harder than necessary. "Don't you worry—our Klokann Kommittee is plenty capable. We'll find out who put Brother Irons in that spot, and we'll deal with him accordingly."

Dale nodded, trying to look enthusiastic.

"Thank you for coming out tonight, sir. We really appreciate you taking the time to support us out here. These are dangerous times, and we all need to band together."

He turned to leave, worried his eyes had betrayed him, or his tone of voice. Or perhaps the Grand Wizard really did have some otherworldly power, could peer into Dale's soul or read his thoughts, maybe through bodily contact, which explained that shoulder thing. Dale needed to save himself, throw out something that might distract this almost omniscient adversary.

"You know, I did think of one thing," he said. "One of the last times I saw Irons, he asked if he could borrow my car. Said he had to do a favor for somebody, but I told him no. I'm kind of particular about who I lend it to, is all. Anyway, he'd said he had to do a favor for some fellow, I want to say he called him Mr. Whitehouse."

The Grand Wizard and Helton seemed to be looking at Dale very intently. And silently.

"It was just an odd name, you know, Whitehouse. That's why I remember it."

Another second, and the Grand Wizard smiled. "Thank you for telling us that, Dale. I assure you, we'll look into it."

22

At ten o'clock, Boggs called in to the precinct from a call box and was told by McInnis to report to an address he knew well: Julie's house. He froze.

"What happened?" His mind raced: an accident, a break-in, those drug users down the block?

"Everyone's fine, but a Julie Cannon says she needs to see you immediately. Consider it your break and make it quick."

Boggs left Smith behind, running the quarter mile to her house. He hadn't yet reached her door when Julie met him in front of the house.

"It's about Sage's dad," she said. "He's come back."

He needed to catch his breath after the run. "Back . . . to Atlanta?"

"He's come by a couple times now, trying to talk to us."

He wanted to ask more but told himself to stop, wait, let her say whatever she was so clearly afraid to say.

She continued, "He's saying that . . . that he wants to be a part of Sage's life now. I told him that can't happen, but he's not taking no for an answer."

Boggs folded his arms across his chest. "Do you know why he even came back? He didn't like Chicago?"

"That's the thing." She looked down. "I'm sorry, but he hasn't been in Chicago all this time." A deep breath. "He's been in prison. He just got out."

"Prison?"

"For five years."

Boggs's mind reeled. He felt that the ground was askew and he changed his footing as if to balance himself against the swales. "He was in the state pen?"

She nodded. Her voice sounded very far away, barely audible. "I'm sorry I lied."

"You're *sorry*?"

"Lucius, I'm scared." Her arms, too, were crossed now, hugging herself. "He came by tonight, when I wasn't here. He forced himself into the house and knocked Mama down. Said he wanted to see Sage, but Sage locked himself in the bathroom 'til some cops came."

"What cops?"

She explained how Dewey and Champ had arrested Jeremiah, sending him to jail in a wagon. Both Julie and her mother had been questioned by the officers.

"Jeremiah," Boggs repeated. "So at least you didn't lie to me about his name. Everything else, though. He has a *record*? Lord God, woman, what are you trying to do to me?"

They had barely ever discussed Sage's father, other than some early conversations to establish the basic details. Or what Boggs had *assumed* were the basic details. She had been amazingly circumspect, never bringing the subject up, a silence he'd taken as a sign that she had no feelings for the ex. He'd attributed her silence to her strong will, her refusal to let life's injustices weigh on her. Now he saw that a different kind of self-preservation had been at work.

"I'm sorry," she repeated, a bit louder this time, yet the words still seemed to dissolve in the air and lose their meaning before they could reach him.

"What did you think, that he wouldn't come back after he got out?"

Later, when he would revisit this scene in his mind, he would realize she'd been leaning toward him, hoping he might embrace her, forgive her, protect her. But he stepped back, turned around, shook his head. He looked up at the dark sky for a moment, then back down at the woman he was now a few feet farther away from.

"His family all moved to Chicago after he went in, so I thought—"

"You thought you could just *hope* him away? What was he even in for—am I allowed to hear that from you, or do I need to pull his record?"

"He worked in the train yards, during the war. He fell in with some boys who were stealing from the cars."

"Great. Excellent. Sage has thief blood, that's wonderful."

"Don't you say that about my boy."

He regretted the comment instantly, but those words were out and he could not take them back.

"And now this man wants Sage? What, he wants to raise him? Teach him to fish? Or does he want *you*?"

"He probably does, but he ain't getting me. And he ain't getting Sage, either."

The *ain'ts* had always grated, but now they were like thorns lashing him. He pinched the bridge of his nose and told himself to calm down. He'd been in the midst of far more dramatic family situations than this, but always someone else's drama. He felt the bottom dropping out of his stomach, felt how hard it was for the people whose lives he was always intervening in and judging.

"So he's in jail now. But he'll be out in the morning. Where is he staying?"

"I don't know."

"Did he ever threaten you or Sage?"

"No."

"Is he dangerous?"

She looked him in the eye, then away.

"Did he ever get rough with you?" He hated even having to ask that.

"No. I never saw him get violent. But . . ."

"But *what*?"

"Jeremiah was always *different*. He was sweet—I mean . . . Some people used to say he was touched."

"Touched, like he was simple? Not right up there?" He tapped his forehead.

"When people felt like being mean about it, yeah, they'd say that. But in my heart I know that's not true—sometimes he'd say things that just didn't make sense, that's all."

"So we've gone from Chicago to convict to crazy convict."

"Some said crazy, some said he was called by God. I don't know. All I'm saying is he was always sweet with me, until the end. He was just . . . He fell in with the wrong people. And they changed him."

He tried to take this in, but every thought hurt. "I cannot believe you kept this from me. Why? What else are you hiding?"

She shook her head. "I'm sorry. How many times do you want me to say it?"

They were outside so perhaps others could overhear them. But that wasn't why he felt he was surrounded. He felt his father was there with them, shaking his head and tut-tutting, his mother fanning herself and raising her eyebrows. *This is why I wanted you to keep away from this woman,* the reverend would be saying. *Not because I'm prejudiced against those less fortunate, but because I have worked so hard to spare you from things like this. I have worked hard to no longer live on the sorts of streets where you're asked for spare change by shifty men who have one hand out-stretched and another in their pocket fingering an ice pick, worked hard to surround you with people who would not be stealing drinks from the liquor cabinet or sifting through our jewelry cases between dinner and dessert, worked hard so you wouldn't have to wonder when a certain relative's parole hearing was scheduled, worked hard to give you a life free of funerals for the young and doomed. Yet here you've chosen to surround yourself with that world, immerse yourself in it. That girl brings with her an entire universe I tried to eclipse from your view.*

Julie said, "I didn't tell you the truth because I knew damn well that if you heard I'd been with a man who was in prison that woulda been the last time I ever spoke to you."

"It still might be."

She flinched. "Don't say that."

"What do you expect me to say? You lied to me. And because of that, I lied to my family! What am I supposed to tell them when this other man shows up one day knocking on our door? Or crashes our wedding? Lord, woman, look at the position you've put me in!"

"I said I was sorry."

"First you lied to me about having a child, and I accepted that, and I accepted you, and you swore to me you'd never lie to me again. But I guess that was just a line, right, another con?"

A hinge turned, her eyebrows shifting from penitence to fury. "Fine! Run back to your snooty parents! I'm too much trouble, huh? I don't deserve their son, do I?"

"You have no right to yell at me, I'm just—"

"Course I have no right, I have no right to be anything but thankful to Mr. Officer Lucius Boggs who swooped up and saved me! I'm just so grateful for everything you did, because without you I'm just a poor ol' nigger girl, right? That's all I am without you, right? And after all your promises, you running off at the first sign of trouble! First sign that maybe life with Julie won't be as easy as you thought, you runnin'!"

His fists were clenched at his sides. Her mother's silhouette lingered in the doorway behind her.

"I never thought it would be easy," he said, keeping his voice down in hopes that hers would join him at this level. "But I thought it would be *honest*."

"No, I'm just a lying hussy, Officer Boggs! Can't trust me for nothing!"

He held up a hand. "Stop it, please. You're making a scene."

"Oh, it was fine when *you* were the one yellin', but not me, huh?"

"Julie, I need to get back to work."

"Yeah, you need to get back, all right."

She turned and walked into the house, passing her mother. Mrs. Cannon stood there staring hard at him, anger writ there, seeing him not as family but as something hostile she needed to protect her daughter from. She shook her head and closed the door.

23

"Pour me some of the good stuff, Feckless, on the rocks."

The bar's owner raised an eyebrow. "I thought you didn't partake."

Smith asked, "You gonna rat me out?"

Atlanta police officers were not supposed to drink. Plenty of white cops did—some while on shift—yet the Negro cops knew that if they dared cross that line, they ran the risk of losing their jobs should someone report it. Smith had reached the point where he was willing to take that risk, small though it was. He was among friends here at the Rook, which had become one of the destination night spots on Auburn Avenue. Packed on the weekends, it hosted bluesmen and jazz bands not just from the South but from across the country, folks like Dizzy Gillespie, Bird, and Thelonious Monk stopping by on tour. Past two in the morning, Smith wasn't the only one who'd clocked out, as members of a local jazz band, silk ties loosened and faces still gleaming after their set, sat around a table eating their late-night snack of fried chicken. A few other stragglers were scattered at tables, Smith the sole man at the bar. Out of uniform, of course, he'd cocked his gray straw boater slantwise to make him harder to spot through the dark of the place, just in case anyone here felt like informing on a cop.

The owner of the Rook, pouring a double bourbon into Smith's glass, was Lester Feck, aka Feckless. As a kid, the daily attendance call of "Feck, Lester" had at some point merged into his nickname. He'd worked moving freight at the rail yards for years. Smith had heard stories that Feckless had not always been an upstanding, law-abiding fellow, that perhaps some of the money he'd used to buy this place had come via illicit pursuits. But that was ancient history. It wasn't where we came from that mattered, it was what we did once we got here. Smith understood that more than most.

"One of those nights, huh?" Feckless asked, pouring himself one as well. He held his glass in a toast. "The hell with today. Here's to showing them tomorrow."

"Amen." Smith wouldn't have minded drinking with Boggs—he felt they could use a few moments like this—but he could only imagine the reaction he'd receive from his partner. *Alcohol? In our bodies?* Just getting the man to shoot the occasional round of pool had been an accomplishment.

Yet in all other respects, life was easier for Boggs. Just was. Born to the right parents. Preacher money and a preacher house, even a preacher car they could borrow in emergencies. Boggs complained plenty about his old man, but he didn't seem to realize how lucky he was to have him in his corner.

Tommy was heartsick for Hannah and Malcolm. They'd both worked so hard, climbing and climbing, hoping to reach not quite Boggs-level society but at least a little piece of the American dream. And when they finally thought they'd attained that much, it was being snatched from them. Violently.

There had to be something Smith could do about the Columbians. Jesus, putting those signs all over Hanford Park like they owned it, no shame at appropriating the symbols of the very country we'd just won a war against.

"Lightning men," Smith's battalion had called the SS troopers. But they were all lightning men. Not just the Columbians but the Klansmen, too, and the neighborhood association that had offered to buy Hannah's house as if that were a legitimate, regular ol' business arrangement shorn of threats. And the other white people, the ones who had allowed those lightning bolt signs to be posted and had not objected, the ones who claimed not to hate Negroes but who surely didn't want to live near them and didn't mind when other whites grabbed bats to settle things—they were all lightning men. Some of them were just more honest about it.

There was no way he or Boggs could go after the all-white Columbians directly. Their only hope was that Rakestraw would keep his word, but that seemed unrealistic. The top Columbians had been jailed when they started talking about overthrowing the government, so maybe the rest would make the same mistake. But maybe they'd learned, and they'd act just mainstream enough that the other white people would accept their occasional violence for the benefits it brought them, benefits like all-white neighborhoods and complacent Negroes. They were no different from the Redshirts who crushed Reconstruction generations ago, just the latest in the glorious Southern tradition of terrorism and lawlessness.

"How's Malcolm?" Feckless asked as he cleaned the marble-topped bar.

"Hospital's gonna let him out in a couple days. He has a long way to go. You hold the job for him, all right? He's good for it once he's on his feet."

Feckless looked insulted. "He don't have to worry about that. Once he's ready, he can get back to work."

That morning Smith and Boggs had driven out to Hannah's place and relieved her of the latest batch of hate mail. Two letters, both of them typed, and both recovered from the trash again, even though he'd asked her to save whatever came. One of them mostly concerned itself with what the writer would do to *her,* rape being but one of the threats. Smith had always seen threats as signs of cowardice, signs that the speaker didn't possess the will to *do* and therefore could only *say,* but reading those letters while Malcolm lay in the hospital showed how wrong he was. The letter addressed to Hannah made him sick, made him want to pound on every door in the neighborhood and force them all to read it, make their wives and children read it.

They had brought the letters to McInnis, asking him to send them to the lab for fingerprinting, along with the lightning bolt sign Smith had torn down. The sergeant's reaction to this display of initiative? Scolding them for collecting evidence pertaining to another precinct's case, for stepping on other cops' toes. *But there are no toes to step on!* Smith had snapped. *They didn't investigate the brick through their window and they probably aren't even investigating this.* McInnis had thought long and hard then, before finally nodding and telling them he'd see what he could do.

Smith read some of the *Atlanta Daily News* in the dim light while Feck cleaned glasses. The front page bore stories about battles in Korea, a controversy over alleged misuse of Truman's loyalty oaths, and a profile of a former member of FDR's "black cabinet" accepting a position at Morehouse. The paper's crime stories, he'd always thought, were terrible: cursory and written with little understanding of how the city actually worked. He'd have to give one of their crime writers, Toon, an earful the next time they crossed paths.

"Listen," Feckless told him. "I appreciate what you're doing. Very much."

Smith just nodded. He felt powerless, not in the mood to hear praise. He asked, "What do you make of Thunder Malley going down?"

"Let's just say I'm not shedding any tears over the fact that he's off the streets. Glad y'all took care of that."

Smith scowled. "*We* didn't kill him."

"I know, but I heard how you brought him in. White folks took care of the rest."

The bourbon in his stomach turned into acid. "It's not like there was some arrangement, we catch the dogs and they put 'em down."

"I didn't mean it that way. Don't take no offense. You wanted him to go to trial, and good for you to think that way. But there were some powerful folks who didn't want that man to ever testify, and that's how it goes."

We should have known that, Smith thought. And maybe he had, he'd just been stubborn. He'd wanted to show everyone, from the white cops to the poorest Negro on the streets, that he could arrest any lawbreaker, no matter how tough or protected the man claimed to be.

Maybe it wasn't so terrible how things worked out. Thunder wasn't on the streets anymore. They *had* sent a message, and the citizens knew who was in charge. Didn't they?

He lifted the glass, nothing but three sad memories of larger ice cubes. "I'll take another."

When Feck returned the full glass, it rested atop an envelope. Smith looked up at Feck, who peeled the triangle away and revealed cash stuffed inside.

"For taking that man off the street. He shook me down plenty, and I'm glad I don't need to deal with that no more."

That there was a lot of money, Smith saw. And for a moment, yes, he was tempted. He thought about his need for a down payment on a house or apartment of his own, thought about his lack of a car, even the worn state of his favorite blazers.

Christ, he'd been drinking too much already.

"I don't do that," he said, looking Feck in the eye.

"Pass it on to Malcolm, then. He could use it."

"He'd be very grateful. But you can give it to him yourself." Smith stood and walked away, leaving the full glass behind as well, and wondering what lay at the end of the road he hadn't chosen.

Two blocks away, McInnis stood alone in an alley off Butler Street, near a squad car he'd spied there. Eddie B.'s was a late-night joint that, he knew, occasionally hosted illegal gambling nights. He'd been there ten minutes when Billy Logan walked through the joint's back door. Logan, a white cop, stopped when he spotted McInnis. No one else was standing around at this hour, and if they were, they were up to something.

Billy Logan was up to something.

"Mac. How are ya?"

"Can't complain. How's Cindy?"

"She's good, she's good. And the boys, they're at Grady already, can you believe it?"

"Time does fly."

A black Pontiac with whitewall tires drove by slowly. McInnis watched it turn down another street and said, "What brings you to my beat?"

"Just needed some information."

"Information you're carrying in your wallet, or in a stuffed envelope, maybe?"

Logan's face soured. "What gives, Mac?"

"I just find it funny, how cops who work a couple miles from here still find a way to make more money in my precinct than I do."

"I never got the sense that was a priority with you."

"That's because it's not. But murder is. Tell me about Thunder Malley."

The change of subject seemed to throw Logan, who paused. "He's dead."

"No kidding. The cop who shot him and the other cop he was supposedly escaping from were both rookies." And both of them, McInnis had learned, were assigned to one of the same squad cars whose drivers had threatened Boggs and Smith in an alley a few nights ago. He kept this detail to himself for now. "I don't see kids that green getting the gumption to gun a man down in the station like that, unless they were following orders."

Logan's shoulders sagged. "You sure you want to get into this?"

"Get into this? Look around you, Billy. This is where I work now. Every day. I *am* in this."

"I just don't think it's a good idea for you to butt heads with some of these fellas."

"Let's try this another way. That money in your pocket? Maybe I should walk right into that club and tell those gamblers they don't need to pay you off anymore, that this isn't your precinct and it's not the way we do things here in Sweet Auburn."

"All right, all right. Your funeral. The Thunder Malley thing, I don't know this for a fact, but I imagine it's Slater. He's the sergeant to those two rookies, and let's just say he's got a nicer house than a fella of his means would normally have."

McInnis shook his head, bad memories returning. "Does he advertise that?"

"He's not an idiot. He ain't living in a mansion, he just knows how to be comfortable without showing it off. Rumor is, Slater has family up in the mountains, cousins who used to run some stills. They've been scaling that back, growing something a tad more profitable."

McInnis mulled this over. "So Slater's cousins up north move their product down here, and Thunder Malley's boys sell it in the Negro neighborhoods, while Slater keeps them all safe for a percentage. Now that Malley's dead, Slater must be scouting for his next opportunity."

"I don't know anything more and I don't care to."

"See no evil, hear no evil? Funny attitude for a cop."

"And it's helped me survive this long, hasn't it? Maybe we aren't all as vain as you, gunning for glory. It's not every cop's dream to run a sting like you did."

"*Vanity*, that's what it was? Huh."

Slater's beat was downtown, yet McInnis knew—from reading arrest reports and officer logs, and from talking to old friends at headquarters—that Slater was a regular visitor to this area.

"Billy, I need you to stop taking your cuts in Darktown."

Logan shook his head like he was enduring an unwelcome joke, and the trick was to wait out the other fellow's awkward laughter. Then he stepped closer so he could lower his voice. "So you want a cut, huh? These are relationships I built over years of hard work. And just because the Department decides to hire nigger cops doesn't mean I—"

"I don't want a cut, no." With Billy fidgeting and talking so quickly, McInnis made a point of being still, speaking slowly. "I just want you to stop getting yours in my territory. I know we go back, but I have a job to do and you need to respect that. Maybe I was inclined to look the other way before, but with people getting shot up, I can't do that anymore."

Quick scowl, a good man deeply offended. "You talking about that shoot-out between your boys and Malley's at Phelps Telephone? I don't know anything about that."

"You say making a little extra bread is harmless, but I recall Slater saying something similar awhile back. Funny how kickbacks can eventually lead to homicide."

"Don't lump me in with that son of a bitch."

"Bottom line, I have ten officers who stick to their beat. I need you and everyone else, including Slater, to stick to yours."

"He ain't scared of them, Mac."

"Maybe he should be a little scared of them. Maybe he should be a little scared of me."

A nearby cat or two made downright beastly sounds to break the long silence.

"You saying you'd use your cops to try to nail white cops? You actually proposing that?"

Doing so, McInnis knew, would violate so many cultural mores that it would be career suicide. And maybe even actual suicide. But perhaps he could bluff them into believing he was just crazy enough to try it. He was aided by the fact that, a few years ago, he in fact *had* led a sting into a numbers running scheme that had been operated by several cops. That investigation—which he'd never asked for, but it had been assigned to him, so he'd done his job—had led to the arrests of a handful of officers and the firing of a few more. It also led to him being hated by most members of the force and exiled to the Butler Street Y. If anyone could be believed to be crazy enough to lay another sting for dirty cops, it was McInnis.

"I'm not going to let other cops shit in my territory and make me and my officers look bad. Now I've asked you, politely. If that doesn't work, there are other tools at my disposal." Then he turned and said good night, walking back to his car.

"You can threaten all you want, Mac," Logan called across the street. "You can't change the natural order of things."

"Let's talk about it over lunch sometime." Realizing that would never happen. "But in a different neighborhood. Because I don't want to see you in this one ever again."

24

Late morning, the house quiet with Cassie and the kids out at a park, Rake read the paper and enjoyed the solitude. An American mine-sweeper had become the first US ship sunk in the Korean conflict; Joe McCarthy was insisting on a more thorough investigation into the Communist infiltration of the top echelons in American government; and officials announced that the mysterious explosions in a Brooklyn neighborhood, initially feared to be a Red attack, had in fact been caused by a gas leak. Then the phone rang.

"Is this Rakestraw, the cop?" A man on the line, whispering.

"Yes. Who's this?"

"You interested in who beat up that colored fella on Oak Lane?"

"Yes. Who is this?"

"Sorry, I ain't leaving no name. That's why I'm calling you at home and not your station." The whispering had seemed urgent at first, but Rake realized now that the man was disguising his voice, less a whisper than a hoarse gasp. This could have been a total stranger or someone Rake crossed paths with every day. "I saw it happen."

Rake reached for a pencil. "What did you see?"

"Three fellas in Klan robes. One of 'em had what looked like a two-by-four. Some plank of wood or something."

"Baseball bat, maybe?"

"No. Didn't look that round."

The caller must have been very close to the attack, to discern that difference.

"Why don't you want to leave your name, sir?"

The man laughed, deeper this time, accidentally betraying elements of his real voice. "You want people like that to come after *you*? I sure don't. Look, I didn't need to pick up the phone, so if you don't really—"

"Please don't hang up. Were they on foot or in a vehicle?"

"It was a sedan. White, I think? Or maybe tan? It was dark out, and the closest light wasn't working or something."

Which was true: that one light had shattered and the city had yet to fix it. Unusual for this neighborhood, and enough to make Rake wonder if the attackers had come by the night before to throw rocks at the bulb.

"Did you see the tags?"

"No, sir. Just heard a screech of tires and then some voices, so I looked through the curtain and saw it. Negro was on the ground by then and they were kicking him, one of 'em got down and threw some punches, and that other fella had the wood. Miracle that boy's still alive."

"Barely alive."

"I don't like that nonsense happening in my part of town. I don't want no Negroes here, but I don't want that, either."

"Was there anything at all noteworthy about them, sir? Was one of them particularly tall or short or fat? Could you make out their footwear?"

"That's all I got, and I've done enough. Good luck to you."

⚡

The sky was clear but the ground damp as Rake walked Charles Dickens. The dog sniffed at a patch of yellow and burgundy coreopsis flowers, lifting his leg in approval.

Police received plenty of anonymous tips at the station, a good deal of them worthless. People who claimed to have seen crimes but were loath to leave their names sometimes had legitimate information, but more often they were neighbors with grudges, cranks venting nonsense. It was uncommon for Rake to get a tip called into his house, however. And the caller hadn't pointed the finger at any particular person, so the grudge angle was out. That made the information more likely to be genuine.

He was surprised, though. He wasn't yet ready to rule out Knox Dunlow. And his main suspect had been Coyle and his fellow Columbians. Rake had spoken to some former colleagues from his time at the mill, where the Columbians had recruited years ago, to see if they were doing so again. They weren't, as far as his old friends knew. And the lightning bolt signs had not yet reappeared. Still, he'd felt it was only a matter of time before they did something stupid again, hopefully leaving more evidence behind to implicate themselves.

And of course he'd suspected the Klan, but their MO was to create a spectacle, inspiring terror in those they opposed. A quiet beating with no attendant publicity—not even a burned cross—did not seem their style.

Then again, neither did Dale's night ride. Maybe the Klan was changing tactics, becoming more secretive than before. What intrigued Rake most was the fact that the Hanford Park attack came so soon after Dale's misadventure. If Malcolm had been attacked by Klansmen, they were likely repaying the neighborhood for Dale's "work" in Coventry. Which meant Rake might discover the true reasons for Dale's mission if he figured out who had attacked Malcolm. But how?

The only other information he'd gathered from neighbors was from one man who lived a few doors down from Malcolm and claimed to have seen a trio of *Negroes* beating him. But this "witness" had been unable to give a description of their car or their faces, and his profuse usage of "nigger" in telling the tale gave Rake the distinct impression the man was just trying to blame Negroes for the trouble. It almost made Rake wonder if Helton had fed the man his lines.

"Beautiful morning, isn't it, Officer Rakestraw?" a voice interrupted his thoughts.

Charles Dickens, who was revealing himself to be sadly lacking in basic canine protective skills, belatedly barked at two men crossing the street. Rake gave the leash a tug, harder than he needed to, and told the dog to hush.

The men's well-shined black leather shoes crunched on fallen leaves and acorn caps as they walked up to Rake. Both wore gray suits. One had the faintest amount of gray hairs along his temple, boyish blue eyes more than compensating. His partner was blond and couldn't have been more than a couple years older than Rake. The one with a bit of gray reached into his pocket and showed off his badge like he was so very proud of it, then hid it again.

"Georgia Bureau of Investigation. I'm Agent Tyson and this is Agent Bradford. Nice dog." Rather than extending his hand to Rake, Tyson crouched down and offered it to Charles Dickens, who sniffed and licked it and was rewarded with some behind-the-ear head rubs.

"What can I help you with?"

Tyson stood back up. "We wanted to ask you a few questions about a shooting we're looking into."

"Sure. There a reason you dropped by here and not the station?"

"Happened to be in the neighborhood." Which Rake smelled for bullshit.

Bradford added, "And most of the folks at your headquarters hate us anyway." Which Rake knew for truth. In addition to the inevitable turf disputes was the fact that the GBI's sting against Atlanta's Klaverns a few years ago had implicated several high-ranking Atlanta police officers. APD and GBI worked together on plenty of cases, but the partnership had been strained during Rake's entire tenure on the force.

"A man was beaten and killed in Coventry a few nights ago, and we have reason to believe the killers lived in this neighborhood."

Oh, he was so smooth, so smart. Mangling the facts that way: *A man was beaten and killed,* when in truth one man had been beaten and another man killed. A deliberate error to see if Rake might give himself away by correcting Tyson. Rake's stomach was tight and he feared he could be facing adversaries smarter than him.

"People I know?" Thinking, *Just talk, be natural, don't think about your reactions because then you'll overreact.*

"We have some concerns about your brother-in-law, Dale Simpkins," Bradford said. Unlike his partner, he edged back the slightest amount from Charles Dickens, whom he glanced at warily, as if awaiting an inevitable pounce.

"Whatever you guys are thinking, just come out and say it. You won't offend me."

"Three Klansmen attacked a man outside a roadhouse in Coventry—attacked a white man, actually, at a very out-of-the-way spot," Tyson said. "They'd about killed him when the proprietor, a woman with a hell of an eye, shot one of the attackers dead with a rifle. The other two Klansmen escaped."

"What makes you think one of them was Dale?"

"A few things. One of which is, he drives the same kind of car the proprietor says they fled in. She didn't get the full tags but recalled a couple of letters, and his tags have them."

"She also may have put some bullets in it," Bradford added, "and conveniently enough, Dale had his rear fender repaired the day after the shooting."

Rake nodded along with these new facts, which revealed how much work they'd already done. He asked, "So, do you want me to talk to him?"

Tyson smiled. "No. We do not want you to talk to him. We want you to tell us everything he's told you."

Charles Dickens started digging near the base of an oak tree. He kicked up dirt, some of which landed against the fine pant leg of Agent Bradford, who scowled and shook it off.

"About this? Nothing. Look, I won't insult your work by noting that the car he drives is a common one, or how many other tags must share *two letters*. I don't see him as the kind of fellow who would drive up and beat on a stranger. But if you do, then go and question him. He's my brother-in-law, but I'll let you do your job."

"Who said it was a stranger?"

Ooops. "Well, who was it?"

"Small-town banker named Martin Letcher."

"Then shouldn't you be talking to people the banker's pissed off up there? What got you to Dale? It must have taken something other than the make of his car."

"He has talkative friends," Bradford said, leaving it at that. Had Mott, the third member of their little goon squad, told anyone else? Rake had been meaning to question Mott, too, to see if he knew anything that might help Rake understand who had sent them, but he'd ultimately decided against it: he didn't want another person to know he was investigating. And this conversation was justifying his paranoia. Was he too late, because Dale had ignored Rake's advice and told someone else, either beforehand or after? Was Rake insane to think Dale could keep anything a secret?

"Look, Officer Rakestraw," Tyson said. "We know a lot about you. You seem like a smart, hardworking cop, on the fast track to detective.

And we know you're one of the rare cops who doesn't have a Klan Kard. Bet you have to put up with a lot of shit for that, right?"

"I can handle it."

"Yes, you do seem like the kind of fellow who can handle things. My concern is that one of the things you can handle is helping your brother-in-law cover his tracks and making sure no other cop gets wise to his trail. You can handle it because he's family and you're a smart fellow, but then suddenly you're handling just way too much, and it all comes crashing down."

His dog-fearing young partner added, "Especially that fast track to detective."

"Then I guess you don't know as much about me as you think. Because I actually don't like Dale all that much, to be perfectly honest, and if he did something that was going to get himself put away, I certainly wouldn't help him out of it." Thinking, *Most of that is true, and I wish to God the rest was, too.* What a fool he was to have helped the son of a bitch.

"You're right, we probably don't know as much about you as we should. Like whatever happened to your first partner, Dunlow. Man completely vanishes and is later declared dead so his wife can get the pension money, and you know absolutely nothing about that, either, do you?"

"And after his disappearance," Bradford noted, "you get a better beat and a more competent partner, almost like someone was rewarding you for it."

Rake stepped closer to Bradford. Charles Dickens picked up on this, must have sensed the tension in his master's muscles, because he moved beside Rake and eyed the strangers, very still, possibly issuing a faint growl at a register human ears couldn't detect.

"I deal with enough bullshit suspicion on that from other cops. I would think you guys were a bit smarter."

"We're smart enough to know that obstruction of justice is a crime," Bradford said.

"I have a spotless record and I'm out walking my dog and you show up to accuse me of a crime. Why is this even a GBI case?"

"Because we're the ones who are so darn chummy with the Kluxers,"

Tyson said, smiling. "We still have enough ears under the hoods to know what goes on with those fools."

"So what are your informants telling you?"

"That it wasn't a hit ordered by any of the Atlanta Klaverns, or the one in Coventry," Bradford said. "There's a couple other local Klaverns we still need to dig into, but this appears to be an unsanctioned attack, which makes it all the more unusual."

They still haven't told me anything about Letcher, why he was targeted. They want me to ask, they want me to show how badly I want to know, and for that very reason, I can't.

"Well, get on and solve it, then. I'm not obstructing a damn thing. I hope Dale isn't involved, and I don't see why he would be, but if he is, do your job."

Tyson glanced at his partner and smiled. He turned back to Rake-straw. "You're absolutely sure you have nothing to tell us?"

Part of Rake wanted to pick a fight with them, let them know how he appreciated their effrontery at showing up and acting like they owned the block. The other part of him realized: *This is how everyone else feels about* me. *They're always thinking, "Damn cops boss us around, don't show us any respect."*

"Don't piss away your career already," Bradford said, and that was all the more insulting from someone so young.

"If I hear anything, I will let you know."

Bored by this human, mostly inert contest, Charles Dickens turned to bark at a squirrel.

"I'm disappointed in you, kid," Tyson said. "We'd heard good things."

They'd been hoping to get something incriminating on Dale, he realized, but they'd also wanted a read on Rake. They'd been testing him, to see what kind of cop he was. He had failed.

Then he had a worrisome thought. What if the mysterious White-house himself was with the GBI? What if the whole affair was another sting, another attempt to take down the Klan? What if these two men before him had been a part of this from the beginning, and they mistakenly thought Rake was just another Kard-karrying kop?

They took a few steps toward their car. Stung by their insults, and newly eager to show his anti-Klan bona fides, he called at them, "So if you have so many ears in the Klan, why haven't you solved the beating that happened here last week?"

"What beating is that?"

He couldn't tell if they were only playing stupid. "Negro by the name of Malcolm Greer was attacked when he was walking home one night."

"Who says it was the Klan?"

"Call it a hunch." He didn't want to mention the anonymous tip, as it would sound thin.

"Well, hunches are nice," Tyson said, "but we prefer evidence. Anyway, we're not here to give *you* information. Unless perhaps you have some information for us, and you want to have an exchange? Because so far I feel like I'm talking to a brick wall."

His partner added, to the dog, "And brick walls get pissed on, don't they, pooch?"

Rake wanted to tell Bradford not to address his dog, but he realized how absurd that would sound.

"Stopping the Klan is mighty tricky when so many of them wear badges under those robes," Tyson said, grinning tightly. Something about that grin sent alarm bells through Rake's skull. *When are they going to question Dale? How quickly will Dale confess to everything, and how quickly will he mention that his brother-in-law Rake had advised him to keep quiet?*

"Before you criticize us," Tyson said as he walked away, "you might want to get your own house in order."

25

It was difficult if not impossible for a Georgia woman to own a business, and indeed the name on all the legal paperwork regarding the Lean-To in Coventry was that of Joe Bleedhorn, Hortense's husband. But five years ago the Lord had seen fit to send some bolt of cerebral lightning into his skull; one half of his body had gone slack, his lips crooked, and the light in both eyes had dimmed substantially. He sat in a wheelchair now and managed to get himself some places one-handed, but for the most part he stayed in their house, where he was tended by a saintly aunt and by Hortense, when she wasn't busy running the bar.

She'd gone by the nickname Tense since her first years. It wasn't terribly fitting. Far from high-strung, she projected a laid-back sense that all would be well so long as she was in charge. And she was. She served drinks, bossed around cooks, and kept the drunkest of her customers from causing too much of a ruckus. And whenever it appeared that causing a ruckus was on someone's mind, well, Tense carried a Colt .45 in her belt and she was never far from the shotgun and rifle she kept hidden on the premises. The Lean-To's regulars tolerated her occasionally surly demeanor and cut her extra slack on account of the misfortune the Lord had dropped on her husband, so she seldom had occasion to display those firearms. When she did, it was usually to deal with folks who weren't regulars, truck drivers who happened to be stopping in town, salesmen looking to celebrate a big score, wayward souls on long, uninterrupted voyages of self-loathing and danger who assumed she was a madam or a whore, or both. She'd been slapped around, fondled, had a scar cut into her right forearm by a blade, and had resewn more than a few torn blouses, but she'd also shot three men and broken more bottles over skulls than she could remember.

Walter Irons was the first man she had killed.

She had lost no great amount of sleep over the killing. She had taken a man's life, but she'd done so in order to save another man's. Martin Letcher was a fellow she knew, friendly enough, funny when sober and funnier when tight and of course less funny when all-out drunk, as all men were, though they believed the opposite. His bank had helped her family out when her husband had first been struck and she'd been dumbfounded by the size of the medical bills. The man she'd shot, however, she did not know. No one did.

That grated on her. As did the fact that he and his fellow assailants had been wearing Klan robes despite local Kluxers' insistence that they didn't know anything about the attack.

Also bothersome was that Willa Mae Letcher, the wife of the man whose life she'd saved, hadn't so much as telephoned to express her thanks. Not a letter, not a brief visit to the Lean-To. Perhaps Mrs. Letcher would not deign to lower herself by visiting such an establishment, which if that were the case, fine. Uppity women could not be talked down from their station, Tense knew. But no phone call, even?

Tense typically opened for business at noon, arriving an hour early to get things moving in the kitchen. She swept some early-to-fall leaves and acorns from the front porch, gazing with approval at two butterflies alighting on the white turtlehead flowers that unfurled from green stalks in the shade cast by the oaks towering above. She looked up when she heard a vehicle crunching its way up the long driveway, which was flanked then as every autumn by thick hedges of orange lantana. An unfamiliar black Ford pickup parked alongside the oak at the base of which the Kluxer had been standing when she'd fired her shots. Two men inside the truck sat there for an unusually long time while she continued with her sweeping. She had been whistling to herself but something about the unexpected arrival made her lose the tune.

Finally there emerged from the Ford two men who were very large indeed. Each of them six four at least, broad across the shoulders. Not portly or overweight, just keep-your-distance big. The driver had a thick beard and with his plaid shirt and overalls looked like a lumberjack in the wrong part of the state. The passenger had clean-shaven cheeks but the same dark hair and as she watched them she spied similarities in their cold blue eyes and the way in which they stared into her.

"We ain't open yet, boys. Gotta wait 'til noon."

"You're Hortense Bleedhorn?" asked the one who wasn't dressed quite so much like a lumberjack. He wore a blue denim shirt untucked over corduroys gone orange in the cuffs from Georgia clay. His voice was pure Bama, though, and a bit higher-pitched than she would have expected.

"Who's asking?"

"I'm Morris. This is my brother Reece."

Reece was looking not at her but at the base of the oak. Something in his gaze suggested he knew where the man had fallen, as there was a forensic nature to it, a calculating of angles.

"Well, Morris and Reece, you're welcome to come by in an hour. 'Til then I can't help you, even if I wanted to. There are laws."

"We know about laws," Morris said, calmly removing a gun from what must have been a holster hidden by that long shirt. "And we know about the breaking of 'em."

She froze. The pistol that was on her person during business hours was tucked into one of the kitchen drawers.

"Boys, I ain't got much money at the moment. I do my banking each morning at ten on the dot, so you're too late."

"We ain't here for money." Reece spoke for the first time. "We're here for our other brother, the one you killed."

She realized she hadn't been nervous enough, because now she was nervous.

Her throat seemed to constrict on her, all the spit gone. It seemed insane that despite all her successful brushes with danger by the darkness of evening, of all the bizarre things she'd seen and endured between the hours of, say, eleven at night to two in the morning, that the fated arrival of the Grim Reaper would come on a brilliantly sunny October morning like this, and her with a goddamned broom in her hand.

"Look, boys, I am sorry about your brother. I took no pleasure in that. But he was beating a man to death with his bare hands, and on my property besides."

Both men walked toward her. Reece sank one of his enormous hands into his overalls and then brandished a gun of his own.

Somewhere nearby a woodpecker was getting out its frustrations.

"We'd like to hear all about it," Morris said. "Lean that broom down on the floor real slow."

She obeyed, and when she'd finished they were standing on the porch, the floorboards groaning beneath their impressive weight. They had seemed large from the distance, but this close it was almost absurd. Their guns were entirely unnecessary. Never before had firearms looked so unthreatening in strangers' possession, petite in their enormous hands. She was accustomed to being in the presence of all manner of rough men, but these two with their massiveness and dead stares and the full thrust of vengeance behind them left her feeling cold in a way she hadn't before.

"Tell us what happened," Morris said. Both of their guns were pointed at the porch floor, as if they were nothing more than metallic fingers.

The Irons brothers had no doubt made note of the fact that only her car was in the yard when they'd arrived. What they hadn't realized was that her Negro cook came on foot each day. Diller was a simple man of about forty who also, she knew, had a gun on him most times on account of that long walk he had to take each night, in a county with far more whites than Negroes. From the porch she and her unwanted guests would have been plainly visible to anyone in the dining room, but the kitchen was on the other side of a wall. There was a small gap in that wall for orders to be placed, and she hoped Diller would glance through it before one of the Irons boys caught a glimpse of him.

"It was late," she said, "and pretty quiet. Letcher had just left and I happened to look out the window, and because it was dark out and with that distance I probably shouldn't have been able to see anything, but those robes being so white I could just make them out, and then I realized, well I'll be, there's a Klan beat-down happening on my lawn and ain't nobody asked me for permission."

She wasn't one to talk so long without a period in the middle of it but she wasn't herself in their presence. Morris stared at her, as if convinced she was lying and determined to spot the exact location where her story diverged from truth. Reece, meanwhile, continued his gnomic way of gazing out at the oak, and beneath the porch banister, and under the two rocking chairs, like some idiot savant detective who can detect a previously overlooked clue so many days later.

"Klan beat-down?" Morris asked. "He was wearing a robe?"

"Yeah, him and two others. They were behind him, and they had guns."

The two remaining Irons brothers looked at each other. Tense felt nausea pulling at her insides like a trapdoor.

Morris said, "We ain't heard nothing about the Klan being involved. Not at the funeral, not from the police."

"Well, the police wouldn't want to talk about that."

"Tell me about this sheriff of yours. He covering something up for the Klan?"

"I don't have any idea. All I know is they were in Klan robes clear as day, yet you're telling me you didn't know about that. If I was the police in charge, then I'd be telling the family of the victim all I knew."

"What a nice sheriff you'd be."

"Sheriff part of the Klan?" Reece spoke.

"Course he is."

"Why would the Klan go after this Letcher fellow? He got a nigger girlfriend?"

"Hell no."

"Catholic? Jew? Red? He in a labor union or some such?"

"He's a banker. I never heard of the Klan beating on bankers. Usually it's bankers *in* the Klan, but things are getting all backwards these days."

The sound of a truck. Both men looked down the drive, and it occurred to her that this would have been her one moment to run. But they'd gun her down in a second, and the thought of trying instead to knock one of their guns away was comical, big as those hands were.

The sound receded, yet it reminded the Irons brothers that they were out in the open.

"Let's go inside," Morris said, motioning to the door. She opened it, the brothers following.

Inside, the smell of onions thickened and even from here they could hear the chopping.

"Who's back there?" Morris asked her, voice hushed.

She could have lied, but she feared the repercussions. Hoping she wasn't condemning him, she said, "My cook, Diller."

Morris raised his hand and pressed the barrel of the pistol into her left temple. She could smell the oil he must have used to clean the gun that very morning.

"Call him out here real natural like."

She tried to swallow but there was no spit to go down. "Hey, Diller?" Hating herself for the betrayal. Hoping he might hear the terror in her voice and reach for his gun, or the one she'd stashed in a kitchen drawer. "Gimme a hand moving this table, would you?"

"Sho' thing."

A moment later the kitchen door swung open, and Diller had barely made it a step when Reece pistol-whipped him. Tense only realized she'd gasped when Morris told her to shut the hell up. Diller was a heap on the ground, motionless. Morris told his brother to drag him into the kitchen, then he pushed Tense forward so they could follow.

The kitchen door swung behind them and she felt even more in danger now. As if being on the porch on a beautiful day was too wrong a way to die, but here, in a dingy and greasy kitchen deprived of windows or ventilation, now here was a fitting place to be murdered.

The drawer in which she'd stashed her pistol was blocked from reach by Morris. But the stove, still on, was topped by a large cast-iron skillet, the onions almost translucent. A pot of lard nearby simmered. Both could be weapons. As could the many knives lying about, and the cleaver that smelled of garlic, not more than two feet from her grasp. She tried not to let her eyes dart toward them, yet a grin streaked Morris's face, as though entertained by his prey's delusions.

Reece dragged Diller by his armpits and dropped him by the back door. Diller stirred and groaned just enough to betray consciousness. Blood ran in a steady stream from his left eyebrow.

"Our brother got himself a whole trophy chest full of hardware from the US military," Morris announced. "He was at Midway and Guadalcanal and half a dozen places a bitch like you never heard of. Shit they didn't see fit to put in newspapers. I was in the Philippines and Reece here helped take Normandy. We done shot up a whole mess of folks and if you think adding some crone to the list gives us pause, you'd best think again."

"I didn't want to kill him." She was almost whispering. "I only meant to scare him off."

"By aiming at his head?"

She didn't have time to explain to him that, if she'd wasted time with warning shots in the past, plenty of drunk bastards would have done plenty of damage in her bar. "I just . . . He was about to kill that man."

"Someone is going to die for what happened. Right now it's looking to be you. Unless you want to point the finger at someone more deserving."

Confusing her, he placed his gun back in his holster, then carefully lifted the pot of lard and poured some of its contents into the skillet. The sound of the sizzling onions intensified and a brief cloud of smoke rose around them.

Then he grabbed her by the hair. With one hand he pinned her head to the countertop, inches away from the stove. She had very long hair, cutting it only twice a year and typically keeping it in a bun, but today she had let it down.

With his other hand he gathered up the length of her hair and placed the ends into the skillet.

"Oh Jesus," she whispered, though only the countertop could have heard her over the sound of the hair crackling. He was frying her hair. He'd pinned her head facing away from the skillet, and she could feel the weight of that hand and nothing else. Within seconds she could smell her hair burning.

"Why the hell was our brother out here miles from home to beat on some banker? Answer me that."

"I don't know, I don't know!" She lost control of her bladder.

"They had some row between them?"

"I don't know!"

"That banker do something to our brother? He have it coming to him?"

"I swear I don't know!"

"Who were the other Klansmen?"

In the warped reflection of a pot she saw him reach with his free hand for a ladle, then dip it into the lard and pour it behind her somewhere she couldn't see. On her hair, she realized. The acrid stench of burned hair grew thicker and it crackled and hissed on the stove.

"Hey, Reece, whaddya think'd happen if I poured some whiskey over her head? I bet it'd drip down like a trail of kerosene."

"Only one way to find out," the other big man said, reaching into his pocket and tossing a flask to his brother.

"I don't know what to tell you!" she screamed. "I don't know what you want!"

"I want to know who we should be paying back if not you! That's what!"

He tugged at her hair again and she could feel the back of her head coming closer to the skillet, could feel the heat in the air and in an instant she knew she'd feel it so much more. She could see Diller watching in horror, and, to her surprise, he spoke: "Those same men beat on my cousin that night."

"What?" Morris jerked at her hair again, this time farther from the skillet.

"The hell you just say?" Reece asked him.

"That same night. Two other fellas in robes beat up my cousin, not more'n two miles from here. No reason at all. Just drove into the yard where he'd been gatherin' firewood and started clocking him. He blind in one eye now."

"I don't give a goddamn about your cousin," Reece said.

"Said they were doing it 'cause they didn't want to beat on no white man like Dale told them to."

"Who?" Morris asked. He released her hair and she slid to the ground. Strands cascaded every which way, the ends burned to a crisp and still smoking. They felt hot on her skin and on her shoulders through her clothes and she had to reach out to hold the mass of it by the parts that weren't afire, trying to keep it from igniting.

"I don't know," Diller answered. "Just what my cousin said. Said they been drinking and were telling jokes about how some fella Dale wanted them to beat up a white man. He didn't know what it meant."

"Who the hell is Dale?" Morris asked her.

She tried to think. She'd known so many men who came here to drown their sorrows, plenty of Donnys and a Danny and countless Davids, but no Dale.

"I don't know," said her broken voice, sounding nothing like herself. She was squatting there in her own filth and her hair smelled of burned onions and worse things and she felt so befouled and destroyed but all she wanted to do was live through this moment.

"Those white men who beat up my cousin," Diller said. "They left a dog tag behind."

"What?" both brothers asked in unison.

"My cousin saw it there next day. Chain musta broke off when they were beating him. Got one of their names on it."

The brothers regarded each other. They may have passed each other secret looks, but she couldn't see them all that clearly what with the hair in her face and the way she was panting and the tears in her eyes.

"She dies, the first person they'll come looking for is us."

"And they know we're in the state."

"Another time, then."

Morris crouched before her. "You look as low as we could've brung you right now. Remember that feeling. Because it ain't the lowest. We will bring you quite a bit lower if you say word one about this to anyone. Got that?"

She told them that she got that. Then Reece picked Diller up by the arms and the three of them exited through the back door. She wondered if she would ever again see her Negro cook of seven years, but at that moment all she cared about was that she was alive and they were gone.

Unsteadily she rose to her feet and removed her pistol from the drawer. She'd never again sweep her porch without it on her person. And if she laid eyes on those giants once more, she would send them straight to their brother.

26

"Records," said one of the voices Lucius didn't want to hear.

"This is Officer Boggs. I need a file pulled, please."

"Boy, I ain't your errand girl." She hung up.

Because the Butler Street officers didn't have access to headquarters or its Records Department, they needed to call when they needed a file. More often than not, they were ignored or denied. Today's particular refusal was relatively mild, thanks to the lack of cuss words.

Boggs was at the Y early, trying to do some research. His next recourse would be to put his request in writing, via McInnis, their liaison to headquarters. But the sergeant did not enjoy the fact that his job duties included delivering mail and other paperwork for his subordinates. And did Boggs really want to put this request in writing?

He wanted to know everything about Julie's ex-boyfriend. Clearly she was scared. Even if Jeremiah didn't have a history of violence, five years of state prison and work camps were enough to make most men develop a predilection for it.

Dewey had spoken to Boggs last night, asking if he was okay and was there anything anyone could do. *We didn't tell anyone,* Dewey had said. *We made the arrest and filed the report, and we mentioned he said he was the father, but we didn't say nothing about her being your fiancée.* Boggs thanked him, embarrassed that his newfound family dysfunction was known to anyone else.

He was a mess. He was so much a mess that he couldn't figure out where the mess ended or started, didn't know what thread to grab and pull first. The heartache and confusion over Julie lying to him again, the sudden limbo that their entire relationship had been thrust into, his own role as Sage's replacement father suddenly in question. It was as though Lucius had known who he was—a fiancé, a soon-to-be father—but now he was neither. He didn't know what was left.

Could he even consider marrying her anymore? He wanted to tell Smith about his dilemma—Tommy had probably experienced every conceivable woman-related predicament, so surely he had some insight—but he felt too ashamed. What did this say about him, that he could be fooled like this? What judge of character was he, and how decent a cop could he be if his own woman could deceive him?

Shame overwhelmed him. And anger, anger at Julie and at himself for being so stupid. What was her next secret? How had he steered himself into this disaster, and how could he get himself out?

Earlier that day, Boggs had tried to hide his despair when he sat down to lunch with his older brother. He didn't dare tell Reginald about Julie's lies. The diner, around the corner from Reginald's office at Atlanta Life Insurance Company, had been buzzing with activity, men in suits loosening their belts as they dined over barbecue sandwiches or pigs' feet and collards. Lucius had been one of the only patrons not wearing a tie.

"Just tell me you aren't marrying her out of some sense of honor," Reginald said.

"What does that mean?"

"I swear, it amazes me you didn't follow the old man up to the pulpit," Reginald said. "It's all about duty to you, right? You see a poor woman and a little boy without a father and now you feel like you've been called to do something about it."

"It's not that simple." Yet he hated how close to the mark his brother's arrows landed.

"But it's part of the story, isn't it? You like being the savior to her. The knight in shining armor. Saving her from that rundown street with the crazy neighbors and her job slaving over white folks."

"I don't—wait, how do you know where she lives?"

"I wrote out half the policies on that block—not that those folks have many. Which is my point."

"What's your point, that she's poor?"

"My point is, you like her because she's poor."

Lucius felt his ire rise. "First of all, I don't *like* her. I love her. Which you seem to be overlooking here, but I see it as a fairly crucial point. Second of all, I'm not marrying her to *save her*. If she didn't have that little boy, I would have proposed *sooner,* a lot sooner. But he deserves a father. What I'm about to do isn't easy, Reginald."

"You've always liked things the hard way, brother. But why's it have to be you? Some other man did that. Some other man walked out. It's not your debt to pay."

He slammed the table. "She's not a debt, dammit. Maybe you can't see love for what it is, you been with Florence so long, her 'loving' you for all those minks and jewels you put her in, you wondering whether she'd still love you if you got laid off one day."

"Whoa." Reginald's expression turned to the kind of cold blankness Lucius had seen on strangers while walking his beat, strangers who were about to throw a punch. "That's out of line."

"You're not holding your tongue about Julie."

"I'm talking about *you*. I want to make sure *you're* doing this for the right reasons. That's all."

"I am. I promise you that. She's not a reclamation project. She's everything."

A few quiet seconds passed, awkwardly, hands in their pockets, afraid to make a disturbance. All the while, despite how strongly he'd spoken, Boggs wondered if he was indeed making a terrible mistake. He couldn't tell his brother about Jeremiah, at least not yet.

"Then I'm glad she'll be in the family," Reginald said. And with that, he lifted his sweet tea in a toast. Lucius met the glass with his. After a pause, Reginald added, "I suppose Florence is getting a tad spoiled."

"I'm sorry I said that. You know I love her."

"It's all right. You say that again, though," and he theatrically puffed out his chest, adopting a mock tough-guy grimace, "and it's fighting words, little brother."

Lucius laughed. "You'd lose that fight, office man."

Heading outside, Reginald asked if they had any idea who'd attacked Smith's brother-in-law yet. Boggs admitted they didn't, but he expressed hope that at least some of the white cops over there would insist on order.

"Well, I hope that's the last of it," Reginald said. "It's more than just housing, you know. A lot of money's at stake."

"What do you mean?"

"One of our vice presidents, Clancy Darden, he's also a big investor in real estate. He built up some lots over by the public housing on the West Side in the thirties. Anyway, this isn't widely known, but he recently bought another big tract of open land northeast of Hanford Park. If the color line keeps shifting and Hanford Park becomes colored, he'll get to build more houses for Negroes on that new land."

"Great." Boggs still lived with his parents, saving money, but he desperately wanted a home for Julie and Sage. He had recently done some house shopping himself with a "realtist"—so called because Realtors didn't admit colored members—but had been discouraged by the prices. The scarcity of housing for Negroes drove up the cost. If more houses, like the ones Darden wanted to build, became available, maybe Boggs could get a place after all.

"But if white folks in Hanford Park fight back and that area stays all-white," Reginald went on, "he'll need to unload that land to white builders, probably for a *lot* less money."

Boggs hadn't thought through the economic implications of the attack before. He thanked his brother for the tip.

Hours later, at the end of an uneventful shift, Boggs called Records again and finally reached the one clerk who didn't hate him on principle.

"Evening, Sheila," he said after recognizing her voice. "This is Officer Boggs."

"How you doing?"

"Can't complain. Still got a job."

"Hey, me, too. We must be doing something right. What can I get for you?"

He had never met her, the only Records clerk who would dare help the Negro officers, so long as her colleagues weren't listening. The third or fourth time they'd spoken, he'd learned her name, but that was all. She'd pulled a number of files for him over the years, most of them routine (if a white clerk actually doing her job when requested by a Negro officer could ever be considered "routine"), but some rather sensitive. She had won his trust, though still he knew to tread carefully. She only called him when the other clerks had stepped away, and she frequently rushed off the phone when one of them returned. He didn't even know what she looked like.

"I'm curious about the arrest records for a Jeremiah Tanner. He's probably twenty-three or twenty-four. Recently got out of Reidsville and I need to know why."

She called him back fifteen minutes later.

"I can have that file over to you tomorrow, but it might not have all you need. You'll have to go to the G-men for that."

"Why?"

"Mr. Jeremiah Tanner, who by the way is twenty-three but has a birthday coming up on November 2, got himself busted for stealing cigarettes off the trains."

"That's a federal crime?"

"It was in May of '45. War was still on." She was talking with something in her mouth, probably a cigarette. "Judging from some of the files of his colleagues here, he was part of a group that had been boosting from the trains while they worked on the freight lines at Pullman Yards. Some of what they'd looted were smokes from army cars headed to Fort Benning. APD did the arrests, but then the G-men must have heard army property was involved. Charged him with smuggling, theft from the military, and aiding and abetting the enemy."

Boggs almost laughed. "Aiding and abetting, are you serious?"

"He plea-dealed his way out of that one but still got the five years."

"Who was the arresting officer?"

"Eugene Slater."

Boggs knew the name: Slater had been friends with Rakestraw's corrupt former partner, Dunlow. Based on association, Boggs figured Slater was just as involved in scams and grafts as Dunlow had been. Did Slater help arrest a gang of Negro smugglers because they weren't paying him a cut, or because they were competing with a similar operation he'd been running?

"Can you send that file over?" he asked.

"Sure, but it's a mess. All higgledy-piggledy." He could hear her shuffling papers. "Oh, *hello*. Gets better. Looks like the fella they really wanted to arrest was one Isaiah Tanner, Jeremiah's brother. But they never got to him, because he was killed first."

Boggs had asked Julie if there was anything else he needed to know, anything at all. The walls in this tiny basement seemed to be closing in on him. "Who killed him?"

A pause as she exhaled, reading. "His murder is marked 'Unsolved.' Looks like Jeremiah was a suspect, but they never charged him or anyone else for it."

Julie told me Jeremiah wasn't violent. She said she'd never been scared of him before. Had she missed something, or had she lied? He tried to make sense of this. Think beyond himself and Julie, ponder a move that might not make things worse for a change.

He asked, "What was the name of the FBI agent heading the case?"

27

Midafternoon and the Rook looked closed. After Jeremiah knocked on the glass door, it opened and a tall, light-skinned Negro in a green sport coat and black tie shook his head at the mere sight of him.

"We're closed."

"I want to talk to Feckless. I'm an old friend. Jeremiah Tanner."

The man stared him down. "Wait here. And you do yourself a favor: call him Mr. Feck." The man had some mild kind of accent, from a city Jeremiah didn't know. "I only hear 'Feckless' from a few folks, and you ain't one, understand?" He closed the door.

Clouds had claimed the skies above Jeremiah, and he feared rain with the animalistic terror of one who has no roof, no change of clothes.

The man returned with a flat expression, opening the door all the way. "Get in. This way."

Jeremiah followed a step behind, smelling wood cleaner, cigarette smoke, and a sour tang from the night before. The floors shining, the maroon-painted walls adorned with framed pictures of Negro boxers and entertainers, the ceiling itself a relief map of intricate plaster molding, the glass chandelier over the dance floor sparkling even with the lights off. A Negro owned this?

"You stink, man." The man cursed under his breath as he led Jeremiah to the gleaming bar, behind which stood a man he'd never seen looking so good. His hair was longer than Jeremiah remembered and combed back with pomade, sleek as any white man's. His medium-toned skin somehow looked lighter than Jeremiah remembered it, but maybe that was just because it was so clean, well shaven but for the narrow mustache above his curling smile. His eyes hazel, Jeremiah remembered that now, lending an almost feline power to his gaze.

"Jeremiah Tanner. Been a long time." He extended his hand. He wore a black-and-gray-checked blazer over a crisp white shirt and red tie knotted in some complicated kind of way.

Jeremiah shook, conscious of the grime layering his fingers, and the funk the doorman had already commented on. Was there anything in his hair? Probably was.

"This your place, huh?"

"It is indeed. You came at the wrong time, though. Come by 'round midnight you want to see yourself a show. Ben Webster's in town, taking some time off Ellington's band to do a little tour of his own."

He could tell this was supposed to be impressive, so he nodded.

"Sit down." After Jeremiah had obeyed, perching himself atop a stool hewn from ash and topped with red satin, Feckless said, "You just got out, didn't you?"

"Few days ago."

"You hungry?"

He did not *feel* hungry, he *was* hungry, to his very core. Hunger was all he'd been reduced to, a physical state so extreme it crowded out any emotion. He hadn't *felt* anything in a day, maybe two. Since the jail slop he'd been give after his arrest at Julie's house, he'd eaten not a single solid meal, begging scraps off some old acquaintances one night and even scavenging food from trash barrels that very morning. He had known hunger in prison, but, without a scheduled meal on the horizon, this was even yet worse, not only a constant sucking at his stomach but also a never-ending headache, a tremor in his limbs.

"Leon, whip me up some scrambled eggs!" Feckless called out to an unseen helper.

"You don't need to do that."

"I don't need to see a man starve to death in front of me, neither."

"Appreciate it." He looked around the place, noticing that the sour-faced doorman was lingering by a pool table, out of earshot but watching. "This place is amazing. Ain't been in something like this in . . . ever. Things worked out for you."

"Timing, son. I used to play drums in a ragtime band, before you knew me. Got me a refined sense of timing. Knowing when to make a move. Seemed to me, time was right to move out of our other business. And soon thereafter, it started falling apart."

He'd always wondered why Feckless hadn't been arrested with the others. Maybe it was as simple as timing—when the FBI came along, it had been a few months since Feckless and Isaiah had parted ways. He couldn't recall the reasons and had assumed there had been some falling-out between Feckless and his brother.

"I moved my money into legitimate pursuits," Feckless continued with his biography. "I invited your brother to do the same, matter of fact. But that wasn't his style. He liked what y'all were doing, didn't cotton to my crazy thoughts about going straight."

"No. Going straight don't sound like him."

"His tragic flaw. See, that world we were in, it don't get no bigger. If you want something on a higher level, you need to move into a new world. That, my old friend, requires the kind of boldness and thinking Isaiah did not possess."

A bald, heavyset Negro in a cook's apron emerged from the kitchen with a plate of scrambled eggs and a heaping helping of grits. The plate held more food than Jeremiah had eaten in two days. Feckless filled a glass of water while Jeremiah tried not to shovel the food in as fast as he wanted to.

"Funny seeing you again," Feckless said. "Like seeing Isaiah, too, that's how much y'all look alike. Like a vision from the grave."

He'd heard people say he and his brother had the same eyes, the same serious brow. He himself had never noticed any similarities, certainly not in their bodies, Jeremiah gangly and long, Isaiah broad and powerful.

Feckless said, "Some folks say you killed him."

So there it was. "Yeah. I heard that a lot."

"Other folks say it was a cop, and you kept your mouth shut instead of telling on him."

"I never hurt my brother," Jeremiah said after finishing the last bite. "I heard some folks say it was *you*. But I never believed that."

Feckless let that linger. "That's good. Means you're not here for some vengeance thing."

"No."

"One thing I've wondered, though. Lotta the old boys from that ring wound up dead. But you didn't."

"Lord has bigger plans for me."

Feckless watched him for a second, in pure amazement, then burst out laughing. So hard his eyes watered.

"Oh yeah, Pure-boy. It really is you. *Big plans,* all right."

When Feckless finally stopped laughing, and had taken a sip of water to wash down Jeremiah's ridiculousness, Jeremiah asked, "I was wondering, you having this place and all, if there was anything I could do for you. I was a hard worker on the rail yards, before that other stuff. 'Fore I was led astray. And you being legitimate now, I was wondering, you know . . ."

His voice trailed off as Feckless changed his expression into a hardened stare, so abruptly Jeremiah wondered if he'd missed something. This new, rougher-edged Feckless said, "You keeping silent all that time, I guess that sort of silence proves loyalty. That what you want me to think? That supposed to impress me? That your résumé?"

"People can think what they want. Including you. I just need work, that's all. If you don't have nothing, that's fine." He stood up. "Thanks for the food, Les. Good seeing you."

He'd made it ten steps when Feckless said, "Hold up." Then he addressed the big doorman. "Hey, Q, do me a favor and grab Pure-boy a mop. Might be we could put him to some use after all."

28

Boggs had known it was a problem when the FBI agent, reached on the phone, proposed meeting at the Rich's lunch counter downtown. Now the reckoning had come.

It had taken only one day but several phone calls to reach the agent who, according to Boggs's secret helper in Records, had made the arrests that eventually led to Jeremiah Tanner's imprisonment. He knew he couldn't expect any help from the APD officer involved, Sergeant Slater, known for being a virulent racist. He was hoping the FBI man wouldn't be quite so hostile.

Boggs took an extra-deep breath as he entered Rich's Department Store. He had shopped here only a few times. He and his family tried to buy what they needed from the Negro merchants in Sweet Auburn, where they were actually allowed to use dressing rooms and didn't have to wait for white customers to be helped first regardless of how long they'd been waiting in line.

He stifled a sneeze as he strode through the miasma of women's perfumes at the cosmetics counter, then past the cases of jewelry, where he was watched very carefully indeed by the white clerks.

The lunch counter was like a small diner grafted onto the side of the store, seven booths and a long L-shaped bar. Three of the booths were occupied by groups of women and some children, and at the bar sat one couple and three solo men. Boggs had never seen a photo of Special Agent Doolittle, who had quipped on the phone, "I'll be the one who looks like an FBI agent," and damn if he wasn't right. He sat nursing a coffee and staring at a newspaper spread regally beside him, as if he had no qualms about taking up the space for three people. He was a particularly pale white man with dark hair combed to the side, slick with whatever product white men used. His suit charcoal gray, his tie black with three diagonal white stripes, he also would have been correct had he predicted, *I'll be the one who looks like a funeral director.*

Boggs was making his approach when the woman behind the counter snapped, "Hey, you can't come in here!"

Special Agent Doolittle looked up from his paper, confused. He glanced first at the irate waitress, then made eye contact with Boggs, who leaned closer to the FBI man, keeping his feet a more respectable distance away.

"I'm Boggs. As you can see, we're going to have to talk somewhere else."

Doolittle stared at Boggs. The entire room was watching them.

"You need to leave!" the woman shouted at Boggs, louder than before. A waiter was hurrying their way.

Doolittle held up his hand to stop them from their energetic enforcement of Jim Crow decorum. Still regarding Boggs, his face calm and unreadable, he said, "I just started my coffee. I'll meet you outside in a few minutes."

Boggs stood outside the Broad Street entrance, trying not to look like a loiterer who might deserve the attention of a passing beat cop. He loathed coming downtown, where simply standing was cause for white people's concern.

Groups of secretaries skirted by on lunch break, fedoras bobbed as three men laughed at inside jokes, taxis dropped off and picked up identical fares. Nearly everyone smoked. A white man in a GI uniform almost bumped into Boggs. He hadn't seen a man in an Army uniform in many months. Judging from the national news, the drama in Korea, it may become a more common sight again, which seemed hard to believe.

After a good fifteen minutes, Doolittle finally emerged, stopping just at the border of what would have been too close.

"So you're Officer Boggs." He paused. "You didn't sound Negro on the phone."

"How do I sound now?"

"Now I don't so much focus on the voice as the face."

Had Boggs expected anything better? Doolittle spoke in a flat, midwestern accent of some kind. If anything, Boggs's experiences with non-Southerners in the army had been even more awkward, as such men weren't used to being so close to Negroes and were unclear as to the most effective ways to demonstrate their dominance.

"I was hoping you could tell me a few things about Jeremiah and Isaiah Tanner."

"Let's walk." They headed south then turned on Peachtree, toward Five Points. Cars honked horns and streetcar brakes squealed as vehicles sat bumper to bumper. Clouds of exhaust and cigarette smoke marred the otherwise crystalline autumn sky. An enormous billboard reminded them that they'd feel better if they drank a Coca-Cola, Atlanta's chief export to the world. "I was wondering why an Atlanta cop would want to revisit that case. Now I suppose it makes a bit of sense."

"How so?"

Doolittle's fedora sat two inches taller than Boggs's. From what Boggs had heard, most FBI agents were in fact desk men, glorified attorneys despite the Hollywood image of intrepid derring-do, but this fellow looked like someone you'd want on your side when you had to knock down a door. "How do you fellows get along with the white cops?"

"We keep to our territory, and they're supposed to keep to theirs."

Doolittle grinned. "You have a lot of territory for ten men."

At least he hadn't said *boys*. "We manage."

"I'll bet. You ever bump up against a white cop named Gene Slater?"

He'd turned to face Boggs when he asked this. They were waiting at the Five Points intersection now, where a streetcar had inexplicably stopped in the center of the street and was now enduring the wrath of horns in all directions.

"Not personally, but I know who Slater is." No need to say more. Boggs knew that white people had little tolerance for criticism of other white people—even someone they loathed—if it came from a Negro.

"Isaiah Tanner was the ringleader of a smuggling operation that had been running for at least two years before we shut it down. And when I say ringleader I mean he was the head *Negro*, operating with the tacit permission of the Atlanta police and possibly some Atlanta business-men. He and his accessories, including his younger brother, had legitimate jobs at the rail yards, and they used their access to take what they wanted. With all the rail lines coming into Atlanta, this city is as good a smuggling hub as any landlocked city could possibly be."

The streetcar finally moved, and they crossed the street.

"They started stealing from cars headed to army camps. Normally, I could care less about small-time crime like that. But we were tasked with protecting and enforcing the law at all factories, plants, ports, and rail yards that were associated with the war effort, and that made it our job to shut down little scammers like the Tanners."

"APD made the first arrests and then called you in, right?"

Doolittle laughed. "No. I don't think APD had much incentive to do that. They were getting a cut from the smugglers and looking the other way. Until we came in. I personally made the first arrest, of Isaiah Tanner's best friend. But not such close friends that he didn't spill that first night, telling us everything about their operation—everything except the name of the officer who kept it in business. He claimed that only Isaiah knew that."

The APD file had claimed that Slater had made the first arrests. Doolittle didn't seem to be lying, so the files were wrong. Boggs had long known that paperwork left behind by white cops was as dishonest as the men themselves, but still the experience was frustrating, like constantly being handed maps to streets that didn't exist.

"We moved quickly to arrest everyone else, including Jeremiah, who wasn't even eighteen at the time. He'd lied about his age to get the job. We couldn't find Isaiah, though; he seemed to have vanished for a couple days. And then we found him, in the backseat of a Ford parked in an alley in Darktown, shot three times in the chest."

"Shot in the Ford or dumped there?"

"Dumped there, with a blanket covering the corpse. Probably killed two days earlier. The car was registered to a deaf old Negro lady who lived two blocks from the Tanners. She'd never seen the Ford in her life."

They stopped at the next intersection. Above them, billboard pasters were applying a new Coca-Cola ad on top of an older Coca-Cola ad. Boggs asked, "Would you mind if I looked at your files?"

"You still haven't told me why you want to know any of this."

"Jeremiah Tanner just got out of Reidsville and he's already caused some trouble. We want to know who we're dealing with. And I was wondering if there was any chance that he killed Isaiah."

Doolittle shook his head. "I don't see it. From what I could tell, Isaiah was in charge and Jeremiah was his loyal assistant, who wouldn't have dreamed of hurting his big brother. I honestly liked him; he was this meek, scripture-quoting kid, far from the surly type. APD tried to get him to confess to the murder—and I mean they *really tried*," and in those three syllables Boggs glimpsed the shadows of batons, rubber hoses, brass knuckles, "but I personally put a stop to that. Besides, they had no evidence."

Boggs wasn't sure if he should feel relieved or disappointed.

"So who did you like for Isaiah's murder?"

Doolittle grinned. "Here we are, federal agents trying to close down a threat to army supply lines, a smuggling operation that we had every reason to believe was sanctioned by Atlanta police, and *right then* is when Isaiah gets himself killed? Far be it from me to impugn the reputation of an Atlanta policeman, but doesn't it sound to you like maybe one of your fellow officers killed Isaiah to keep him from talking?"

He never thought of the white cops as his *fellow officers*. "Of course it does," Boggs said.

In fact, it was exactly like what had happened to Thunder Malley. A dirty cop helps protect a smuggling racket, and when an outside force—the FBI in '45, Negro cops today—moves to stop it, the Negro atop the chain is killed before he can inform on the corrupt cop.

"I'd love to see those files," Boggs said as they stopped in front of an office building.

"I'll see what I can do." Which seemed to be his polite, WASP way of saying, *No*.

"Did you look into Slater?"

"Again, it was our charge to defend America's war-industry rail yards against all sabotage, including theft. We did that. Drawing up a sting to root out corrupt municipal police wasn't on the table." He put his hands in his pockets, perhaps embarrassed to admit the G-men's inaction.

"Were any women involved? Did you ever talk to someone named Julie Cannon?"

"None were charged, no. We interviewed some relatives, but I don't recall that name." Doolittle paused. "So tell me, what did your sergeant say when you asked him about the case?"

"I haven't asked him yet."

Doolittle watched Boggs for a moment, and Boggs wondered if he'd made himself look amateurish with that admission. "Probably a good idea not to."

"Why is that?"

Doolittle smiled. "He was Slater's partner."

29

Julie was readying for bed when the phone rang.

"I'm sorry I yelled at you," Lucius said.

They hadn't spoken in days. That wasn't so unusual, as their incompatible work schedules made even brief phone calls a challenge during the week. But this particular silence had felt all the more chilled given their last talk, her admissions to him, his storming off afterward. "I know I didn't handle that as well as I could have."

"I'm sorry I didn't tell you the truth," she said.

Silence for a few seconds. "I just wanted you to know, we're going to keep our eyes out for him, and we'll keep our eyes on your place. Another officer, Champ Jennings, is going to drop by later to get an additional statement from you."

"Why?"

"It's standard. We need a report that this man has been hassling you, and that can justify certain things on our part."

"What are you . . . ?"

"I thought you wanted us to protect you and Sage."

Us. That word had never seemed so distant, so exclusionary. As though he were calling on behalf of the Atlanta Police Department, not himself. "I don't think he wants to harm us, Lucius. He wants . . . He wants to turn back the clock."

"Just answer Officer Jennings's questions when he comes and we'll take care of the rest."

"Okay."

"Julie. You neglected to mention that Jeremiah's brother was killed." *What to say?*

"And that it was never solved. I asked you specifically if you thought

Jeremiah was violent, and you said no. Do you think there's any chance he did it?"

"No. No chance. He never, ever would have done that."

"Why didn't you at least tell me?"

So the conversation had begun with him apologizing, but the focus again was on all that she had done wrong. That she'd grown used to this didn't make it any more pleasant.

"Everyone says the cops did it. They tried to pin it on Jeremiah."

"So that's the new complete truth, as of this evening. What's the new complete truth going to be tomorrow?"

She sighed. "Jeremiah made some bad decisions. When we started seeing each other, he had a job at the rail yards. He had money, but not so much that I thought he was mixed up in anything bad." She remembered their Christmas together. He'd actually bought her a dress. Who bought his girlfriend a dress? But he'd had two sisters, and the money, so apparently they'd all gone to one of the downtown department stores. Yellow cotton with short sleeves, lace trim on the collar and hem, not right for the season at all, and dressier than anything she'd ever owned, but she wore it as many times as she could the next spring, until he was arrested.

She went on, "First he told me how his brother and some friends were stealing from trains, but *he* wasn't. I told him to stay out of it, told him theft is theft. He had a decent job and should be happy with that. He told me he wouldn't get involved."

"So what happened?"

"He went along with his brother, I guess. One day I'm at Jeremiah and Isaiah's place and they have some friends over telling stories, and I put one and one together. I mean, Lucius, I was seventeen. I wasn't going to jump up and confront him in front of all those people. But later, when we had a chance to talk alone, I told him I was upset. Told him I might not even want to see him if he kept up with that. I didn't want to be with a criminal."

"What did he say?"

"He apologized. Said he'd back out, but he wasn't sure how. He couldn't afford to leave his job, and he felt . . . beholden to his brother. And intimidated by him."

"So when did you . . . find out about Sage?"

He could be so awkward sometimes. "I didn't know for sure that I was in the family way 'til he'd been arrested."

He seemed to think about something for a moment. "Did you ever meet a white man, a police officer, named Slater? Or McInnis?"

"Meet a white cop? No."

"Did Jeremiah ever talk about them having help from the police? A cop at the top of the pyramid, calling the shots or keeping them from being arrested?"

She sighed. "I didn't ask for details about what they were doing—I didn't want to know. You're making me feel like I'm being interrogated all over again."

"Police questioned you?"

"Yeah." He was infinitely more polite and gentle than the cracker cops who'd terrified her back then, who'd made jokes about Jeremiah, who'd grabbed her ass when they'd escorted her into their dimly lit room and had given her every indication that they'd take advantage of her sexually if she didn't cooperate. She remembered those two cops quite well, not their names but certainly their faces, and it wasn't until an older cop had shown up that the two dropped the suggestiveness and stuck to the facts, though they remained plenty hostile. "They asked what you're asking, and I told them I had no idea."

"I'm sorry, I just . . ." He sighed. "I have to handle so much, Julie. I can't handle all the lies on top of it."

"Sometimes people lie because they have good reasons for it." She didn't want to rehash this, didn't even want to remember it. It wasn't a part of her anymore. That was one of the many reasons she was with Lucius, so that time in her life could officially be over. Yet he seemed to enjoy reminding her of all her mistakes.

"I'm sorry you went through that. It must have been hard."

He had no idea, Julie thought. To have your own man put away like that, and you can visit him but on the other side of bars, can't even hug him, and you have to listen to all the guards' comments when you see him, such disgusting things you decide you can't go back there again. So you feel guilty for not seeing him. This was all before the trial—she never dared visit him once he was convicted. Lucius didn't know what it was like for everyone to say the people you love are mixed up in that, that they're dirty criminals, and you probably are, too. He didn't know what it was like to lose a job or cause your family to get thrown out of an apartment because no one likes to see an unmarried girl who's expecting. Come home one day and all your things are on the sidewalk, not even in boxes, just tossed there, and your daddy's pleading with a stranger and Mama's crying and there's nothing you can do. He didn't know what it was like for most of your friends to turn their backs on you.

She said, "I'm sorry, too. Look, I can't promise to let you in my head all the time. Sometimes there are bad things in there."

"I thought I was clear that I loved the whole you. Whatever else you're carrying inside."

Perhaps she was overthinking, but why had he said *loved* instead of *love*? "I guess I was afraid to put that to the test," she said.

"Well . . . life has a way of testing us anyway. Look, I need to go. Good night."

And that was it. No *love you*, no explanation about what this meant for them, whether there even still was a "them." She had no idea who they were to each other anymore. She knew only that it was late and she was alone.

～

"I've got a problem with Julie," Boggs finally told Smith, unable to keep it inside any longer.

"You'd best get used to that, once you're married. Can't walk away from those problems no more."

That's how easy it must be for his partner, Boggs realized. Win a woman, take what you want, enjoy it for as long as it goes, and, once she's "a problem," drop her for the next one.

Smith's response almost made him reconsider saying any more. Yet he told his partner what he'd learned: about Jeremiah, about his criminal past and involvement with schemes overseen by Sergeant Slater, about all Julie's lies.

"I don't know what to do. My father nearly disowned me for proposing to her. Thinks I'm crazy to 'trade down' like this. If he finds out Sage's father is back in town . . ." He shook his head. "She's *humiliated* me, Tommy. I don't think I can just let that go."

"A man needs an audience to be humiliated. *She* laughing at you?"

"Of course not."

"Anyone else know?"

"Not yet, but if the father stays on the scene, it's only a matter of time."

"Then you need him escorted off the scene."

"You mean, arrest him again? For nothing?"

"If he's threatened her, we can get him for that, right?"

Boggs couldn't tell if he was being indecisive and weak to equivocate like this. But it felt wrong to use their position this way. It wouldn't solve any problem other than Jeremiah's physical presence, when the problem felt so much larger to him.

Smith said, "You're overthinking. As usual."

"I'm wondering if this is a sign. That our whole relationship's been a mistake. That I was a fool to let it go this long, and Jeremiah showing up like this is a second chance God is giving me to make right, just in time."

"Well, that's different, then. I was going off the assumption you cared for her."

He felt that like a slap. "I *do*. But that's not the point."

"Then what the hell *is* the point? What are we talking about? You don't care for her, you leave her. Let her get with that other fellow. What's the problem?"

The problem was whether he could ever trust her again. She was giving him every sign that she was bad news, hardly a woman to marry. Was marital strife inevitable with a woman like that? As much as he loved her, and cared for Sage, didn't he *need* to walk away from her, to spare himself—and them—further harm down the road? Or was he being too proud and unforgiving, too much his father's son?

None of that entered Smith's thinking, apparently. Boggs shook his head, marveling at his partner's straightforwardness. "Things are so simple for you, aren't they?"

Smith's chin dropped. "Yes, suh, things is mighty simple with me. Not as complicated as you high-rollin' Negroes, suh."

"I didn't mean it like that."

"Then how *did* you mean it? I don't come from your home-owning family with all those big expectations on your shoulders? I don't have a reverend father to disown me for marrying a maid? You got any idea how many maids I've known?" A cocky grunt. "In the biblical sense?"

"I didn't mean to insult you, all right? I'm sorry. I figured you've been in all kinds of messes with women and would have some advice."

"I can't tell you how to feel, man. But if *I* loved a girl, and another man tried to get in on the scene?" Another grunt. "I would remove that problem right quick."

Boggs looked into his partner's eyes, trying to sift through the layers of meaning there, which was difficult when the look in those eyes was so hard, so definitive. He wondered what he could do, what he was capable of, reeling at the array of possibilities he'd never before considered.

"There's a few other things," Boggs said. He explained how the FBI file, a copy of which Doolittle had indeed sent over, listed Lester Feck as a past associate of Isaiah Tanner. Feck had once worked at the rail yards with Isaiah; the feds believed he may have once been a part of the smuggling ring and had even questioned him when they made the other arrests, but by that point Feck had had a falling-out with the Tanners and bought his club. Feck, whose nightclub Smith seemed to frequent, hadn't given them any dirt on Isaiah, and they'd never had enough evidence to arrest him for what he may have done in the past.

And Boggs explained how McInnis had once been partners with Slater, the crooked officer who'd been involved with the smugglers.

"I don't . . . I can't see it," Smith said. "McInnis is clean. He's never struck me as the type to take bribes; he even led that anticorruption thing awhile back."

Boggs tried to peer through all the lies and half-truths he'd been told by so many people lately: his fiancée, his boss, and, no doubt, several other people. He asked, "You really trust him?"

Smith nearly laughed. "Whoa, I said the man's clean, but do I *trust* him? A white man?" He shook his head. "Of course not."

30

Two knocks and the door opened without being invited.

"Hello there, Jeremiah."

He thought of the white man as Officer Tall. He actually wasn't all that tall, Jeremiah realized now, but something about the way he carried himself made him seem more imposing, as if he were perpetually standing on something. He'd been a distant, lingering presence years ago, this cop who would show up and take money from Jeremiah's brother.

"Hello, Officer, sir."

Jeremiah had been sitting on the wooden shipping pallet that, adorned with a thin blanket, was his makeshift bed. He took the Bible that had been on his lap and put it on top of the cardboard box that served as the only other piece of furniture in his room, his home, this tiny space in the basement below a smoke shop. The shop owner rented the space from Feckless, who owned this building one door down from his club. Feckless was letting Jeremiah sleep here temporarily, until he found a place. His new job was nothing special, cleaning the club and doing dishes, grunt work, but at least the days ended with a bit of money in his pocket.

"It's 'Sergeant' now." Officer Tall closed the door behind him and Jeremiah could immediately smell what was in the brown paper bag the white man carried, could see the grease stains of the fried chicken. "Good to see you again, boy."

Jeremiah wasn't sure if he should stand, if that would be more polite, or if Officer Tall would see that as a threat, so he stayed put, hands at his sides. He was wearing the same clothes he had worn for as many days as he had been out of prison.

"It's good to see you, too, Sergeant, sir."

Officer Tall looked around the room. "I heard you had fallen far, boy, and I'd say this confirms it. You hungry?" He offered Jeremiah the bag.

"Yes, sir. Thank you, sir." The bag seemed incredibly heavy—was there an entire bird in there?

Officer Tall watched him for a moment, a strange look in his eyes, at least as far as Jeremiah could tell based on the tiny quick glances he allowed himself. You were not supposed to look white folks in the eye, certainly not police officers.

"I know you were in there a long time, boy, but I hope you never forgot you could've been a lot worse. Could have been dead. I do hope you remember that."

"Most definitely, sir. I'm very grateful to be alive. Thank the Lord."

"And thank me as well."

"Yessir. Thank you."

Officer Tall looked at the tiny space, basically a closet. A lone lamp was plugged into an outlet in the hallway thanks to an extralong cord. To use a toilet, Jeremiah had to creep upstairs and out the back door, then walk to the Rook's restroom. He'd used the alley a few times when the Rook was closed.

"It's a shame what happened to your brother. I know there have been whispers it might have been me who done him in, but I never did kill Isaiah. What happened to him was tragic."

Jeremiah wasn't sure what he was supposed to say. He opted for, "Yessir."

"I been keeping my eyes out for who mighta killed him," Officer Tall continued. "Couldn't mount a real investigation at the time, on account of all the trouble that had been kicked up then. Had to keep a low profile."

"Yessir." *You haven't even thought of my brother until you heard I got out.*

Silence for a few seconds, Officer Tall staring at him, perhaps to see if Jeremiah would give something away. He prayed to the Lord that he not give anything away. He shouldn't even think bad thoughts about Officer Tall; white people had a way of reading your thoughts. They had powers Negroes did not possess, and Jeremiah needed to be careful.

"I understand your family situation is rather complicated right now."

He must mean the Negro policeman, Jeremiah thought. He didn't know how to respond, couldn't think of words that would do justice to his feelings.

"He ain't going to just walk away from her, you best understand that. You want to raise that little boy, there's but one way to do it."

"Yessir." Not understanding.

"You like the thought of him climbing on top of your woman?"

"Nosir."

"He's a hell of a nigger. Acts all churchified and high, I suppose there's a *chance* he ain't stuck himself in her yet. There's a *chance* you can have her back before he's spoiled her, understand?"

Jeremiah had never been one for such coarse talk but he said, "Yessir," in hopes that would stop Officer Tall's comments.

"Eat, boy. I know you're hungry."

How did he know? Jeremiah was given some food at the club during his break, but barely enough to keep him going. He hadn't wanted to spend all his meager pay on food, knowing he needed to save money to win Julie back, so he'd barely eaten, and not in many hours.

Despite his nerves to be in the officer's presence, despite the tightness that had not yet released his chest, he opened the bag. He reached for the waxed paper and picked up the top portion, a fat drumstick attached to a thick breast. Good God, it smelled delicious. He tore into it and hated how he must look, the fierce bites and the grease on his lips, using his sleeve as a napkin. He hated how self-esteem was a luxury.

"These colored cops, they think they run this city now," Officer Tall said. "Think they can rewrite our laws, redraft our traditions, retell our culture."

"They bad news, that's right." It wasn't himself speaking, he was just reading the lines that he knew the white man had set before him, as though Officer Tall were pointing with his baton at cue cards.

"Ain't but one way to stop them."

Jeremiah was wiping his lips on his sleeve again and wondering where to put the last of the picked-clean chicken bones when Officer Tall said, "There's more in there, boy."

Jeremiah reached into the bag. His fingers touched steel. He looked up at the officer for a second, momentarily forgetting the protocol.

Officer Tall smiled as Jeremiah removed from the bag a small revolver. So that's why it was so heavy.

"There is but one way to rid yourself of the problem of Negro Officer Lucius Boggs." Then he took something from his pocket and tossed it at Jeremiah. A smaller bag, rolled tight. "The bullets. You didn't think I'd hand you a loaded weapon, did you?"

Officer Tall laughed and Jeremiah fake-laughed along with him.

"No one will ask questions when it's done. In fact, the police department will be on your side this time. Win yourself quite a few favors, boy. More importantly, you'll get that girl back before he spoils her."

He felt sick to his stomach. Why was Officer Tall asking this of him? *Why me?* Surely a man this powerful could do the deed himself. Jeremiah felt small, a thing to be played with.

Officer Tall told him Boggs's address. "There will be two hundred dollars in your pocket once you do the deed, boy. You imagine all the things you could do with two hundred dollars?"

"That's a lot of money." Life-changing money. Family-making money. Surely the offer wasn't sincere?

"But you'd best hurry, 'fore someone else beats you to it."

Officer Tall was leaving when Jeremiah said, "I'm not a fully formed thing. I'm still clay."

"What?"

"I mean, the clay hasn't hardened yet." He scrunched his eyes shut, knowing he couldn't explain.

"Boy, I haven't a clue what you're saying."

Jeremiah shook his head and held his breath a moment, tried again to make sense of this world and his role in it.

"You understand all this? Do I need to find someone else, or are you my boy?"

"I understand, Sergeant, sir. I'm your boy."

31

Early the next evening, the Rakestraws were taking an after-dinner stroll with Charles Dickens on one of Rake's rare nights off. All above them was lavender and pink. Skies, Rake thought to himself, did not come any more feminine than this.

In a few more weeks it would be dark at this hour, so even though the baby had been cranky during dinner and Denny Jr. tended to complain that his feet hurt after making it a single block, he and Cassie believed in the importance of family rituals. Cassie talked to the pram-bound baby about the busy squirrels, and Rake pointed out to his son the contrails of some jet thousands of miles above, a celestial slash mark in all that pink.

Rake felt like these were the sorts of family moments that looked more idyllic than they actually were—because, true to form, Denny Jr. was already asking to be carried, and Rake's polite refusal had the boy on the verge of a tantrum. Rake wasn't sure if this observation was true of parenthood in general or was he perhaps doing it wrong, not as emotionally invested in this as he was supposed to be.

"I had four Negro sightings today," Cassie said. Ever since she'd attended that neighborhood association meeting, she'd been recording, in a small notebook she kept in her purse, any "sightings" she had of Negroes in the area. She'd been jotting down descriptions along with makes and models and times of day.

"People do have maids, you know."

"I *do* know. I recall telling you we should get one, Mr. Tightfisted." He let that one slide. They couldn't afford domestic help, but maybe if he made detective. "I'm not counting 'em if they look like maids, and anyway maids take buses. Folks I've been spotting are in cars, usually men, sometimes being driven around by another man. Realtors and such, up to no good. Anyway, four today, that's the most yet."

"Cassie, I don't know that you need to be—"

"I shooed some off today, too."

"You *what*?"

Undeterred, she smiled, proud of her gumption. "Me and Sue Ellen were walking with the kids this morning and we saw what I'm sure was a Negro realtist out with a Negro couple, by the Richmonds' place. So I very calmly and politely informed them that this was not a transitional area and that they'd been misinformed, and they'd best be on their way. They left."

"Cassie, you should not be walking up to random Negroes like that."

"Why not? Cause they're dangerous? You're always insisting they're not."

"That's not the point."

Denny Jr. started to say something about a neighbor's cute dog, but they ignored him. "If most of the neighbors were *half* as vigilant as me," Cassie said, "we wouldn't be having this problem."

"I do not want you—"

He was interrupted by what a less experienced man might have thought was the sound of a car backfiring. Then a two-second pause, then two more shots.

Cassie put her hand to her mouth. "Lord, it's worse'n I thought."

"Take the kids back home," he told her, handing Denny Jr. the leash.

Before she could reply, they heard the sound of tires squealing, then shouting.

He ran down the street to the next intersection, turning left toward where he believed the shots had been coming from. Here he saw more people, some still emerging from houses, and three men talking in the street.

One of them held a gun.

He ran toward the trio, who were stepping back to look in all directions as if they were surrounded by something invisible that might attack them at any moment.

"I'm a police officer!" Rake yelled as he ran toward them. "Put that gun down!"

He was very aware of the fact that he had no weapon of his own, no uniform or even badge, that he was running toward a firearm, with no idea what was happening. But something about the men's posture suggested they weren't arguing with each other, that whatever altercation had occurred was already past. They looked up at him as he said, "Sir, you need to put that gun down and step back."

One of the men Rake recognized from church; they'd chatted at a punch social once or twice, but apart from that Rake couldn't recall much. Short and slight, nothing to worry about. Another man, much older and with old-fashioned pants hitched halfway up his chest, was a stranger. The fellow in the middle, the one who—enragingly—was still holding a revolver, was the local plumber, Paul Thames. The one who, Cassie said, had come by a few nights ago in search of donations for the neighborhood buy-out-the-coloreds fund.

"This is my gun," Thames said, his voice shaking a bit, "and I'm on my property."

Rake kept his hands at his sides. The other two men each backed up another step. If Rake lunged forward to knock the piece away, he'd probably get shot first.

"You're in the middle of the street, sir, and that gun's making me just a bit nervous. So put it down, please."

Thames looked down at the asphalt below them. Which was when Rake realized they'd gathered here to take in the fresh black skid marks, no doubt left behind by the squealing tires he'd heard a moment ago.

"I own this gun square and I don't have to give it to you."

The barking of neighborhood dogs, roused by the gunfire, added to the chaos.

"Paul, c'mon," the man from church said. "I know Officer Rake-straw. If he says put the gun down, put it down."

Thames nodded, then bent over—grunting from creaky joints—and laid the revolver on the street. "Sorry. I'm a little heated up, I guess."

Rake picked up the pistol. It, too, was heated up. He would check how many bullets it had later, not wanting to do so in front of Thames. "Now, what's going on, gentlemen?"

The older man said, "Coloreds broke into his house."

Thames nodded. "That's right." His mind seemed slowed, unable to take hold of all that had occurred.

"What happened, Mr. Thames?"

"I was in the parlor reading after dinner. I heard a crash coming from the bedroom. Martha Ann's at her bridge club tonight. I grabbed my gun and ran to the bedroom and there's this nigger going through my things."

"You shot him?"

"No, I just shot into the ceiling the first time. I thought about it, but I couldn't quite bring myself to it. Then he jumped out that window he came through. I coulda shot him in the back, I guess, but . . ."

"That's all right, Paul," the older man said. "It's a hell of a thing to do."

"I fired again as he slipped out; wound up shooting up my own wall just to scare him I guess. Never had anything like that happen before. It was so fast. And then he made it into some getaway car and off they went."

"You get a good look at him?" Rake asked.

"Yeah, which one you think it was?" the man from church asked before Thames could answer. "That young one down the block? Or that ornery one on Oak Lane?"

The "ornery one on Oak Lane" just got out of the hospital this morning, Rake thought.

"I don't . . . I gotta think."

Rake asked the others if they'd seen anything. The older man said no. The man from church, who lived across the street, said he saw a Negro run into a red car, a longer model ("maybe a Plymouth?"), and drive off. He didn't get a clear enough look at anyone's face, just enough to see the skin color ("jet black, and real sweaty lookin' ").

More people gathered outside now, some of them almost close enough to overhear the conversation. Rake recognized many of his neighbors, men who spent their weekends fixing cars, cleaning gutters, and playing ball with their children. Mailmen and rail yard workers, carpenters and masons, truck drivers and firemen; he didn't see any of the other cops, yet.

Rake told one of the men to call the police from his house.

"What's going on?" one of the many onlookers asked.

"There was a break-in, sir, but the perpetrators have driven off. I'm a police officer, and more will be arriving shortly. In the meantime, everyone should stay in their homes." If there were more witnesses, the responding officers could find them later. He didn't need a mob gathering, trading bits of misinformation that might color what witnesses would later claim to remember.

"Someone break into your place, Paul?" another man asked, ignoring Rake's command.

"Yeah. But I'm okay."

"Please head on back home, folks." Rake felt the futility of these words even as he spoke them. Upward of two dozen people spread across the length of the block now, staring, passing on news, gesticulating. The world had grown darker, purple sky gone to deep indigo, porch lights flickering on. In minutes it would be full-on night, and an angry crowd would be all the more able to spin beyond control. He hoped the nearest squad car was very near indeed.

"What'd the niggers steal from you?" someone called out to Thames.

"I don't . . . I don't know yet," Thames said. Then a look of horror stole across his face. "Oh no." With that, he turned and ran toward his front door.

Rake told the crowd again, "Y'all go home now, please." Then, needing to see whatever Thames might next do in this house that had become a crime scene, he followed the plumber inside, locking the dead bolt behind them. "Mr. Thames?"

"I'm in here! Oh Lord Jesus!"

Rake walked through the overdecorated parlor—he or his wife was quite the watercolor painter, landscapes of all hues and geography filling nearly every inch of wall space—and down the bungalow's short, unlit hallway, following the lamplight into one of the bedrooms. Thames stood before an old dresser, his reflection in the mirror doubling his sense of loss.

"It's gone! They took the CAHP money!"

It took Rake a minute to understand the word, remembering the leaflet Thames and his wife had left behind when they'd come by seeking donations.

"I keep it in an envelope in here!" He was motioning to a small pile of men's underpants, any sense of embarrassment absent amid the greater tragedy. He'd kept the money in the top drawer, the first place a thief would look.

"How much was it?"

Thames closed his eyes. "Five thousand one hundred and twenty-seven dollars."

Jesus Christ. Hadn't the man heard of banks?

Rake assessed the room. The window was open, the panes overlapping, both of them shattered. Half-unfolded blankets that perhaps had been stored under the bed were thrown across the floor. Coins lay scattered atop the man's dresser, and the drawers of a ladies' dresser on the far wall had similarly been rifled through.

"Oh dear Lord, they're gonna kill me."

"Who's going to kill you?"

"Everyone who donated money! Everybody standing out there! Five thousand dollars! I had it and now it's all gone! They're gonna kill me!"

"No one will be killing anyone, Mr. Thames." Still, he was glad he'd taken the man's gun away—the plumber seemed less stable every second. And though Rake was reasonably sure no one would try to punish Thames for being the victim of theft, he was far more concerned about the safety of Hanford Park's three Negro homeowners.

Alone in the kitchen, he called headquarters to check on the squad car and was told two were on their way. Then he called Cassie, assuring her all was well but explaining he'd be awhile. He popped open the gun's cylinder and confirmed that the six-shooter was half empty. He spun it to an empty chamber, then slid the still-warm gun into his jeans pocket.

Ten minutes later, two officers interviewed Thames in the parlor. Rake had been at the academy with Officer Al Wilkins, a cocky and energetic kid who struck Rake as the sort never to back down from a challenge. His partner, Officer Henry Dallas, maybe ten years older and possessing the slow drawl of someone used to being in charge, was short but muscular, and Rake appreciated the steady calm the man conveyed as he asked his questions, looking Thames in the eye the entire time while Wilkins took notes.

Dallas had allowed Rake to hang around, provided he not interfere. Rake had given them Thames's gun and stood by while they noted the condition of the man's bedroom, one bullet hole in the ceiling and a second in the wall beside the window. Just in case, Wilkins called Dispatch from their squad car and requested they inform the Negro hospital to keep watch for anyone with a bullet wound.

While they questioned Thames, Rake wandered into the kitchen, where a pile of hand-drawn maps of the neighborhood sat on the table. Three of the houses were circled to indicate where Hanford Park's Negro inhabitants dwelled. He folded one in half and slipped it into his pocket.

Outside, the officers and Thames inspected the yard. The squad car was parked diagonally across the center of the street to discourage onlookers from getting too close. The neighbors had indeed backed off, but it didn't appear that anyone had actually retreated into their houses. Under the shroud of darkness, what might have been idle gossip took on a conspiratorial air.

Wilkins held his flashlight as Dallas took note of the shattered window. They didn't appear to have found any footprints. Grass or pine straw covered the dry ground everywhere, no exposed dirt for a sole to imprint itself.

"Who knew you were keeping that money there, sir?" Dallas asked.

"There in that spot? Only my wife. But the whole neighborhood knows I've been collecting it. I got a master list in there of every house I've knocked on and everyone that's given. They knew I had it. And the coloreds knew, too."

"You'd approached them already?"

"Yeah, the one on Oak Lane and the one on Spruce. I haven't had a chance yet to talk to the ones on Myrtle Street, but I imagine they all passed word on to each other."

"How'd it go when you made the offers to 'em?"

"Not good at all. They weren't inclined to listen to reason. Damn it all, the plan was to use the money to buy them out, then resell to white families, and everyone would get their money back, or near enough. It might cost us a few percentages, but it would have been worth it to get them out. Now it's gone, how are we supposed to get them out?"

"Let's try and stay focused a minute," Dallas said. "Can you identify the one who broke into your house?"

"I don't know, maybe. It happened so fast. But it must be one of the ones in the neighborhood, or one of their friends or relations. How else would they know I had that money?"

Rake counted thirty, maybe forty people gathered down the block as a second squad car parked on the curb in front of Thames's neighbors. Out of shotgun came another young officer Rake had trained with, Barnwell. Then emerged the driver, Brian Helton, best friend to Rake's former partner.

"Grits Rakestraw," Helton said to Rake as the officer huddle split up. An old insult that only Helton still used. "Looks like your neighborhood's going to shit."

"What a surprise, with a professional like you keeping watch."

"I keep watch just fine." Rake didn't care for the way he was staring, as if trying to peer into some truth Rake was hiding. *I have no idea what happened to Dunlow two years ago,* he had told Helton many times. *I don't know where the man is, I don't know if someone killed him or why.* Yet Helton clearly suspected him in some nefarious dealings; he was reasonably sure Helton had investigated him, discussing Rake with his then sergeant, thumbing through his daily reports for evidence of any scheme.

Rake already had enough of Helton, so he walked back to where Dallas and Wilkins were talking to Thames. He put a hand on Wilkins's shoulder and gently pulled him aside.

"This isn't good, Al," Rake said. "That was communal money that got stolen. It's not just a theft from one man. We're gonna have a whole neighborhood of people feeling victimized and wanting revenge."

Wilkins agreed but said they needed a few more minutes with Thames. Rake walked over to Barnwell and Helton and told them he'd try to get people to go home. Rather than assist him, they stood by their squad car, unimpressed or uninterested, as Rake walked toward the nearest group, five men in a semicircle. He knew one of them, Bobby, a lanky blond, from his brief time at the mill after returning from the war. Bobby had been a joker at the mill but here his face looked dark and ready to give in to motives that were far from comic.

"What's the story, Rake?" he asked.

"Story is, there was a break-in." Rake let his eyes move across all five men's faces. "No one's hurt, and we're going to find out who did it. But it's time everyone headed back home."

"When you gonna arrest the niggers?" one of the men asked.

"Where'd you hear they were Negroes?"

"Joe over there said he saw one at the wheel of the car," he said, motioning with his head to some other group, somewhere else, wherever it is rumor or fact comes from, who knows. "You-all gonna get 'em, or do we have to?"

Rake kept his arms at his sides, trying to stay friendly and affable but unquestionably in control. "Crime's not but an hour old, fellows. We'll get 'em."

Another man said, "You gotta open your eyes. We got coloreds moving in and already we got a break-in."

"Last time they moved in, they got burned out," another said. "That's the only way."

Rake folded his arms, surrounded by a circle of five angry men, and behind them the other groups had seemed to coalesce, as if waiting for some signal that the time for impotent porch chat had passed and now the real men could take control.

And they didn't even realize yet that the money that had been stolen was theirs.

"I'm not a fan of talk about folks taking the law into their own hands," Rake said. "I live here, too, you know that. We won't let anything happen to this neighborhood."

The voices came too quickly and angrily for him to reply:

"But it *is* happening!"

"They can't move in here and bring Darktown's problems to our doorstep!"

"I didn't fight in a goddamn war to have my own neighborhood taken over by them!"

"Hey, hey, hey!" Officer Dallas had quite a set of pipes when he used it right. Rake felt it in his chest. "People! My partners and I have a job to do right now, and it isn't made any easier by all of you standing around here." As he said this, Officer Wilkins slowly walked to Rake's left, a gentle pace and with both his palms raised at his chest, but walking forward nonetheless, like a slow-motion football blocker who only needed a few feet of air to propel opponents backward. Helton, perhaps reluctantly, was doing the same thing.

Dallas told everyone to go home, using people's first names, seeing Fred over there and Jason over here, Mikey and Mikey Jr., calling them out and thus reminding them that they could not dissolve into anonymous parts of a soulless mob and instead were still imbued with, and weighed down by, their consciences. Rake stepped back so the uniformed officers could take control.

He was standing on Thames's yard again, which rose a bit from the street level, and from that vantage he could see, at the periphery of the crowd, a familiar face: Delmar Coyle. Standing beside him was his pal Neville. Two Columbians, neither of whom lived anywhere near Hanford Park. Either they had a sixth sense for racial disturbances, or they made a habit of patrolling the area like they'd done to other "transitioning" neighborhoods a few years back, or they had known something would be happening tonight.

Rake remembered the incidents from a few years ago, when Negroes moving into other formerly all-white areas had been attacked by Columbians at night, some of their houses firebombed. Maybe some of those nights had started this way, with some unrelated crime providing the spark the Fascists needed to harness the crowd's anger and unleash anarchy.

Then Rake saw the most galling sight of all. Approaching the two Columbians was Dale. Who smiled and shook hands with Coyle like they were old friends.

Later, Rake and everyone else had finally returned to their homes. He called the police switchboard again and asked to be transferred to the Butler Street precinct. The Negro cops.

"Atlanta Police, Sergeant McInnis speaking."

"This is Officer Denny Rakestraw, from the Sixth. I need to get a message to Smith."

"He's walking his beat. Can I help you with something?"

He was glad Smith wasn't available to speak. After all, he'd told

Smith and Boggs he would help look into the beating of Smith's relative, yet he'd done little beyond keeping an eye on the Columbians and the Dunlow brothers. When chatting with neighbors, he'd asked if they knew anything, but he would have done that regardless.

"He needs to get word to the Negroes in Hanford Park. They're not safe here tonight." He gave McInnis the basics, ending with, "We've calmed people down and got them to head home, but we can't stand watch forever."

"Hanford Park's not our beat."

"I'm trying to do the right thing here. I'm not saying I want Negro cops to come out and patrol—Jesus, that's the last thing we need." He couldn't understand why McInnis was being so obtuse. Maybe he thought Rake should knock on their doors himself, which Rake had considered. But that might antagonize the rest of the neighborhood, like he was taking the Negroes' side; he'd lose whatever local authority he was clinging to. "I just need them to get word out; the Negroes here might want to sleep somewhere else tonight."

A long pause. "We'll get the word out, Officer."

32

Jesus said it was easier for a camel to walk through the eye of a needle than it was for a rich man to enter heaven. Nearly as difficult a task was accessing the alcohol stash of Reverend Daniel Boggs. The Baptist minister did not partake of the stuff, but he had secreted a few bottles in his house, as he often entertained local and visiting luminaries, and surely the Lord did not object to such consumption by laymen. One of the brightest such luminaries was sitting in the study right now: Thurgood Marshall, swirling rye in his glass as he told his latest tale.

"They have any evidence at all?" asked Lucius, holding a glass of Coca-Cola.

"They claim to have molds of footprints one of the men left at the scene of the crime," Marshall said. "But I have an expert saying that one of the cops must've taken the boy's shoe after they arrested him, then made the footprint and took the mold."

Lucius shook his head. "Can't trust any evidence from a Southern cop."

"Said the Southern cop." Marshall laughed. The lead attorney for the NAACP's Legal Defense Fund, he'd stopped in town for a day of meetings on his way to Groveland, Florida. Deep in orange country, two Negro men had been convicted of rape under deeply suspicious circumstances. Originally three had been charged, Marshall explained, but the third had been hunted through the cypress swamps and killed by as many as a hundred vigilantes, his body riddled with bullets. The two who hadn't been shot that day had lost their case in a small-town court and been sentenced to death by electric chair, but Marshall was appealing.

Bach played softly on the record player as Lucius, his father, and his brothers chatted with Marshall. The attorney's tie was loosened around his neck and his shirt was nearly untucked after enjoying Roberta's feast of brisket, collards, and corn bread.

"I have a doctor saying he doesn't think there even was a rape," Marshall said. "She'd been out drinking with her estranged *husband* that night. One of the men they charged, they only picked him up because he wanted in on a gambling operation the cops down there control. So they pinned a rape on him, and when he ran, they chased him through the swamps and took target practice on him."

This brand of justice sounded distressingly familiar to Boggs.

"We'll have to get you in our courthouse one of these days," Reginald said. "That'd be a sight."

"Just tell someone in your daddy's congregation to get in some trouble."

"How are those school trials going?" William asked. Normally he slept at the Morehouse dorms, but a visit from Thurgood Marshall was not to be missed.

"The wheels of justice are slow, son, but they do churn if you keep pushing from behind and don't mind getting mud and horseshit kicked in your face. Might take another few years, but we'll get there." A few months ago, the Supreme Court had ruled in Marshall's favor on two cases involving Southern Negroes and white graduate schools. The Justices had avoided striking down school segregation en masse, but Marshall explained that he'd put his foot in the door, which he would soon force open. "Once we win on schools, everything else will follow."

"You truly believe that? That segregation will end?" Lucius asked.

Marshall looked surprised by the doubt. Lucius's own job was a sign of progress, supposedly, but the very difficulties that he confronted day in and day out were wearing away at him. An unending tension, this awareness that he was a statistical oddity the law of averages would soon correct.

"I do, son. Every day I believe it. Or I'd be a crazy man. I got you the vote, didn't I?" He winked.

It was true. A few years back, Marshall had argued before the Supreme Court that all-white Democratic primaries, like the one in Georgia, were unconstitutional. As a result, Lucius's father and other local leaders had registered thousands of Negro voters, providing the leverage they'd long needed to get Mayor Hartsfield to hire Negro policemen. Which meant Lucius literally owed his job to the man sitting before him.

"Got me a lot more than the vote," he said.

Marshall lifted his glass to acknowledge the compliment. "I'm kidding, you know that. Constitution gives you the vote. But they kept it from you, that and a lot else. We'll be getting it back, I assure you." He smiled again. "We'll get you backward Southerners to catch up with the rest of the country yet."

"I've been asked to mediate the matter in Hanford Park," Reverend Boggs told Lucius in the kitchen. They were foraging for snacks, as Mrs. Boggs had retired for the evening. His brothers and Marshall were laughing about something in the parlor. "A white man by the name of Gilmore sent word through one of my congregants. They realize things are getting tense there, and they know that one of the Negro families who moved in are members of my congregation." It wasn't unusual for Reverend Boggs or other Negro men of the cloth to be invited to unofficial councils like this; with no colored elected officials, the ministers and local businessmen served that role instead. "He said the neighborhood wants to negotiate."

"What do you know about Gilmore?"

"He owns a hardware store in Hanford Park. Says he's the head of the neighborhood association." He scanned the countertops. "Now, where does your mother hide my pecans?"

"Negotiate what, exactly?"

"The color line, I'm guessing." The pecans weren't in the cupboards; they weren't behind the toaster, either. "My money says he's going to show up with some maps and pencils and he's going to propose where we redraw the line between white and colored."

Lucius smirked. "He wants the reverend to play God with the land."

Reverend Boggs checked the top of the refrigerator: nope. "It's not playing God, Lucius. It's keeping people safe. You should know about that."

"I also know about arresting criminals. How do we know this Gilmore fellow isn't involved in what happened to Malcolm?"

"We don't. But the point is, they want to negotiate." He checked the bread box: nope. "That, in the end, is a good thing for us. It means they're willing to concede some of the neighborhood."

"I want to be at the meeting."

"Hold on. This is a delicate matter as it is. Bringing a policeman, especially a—"

"I won't wear my uniform. Look, even if he didn't take part in what happened to Malcolm, he's likely to at least know something. None of the white people will talk about it, especially not to us. But I want to see if he lets anything slip."

The reverend opened a tin marked Baking Soda, something he would never otherwise look in. "Ah-ha." He took a bowl from the cupboard, then emptied into it the true contents of the tin: a good half pound of candied pecans. "Woman's not as sly as she thinks she is."

"This Gilmore probably isn't, either. Come on. I'm not saying I'll interrogate him, I just want to be able to look him in the eye. See what he gives away."

The reverend held out the bowl. Lucius took a handful. They were sweet and delicious and he himself could eat piles of them if given the chance.

"I suppose you're the last person I should remind, but: you should be careful what you wish for. And yes, you can come to the meeting. Tomorrow morning at ten."

By early evening, William had returned to Morehouse and Reginald had retired to his wife and children. The early rising reverend had turned in as well, and Marshall was perusing the family's book collection in the study while Lucius handed him another rye. The job's late hours made it impossible for Boggs to go to sleep early even on his one night off. Normally he would have a date with Julie, but he had pointedly let this night come without setting something up. He still wasn't sure what to do.

"How are you taking to the job, son?"

Boggs thought for a moment. "There was a spell in the beginning when I thought it would get easier with time. I don't think that way anymore."

"Which part you find harder, the white cops who hate you for thinking you're as good as them, or the colored folk who hate you for 'acting white'?"

How freeing it felt to talk with someone who could actually understand his experience. He tried to imagine how it felt to stand, as Marshall had, before a rural judge and jury, where the simple facts of his suit and tie and proper diction must have enraged them.

"I knew the white cops would be awful. But knowing it and feeling it every day, right in your face . . . That's something different."

"Your father protected you from a lot of that growing up, huh? Sweet Auburn. This is a special place. Reminds me of Harlem, only smaller. And with better weather."

"And better-looking women."

"Ha!" Marshall leaned forward. "Get yourself to Harlem, boy, and you'll see some women. Hell, we have half of the Georgia-born girls by now, so many are coming north."

Lucius smiled—Marshall was one of the few people who could cuss in this house and not be chastised for it. "I suppose my father did protect us." The thought did not warm his heart. Earlier in the evening, when they'd been exchanging news, Lucius had noted how his father bragged to Marshall about William's latest academic accomplishment and Reginald's promotion, had even mentioned a recent school recital by one of the Boggs grandchildren, but had failed to mention Lucius's engagement. The old man was refusing to admit the marriage was possible. It was as though he knew, somehow, that something would happen in Julie's life, some past sin revisiting, to chase Lucius away.

"I could put you in touch with some Negro cops up in New York if you ever need someone to compare notes," Marshall said. "Trust me, it ain't no cakewalk up there, either."

"So even if you get us backward Southerners to catch up with the rest of the country, that's no cakewalk?"

"They still find ways to have segregation even when it isn't explicitly written into the law. Smart fellow like you, I can't be telling you anything you don't already know."

"I just . . . I want to believe there's a better place to strive for. I want to believe it's real."

"I'm not saying it's not real. Just that winning one battle doesn't make the next day as easy as you might hope. Biggest case I ever won, I celebrated and had a few too many of these," and he swirled the rye again, "but the next morning I woke up and still had a case to fight somewhere. With a hangover."

The phone rang, very late for a call. Boggs hurried into the kitchen and answered it during the second ring. "Boggs residence."

"It's Tommy. I need you to steal your old man's car and get over to Hanford Park, fast."

33

Past midnight, Boggs saw a trio lingering outside.

Malcolm must have noticed from the way Boggs's shoulders had tensed, or maybe he'd spied the reaction in Boggs's eyes, though that would have been tough given the room's darkness. Malcolm scooted toward him. They were sitting on the floor of the front parlor. Curtains drawn, lights out. Hannah had finally gone to bed no more than half an hour ago; she'd agreed only when they said they'd wake her in two hours so they could rest in shifts. Boggs was holding his pistol and Malcolm had a Winchester repeating rifle.

"I don't see any guns," Boggs said softly. When he'd arrived an hour ago, he'd drawn the curtains in such a way that he could see through a tiny sliver, just enough to keep watch. Malcolm had been looking through one of the side windows, which afforded a view of an intersection to the north.

Boggs had arrived here in his father's Buick, pistol in his pocket and a knapsack concealing a rifle that now sat just a few feet behind him. He had driven as fast as he could until he was at the edge of the neighborhood, at which point he had decelerated to a crawl so he could scope out the area. He'd noted a larger-than-usual amount of light on in people's homes for such an hour, but no one had seemed to be out on the street.

He'd slouched low as he'd driven, knowing that his skin color would be seen as a provocation to the sorts of people he was hoping to protect the Greers from. When he reached their house, he pulled all the way into the driveway and quickly walked to the back door, knocking six times, as he'd told them he would.

An hour later he was watching the three white men. They weren't directly across the street but were one house over, a good twenty feet from the nearest streetlamp, making it hard to see any details. Two had hands in their pockets—a chill had descended on the city—and Boggs still saw no weapons. Then one of those hands emerged with a flask. The man took a snort and passed it around. Not a gun, but not a good sign.

"Know any of them?" Boggs asked.

"One in red lives in that house, I think. Never said a word to me one way or the other."

Malcolm had been discharged from the hospital that morning. His face still showed signs of the beating, not that Boggs had gotten a good look at him: every light in the house was out, at Boggs's instruction.

The three white men each took a slug from the flask. Someone took a second. It would be empty soon. They were talking, not terribly animated. Boggs had cracked the windows open when he arrived, but the crickets and locusts—quieter now, a vestige of summer not yet removed from the cool October nights—were just loud enough to conceal whatever the men were discussing.

All his life Boggs had heard stories of the horrible few nights in '06 when the white people had rioted through downtown. His father had been a child, yet the reverend vividly recalled the night when his own father, a postal carrier, had run into his house for refuge at midday, and several other relatives and friends had hid there while the white people raged. Reverend Boggs's adult relatives had sat sentry all through those nights, holding rifles should any white people attempt to storm the house that the family had owned for years. And here Boggs was, nearly half a century later, on the verge of seeing the same madness. No one in his family had died that night, but dozens of Negroes had been murdered during the riot, countless others beaten and maimed. Whole neighborhoods of Negro-owned houses and businesses had been torched. In the ensuing months, the colored residents of downtown fled east, settling in what would become Sweet Auburn. Decades later, they had created their own, separate community. But the city was too crowded now, and there wasn't room for all of the Negroes in Sweet Auburn and Summerhill and Buttermilk Bottom and Darktown and the other areas whites had restricted them to. Had Malcolm and Hannah and the other two Negro families had any choice but to try living here?

Was there really a choice between taking this chance and living in a hovel in Darktown, in a third-floor walk-up with a door accessible only through a lightless alley, where men smoked marijuana on their front stoop even before dark, where drunks harassed them and boys with knives tried to take what was theirs, where only ten Negro cops tried to protect thousands upon thousands? All to live in a tiny apartment with a shared bathroom and no kitchen sink?

Malcolm crept to a side window. "No one else is coming, I don't think." He scooted back to Boggs. "Pulled a lot of late nights in the Pacific. Did a lot of watching out at nothing. Didn't think I'd have to do it in my own city."

The white men gazed at Malcolm's house. Boggs knew they couldn't see inside, yet still he felt their predatory gaze. The men smoked, the ends of their cigarettes dancing like fireflies. Sometimes they laughed.

Boggs watched in silence, seething. He wished he could stand out there with a partner, in uniform, but the mere sight would drive the neighbors wild. The line of how to wield power without provoking greater backlash was so narrow as to be invisible.

In ninety minutes, Smith would be off duty and would catch a ride to Hanford Park with Dewey. Until then, Boggs was the only cop here.

The three white men looked to Boggs's right. Another group was approaching. Three more men, in what appeared to be uniforms. Khaki or olive, hard to tell given the dim light. Then Boggs saw the lightning bolt patches on their sleeves.

"Lord. The Columbians."

"The who?"

Boggs told Malcolm about them. "Have you seen them around here before?"

"No."

One of the white men from the first group pointed at the tall Columbian who stood in the middle and carried himself with the gait of a leader.

Boggs had called Hanford Park's other two Negro families, warning them. They had exchanged numbers with Malcolm and Hannah when they'd first moved in, trading pleasantries about future cookouts or cakewalks, not realizing that the first time they'd call would be to warn each other of danger. One of the men Boggs talked to had said he would take his wife and two children to his brother's house in Mechanicsville for the night. The other, though, had insisted on standing firm; Boggs hoped all was quiet at that house, a block behind this one and out of view.

"You recognize them?" Boggs asked. He still suspected the Columbians were the ones who'd beaten Malcolm. "From that night?"

Malcolm nudged Boggs aside so he could get a closer look. "I just didn't see anything. I keep thinking maybe I'll see somebody and it'll jar some memory. But they got me from behind. Didn't see a damn thing."

Boggs wondered if Rakestraw had spoken to any of them, checked their alibis. Would he really investigate a white person's crime against a Negro in his own backyard? It would be so much more convenient for him and his family and his bank account if he simply ignored the crime, or helped cover it up.

Headlights. Boggs let the curtains close even more, narrowing his view. He watched as a car approached from the south. A squad car. It pulled in front of the six men, its red lights off.

Boggs couldn't make out the driver, as the window was up and the faint amount of light reflected off of it. One of the men pointed at Malcolm's house. He could hear raised voices but couldn't make out what they were saying.

Then he saw the men laughing. The squad car pulled away.

"What's happening?" Malcolm asked.

"Good ol' boys being boys." But the fact that the squad car had left made his heart sink.

Only minutes later, his feeling was confirmed: the six men outside were joined by three more. Then another, and another. None of these were in those Nazi getups, but still, they all looked quite comfortable out there together.

Then a group of four more. Soon Boggs counted more than two dozen, including a few women, arms crossed, and a couple of teenage boys. He didn't see any weapons yet but he couldn't see everyone, couldn't see their belts or bulging pockets. And with this many, they'd barely even need weapons. Rocks weren't hard to find. And most of them probably had lighters in their pockets, matches.

Some looked angry but many were smiling, entertained. Like they'd been invited to some climactic event and they couldn't wait to see it commence.

"Jesus," Malcolm said. "What do we do? Should I fire a warning shot?"

The gun handle had gone slick in Boggs's hand. *"No."*

"Then what do we *do*?"

Boggs tried to sound calm. "We wait."

The whites of Malcolm's eyes had grown. "Until *when*?"

He took a breath. "Until we stop waiting."

34

That same night, Dale's one-time friend Iggy was in the midst of one of those rocky stretches in his marriage, during which his wife decided she and the kids should best live elsewhere. Her folks were only three miles away, so for Iggy it felt like a short vacation. The house to himself, no one complaining or turning minor disagreements into crises. He knew he would have to drive to the in-laws soon, go through the song and dance of apologizing to win her back, but frankly he was enjoying the silence too much.

He'd stopped at the bar on the way home from work, only meaning to have one, yet somehow he'd managed three—or was it four?—by the time he left. He'd been leaving the front door unlocked in case his wife decided to return, as she chronically lost keys and purses and matches and cigarettes and other items of importance, and he didn't want her to come back only to find herself locked out, though there would have been justice aplenty in that.

He opened the door, stepped into the bungalow's small foyer, and hit the light switch. Nothing. He cursed—was there an outage? No, the streetlamps were on. Maybe it was the bulb.

Then his head exploded and his knees liquefied. He landed on the floor, his body numb.

Sensation returned in time for him to feel something grab him by the armpits, dragging him into the familyless family room. He tried to push it away, tried to stand up, but two blows to his ribs left him flat on the ground again. The pain made him dizzy, and together with the darkness and his drunkenness he found himself imagining a grizzly bear loose in his house, mauling him to death.

Then the small lamp his wife liked to read by flickered on. Before him loomed a bear-sized man in a plaid shirt and jeans. The butt of a pistol stuck out from beneath his belt buckle like some terrible metal phallus.

Something pressed on Iggy's back. He couldn't see behind him but it was most likely a foot belonging to another man. Or possibly a bear.

"Inman Daniel Christiansen," the man by the lamp said. "Aka Iggy."

"The hell's going on?"

"You beat up some coloreds in Coventry a few nights back."

"Like hell I did."

Perhaps he'd had more than four beers after all. This was a fever dream, like delirium tremens, only he was drunk. Surely it was a hallucination of some kind. He'd always been terrified of bears.

"You left these behind while you were there." The giant dropped something onto the floor, just in front of Iggy's face. Something metal and shiny and spinning. No, the metal thing wasn't spinning, Iggy's drunken perspective was. The thing on the ground was still. His dog tags! With his name imprinted on them. He'd realized they were gone a few days ago, had looked everywhere for the damn things.

"Those ain't mine."

The giant kicked him in the ribs. Iggy thought he might throw up.

Then a foot nearly stepped on Iggy's head, and the old floor creaked beneath the man's shifting weight. He was bending down, lowering his head to almost Iggy's level.

"Me and my brother really don't care if you beat on a couple niggers. What we do care about is our other brother being killed in Coventry that same night, something that nobody, not even the cops, can tell us shit about." The man paused for this to sink in. "We're awfully keen on figuring out what exactly happened. Care to tell us?"

35

Three miles from Hanford Park, it seemed fitting Jeremiah would find himself back at the rail yards for today's shift of "work." Not normal work, he knew, and not even day, as darkness shrouded him.

That afternoon Jeremiah had reported to the Rook for another night of washing and rinsing, but Feckless had stopped him at the door. Turned out, he didn't really need that kind of help. He'd only given Jeremiah those first days of labor out of pity. No, if Jeremiah really wanted to earn money from Feckless, he would need to do something altogether different.

A week earlier, perhaps Jeremiah would have said no. But days of being told no while pursuing other employment, days of barely finding food to eat, days of sleeping in a rat-infested basement, had swayed him.

So Jeremiah was driving a tan GMC pickup. In back, a canvas top obscured what they were hauling: a quartet of trash barrels, two of them empty. In shotgun rode Cyrus: light-skinned, maybe twenty, and quite thin. Jeremiah couldn't tell if Cyrus's eyes were a bit larger than normal or if he was just perpetually on alert.

"You done time, huh?" Cyrus asked after Jeremiah had been driving for ten minutes.

"Yes."

"How long?"

"Five years. One month. And six days."

Jeremiah was facing forward but he could tell Cyrus was staring at him. After a two-second pause, Cyrus laughed. "Damn, you strange."

Funny that he was being teased. He had thought his time would lend him some status around hoods like this. But it never worked that way with Jeremiah. He wasn't sure why. People sensed in him some goodness, which many took for weakness, and no one took seriously.

Cyrus had bragged earlier about the pistol in his pocket, implying that Jeremiah would be unwise to challenge him. He apparently hadn't realized Jeremiah carried one as well.

How strangely life was twisting before Jeremiah.

He had expected to be washing dishes again, yet instead he was doing this, something that made use of his past experience. He wanted to stay true to his promise to the Lord, true to his promise to Julie so long ago, that he would not do the devil's work again. This morning he had woken up thinking that the strange nocturnal visit from Officer Tall had been a dream (how had he known Jeremiah was camped out in that basement?) until he saw the gun lying there. Not a dream, then, but something that had been somehow preordained, scripted in advance. He had told the Lord he would walk a righteous path, yet this messenger had been sent to him, bearing food and a lethal gift and a distinctly nonrighteous command: kill Boggs. He knew it was wrong, crooked, diabolical, yet it also felt so simple and straightforward, after days of the free world's puzzling complexity.

It all had seemed to happen so quickly, and he had no alternatives, and if the Lord had wanted him to do something different, then surely an option would have been revealed, wouldn't it?

So difficult to avoid temptation when it tenaciously sought you out.

He could do this job for Feckless a few times, he figured. Make some money, show Julie he was a workingman. Prove he could provide for her and the little one. Surely that wasn't too much to ask of the Lord. But, killing Boggs—could he do that? If that's what it took to re-win Julie and raise his son? Was this a test from the Lord? What was expected of him?

"Turn left here," Cyrus said.

"What happened to the fellow who used to drive?" Jeremiah dared ask.

"Don't worry about it."

At one in the morning, twenty minutes after the arrival of a certain freight train from New Orleans, Jeremiah drove the truck along a narrow street that cut through two sections of the rail yard. A gangway above allowed for rail workers to walk over the road. Fences topped with barbed wire loomed on either side.

Jeremiah and Cyrus wore gray canvas custodial uniforms. Smelled foul. In their pockets were letters from a fictional employer certifying that these two Negroes had legitimate reasons for being out so late after the city's unofficial curfew for the colored.

Driving back on the narrow road, this time Jeremiah's headlights revealed a solitary figure standing on one of the gangways, directly above two Dumpsters. He had dragged behind him several trash cans and four cardboard boxes.

Cyrus reached out the window and flicked his lighter once, the signal, then the man above poured the contents of his barrels and threw the boxes to the Dumpsters below. He aimed well, the boxes landing just *outside* the Dumpster. Jeremiah pulled alongside it, killed his headlights, and jumped out. He picked up the surprisingly light boxes and carried them to the back of the truck, where Cyrus met him, switchblade in hand. Quickly now, just as they had rehearsed, Cyrus tore the boxes open while Jeremiah took the four trash barrels from the back of the truck. Cyrus poured the boxes' contents, two packages wrapped tightly in brown paper, into the empty barrels. Jeremiah could barely smell the herb's aroma. Then Jeremiah, donning gloves, opened one of the trash barrels that actually *was* filled with garbage, and by hand he redistributed some of the trash so that the bundles of marijuana were covered in it. Should any cops pull them over, they would find two night janitors hauling garbage.

Minutes later, south of downtown in Summerhill, they circled a certain block once, looking for cops, then pulled behind a small brick building, a defunct grocery store. In the back, a door opened and out walked a tall, very light-skinned Negro clad in a white dress shirt, light-gray slacks, and a matching vest. The Rook's doorman, whom Feck had called Q.

They climbed into the truck, picking up the two barrels in the back.

Q motioned to the door, through which Jeremiah and Cyrus carried the barrels. Q closed the door behind them and hit a light. This had once been a store, but now it was empty—other than a crate in the middle of the floor, Jeremiah saw nothing but dust bunnies and cobwebs.

Cyrus dumped the barrels, garbage spilling everywhere. He tossed it and reached into the trash for the paper-wrapped bundle, which he transferred into the crate. Q watched as Jeremiah did the same. Then he silently handed Cyrus a small envelope and took out a set of keys, apparently anxious to lock the door and usher them out.

"Got an envelope for me?" Jeremiah asked.

"What?" Q stepped closer, staring into Jeremiah. It was the first word he'd spoken. "What in the hell you just say?"

Jeremiah knew he was bad at this. The pecking-order, tough-guy thing. He'd been teased in his brother's gang, and again at Reidsville. There were rules he didn't understand, even when the occasional, pitying mentor tried to explain them to him. So he tried not to sound argumentative as he hazarded, "I should get paid, too, right?"

A hand disappeared behind Q's back, then reappeared so fast Jeremiah barely had time to see the gun before it slammed into his head. Jeremiah hit the ground, pain leveling his world.

"Y'all figure out how you divide that on your own, goddammit!" Q shouted.

"He's new, Q," Cyrus said. "He didn't mean nothing."

When Jeremiah looked up, he saw the gun was pointed at him. "I know who you are. They said you done in your brother. I don't know why Feck would bring in someone like you, cloud over your head and all. But you give me lip one more time, Cyrus here'll be taking you out in one of those trash barrels, understand?"

Jeremiah tried to nod, but it hurt too much. "Yeah. I understand."

"Now get out of here."

Cyrus helped him up and guided him out by the arm. Once outside, they heard the door lock behind them.

"Who *is* that?" Jeremiah asked. During his time smuggling cigarettes, tempers had flared on occasion, usually his brother's. And Isaiah hitting him hadn't been noteworthy—he'd done that all his life. Out of fear of Isaiah, however, no one else had ever touched Jeremiah.

"That's Quentin Neale. Or just Q. He don't usually have much to say, but when he do, you'd best listen real good."

Jeremiah glanced at one of the empty barrels and tried not to imagine himself stuffed inside one.

36

Smith caught a ride from Dewey to Hannah and Malcolm's, arriving past three in the morning. His sister asleep in the bedroom, Boggs and Malcolm sat watch, grim and in darkness.

They caught him up: a crowd had started gathering at half past midnight, seeming to materialize right after a squad car's most recent pass. As if the cops' exit had been a predetermined signal. The crowd had grown to fifty or sixty people, by Boggs's best guess. Then at about one o'clock the same squad car returned, with a second. To Boggs's surprise and profound relief, the cops had gotten out and warned people to return to their homes. Much arguing had ensued, yet the cops had stood firm. By two, everyone was back inside.

Then the squad cars had left again. Another hour had passed now, but they wondered when the crowd—or even a single, emboldened person gripping a Molotov cocktail—might emerge next.

Smith thanked Boggs, then he insisted his partner head home to bed.

"You sure?" Boggs asked. "I don't think it's over."

"Get some sleep. I'll call if things look bad." Boggs obeyed, and Smith took over his position.

After twenty minutes of uneventful silence, some of the adrenaline drained from Smith, and he noticed a heaviness to Malcolm's lids, tiring after so many hours of hyped-up vigilance. It felt like the best time to say, "I'm only gonna ask this once. You take that money?"

"Are you serious?" Combination of shock and deep offense.

"Pretend I'm asking as your brother-in-law and not as a cop."

"Tommy, I did not take that money! Didn't go anywhere *near* that man's house. Can't believe you'd even ask me that."

"Just wanted to be sure I was risking my life for a good reason."

"Oh, if I *had* stolen some money then I'd deserve to be lynched?"

"I had to ask, all right?" This was already off to a bad start, and he hadn't gotten to the tough stuff yet. "Blame the cop in me after all."

A sound, a car door slamming. They checked their windows, saw nothing. Smith scooted to another window, facing south, and saw a figure moving three houses away. A moment later a front light illuminated the man, in overalls and a work shirt, unlocking a front door.

"Nothing," Smith reported, "just a fella coming home from work real late."

They settled back into their positions. Smith eyed the rifle Malcolm held. "You a good shot with that Winchester?"

"Good enough."

"Better'n that, right? Didn't you get a medal over there?"

"That was for more than marksmanship, but yeah, I can shoot."

"How 'bout a man across the street, maybe forty yards? At night?"

Malcolm glanced out the window, not realizing where Smith was leading him. "Forty wouldn't be a problem, but the street's not that wide."

"That uses .30-.30 bullets, don't it?"

Malcolm looked at him. Finally catching on. "Yeah. It does."

Smith maintained the stare. "Last week, when I came by here asking you about the drug trade, you didn't think there was maybe something you ought to tell me?"

Another car door. Malcolm looked outside but Smith didn't move. "Tommy, we gotta concentrate."

Smith glanced out the window and saw just another late-shift worker trudging home.

"Malcolm. I am out here risking my life for you, and you don't have nothing to say to me?"

"Tommy, I . . ." Malcolm looked down. "That wasn't supposed to happen."

"*What* wasn't supposed to happen?" Raising his voice more than he should.

Malcolm couldn't answer, so Smith told the story, one he had just figured out a few hours earlier. "The night me and Boggs broke up that smuggling drop at the telephone factory, somebody got shot dead. Because someone *else* was stationed across the street, shooting with a Winchester. We assumed the shooter was part of the operation, a lookout, firing at us and accidentally hitting his own man. But no, the shooter *wasn't* part of Malley's gang, was he? He was part of a whole *different* crew, the crew that's been trying to take over Malley's turf. You been working with Quentin Neale, and you were stationed there as a sniper to take Malley's boys out. Me and Boggs just happened to walk into it."

"I didn't know you were going to be there. As soon as I saw you two, I took off."

"And that makes it okay?" They were sitting on the floor, ten feet apart. The fact that they were both gripping firearms loomed large in Smith's thinking. He needed to confront Malcolm without threatening him, a tough balance, doubly so given their exhaustion.

"Tommy . . . I didn't mean for that to happen."

Smith prided himself on being intuitive and quick, but the truth had eluded him for so long because it hid in his blind spot. His own family.

A week ago, boxer Spark Jones had given Smith and Boggs the name Quentin Neale, a potential rival to Malley. And then today, hours earlier, the final piece of the puzzle: Smith had leaned on an informant who told him Neale was known for bringing his drugs and liquor not from the mountains like Malley, but from New Orleans via freight lines. The rail yards—the same place that Jeremiah had worked back in '45. Smith had heard rumors that Feckless hadn't always been a legit businessman, but he'd wanted to believe a fellow could rise from humble and even twisted roots to become respectable.

So when Feck had tried to offer Smith that envelope of cash the other night, Feck had been feeling Smith out, trying to see if he would take a bribe and look the other way, just like Malley had done with the white cops. Feck knew how to exploit the rail yards from his time with Isaiah Tanner, he had money and workers thanks to the Rook, he had an open market now that Malley was dead . . . The only thing he lacked was police protection.

Smith hadn't put it together until the informant mentioned that one of the men who usually managed Feck's rail yard deliveries had been beaten to a pulp a few nights back.

"Folks who beat you up, they weren't angry white neighbors or Klansmen, were they? You remember just fine, I bet. It was someone from Malley's gang, paying you back for the shooting."

Malcolm looked down again. "I . . . I didn't remember at first. Honest. But then, yeah. I took the bus home from the Rook and they must have followed me in a car. Waited 'til I got off and walked to a quiet block, no one around."

"You were happy to have me running around thinking it was white folks, just to keep me away from what you were up to. You been lying to me the whole time."

When Malcolm had finally found work at the Rook, Smith had been so relieved for his sister that he hadn't questioned their newfound prosperity. And when they'd told him they'd bought this house thanks in part to a sudden inheritance from some uncle in North Georgia, Smith had actually believed them.

"I wasn't trying to kill no one, just shoot out the wheels of their delivery truck. We were gonna show up in force and scare Thunder's boys off, let 'em know to keep out of our area, that this was Q's territory now. Then we'd keep the goods. That's all. But when *you* showed up out of nowhere, that fellow ran into my line of fire."

"It's my fault? All you were doing was firing a rifle across the street, and you're surprised a man got killed? You know the white cops wanted to charge *me* with murder?"

"I know it's bad, all right? And why do you think we bought a place over on this side of town, huh? I been wanting to get away from the business, cut ties with all them. I know a guy does construction out here, helping one of those crews put up new places—he said he could get me a carpentry job once they start building this new complex. I swear, I'm trying to put that stuff behind me."

"Behind you? It was barely two weeks ago." Smith was disgusted, and as angry as a sober man can be at half past three in the morning. "Can't believe you let yourself be muscle for that kind of nonsense."

Eyes gone cold. "I did a lot worse in the Pacific."

"That's different."

Malcolm looked away, out the window again. "So, you gonna arrest me, Tommy? Is that it?"

This was the question Smith had been asking himself for hours.

He took a breath, then said, "You need to get rid of that rifle. Immediately. It can link you to murder."

Understanding what this meant, Malcolm nodded. "Tommy, thank you. I'll get rid of it, first thing tomorrow."

Smith would have preferred he do it right then, but that was out of the question. Tonight it might save Malcolm's life, but if he did indeed have to use it, he'd produce shell casings that could get him sent to the electric chair.

"Get yourself another weapon, in case we have to do this again tomorrow."

Malcolm closed his eyes, either in relief he wasn't being arrested, or in horror at realizing that, even if he survived this night, the sun would set again tomorrow. He opened his eyes. "I'm sorry, Tommy. I tried to keep you out of it."

"Sorry don't cut it."

"What would you have me do? You know how long I looked for work? All them skills I came back with from the war didn't matter to nobody. Couldn't even get a damned *janitor* job. Feckless took a chance on me, and the one skill that I could make money with, it worked out for both of us. It ain't what I wanted, all right? But it's all I could get."

They heard another car door and checked the windows again. It seemed an unusual amount of doors opening and closing given the hour.

"Malcolm, you want to stay a free man, you want me to keep quiet about this? You're going to have to give me two things. One is your word that you will not set foot in Feckless's place or talk to him or Quentin Neale ever again. You're done with them."

A longer pause than Smith would have liked. "All right. I'm done with them. What's the second thing?"

"You hand those sons of bitches over to me."

37

"Denny, we need to consider leaving the neighborhood."

"Are you serious?" He and Cassie sat at the kitchen table while, below, Denny Jr. played with his train and Maggie gummed a toy on a blanket. In the midst of this rare peaceful moment with the kids, Cassie's comment was a thunderclap.

"Don't be stubborn. You see what's happening. Maybe you're used to this sort of thing because you have to see it all day, but we shouldn't have it in our own neighborhood."

He was still trying to make sense of the previous evening. The mood of the crowd had been close to violence, he'd felt it, that need to lash out against the forces that had struck them first. Rake had successfully kept Thames from telling the neighbors what had been stolen, but how long could he hold out? A day? Once they found out, a sense of unjust victimhood would overpower them, forcing them to do whatever was necessary to restore order.

He'd called the Department first thing in the morning. One of the officers responsible for Hanford Park, an older fellow who sounded annoyed that a cop from another beat was bothering him, assured Rake they were working on it, hanging up quickly.

He wasn't sure how much to tell Cassie. He knew she had been raised differently, had heard her parents drop the N-word as natural as drinking sweet tea, knew the way her brothers felt about shiftless Negroes perpetually on the verge of taking their property, their jobs, their women. For the most part, he and his wife had avoided conflict on race matters. Yet the events of the last couple weeks were bringing it to the forefront.

"Our neighborhood is damn near rioting," he said. "I'd like to hear a more rational opinion within my own house."

"You want rational? Here's rational: three Negro houses will turn into six, then twelve, and each time that number goes up, our home value goes down. A Realtor was here the other day asking if we wanted to sell, and the number he offered was less than it should have been."

She explained that a young, well-dressed Realtor ("a white one, at least") had come armed with documents describing what had happened in an Atlanta neighborhood that had turned Negro a year ago. It had been white for generations, yet, like a lunar eclipse, it had gone completely black mere months after the first Negroes moved in. Whites had to sell against their wishes as the blocks were besieged with Negro families, multiple generations piled into bungalows, broken-down cars parked on the front lawn, livestock in the back. Those who'd sold first had escaped with close to what their houses should have been worth, the Realtor had warned, but the ones who'd waited too long lost up to half the value of their home. She retrieved from the kitchen some paperwork that backed the man's claims and handed it to Rake.

"Those people are vultures, Cassie. They're just trying to scare you."

"I don't scare easy, but others do and that's what worries me. The Bartletts and Caseys are about ready to sell—I had lunch with the ladies the other day. Folks who bought most recently, like them, are more willing to pull up stakes. We've only got four years into the mortgage, so we should think about it."

"I can't believe you're considering this. We just got the bedrooms and the kitchen the way you wanted them." He had spent hours rebuilding cabinets with his father, had stained and repainted furniture they'd inherited from her grandmother, had planted two trees in the front after a century-old oak had fallen last spring, barely missing the house. All that sweat and time had made the house feel like an extension of himself, not something that could be so idly shucked off due to vague fears.

"Hopefully those Negroes will take the offer from the neighborhood and will sell their houses back, and soon," she said. "But if that doesn't happen, we do need to consider leaving."

Denny Jr. wandered over to tell them something his imaginary train conductor had done, asking Daddy to come play. Rake promised to be by shortly and shooed him away.

He hadn't grappled with the big picture, he realized. From his time as a soldier to his time as a cop, he'd operated a certain way: get orders, execute them, move on to the next task. He realized he wasn't as good at stepping back and considering all the angles, the tectonic shifts under his feet that determined which orders he was even given. When the Negro families had first moved in, and people like Dale had dropped hints about violence, he had been hoping the neighborhood would settle again into some sort of equilibrium. The Negroes would stay put, but they weren't on his block, so he didn't mind. Which was ridiculous, he understood now, because if three Negro households were able to live safely here, those three would become six, then twelve—Cassie had been right about that. He'd agreed to help Dale not just because Dale was family but because Rake hoped that, if he'd solved that mystery, he could root out the instigators and contain the violence. He had eventually capitulated to her and gone along with CAHP's money-raising scheme, even though he'd feared it was just a different finger on the same hand that would inevitably strike out against the Negroes—and he believed that now more than ever.

So he said to Cassie, "I want to tell you something, but you need to keep it between us." She nodded. "What those burglars stole was the neighborhood money, what Thames had been collecting. It's gone. So no one's going to be able to buy the Negroes out."

She brought her hand to her mouth. "Oh my Lord. They got *all* that money?"

"Supposedly."

"What do you mean, *supposedly*?"

"I think there's more going on here than anyone realizes." He was afraid to say more, afraid what her reaction would be. He needed proof first, otherwise his accusation would risk tearing a deeper fissure between them. "I just need to figure a few things out."

"You've got to find it, Denny. You've got to get it back before they blow it on booze or whatever and then we're all out of luck."

"Cassie . . ." He tried to proceed carefully. "The neighborhood is going to be fine, and we aren't going anywhere. But in the meantime, please do not repeat any of this. I need to find that money before anyone else hears it ever went missing. Otherwise . . ." He didn't want to even imagine it. "In the meantime, just, don't talk to any Realtors, all right? Give me a day."

Thinking, how much worse could things get in one day?

⤙

He needed to talk to Dale again. It had been only yesterday when the GBI had spoken to him in the park; he'd planned on heading over to Dale's that night after the kids went to bed, but the robbery and subsequent chaos had quashed that plan. Then, of all things, he'd seen Dale chumming it up with the goddamn Columbians.

Wary of leaving any phone records the state cops might be able to trace, he headed outside without bidding Cassie good-bye, driving to a pay phone three blocks away. He called Dale's mill. Told that Dale was unavailable on the floor at the moment, he claimed to be a neighbor and said Dale's wife was very ill and needed him immediately.

Three minutes later, Dale was on the line, out of breath. "Hello?"

"Dale, it's Rake, but don't say my name out loud. Sue Ellen's fine. I lied. But you and me need to talk immediately, in person."

⤙

Twenty minutes later a rather steamed Dale got into Rake's Chevy, where Rake had pulled over at the northern end of the park that lent Hanford Park its name. He slammed the door.

"That wasn't a very nice stunt, Rake. You like to have given me a heart attack."

"You need a heart for that." Rake pulled away, eyeing the mirrors carefully. He'd taken a circuitous route here to make sure he wasn't being followed.

Five blocks from the mill, Rake pulled into the narrow alley that ran between a restaurant that had recently closed down and a bar that wasn't open yet.

"Why are we talking here?" Dale asked as they got out.

Ignoring the question, and confident they were alone and unobserved, Rake asked, "Has anyone from the Klan gotten in touch with you?"

"No. You told me to lay low, so I've—"

"The Negro that got beat up the other day, what if that was in payment for what you did up in Coventry?"

"I thought that, too. But if that were the case, they woulda said something at our last meeting."

"What last meeting?"

Dale looked sheepish. "Our Klavern. We met the other day—"

"I told you to stay the hell away from them."

"If I skipped a meeting that woulda looked suspicious, wouldn't it?"

He hated the fact that his brother-in-law might actually be right. Perhaps Dale's being at the meeting was good—it was like having a spy there, if a moronic one. "What did you hear at the meeting?"

"They were right upset about what happened to Irons, and they asked if anybody knew anything, but I kept quiet. They barely mentioned what happened to that Negro here."

"Who have you talked to about that night in Coventry?"

"Nobody. You told me to keep quiet and I have." Rake was about to say *Good* when Dale added, "The only people who know other'n me and Mott are Iggy and Pantleg."

"Who?"

Then Dale sketched an even worse picture, explaining a part he'd left out before: originally *five* Kluxers had ventured to Coventry, but then two had abandoned the plan, not wanting to beat up a white man, instead choosing to cause even yet more trouble elsewhere.

Rake was agog. "There were *two others*? You forgot to mention this before?"

"I . . . I guess I thought I told you."

"No, no you did not fucking tell me. So there are *three* people who know you went up there that night? Jesus. Who else have *they* told?"

"Nobody, Rake, they know better."

Rake couldn't believe what a fool he'd been. There had been a clear option when Dale had first asked for his help: turn him down. Better, Rake should have taken Dale to the station himself. Referred him to a decent lawyer, told him to explain things as accurately as possible to the Homicide detectives. Dale might have gotten off with aggravated assault, perhaps less if he'd convinced a prosecutor he was a good ol' boy enforcing Christian virtues. Jesus, Rake had failed such an obvious ethical test. Despite being so sure of his moral compass, and thinking himself so much better than crooked cops like Helton or his ex-partner, Dunlow, he'd botched things, horrifically. He knew better than to be motivated by greed or lust, to accept bribes or take advantage of helpless women. That's not where his faults lay. He had been trying to aid his sister, which he'd thought lent his actions a certain nobility. So he had failed to report a crime and he was in danger of losing his job once word got out, which, he now understood, it inevitably would.

"Dale, this is goddamn hopeless." He hoped his tone of voice did justice to what he was about to say. "You need to turn yourself in."

"*What?* I can't do that."

"You have no choice."

Dale looked terrified. Worse than the first day, when he'd still been in shock. "We can keep quiet about it, Denny, I swear."

"You cannot keep quiet. It's not in your nature."

"Denny, I swear to you—"

"Even if you could, those other two have less to lose. They weren't part of the actual attack where a man was killed. If they get leaned on, they'll point the finger at you."

"They're my friends."

"Your best friends in the whole wide world? They love you so goddamn much they'd go to *jail* for something they *didn't do* while keeping their mouth shut so that *you* could stay free? Do you realize how crazy that sounds?"

Tears in Dale's eyes now. He put his hands together in prayer. "Denny, please."

Seeing him like that, broken down and desperate, defenses long gone, this was the best possible time to ask, "And what were you doing chumming it up with the Columbians last night?"

Dale shook his head, thrown by the change in subject. "You mean Coyle?"

"You know him?"

"Yeah. You know I almost got mixed up in that once, but, Jesus, that was years ago."

"What was he up to last night?"

"Same as everyone else, I expect. I just saw him out there and said hi. I hadn't even known he was out of prison."

Dale looked too pathetic to lie convincingly right then, but Rake had been wrong before. "Stay the hell away from them."

Dale wiped at his eyes, regaining control over his emotions now that they weren't discussing his inevitable imprisonment. "They're just trying to help the neighborhood."

"Help how, exactly?" Rake stepped closer. "Were they the ones who attacked the Negro the other night? Or broke into Thames's house?"

"I don't know! Look, I felt like they were speaking a lot of truth when they stood up for white neighborhoods a few years ago, but when they got arrested for *treason* or whatever it was, I kept my distance. I don't wear the uniform or go to their secret meetings, okay?"

"They have secret meetings?"

"It was just a figure of speech! Lay off, goddammit." He shook his head, his fear as usual turning quickly to anger. "You really want me to turn myself in? Tell the truth and all? Then I'll have to tell the whole truth so help me God, and that would include how I talked to my brother-in-law, Officer Denny Rakestraw, and told him all about what happened in Coventry, and he advised that I keep my mouth shut. So I obeyed."

Rake kept very still. He could hear children playing, recess beginning a couple blocks away, a gentle breeze carrying the sound.

"Are you threatening me, Dale?"

"I would never threaten a cop. I'm just saying, if it ever got so I had to tell the complete and whole truth, well, I guess I'd just have to go and do that."

Rake punched him in the stomach. Only the slightest amount of better judgment restrained his hand from punching much higher, from breaking Dale's nose and leaving his face with evidence of this encounter. Dale doubled over and Rake caught his shoulders, lifting them up and pushing him against the wall. Then he hit him again in the same spot.

He backed up so Dale could fall to his knees and start coughing. He thought Dale might throw up but he didn't. Rake got down on one knee, from where he was still inches above Dale, who was barely holding himself up, hands on the alley floor.

"If you even think of implicating me in any of your nonsense," he said quietly, almost whispering in Dale's ear, "I will beat you to death. Slowly. I'll do some of the things the Nazis did over there. Things we had to copy sometimes. So keep your goddamn mouth shut."

Back in the Chevy, keys in the ignition, he reversed all the way, giving Dale one last glance, still facedown in the alley like he'd been beaten into a quadruped.

Later, when his adrenaline faded and his anger slightly cooled, Rake would realize he had accomplished nothing, worse than nothing, because he honestly had no clue what Dale might do next.

38

Hannah rose from the bed gingerly, head pounding, as if sleep were something that had assaulted her. The clock read half past nine. The headache wasn't from sleep, it was from too little. She, Malcolm, Tommy, and Boggs had traded shifts throughout the night. She'd never held a gun before, had never wanted to. But last night, Lord, that gun in her hand, its cold hardness, its undeniable power, may have been the only thing that kept her from breaking down.

She stretched, her back sore. Sleep had grown difficult enough due to the baby, even without the fear of death. She used the bathroom, which she needed to do every hour or so now. She sipped some water and could feel already the heartburn in her stomach; nothing would taste good today.

Apologizing, but needing to get home and check in with his colleagues, and maybe nap before his shift, Tommy had already left. With the sun up, he believed, they were safe. She wished she agreed, but it wasn't vampires or werewolves that were hunting them. The white people stalking them were all the more terrifying because they could strike at any time.

She and Malcolm had both crawled into bed soon after Tommy left—at first they'd been afraid to, but something about the morning's unceasing echo of neighbors' front doors opening and closing, and the attendant parade of automobiles winding their way out of driveways and down the road to this office or that factory, the sheer normalcy, made the call of their warm bed irresistible. They'd lain down in their clothes, asleep in seconds.

Malcolm was still snoring, so she crept silently into the kitchen to fix herself some coffee. The floor cold on her bare feet, she felt crumbs that she'd been too distracted to sweep last night. And what would happen tonight? How many midnight vigils would they need? Tommy's one night off was a few days away, so again he wouldn't be able to join them until past two in the morning. He had said another Negro officer would help, but what if that cop decided it wasn't his problem? How long could they hold out?

She thought about the white couple who had visited them not long ago, offering to buy back the house "on behalf of the neighborhood." As if "the neighborhood" were a thing separate from her and Malcolm. "The neighborhood" so wanted them gone that it would do them this favor, if they knew what was good for them. They had dared to decline. Then the white couple, without issuing any epithets or overt threats, nonetheless left the clear impression that the easiest, safest route had just been closed off, and only dangerous roads remained.

The coffee not yet finished, her head still pounded when it was joined by a more physical pounding—the front door. Three heavy knocks accompanied by *"Police! Open up!"*

She tried to both whisper and scream—*"Malcolm!"*—to wake him without being overheard outside. Were they really police? And did it matter? She hurried into the bedroom, shaking her husband by the shoulder. "Someone's knocking on the door! Says they're police."

First he was as hard to rouse as a dead man, then he sprang up as if electrocuted, grabbing the revolver from his bedside table before his feet had touched the floor. He popped out the chamber to double-check the rounds—quintuple-check was more like it, as both of them had done so many times last night—then stuck it in his pants, his flannel shirttails concealing it.

"If you don't open right now, we'll kick it down!"

In the front parlor, Malcolm's Winchester lay on the sofa. He moved a few of the cushions to conceal it. Then, positioning himself beside the sofa, told her to open the door only a few inches.

She realized her hand was shaking as she turned the bolt, then the knob, so overwhelmed by even these most rote of tasks that she forgot to offer a quick prayer to the Lord, not that the Big Man hadn't been hearing from her plenty of late.

She opened the door just enough to let them see her—unwashed, hair a mess, great with child, terrified. Two white policemen. She didn't get a chance to ask what they wanted when the one in front demanded, "Where's your big buck, girl?"

He pushed the door open, almost hitting her belly. The officers walked into the parlor as if it were theirs, like they'd celebrated holidays here, said their prayers and raised their children within these walls.

"Well, hello there," the lead officer said. He was perhaps forty-five, tall and ruddy, auburn hair visible beneath his cap. His partner was younger, and something about his doughy cheeks and fast-moving eyes reminded Hannah of a bulldog, as did the thickness of his chest and neck. Tommy had told her to always try and get the names of officers who spoke to them, but they didn't wear nameplates and she could only imagine how they would respond if she dared ask.

"Morning, Officers," Malcolm said. The cops fanned across the room, into and out of his personal space, but he stayed cemented in place.

"Malcolm Greer, correct?"

"Yes, sir."

"Where were you last night, boy?"

Hannah felt the bulldoggish one watching her.

"Here. We were here all day, all night."

"How about around six, six thirty last night?"

"We were eating dinner together."

The lead cop stepped closer to Malcolm. "Anybody else can vouch for that?"

"I can," Hannah said. Both cops stared at her, stunned that the woman dared speak.

"Someone *other than* the two of you, I mean."

"It was just us," Malcolm said.

The cop looked him up and down. Hannah imagined what he saw: an exhausted Negro still bearing the marks of a severe beating, the bridge of his nose crooked and the skin above his right eye lower than it should be. He was missing two front teeth—the dental work was going to cost a fortune—and it lent him a slurred speech his own wife barely recognized.

"Someone broke into a neighbor's house last night," the cop said.

"Stole quite a lot of money. Two Negroes, one of them the break-in man and one of them driving a getaway car, who mighta been a woman. So the two of you had best have a better alibi than keeping each other company, or we're gonna have a few more questions to ask at the station."

"Why would we steal from a neighbor?" Malcolm asked.

For all Hannah knew, these were the very men who'd beaten Malcolm. Nearly killed him.

"Oh, I can think of a few motives. Fellow whose house got broken into was a man you had a bit of an altercation with recently. And that—"

"It wasn't an altercation," Hannah said, "we just said we—"

"Hush your mouth, girl!" the bulldog called out.

The lead cop asked Malcolm, "Are you gonna let her keep talking or are we gonna have to hush her next time?"

"Hannah," Malcolm said, eyes down. "Just let me . . . let me talk to them."

The lead cop smiled. "You both knew that Mr. Thames had quite a bit of money in his house, and you decided that instead of selling your place for it, you'd just up and take the money instead. Ain't that right?"

Contradict them, and they'll snap. Admit a wrongdoing you didn't commit, and you go to jail. Stay silent, and they'll be just as furious.

Malcolm said, "I was discharged from the hospital yesterday at ten in the morning. We haven't left the house once since then. I can barely move around, let alone break into a house."

The lead cop stayed motionless for a spell, watching Malcolm. "Well, Officer Barnwell, it appears the subject is unwilling to confess his crimes here. We'll be able to get the truth at the station. Cuff him."

The bulldog, Barnwell, grabbed Malcolm by the shoulder and spun him around. He was pulling Malcolm's wrists behind his back when Hannah screamed, "You can't do this! My brother's a policeman!"

"I can't do something?" the lead cop barked, stepping closer to her now. "Are you telling me what I can and cannot do, you black bitch?"

"Don't you call her that!" Malcolm snapped. His hands not yet cuffed, Malcolm tried to shake Barnwell off, turning to face the one who'd insulted his wife.

Things were moving too fast for Hannah to follow, but to the lead cop this must have been an all-too-predictable response to his comment. He turned to Malcolm and did not seem the least rushed, surprised, or even bothered as he calmly punched Malcolm in his barely mended cheek.

"Don't touch him!" Hannah screamed.

There was another sound, one she didn't yet understand, as she screamed at them and Barnwell leaned Malcolm into the sofa and grabbed his wrists again, this time cuffing him. The other cop slapped her in the face. Not since she was eight or nine, fighting with a friend she'd never speak to again, had she been struck. Her cheek felt hot and there were tears in her eyes and her whole body had shifted a few feet to the right. When she was able to look up again, she saw through watery eyes that the lead cop was crouched on the floor and holding a gun.

"Well, look what we have here." Malcolm's revolver had fallen from its perch when the cop had slugged him. The cop stood all the way up, gripping it by the handle.

"I have papers for that," Malcolm said, still bent over the sofa.

"Brother's a policeman, huh? Well, there's yet another motive. You're getting all uppity, thinking your family's above the law. Thinking you can bust into houses and steal from the good white people of this neighborhood."

Then, in a motion that would be seared into Hannah's memory forever, in a pose that would wake her in the middle of countless nights, he pointed the gun down, to the back of Malcolm's head.

"No!" she screamed, so loudly she wet herself, so hard the muscles around her ribs would ache later.

He held the gun there and smiled. Malcolm couldn't see what was happening, and he started to say "Hannah" just as the lead cop laughed.

He put the unfired gun into his pocket and nodded to Barnwell.

"Cuff her, too."

39

Just past noon, after Rake's tussle with Dale, he had just finished roll call when his partner, Parker, told him the latest on the Thames robbery.

"Helton made an arrest a little while ago. It was one of the Negro couples who'd just moved in, Malcolm Greer and his wife."

"The one who got beat half to death? He's cousins with Negro Officer Smith."

"I didn't know that. How did you?"

"Just heard it around." Rake shrugged, working a fake dose of nonchalance into his very real anger. "But why them, what's the motive?"

"For a burglary? The motive was money. They knew he had a lot of cash lying around because he'd offered some of it to 'em to buy their house back. Pretty stupid move, robbing from one of your neighbors. Don't shit where you eat, but maybe Negroes don't know that expression. Anyway, the victim positively identified Greer in a lineup a few minutes ago."

Helton had closed his case quickly and efficiently.

"Parker, that money wasn't even stolen—at least, not the way Helton thinks. Thames staged it."

Parker looked at him like he was crazy. "Come again?"

"I was first on the scene. There was a hell of a lot of glass outside his window, on the lawn, and just a tiny amount inside. He claims the intruders broke the glass to gain entry to the house, but it had been broken from the inside. Either Helton's being played, or he's playing along deliberately."

"Maybe they broke it on the way out, too."

"That's not what he said. I was there, I could see it in his eyes."

Parker tried to follow Rake's logic. "So he ran a neighborhood collection to buy out the Negroes, then he pretended to rob himself so he could keep the money?"

"Yes. He claimed it was two Negroes, but I smelled shoe polish strongly in that room. I think he had two friends over, who came in and slathered on blackface, then one got into the car to act like the getaway driver." Committing crimes in shoe-polish blackface was not unheard of, especially at night and in white areas, where people weren't all that used to seeing Negroes and often couldn't tell the difference from a distance. "Thames fires a couple shots into the wall to attract attention, then the accomplice runs off into the car, to confuse any witnesses. Thames was acting so damn strange, and I couldn't help realizing how convenient it'd be for him if that collection of other people's money just happened to vanish into his own bank account."

"I don't know, bud. You told me you didn't much like that fellow, remember?"

"Yeah, there was something about him that didn't wash, and now I've figured out why. Think about it: Helton's pinning this on those Negroes. Why chase them out of the neighborhood when you can jail them for a trumped-up crime? And as an added benefit, it'll probably scare the other two colored households away, too."

Parker shook his head. "You're basing this on how glass fell and the scent of shoe polish in a man's bedroom. A man who has every right to polish shoes in his house. What Helton has is a Negro couple with reason to be vindictive against the victim," and he counted on his fingers, "reason to suspect he had a lot of cash, and, oh yeah, the victim has *positively identified* them."

"To frame them and cover his tracks! I bet if someone looked into his bank records, they'd find something—for all we know he has gambling debts or a drug habit, or he's about to go buy a bigger house with his sudden windfall."

Parker frowned like a sage father who was through indulging his son's well-argued but futile case for more allowance. "Glass falling isn't strong enough, and a judge would never okay looking into the man's finances. Even if Thames does have money problems, that kind of case would take far too long to work out, and time is the one thing we don't have. You know it, just like Helton does: if the sun had set one more time on Hanford Park without an arrest, folks would riot. Houses would get burned down and maybe someone would get lynched. Do you want that? You want to explain to your little boy what that body hanging in the tree is? Maybe fate dealt this Greer boy a bad hand, but busted for burglary beats being barbecued and having his dick chopped off." He paused at the image. "You may not like it, but Helton did what he had to do to stabilize the neighborhood and restore order."

"What if a crowd gathers tonight for vengeance against the other Negro houses? The arrest doesn't solve anything if Greer's innocent. No matter how well Thames lies, that money needs to turn up, or we'll still get that riot."

"Nah. If anyone complains about their missing money, Helton and his boys'll assure them that the perpetrators are in custody and that the slow gears of justice are moving. By the time Greer's found guilty, months will have passed and no one will be so incensed about having lost twenty or fifty bucks that they'll do anything rash." He adjusted his cap. "Like you said, those other Negroes will get the message and clear out, so folks will be happy, no matter what the hell really happened with their money."

Rake and Parker were about to head out when Rake got a call.

"Why is my cousin in jail?" Smith demanded.

Rake motioned to Parker that he'd be a minute. Once he was alone, he said, "This is a delicate situation. I'm sorry for him, but there's a lot going on right now."

"Tell me about it. I was up all night at his house holding a rifle."

"*What?* Boggs told me you wouldn't come around Hanford Park again—that was part of our deal."

"The deal got revised when a mob of white folks took to the streets."

"You standing around with a rifle is not a good idea. I don't want things to escalate and—"

"Escalate? That was self-defense. We were *in* his house standing watch. Some other people were going to do it again tonight, but I guess they don't have to since the Greers are in jail. Or maybe that was the plan all along? Get them in jail so you can torch their house and not have to feel guilty for killing someone?"

He couldn't stand Smith. Boggs you could deal with, well spoken and polite, but trying to reason with this fellow was like juggling grenades. "I've been trying to help you, goddammit."

"He's been arrested. How is that helping?"

Jesus Christ. Especially after the attack on his brother-in-law, how could Smith fail to realize what he was dealing with? On one side were whites like Dale and the Columbians and the Klan, thugs who were itching to stomp the Smiths of the world into oblivion. People like Rake—outnumbered and not thanked—were barely holding those forces back, and what Rake gets in return is Smith's outraged attitude.

"I've been sticking my neck out for you," Rake snapped. "I've been asking uncomfortable questions and putting myself out where I shouldn't. And *I'm* the one who kept that mob from spinning out of control last night. Rifle or no rifle, you wouldn't have had enough bullets, trust me. All this has gotten me is a hell of a lot of dirty looks from my own neighbors and other cops."

He was keeping his voice down, but still he worried others might overhear. It was like he'd been turned into a spy against his own race. How had he let Smith and Boggs do this to him?

Smith said, "I appreciate that you're in a tough spot. So am I. I have people to answer to, and they're wondering why my relatives, who aren't thieves, are in a *cell.* We got a lawyer heading over there; I wish I felt confident that they'd be *safe* once they're bailed out, but something tells me that's asking too much." Rake did not appreciate the acid tone. "Now, what can you tell me about the arrest? They got any kind of fake evidence whatsoever?"

"All I'm hearing is that the victim ID'd Malcolm in a lineup."

"That's crazy."

"I don't like it, either." Rake could have told Smith his suspicions about Thames. But clueing a Negro in on the internecine conflicts of whites did not seem wise, especially now. And Smith's tone during this conversation was not lending Rake an overwhelming desire to be forthcoming. "If you're waiting for me to apologize for not finding out who roughed up your cousin, don't hold your breath. Doing favors for you hasn't exactly been good for me. If I find anything that helps your family, I will let you know immediately." He hung up before Smith could criticize him again.

Next he put in an overdue call to an old buddy who wrote at the business desk of the *Constitution,* Chip Weathers. He'd called Chip a few days ago and asked him to look into Letcher's business, which Rake wouldn't have known how to research or even understand.

"Have you learned anything about Letcher?"

"Oh yeah, been meaning to call you. Interesting fellow." But Letcher *wasn't* interesting, at least not as far as Rake could tell; he'd already looked up Letcher's legal records, finding little of note. "Owns quite a bit of property in Atlanta."

"Including a stake in Sweetwater Mill just down the road from me."

"Correct, but he's been making out particularly well with residential real estate. It took some digging, but turns out he's one of the owners of a firm that bought a number of properties in '47 and '48, *all* of which it resold within a year." When Chip explained where exactly those properties were located, Rake leaned back in his chair.

"Those neighborhoods all went colored," he realized, hating himself for having missed this, the connection that linked Letcher to Hanford Park. Letcher made a business of profiting off neighborhoods that changed color, buying houses low from panicked whites and reselling them high to incoming Negroes.

"I was talking about him the other day to a buddy of mine here, on the crime beat," Chip said. "The Letchers have quite a bit of money—his daddy made a ton before the Depression, and managed to hold on to it—but they've had their share of kooks in the family tree. One of his cousins, matter of fact, was one of those Columbians got put away a few years ago. Let's see, where'd I write that name?"

Rake's mind raced. Letcher's moneymaking scheme would not sit well with most Atlantans—and especially not with the self-appointed guardians of white Atlanta, had they realized he was behind it. Letcher was wise to have kept it a secret, buried behind complex financial relationships that only a journalist could ferret out. A journalist, or maybe a relative who happened to overhear something once.

"Sorry," Chip continued, "I'm still looking for that notebook, it's here somewhere . . ."

Rake guessed it, his voice dry: "The cousin was Delmar Coyle."

"That's the one."

40

Clancy Darden liked stripes, Boggs noticed. He wore a dark gray suit with thin pinstripes over a white shirt with black pinstripes, his red tie had black stripes, and when he smiled his forehead wrinkled in an undulating stack of horizontal lines. The vice president of the Negro-owned, million-dollar insurance company where Boggs's brother worked, Darden smiled a lot, even though his smile appeared very nervous indeed.

Boggs sat with his father, Darden, and Reverend Holmes Borders of Wheat Street Baptist. They were the three wise men of the Sweet Auburn community who had been invited to sit down with the white leaders of Hanford Park to discuss the deteriorating situation.

Sitting opposite them were three white men. Don Gilmore, the hardware store owner, headed the neighborhood association, which had not existed until the Negro families started moving into the area. He had gray hair and the physique of someone who'd made his living building and fixing things; the plaid tie over his white dress shirt appeared to be a clip-on. Beside him sat Richard Puckett, silver-haired and bedecked in a gray business suit, meaning he was as well dressed as the Negroes here. He was a lawyer and former city councilman with an air of authority about him; surely he himself didn't live in blue-collar Hanford Park. The third white man, John Vanders, a foreman at Sweetwater Mill, crossed his arms over his denim shirt and thick chest; unlike his colleagues, he didn't see the point in smiling.

They sat at a long table in a conference room in Puckett's downtown law firm. Boggs had felt very conspicuous indeed as he and his fellow Negro ambassadors had entered the fine lobby a moment ago. The elevator operator, a Negro barely out of his teens, had seemed flummoxed when they entered his car. Several white people behind them had opted to wait in the lobby rather than share the elevator.

"Thank you for coming, gentlemen. I admit this is awkward timing," Puckett said. "I understand there was a robbery in Hanford Park just last night."

Boggs wondered exactly how much these white men knew about it.

"It's very unfortunate," his father said. "Sin certainly knows no borders."

"Well, Hanford Park has been crime-free for years," said Gilmore. Boggs very much doubted that: what area could ever be completely crime-free? "Look, I'm a businessman; I sell my goods to both races. I want no trouble in the neighborhood, I want no property damage, and I want no more nights like last night. Now, given that we're already talking about three families, and given that the area a few blocks south has gone from mixed to mostly Negro over the past two years, it doesn't seem likely we can get that genie back into the bottle."

"We feel that restoring natural borders between the races is the smartest and safest strategy," Puckett declared in his lawyerly voice as he removed a map from a folder and spread it before them. "What had been the border, Beacon Street, is no longer serving as such, as we now have three Negro families living north of it." Beacon, a main thoroughfare that ran all the way downtown, flanked by businesses, had separated the races for decades.

"But this only works," Vanders said, his tone a bit more forceful than his colleagues', "if y'all respect the new borders we draw today. Doesn't do any good to draw a new one and retreat and then a year from now three other colored families break the border."

Boggs had the sense Vanders's words weren't directed solely at the Negroes but at the other white men as well. There seemed to be a difference of opinion on that side of the table as to how bright of an idea this meeting was.

"The greater issue is that there is a severe shortage of housing for Negroes," Reverend Boggs explained. "Much of the existing properties in Negro areas are substandard at best, and we have thousands more people moving into the city. *No one* wants to live in a dilapidated shack in Darktown or a hovel in Buttermilk Bottom that doesn't have plumbing."

"All that new public housing was supposed to remedy that," Gilmore said.

"It has helped, but there is still a shortage," Darden said. "Particularly for those Negroes with means beyond what public housing offers."

Boggs remembered what Reginald had told him: Darden had spent a not inconsiderable amount of money on a wooded parcel northeast of Hanford Park, not far from one of the public housing complexes put up during the New Deal. He planned to build single-family homes and an apartment building for Negroes. Any decisions about the future of Hanford Park would have a huge impact on Darden's nearby investment.

"We may have differences of opinion on a lot of things," Puckett said, "but one thing I'm sure we agree on is that we want to avoid violence. We don't want people taking up arms and rioting because things have gotten out of hand."

"There's already been violence," Boggs pointed out. "One of the Negro residents was nearly killed."

"None of us condone that," Gilmore claimed, "and none of us want anything like that to happen again. That's why we're here."

They're so slick, Boggs thought. With one hand they beat Malcolm and nearly run riot like last night, and with the other they offer bland sentiments and claim to be moral and just, all the while warning you that the first hand is still clenched and ready.

"One of the things we had been planning to put on the table today was an offer to have the neighborhood association buy back the properties those three Negro households bought," Gilmore said. "But, ah, as I understand it, just last night the money was stolen."

Boggs knew about the break-in, but he hadn't realized what exactly had been stolen.

"Now, I do hope the money will be recovered," Gilmore said. "But if it isn't, then I'm afraid we will not be in a position to buy those properties."

One of the Negro families had temporarily moved out of their home, but Boggs had told his father not to disclose that. *If we let the white people know that they've bullied Negroes away, they'll be emboldened. And if word spreads that one of the houses is vacant, it's more likely to be torched.*

"We feel that the needs of the greater community could be met *and* more housing could be available to colored families if we began to treat Magnolia Street as the new border," Puckett said, removing from one of his folders another map. Sure enough, the area north of Magnolia was marked White, with Colored to the south. Magnolia wasn't a main road like Beacon, but it ran along the southern end of the park, making it a logical border in the white people's minds.

Boggs said to his father, "So they're asking us to sign off on restricting Negroes' right to live where they see fit? Didn't the Supreme Court already have something to say about that?"

A flash of anger in his father's eyes, but before he could reply, Puckett did.

"First of all, we're not a housing authority or the state senate, we're just a group of private citizens having a conversation. There isn't a court in America that has a problem with that. Secondly, no one will *sign* anything. And third, as Mr. Gilmore just explained, you aren't the only ones who would be giving something up. You agree that the Negroes stay south of Magnolia, and we agree that those whites who now live on those three square blocks—and have been for decades—will move out."

"That's not a minor sacrifice," Gilmore said. "It's three blocks down and five across for you all. And *we'd* be the ones who'd have to tell those folks they have to sell. I assure you, those are not conversations I'm looking forward to."

Puckett said, "Just like you, we are trying to avoid bloodshed and chaos."

"And those white people would all move because you tell them to?" Boggs asked.

"They would be extremely foolhardy not to," Puckett said. "No one wants to be the last white house in a neighborhood of Negroes."

"Lucius," Reverend Boggs said, "I left my briefcase in the car. Could you get it for me?"

He felt the blood rise in his cheeks. He was being banished.

"Yes, sir. I'll be right back." He walked slowly through the hall and back to the elevator and its nervous young operator. Out the lobby and down the block to the car. There the briefcase sat, no doubt left on purpose, just in case his father needed to employ this ruse.

By the time he returned to the room, everyone was shaking hands. Not celebrating, exactly, but difficult business had been worked out, and the grown-ups had restored order.

He endured a lecture from his father during the drive home. "This is how we do things in Atlanta. This is why we've had peace for so long." It made Boggs sad, as if the city should congratulate itself by posting a knockoff of one of those factory signs, "Welcome To Atlanta, 44 Years Without A Race Riot!" "I know it feels wrong to concede anything when you're sitting across the table from them, but that's the thing: *we were across the table from them.* In most Southern towns, white folks wouldn't *consider* sitting down with us. Don't you appreciate how rare that is? I have worked very hard for a very long time to have earned my seat at that table. I can't have hotheaded talk jeopardize that, badge or no badge."

He was not in the mood to fight with his father—his father who might have been right about Julie all along, his father who would no doubt *never* let him forget making such an error in judgment. Boggs feared he had many days of penitence to go, so he needed to choose his battles carefully.

They were pulling into the driveway when they saw Boggs's mother in the front yard, hurrying toward them, her brow creased with worry.

As soon as they stepped out, she walked past the reverend and right up to her son. "Tommy Smith called. His sister and brother-in-law are in jail."

41

Smith drove slowly down Malcolm and Hannah's block. Midmorning and gorgeous, the purple and white aster blooming in more than a few front yards, a young woman planting bulbs in a bed alongside her driveway.

Malcolm and Hannah had been arrested about two hours ago. He saw no squad car in front of their place, no yellow tape barring entrance, no police presence of any kind.

He had borrowed Dewey's car to get here, lying when Dewey asked if he had a license. He'd only driven in the States a few times, but in the war he had driven not only a tank but also various trucks, so he had a good enough knack for it. The engine did not appreciate the way he used the clutch, based on the noises it made, but he hadn't hit anyone or been pulled over.

Smith pulled into the Greers' driveway and parked beside the house. He exited quickly and made for the back door, less likely to be spotted. With a spare key they'd given him, he let himself in. He didn't call out hello. Apart from the hum of their refrigerator and the birdcall from some opened windows, he heard nothing. The place smelled of stale coffee.

First he checked to see if they'd left the rifle out in the open, but if they had, the white cops would have found it. In which case Malcolm was already doomed. He didn't see it, so next he checked the obvious places: the closets, under their bed. Then, back in the parlor, he looked under the sofa. Where was it? He sat down, and then he felt the rifle, stuffed behind the cushions.

The white cops must not have been looking for it. They'd simply come to pin a burglary on Malcolm, not realizing he had committed a much worse crime.

Smith wrapped the rifle in a spare blanket from the bedroom closet. Then he exited through the back door and hid the rifle in the trunk of Dewey's car. He slowly backed out of the drive, scanning every near window and yard as he did, hoping to slip out unnoticed.

Speed limits obeyed, rear mirrors checked constantly, yellow lights humbly acquiesced to, he made it to his side of town in twenty minutes.

He was beyond exhausted. His eyes hurt, pulse pounding in his temples. He had gone from his night shift to his overnight vigil with Malcolm, leaving at sunrise around seven, then managed barely three hours of sleep before being woken by pounding feet from the upstairs neighbors, informing him of the phone call, which was Hannah calling in tears from jail.

He was still reeling from his revelation about what Malcolm had done for Feckless. (Did Hannah know? He hadn't dared ask last night.) He knew that he himself was wading deep into morally suspect waters just by agreeing to keep silent about it.

But knowing that the white cops were pinning the burglary on the Greers, using their power to so casually eliminate the problem of Negro neighbors—it was more than he could bear. The white people had gone too far. He knew they went this far quite often—even further—but this was *his family*. He needed to protect them from the sheer evil of the other cops, of their new neighbors, of all those lightning men in their various uniforms. He would protect them, even if it meant also protecting them from the consequences of Malcolm's dirty work for Feckless.

He couldn't imagine what his straitlaced, preacher's-son partner would say if he'd told him about this. The hell with Boggs. As much as Smith loved him for sitting vigil with the Greers, for putting his life on the line for his family, he knew this was more than Boggs could ever condone or forgive. For God's sake, Boggs was about to drop the love of his life, all because she'd once been with a man who'd smuggled cigarettes! The perceived purity of the Boggs line was more important to his partner than a happy life with Julie. No, Boggs wouldn't understand this at all. Smith hated what he was doing, and he *despised* how Malcolm had turned himself into a drug dealer's goon, and perhaps if the situation had been different, he would have let the arm of the law take Malcolm all the way to the electric chair, would have allowed his pregnant sister to become a widow. But what good would that do? Who would that possibly help? It would be a victory for the lightning men, and he could not abide that.

Fifteen minutes later, the city vanished, overtaken by red-clay forest, the autumn sunlight sharply cutting through the boughs. Tar paper shacks down here, dirt-poor Negroes living without plumbing in an area that seemed so many worlds from the unseen capitol building, which Smith had passed a moment ago. Then farther south the road straightened and he passed the local prison, trying not to think about the murder weapon in his trunk or stare at the razor wire and the armed guards on those watchtowers, trying not to think of some boys from his childhood he knew were inside, there but for the grace of God or sheer luck, there but for better parenting, there but for the fact that they were offered a quick way to make some cabbage and I wasn't, there but for the fact that I was too afraid to run with those boys, or too square, there but for the fact that I got hired for this job when I applied but Malcolm didn't, he told me so when I got the job, we hadn't even known the other had applied, and if the Department had chosen him instead of me, where would I be right now? Would Malcolm be disposing of a murder weapon for *me*?

He needed to hurry back to the city, see if the lawyer Boggs had recommended had visited Hannah and Malcolm in jail yet. Like with Thunder Malley, he feared someone in the Department would have reason to permanently silence Malcolm. He couldn't imagine how his pregnant sister was being treated.

He came to an old quarry, some of which had been filled with water in a sad attempt to turn these trash-strewn woods into a pleasant escape for city folks. No cars in the gravel lot. He hiked along the trail ten minutes before cutting into a narrow, untended side trail he'd walked once before, ignoring the Warning signs until he came to one of the still-empty pits. A great wound in the earth, the striations of orange and red and so many shades of brown he was amazed to see them all, a veritable rainbow of brownness, and beyond that, black, a pit of endless depth.

He used the blanket to wipe the gun down once more, then tossed it. A full five seconds until he heard it strike anything. A cool breeze hit him then, as if coming from the pit, and he wrapped the blanket around his shoulders like some vagabond as he walked back to the car.

42

The location of Joe's Ribs, one block from police headquarters, meant that the barbecue joint was responsible for countless failed physicals. Sergeant Gene Slater was a regular patron, though he'd managed to eat there for two decades without putting on a spare tire. Tall fellows were like that sometimes, McInnis noted as he slid into the chair opposite his former partner.

Slater was dressed in his uniform blues, this being his break. McInnis had a few hours to go, wearing a white polo shirt with the police crest in the corner.

"That still your old Plymouth parked at headquarters?" McInnis asked. "I heard your wife has herself a Chrysler convertible."

"It's not a good idea to drive something like that to the station. Hello to you, too."

"These last few years have been good to you."

"Can't complain."

"Must be nice to supplement one's salary like that."

The pert waitress took McInnis's order—pulled pork, collards, sweet tea—and left.

"Feeling left out?" Slater asked with a smile. "You had your chance, Mac. Plenty of chances. I seem to recall a certain high-and-mighty attitude, an unwillingness to play by the same rules as everyone else."

"I don't regret my decisions."

"Yet it's why you find yourself working down in the Congo." Slater leaned back and laced his fingers behind his head, still smiling. "How the hell were we ever partners?"

"We had a few similarities then. You were a fairly good cop, for one. Just a tad greedy."

"You think *I'm* the one who changed? Please. You were a good cop then, too, 'til you decided you liked informing on others so much."

McInnis looked around the joint for a moment—crowded, half of the clientele cops. It smelled like heaven set on fire. "Gene, you and your boys need to find a new way to supplement your income, outside my precinct, effective immediately."

Slater sipped his tea. He looked entertained. "Men who sell liquor and drugs sell 'em to those that use 'em. Coloreds love that stuff. Just good business, Mac."

"Be that as it may, your business is making things difficult for my officers."

"Shit, *your officers*. You make it sound all professional, not like the laughingstock it is."

"They are men working under my command. And maybe you don't give a damn, but they can't do their job while officers under *your* command are helping move drugs into their beat."

"Who says my men are doing anything like that?"

So Slater was calling McInnis's bluff, but that wouldn't stop McInnis from bluffing some more: "Are you asking me to provide evidence? Is that really what you want?"

"You're right, I don't give a damn about your boys. You keep on about this, and I'll start feeling the same way about you."

"In that case, let me rephrase it without a question mark at the end. Wait, no, there wasn't one to begin with. So I'll just make sure it's real clear for you. If you and your boys don't stop protecting bootleggers and dealers in my precinct, then the taxpaying citizens of Atlanta will soon be reading yet another front-page story about corrupt officers being busted."

Silence while Slater sat there, watching a man he thought he once knew.

"You're serious?"

"I've never been accused of being a very comedic man."

"Then you're suicidal."

"Nah, that's un-Christian. Anyway, I just wanted to let you know, as a courtesy, that, two years in, we're done arresting the little fish and we're moving up."

"Like Thunder Malley, huh? That didn't work out too well for anyone."

"No, it didn't. We've got enough murders to clear without having to deal with turf battles between rival groups moving dope, to say nothing of cops getting their hands dirty."

"You think I'm to blame? That's what you came here to accuse me of? Why would I do something like that?"

"I don't know. Maybe I should have asked Isaiah Tanner a few years ago."

McInnis felt right then that the scathing look in Slater's eyes was something that few other men had ever seen and survived.

"That is ancient history," Slater said, "and not worth bringing up."

For someone who spent so much of his time putting away criminals, it was galling to have this conversation, speaking in code like this. How badly McInnis wanted to just come out and say it: *Slater, your MO is to protect smuggling rings in colored neighborhoods, taking your cut while you do what you can to dissuade other cops from taking a closer look. And when, alas, things do go sour—due to an FBI investigation into wartime theft in '45, or due to Negro cops stopping a drug shipment this month—you cover your tracks by killing off whoever might be able to identify you, lay low for a bit, then start again with the next group.*

The waitress passed by and Slater asked for his order to go, on second thought. McInnis said the same.

"I understand the relatives of one of your officers were just arrested," Slater said. "Smith, right? Sounds like my ol' buddy Helton has an iron-clad case against them for B and E. They'll do a lot of time for that. And don't we have rules about not hiring people with felons in their family?"

"That doesn't apply retroactively, you know that."

"Well, that's true when it comes to white cops. I daresay the chief'll feel different about it when it comes to a black cop with a thief for a sister."

McInnis told himself to stay calm. He usually didn't need to remind himself. "Smith has a perfect record under me. Nice try, but that won't happen."

"Don't be so sure. How's he gonna feel knowing his relations could get sent away for, oh, five years? His cute little sister, chained to a grueling work camp. Ruin her life. But, wait, maybe there's some way we could pull some strings for 'em? Unlike *you*, I have quite a few friends over there. Maybe I can get the prosecutor to let them out on a technicality. Probation instead of time. Wouldn't that be nice?"

It almost made McInnis wonder whether this had been the plan all along. White cops were always trying to point out perceived violations by the Negro officers in hopes of getting the chief to nix the colored experiment. Now they'd moved on to blackmail.

"Good talking to you, Gene. But no deal. I'd hate for any arrests to lead your way, or toward any white officer at all. I know that sometimes those arrested Negroes wind up conveniently killed in jail, but I don't think that can happen too many more times before the folks in Internal Investigations get curious. Or even the chief, or the mayor. This is my final warning."

Slater lowered his voice. "You son of a bitch. After that sting you helped with, there were plenty men ready to mess with your brakes one day so you'd have an unfortunate accident. *I* held them back. *I* believed you were still a decent fellow. Looks like I was wrong."

"You're wrong about something," McInnis said just as the waitress came by with two paper bags. He grabbed his hat and stood to leave, Slater following.

Outside, Slater said, "Know what I think, Mac? You're just a pussy who's found you'd rather stab cops in the back than risk his life going after real crooks."

McInnis dropped his bag, turned, and threw a fist Slater's way. Another bag hit the ground as Slater dodged it, having expected that reaction. A southpaw, he punched once with his left, catching McInnis in the jaw. Already off balance from his miss, McInnis stumbled back, into a parked car.

Slater stepped forward, intending to make his point more emphatic, but McInnis pushed off from the car, launching his head into Slater's midsection and charging. He slammed him into the brick wall. Through a window McInnis could see cops with full mouths staring.

He hit Slater as hard as he could in the stomach, twice. He was at least two inches shorter and maybe ten pounds lighter than his ex-partner, yet this was the first time they'd ever fought. Both had wondered how it would go down. Slater wrapped a hand around McInnis's head, trying to wrench him away, and McInnis drove another fist into Slater's ribs. Slater released him, McInnis backed up a step, and they stared at each other.

Slater swung first, a right that McInnis mostly dodged, then McInnis drove a fist into Slater's nose. A tornado of cops whirled upon him then, holding back his arms and pushing against his chest. Another group held Slater back, cops everywhere calling out *Hey* and *Mac* and *Stop that*. McInnis pushed them away, demanded they release him, and finally he had his body to himself again. He ran his fingers through his mussed hair and spat on the sidewalk. No blood. Someone had stepped on his to-go bag. McInnis picked it up anyway and refused to look at any of the gathered men, who'd all but disowned him anyway. He kept his gaze on Slater.

Then McInnis turned and walked away, refusing explanation. He told himself not to listen to their comments as he crossed the street toward headquarters, nerves afire.

43

During what should have been his break in the late afternoon, Rake lied to his partner, saying he needed to run an errand. Then he drove in search of Delmar Coyle, local Fascist. He didn't trust Parker enough to have made this errand while on the clock. If he was going to solve the dilemma Dale had set before him, he'd need to do it on his own.

No one answered the door at Coyle's shack, so Rake knocked on the neighbors' doors. One of them was answered by a man in his sixties, who claimed Coyle had been leaving his house most mornings, perhaps going to work, like any normal fellow.

Rake returned to his squad car, which he'd parked around the corner so as not to alarm Coyle, and waited. He'd sat there only twenty minutes when a brown pickup, fifteen years old at least, pulled in front of the Columbian's place.

Coyle stepped out. He was clad not in his Nazi Brownshirt getup but another kind of costume: white collared shirt, red tie, slacks. In disguise as a respectable American.

Rake walked over to him. "I almost didn't recognize you in that."

Coyle froze. Recognizing Rake, he said, "Yeah, well, some of us have to earn a living doing real work."

"But who'd hire you?"

"Why is it any of your business?"

"Just answer me."

"I got a cousin high up at a shipping outfit by Terminal Station. They needed a junior accountant, and I've always been good with numbers."

"They hired a known felon?"

"Like I told you before, I've paid my debt. And people stick by their family."

"That's funny coming from you."

"Why's that?" He looked over Rake's shoulder and to the side, checking for other cops.

"Tell me about your cousin, Martin Letcher."

Coyle's reaction was the lack of one, his face blank. "Been doing some research, huh?"

"You're a bit smarter than I thought. But still not as smart as you think you are."

"My cousin Marty is a damned *crook*. He's the one you should be bothering, not little ol' me. He and his cronies, the other bankers and real estate men, they got this whole system worked out, see? They pick a neighborhood, then they sell a couple houses to niggers there, telling them it's a 'transitional area' and okay for them to move in. Then they run to all the white folks and tell 'em that, oh gosh, the neighborhood's turning, so you'd best sell your place fast or you'll lose even more money than you already have. They get those white folks to sell to 'em at rock-bottom prices, then they turn around and resell to the niggers for a big markup. Presto, it's an all-African neighborhood and Marty makes out like a bandit."

"And you decided to teach him a lesson. But why use the Klan? Didn't have the guts to do it yourself?"

"The Klan," and he laughed bitterly. "Klan's a bunch of traitors. When us Columbians stepped up to try to make this city safe for white folks, all the Klan wanted to do was hide. They were all worried after that GBI sting, worried they didn't look 'respectable' anymore—one of them actually said that to me! They turned their back when the cops arrested us, and I know for a fact that some of those cops were Klansmen themselves. They didn't understand that we could have been their allies. They'd rather tease us for our uniforms—as if *theirs* aren't the silliest damn things grown men ever did wear—and call us Nazi stooges, when really they were just jealous, *jealous* that we dared to say what we believed in, in broad daylight, 'stead of running around with pillowcases over our heads."

"So you wanted somebody to teach Martin a lesson, let him know that his blockbusting was not appreciated by tough guys like you. And you picked a moron Klansman to do the dirty work for you, out of some sense of poetic justice."

"I'm not confirming a damn thing," Coyle said, grinning. "But I'll say this," and the Columbian chose his words carefully. "There are reasons the Klan hasn't been doing enough to stop what's happening in Hanford Park: they're the same kinds of rich folks who are making *money* off that, so why would they stop it?"

Rake had to admit Coyle's plan was smart: it kept the Columbians clean of the attack, it gave Letcher reason to fear Klansmen even though the Klan hadn't actually been angry at him, and it caused widespread confusion within the Klan, making them look all the more foolish and incompetent. In one move, Coyle had beaten one foe and debilitated a rival.

"You picked my own brother-in-law, you son of a bitch. Though I doubt you realized he was related to a cop. Only thing I can't figure is, who was Whitehouse?"

"You got any proof of any of this? I've never known a man named Whitehouse. Sounds fake to me. But, you know, I do have plenty of allies. And we aren't all young."

"You're very proud of yourself, aren't you?"

"Come on, you don't care about some nigger getting beat up—what you've been doing all along is trying to protect Dale. Who, by the way, you're right about being a moron. But you're not too bright, either. *Your* brother-in-law got mixed up in a killing, and you've been trying to find a way to help him out of it ever since."

Rake stepped closer. "Watch it."

"You don't have anything on me I don't have on you. You try and arrest me for anything you just said, then the whole story comes out. Including how you've known all along what Dale did. Instead of turning him in, you kept it to yourself. You put your family first. Family, clan, blood, race. That's how life works, so why are you fighting it?"

Rake was tempted to end this conversation the same way he'd ended his talk with Dale—punch the son of a bitch a few times. He wanted it so, so badly. Yet he was standing there in his uniform, and he would not allow himself to descend to the same level as his former partner, administering beatings whenever he couldn't solve problems with his brain.

"I hope you're not threatening me, Delmar."

"What are you so bothered about? Hell, I've been *helping* you. Marty's trying his dirty business in Hanford Park now, in *your* neighborhood this time, and you can't even see what's happening. You're too busy wanting to be mad at *me,* 'cause you think you're better than me, just like those damn Kluxers. I've been trying to keep your neighborhood white, but in another week or two, every other white family but you will be moving out."

"That's not happening."

"The hell it ain't! Call Marty and ask him, I dare you. Or talk to your neighbors and find out how many have decided to sell. I hear some neighborhood association just sat down with some head niggers or some such to redraw the race line officially—if that's true, you'd best believe your house is on the wrong side of that new line. Christ, stop worrying about Dale and me and worry more about yourself. Whose side do you want to be on?"

Rake shook his head. Seeing Coyle in that respectable getup, looking to all the world like a perfectly harmless, well-functioning part of the American workforce, was nauseating. There had to be some way to punish Coyle without seeing Rake's own career go down in flames.

Yet Coyle was right about Rake's neighbors fleeing Hanford Park. Cassie had said as much that morning.

Rake said, "Much as you may hate your cousin, he isn't doing anything illegal. Stay away from him, and from Dale. And from Hanford Park, understand?"

"Marty may not be breaking *your* laws, but some of us answer to a higher law," Coyle said as Rake walked back to his car. He sounded so confident, so right in his cause. "And you'd best believe, the reckoning's gonna come quick."

44

"I spoke to the prosecutor," McInnis told Smith and Boggs in his dank, mildew-scented office. When the Y basement had been turned into their de facto precinct, the city had paid to put three walls and a door in the corner for the sergeant. Usually McInnis only spoke to someone in there if that someone was in trouble, but Boggs and Smith had asked to meet there before roll call. "He's going to recommend that the Greers be held without bail for their own safety."

"No bail, for a B and E?" Smith had been sitting, but he nearly shot up. He felt just a few degrees below boiling. "That's crazy!"

McInnis held out a hand as if he could contain Smith. "Given the tensions in the neighborhood, he's afraid that if they're released, something will happen. I know jail's no fun, but it beats a lynch mob."

"So because white folks can't control *them*selves, two colored folk have to stay in jail?"

"I realize it's wrong. But do you want to see your relations strung up?"

"I want to see them dealt with fairly."

"Unfortunately, a lot of other factors are being placed on the scales right now."

"Sir," Boggs finally spoke, "his sister's seven months pregnant."

"I've greased some wheels with the jail warden. There are still a few folks over there who owe me favors, and I've been guaranteed no one will hurt them. We've made things as good for your family as we can expect until we get a better handle on things. They're safer there than they'd be encountering some linthead neighbor with a grudge and a baseball bat."

Smith leaned over and put his face in his hands. He felt on the verge of collapsing, overcome by the sheer stress of the past twenty-four hours, and the uncertainty of the many hours to come. It was all he could do to lift his head, looking straight at his sergeant.

"You need to get back on the phone with that prosecutor," he said. "Malcolm and Hannah *aren't* safe in there, and I need them out before they're killed."

McInnis seemed thrown by his officer's blunt command. "What aren't you saying?"

"I just figured this out last night, while we were sitting watch together in his house." He told them what details he dared, leaving out quite a few. He explained how Malcolm worked at the Rook as a doorman and bouncer. In that capacity, Smith lied, Malcolm had learned that his boss, Feckless, was involved in more than running a legitimate nightclub.

"Feck also works with a man we've been hearing about, Quentin Neale. Me and Lucius got some tips Neale was part of the gang that opposed Thunder Malley. Now I've learned, according to Malcolm, Neale spends a lot of time at the Rook, and he's always there when some mysterious deliveries show up in back."

"Keep talking."

"Malcolm was recently asked to tag along on a late-night errand to pick up something at the Pullman Yards. He declined because he thought it sounded shady. He asked around and figured out what his boss is really up to. Lester Feck, the Rook's owner, smuggled from the rail yards during the war, and now he's starting to smuggle marijuana in from New Orleans. So, first Feck and Neale tried to take down the competition, Thunder Malley, who had protection from white cops. We inadvertently helped him there."

Smith noticed McInnis sit up a bit straighter at this news. "Where'd you hear the part about smuggling during the war?"

"From Malcolm. *He* wasn't a part of that—he was in the Pacific back then—but Feck was here making money from stolen smokes. Then Feck decided to go straight just in time, buying a nightclub and walking away from smuggling."

"Shortly after Feck walked away," Boggs said, watching McInnis carefully as he said this, "the smugglers got shut down by the FBI.

In '45. An Isaiah Tanner was the ringleader. The FBI arrested Tanner's men, but didn't have anything on Feck. Tanner himself was killed. In an unsolved murder."

McInnis looked distinctly uncomfortable. "How do you know all this?"

Boggs said, "Tanner's brother, Jeremiah, who got put away for five years—I'm engaged to his ex-girlfriend."

"Well I'll be."

"And, Sergeant . . . We're pretty sure the cop who was helping Thunder Malley was Gene Slater, the same cop who was probably helping Isaiah and his ring back during the war." He paused, but he'd gone this far, so why not? "And you were Slater's partner back then."

"So all the cards are on the table now," McInnis said, still sounding calm. "I saw Tanner's name on the arrest report Jennings and Edmunds filed last week, so I knew he was out of Reidsville. I didn't know about your connection to him. And I didn't realize my own officers were digging into my past."

"I was only looking into my fiancée's ex-boyfriend, to see who I was dealing with. I didn't expect to find . . ." He didn't seem to know how to say it.

McInnis nodded and stared at his desk for a moment, eyes inward. "I like to think that one of the reasons I'm the cop I am today is because of Slater. Because he showed me exactly who I did not want to become."

Boggs and Smith waited. McInnis broke a long silence with, "He was my second partner, after I'd been on the force a few years. I realize now I turned a blind eye to the seriousness of what he was doing. First it was taking a little cut, protection money, which was bad enough. I told myself there were worse cops out there. I didn't lift a finger to help his little smuggling ring, and I didn't take a cut. But I didn't stop him, either. Otherwise, we worked well together. Then, when the FBI came in, Slater panicked. He told me he was going to kill Isaiah to make sure he couldn't be implicated. But first, Isaiah vanishes. Slater says he can't find him. Then, two days later, a beat cop finds Isaiah's body decomposing in a car abandoned in an alley."

"So . . ." Boggs tried to work this out. "Slater killed him?"

"I don't know. He had all but said he was going to. Then he said he couldn't find him. Then the body turns up. He never told me he did it, never spoke about Isaiah again. Maybe he just couldn't say it, or didn't want to."

McInnis rubbed away pressure along the socket of his eyes, as if pushing back a memory. He continued, "When they arrested Jeremiah for the smuggling, they tried at first to get him to confess to killing Isaiah. That is about as low as I have ever felt, knowing they were doing that, when there was a chance my own damned partner was the killer." A pause. "Jeremiah didn't confess, didn't get charged. And I didn't point the finger at Slater when I could have. A couple months later, we were assigned to new partners, and from then on we avoided each other."

This was all rather illuminating to Smith, but he said, "I don't mean to slam the door on your past, sir, but it's my family's future I'm worried about right now."

McInnis shook his head. "Slater is an opportunistic and slippery son of a bitch, but he has no desire to be put inside of a jail cell. He may have taken his cuts from Malley, and Tanner before that, but I don't think he'll be moving on to Feck. I'm confident we've shut him down."

" 'Shut him down,' that's our goal?" Boggs asked. "He's racked up a heck of a body count for us to settle for shutting him down."

"I agree, and if I felt I could get the Department to seriously look at him, I would. We can keep gathering evidence and hold on until a prosecutor cares enough to make another case against corrupt officers. In the meantime, we've shown him that it's going to be too much trouble for him to start another operation."

"What if you're wrong, and he does start taking cuts from Feckless?" Boggs asked.

"Then we pounce," McInnis said. "Meantime, I'll get on the line with the prosecutor and do whatever I can, without giving away much about our source. And if you have reason to suspect this Quentin Neale killed Forrester and Crimmons, you need to find him. Did Malcolm tell you anything about how they handle their deliveries?"

"Yes, sir, he did."

Once they were outside and a safe distance from the Y, Boggs stopped on the sidewalk and asked Smith, "When did you learn all this about Feckless and Malcolm?"

"Sitting watch with him last night."

"There's more you didn't tell McInnis."

"That's right." Smith tried to convey that Boggs was wandering into dangerous territory. "There are things he can't know."

"What about me, your partner?"

Maybe he'd been a fool to think he could keep anything from Boggs while working with him so closely. Perhaps he'd been a fool to tell McInnis anything. If he really wanted to protect Malcolm from the consequences of what he'd done, he'd need his partner's help.

Smith asked, "We trust each other, right? I can rely on you?"

"Of course you can."

"The shooter from the night at the telephone factory? The one camped out across the street? It was Malcolm."

After Smith sketched out the details, Boggs shook his head. "That's *murder*, Tommy. Family or not, we can't bury a murder."

"Can't we? Didn't you do that once? I helped you then, didn't I?"

Boggs didn't seem to appreciate the reference to a horrible night they'd shared two years ago, when they were rookies. "That was different. This isn't self-defense we're talking about."

"He says it was an accident, and besides, no one can prove anything. No one saw him."

"Where's the rifle?"

"Where no one can ever find it. I made sure of that."

He'd never realized how big Boggs's eyes could get. "*You* did?"

"Like I said, I only figured this out last night. Then I come home and barely two hours later he's arrested for the theft, which I *know* he didn't do. He hadn't had a chance to get rid of the gun yet, so I had to do it for him."

"You *had* to? You *had* to obstruct justice? Do you hear what you're saying?"

"Don't you quote the criminal codes to me, preacher's son. Or the Bible. Aren't you the one who was telling me how special family is? Aren't you marrying a girl who got mixed up in this same kind of thing?"

Boggs's jaw dropped but he couldn't seem to find words to fill the space. Finally he said, "She didn't commit *murder*, Tommy. Good God, don't you see the difference?"

"Maybe I *do* see the difference, and I'm tired of how much better it looks from where you're standing! I *hate* what he did, Lucius. All right? I hate that he got mixed up with that nonsense and I hate that he pulled the goddamn trigger on someone. And I know we hear all kinds of bullshit, but what he was telling me about only getting involved because he couldn't find a real job, and wanting to get back out as soon as he can—I don't know if I believe that, but *he* does. Now, it's bad enough he's gotta sit in jail for this bullshit robbery, but if he gets a murder charge added to it? I'm not taking chances with my brother-in-law's life. If the choice is letting him walk for a murder or having him killed in jail, then yes, I'm letting him walk."

They stared at each other for a long, uncomfortable moment.

"Tommy . . . Are you honestly proposing we let him get away with what he did?"

"I'm saying I've already made my decision. So now *you* get to decide whether or not you're going to go after him, and get me charged with obstruction while you're at it."

"That's not fair. We're in this together."

That phrase had never sounded so meaningless.

"Are we? Are we together, Lucius?"

45

After his shift, Rake drove in circles throughout his neighborhood, partly to see if there was any more activity and partly because he wasn't sure what his next move should be. Already today, both Coyle and Dale had threatened him with the same thing: talking about his own involvement if he dared arrest either of them. He'd allowed himself to be compromised. The weapons usually at his disposal had been rendered useless.

He finally stopped by a pay phone near the park and called Dale.

"I know who sent you to beat up Letcher. It was your buddy Delmar Coyle." He waited a few seconds for it to register. "He's not your friend, Dale. He used you as a pawn, because he knew you'd fall for it."

He explained the rest, reveling in Dale's silence and empty denials, his expression of shock that someone he thought was an ally could do that to him.

"You don't believe me? Fine. Go talk to him yourself." He gave him Coyle's address and hung up.

Three hard knocks and the plumber's door opened. Thames looked alarmed to see Rake, but that may have been because Rake had nearly punched a hole in the door.

"Can I help you, Officer?"

"Yeah, I need help dislodging some shit. Yours."

"Excuse me?"

He looked over Thames's shoulder but couldn't see enough to know if his wife was in.

"You were not broken into yesterday. Own up."

"I don't know what you're talking about."

"I'm talking about your master plan to abscond with money belonging to the community. Including some belonging to me."

"I'm sorry, I—"

"You staged the break-in and made a false statement to police. You made another false statement this morning when you ID'd the Greers as the thieves. That's a serious offense, especially considering that two innocent people are in jail because of it."

"I . . . I don't know what you're talking about."

"You framed them. And if you're too much of a coward to admit it, I will prove it by the end of the week, because you're a damn fool and your accomplices left behind plenty of clues." A bluff, but one he hoped would goad the plumber into talking. As Parker had pointed out, Rake had no evidence other than the fact that glass had fallen the wrong way, and, worse, no officer had taken any pictures of it. He needed Thames to believe he was on the verge of arrest. "Unfortunately for you, I live here, and I take what happens in my backyard seriously, so I'll be doing the real detective work. If you want to make things easy on yourself, now is your chance to confess."

Thames looked scared. That might—*might*—have been because he had an angry cop on his doorstep, but Rake chose to believe it was the guilty kind of fear. Thames now understood that not everyone had been conned by his get-rich-quick scheme.

After a long silence, Thames said, "I'm gonna have to ask you to leave."

"Sure. You have one day to turn yourself in, Mr. Thames, or you're looking at serious jail time and an entire neighborhood full of people who'll want to see you punished, severely. As you know, I live one block away, and I excel at punishing people. You have a good night's rest."

46

"Are you Jeremiah Tanner?"

Jeremiah had just finished his supper of hamburger and a Coke at a diner around the corner from the Rook when a Negro policeman walked in from the street and straight up to him. The policeman looked a few years older than himself, his skin a shade lighter, and his uniform was crisp, like the shirt was mere minutes from its latest date with an iron. Brass buttons shone, as did the badge at his breast and the crest on his perfectly centered cap.

"Yes."

"I'm Lucius Boggs. I think we should talk."

"*Officer* Lucius Boggs," Jeremiah corrected. Who possessed some of the straightest and whitest teeth Jeremiah had ever seen on a Negro. He took off his cap and sat down opposite Jeremiah, folding his hands on the table almost as if in prayer. His nails were uncracked.

Jeremiah quoted, "One's pride will bring him low, but he who is lonely in spirit will obtain honor."

"Proverbs. Yeah, I heard you knew your Bible. Well, my father's a preacher, so there's nothing I haven't heard. Any lesson or quote, it's been imprinted in my skull." He tapped the side of his head with one of those perfectly manicured fingers. He was one of those front-pew Negroes, his mama with a wide-brimmed hat she bought at some Auburn Avenue milliner, cost enough money to have clothed Jeremiah's whole family for a year, and his daddy passing around the collection plate, money for their clothes and jewelry and watches, not to mention their house and car. The Lord had been good to them, so much better than to others.

"We went to Pentecostal Holiness," Jeremiah said.

"I know the place."

"Probably think we were all snake-stompin' fools, right? That what you high rollers call it?"

"Just different ways of worshipping."

"Yeah. How I worship, I try to do good things. Try to remember He looking over my shoulder, telling me, *Jeremiah, there is a path. You got to find it and walk it and not be led astray.*"

Boggs nodded slowly, like he was trying to understand.

"Jeremiah," Boggs said in a voice that meant *We're changing the subject now,* "you know why I'm here."

But do you know I have a revolver in my pocket, Officer Boggs? Do you know that the bullets Officer Tall gave me have since been put into the chamber, by myself? Do you know which pocket the gun's in? Do you know how close your forehead is to the barrel?

"Do I?"

"Yes," Boggs said. "You do."

This was how Boggs's life worked: for days he'd been hoping to find Jeremiah, without success, and then tonight when he and Smith needed to get to another part of the city quickly, who should he happen to see through the window of a diner? He had stopped on the sidewalk involuntarily, knowing he didn't have time for this. Feckless's shipment was due to the stash location in Summerhill in two hours, if Malcolm's information was correct. But Boggs couldn't walk past Jeremiah. He'd told Smith to give him a minute; Smith stayed outside, observing the exchange through the window, should the need for assistance arise.

But what could he reasonably expect of Smith anymore? He was still reeling from what Smith had said about disposing of a murder weapon for Malcolm. Was this who they'd become? He couldn't believe that they, of all people, were working around the law. For decades Atlanta Negroes had policed themselves, taking important matters to their preachers or business leaders for adjudication, or settling disagreements with their fists. Those days were supposed to be over now, thanks to Boggs and Smith and their colleagues. It was their job to step in and help their community, to solve problems using *the law*. Yet Smith was helping Malcolm conceal a crime, and he'd given Boggs similarly illicit advice about Jeremiah, recommending that Boggs find a way to "remove" Jeremiah from the situation.

Now Boggs found himself face-to-face with his adversary. He said, "You need to stay away from Julie."

A charged moment of eye contact. Then Jeremiah looked away again. "She's got my boy."

"You need to stay away from him, too."

"Says you?"

"Yes, says me. I can give you lots of different reasons to choose from. The *legal* reason is, she signed a restraining order after you busted into her house, and that order means you'll get arrested just for getting *near* her, you understand?"

Jeremiah grinned. Boggs had grown accustomed to that damn grin, the one so many men wore when they were hearing things they didn't like and couldn't stop. Boggs continued, "And the *moral* reason is that boy. He doesn't need to see you. Doesn't need to see what you became and where you've been. He deserves a chance, deserves to believe he can be anything and do anything. He shouldn't have to think he comes from the gutter."

The grin was gone but Jeremiah still wasn't looking Boggs's way. The tabletop and whatever was happening on the sidewalk outside seemed to hold more interest for him.

"Some folks call it the gutter. Some call it the alley. Some call it Darktown. We can't help where we born, Officer Lucius Boggs."

"But we can help what we do. You chose to run with the crowd you ran with. You chose to steal—from the military, of all places, with a war on. You had a job that paid and you went and ruined it, so you could look big to a group of fools."

"Easy for you to say, preacher's son."

"Don't give me that. Two of my fellow officers grew up on that same block. They didn't turn out like you did, so don't blame your address. Blame your choices."

Eye contact again. "What else Julie tell you about me?"

Even though she was the subject of this conversation, Boggs didn't even want to hear her name on his lips. "*She* didn't say that, your record does. I've seen the files, read the transcripts."

"What the white people say." Jeremiah rearranged himself again. At first he'd been fidgeting, reaching for a packet of sugar and then dropping it back on the table, at one point scratching at the stubble on his chin. But now he was very still. His threadbare coat hung open, a white undershirt beneath it, dirty and yellowed in places. His left hand fell to his side and his right rested in his lap, both blocked from Boggs's view by the table.

"Keep your hands where I can see them."

"There a law against having my hand in my lap?"

Boggs very slowly leaned back so that the table would not be an obstacle if he needed to reach for the gun in his holster. More forcefully now: "Keep your hands where I can see them."

Jeremiah lifted his hands, both of which were empty, and he held them there a moment, palms up, like a preacher beseeching the Lord to help him deal with the madness here on earth. Then he let them fall to the table.

"You may have been let off for Isaiah's murder, but you still did plenty. So if I were you—"

"I paid my debts."

"I were you, I would think about all those other cities that aren't Atlanta. I would think of all the opportunities you might find if you weren't in a town where the people who know you suspect that you killed your own brother. I would think this is the perfect time for you to start over, clean the slate."

"Officer Lucius Boggs wants me gone."

Hearing his name said that way reminded him, in a sickening way, of how Julie had done the same when they'd first met. She'd called him by that full, official name, in a singsong way that fell between mocking and flirting. Hearing Jeremiah use all three words, mimicking her without even realizing it, left Boggs cold.

"What I want is no trouble. You've done your time and I respect that. But I don't see any reason to think you're suddenly going to become an upstanding fellow. You have a job? You have a place?"

Jeremiah eyed him again. "Boy is my son."

"Not anymore. You forfeited that right."

"Never seen anything about that in the Bible. Never heard Jesus say a man forfeits his child."

"There are cold hard facts you need to accept. There are conse-quences to your actions."

"That boy, *he's* a consequence to an action." He eyed Boggs again, some viciousness there that hadn't been visible before. "An action be-tween two people, neither of 'em you."

Boggs leaned forward. "You want to get dirty, now? That make it sit better with you? That give you the satisfaction you can't get anywhere else? All right, Jeremiah. You had something, something *good,* and you lost her. But you talk dirty 'bout her one more time, you'll be picking yourself up off the sidewalk an hour later."

The viciousness still glinted in Jeremiah's eyes. He held his head at a jaunty angle, his chin low, looking almost sideways at Boggs. "Been talking 'bout five minutes and now you get to the threats. Surprised it took you so long."

Maybe Tommy was right: there was only one language a man like this spoke, and Boggs had been wrong to waste those first five minutes. He leaned back again, slowly, hoping it conveyed power and assurance, but worried it merely showed that he wasn't sure what to do next.

"I hope I've made myself clear."

"Maybe I like Atlanta," Jeremiah said. No way was he going to give this traitorous house Negro the satisfaction of thinking he could be intimidated. "Maybe my old friends want me to work with them still."

"That would be a mistake."

"Maybe you ain't the only cop I know."

"Oh, you're gonna sic the white cops on me? You think that scares me?"

No, Officer Lucius Boggs, the white cops are gonna sic me *on* you.

"Maybe it should."

And maybe I should scare you, Officer Lucius Boggs. Maybe Julie should scare you. Yes, her. Because now I know your weakness, now I know what you fear. You fear sin. You are surrounded by it, and you have invited it into your family, so let's see how you like realizing that.

Intrigued, Boggs said, "You know a lot about white cops, don't you? Like Slater. What can you tell me about him?"

Jeremiah looked even less comfortable than before. He sat up straighter. "I don't know."

"But you know the man, don't you? You and your brother were working for him."

"I don't know."

"When the feds stepped in, everyone got arrested, but they let the dirty cop walk. How did that make you feel?"

"I was in jail. Didn't feel nothing but being in jail."

Boggs leaned closer. "Do you have anything on that man? Anything that could help put a dirty cop away?"

Jeremiah watched him carefully, as if he expected Boggs to bust out laughing at some practical joke, or pull a weapon. Boggs had played this badly, he realized; surely Tommy would have known a slyer way to ask.

When the silence finally grew too heavy, Boggs said, "No, I figured not. If you had anything on him, he would've killed you like he killed the others, right? Like he killed your brother?"

"Man like Slater isn't someone to trifle with, Officer Lucius Boggs. Man like that . . . can do things."

Boggs tapped the table. "So can I. If you do one day decide you can help get that devil off the streets, you call me. Otherwise, you stay very, very far away from Julie. You hear me?"

No reply. Boggs wasn't going to ask a second time. He was about to stand up when Jeremiah finally spoke.

"You think I want to hurt her, Officer Lucius Boggs? If I wanted to hurt her, I wouldn't need to use my body." He lifted his hands up, palms out, in a way that attracted attention from a couple sitting at another table. His tone had always seemed odd but now something had shifted. The door opened behind him as a man walked in and Boggs felt a cold breeze in his face, a chill up his neck. Smith was still out there, watching. "I wouldn't need to use these hands," Jeremiah said—then he let his hands fall back into his lap and out of view.

"I said *keep your hands where I can see them*," Boggs said through gritted teeth. Not wanting to yell in here but not wanting to make a grave mistake.

"But I don't need to use them."

Boggs moved his right hand into his lap, placing it on the handle of his revolver.

"*Show me your hands, now!*"

"All I'd need to use is my mouth, Officer Lucius Boggs." Jeremiah lifted his hands back onto the table, slowly. They were empty. "If I really wanted to harm that girl, all I need to do is tell the truth."

Boggs still gripped the handle of his revolver but hadn't drawn it yet, so deeply confused by those empty hands, the calm tone that still seemed to be voicing threats, everything all wrong. "What are you talking about?"

"I'd just tell the truth and Julie would be put away for a long, long time. I coulda done that before, but I didn't want to." Staring straight into Boggs's eyes. "You think I should change my mind?"

Behind him, the door opened: Smith entering, hand by his pistol handle as well. Alarmed by the look on Boggs's face and Jeremiah's movements. Boggs shook him off, not wanting Jeremiah to stop but also not wanting Smith to overhear whatever was coming.

Jeremiah continued, "I made myself the sacrifice for her. Because that's what love is, Officer Lucius Boggs. Love is five years and one month and six days so my girl could walk free. If I lost that love, she could lose that freedom."

No.

Jeremiah smiled as Boggs understood, the realization no doubt scarring its way across his face. "See? I don't need no gun to hurt *you*. All I needed was the truth."

Boggs glanced up at Smith, still standing a few feet behind Jeremiah. Had he overheard?

"You're lying," Boggs insisted.

Jeremiah seemed to be marveling at Boggs's expression. He didn't know Smith was lingering a few feet behind him. "The truth can do so much damage. Ask her yourself. My brother, you see, he was a man of appetites. They got him in a lot of trouble. He treated me mean sometimes, but he was my big brother, he taught me things, too. That's how family is." Tears welled in his eyes. "He didn't respect no boundaries, no lines. What was mine was his. I wish I'd been there to protect her that time. It was just the one time, she said. And I'll always blame myself for not being there. He did what he did, didn't care that she didn't want it. Only he didn't see that he'd left his gun right beside the bed when he did it. So she did what she did."

"I don't believe you."

"I helped her move the body, that's true, and I made up a story for her. That's what a man does; he makes sacrifices for his woman and child."

Boggs felt dizzy, hot. Sick to his stomach.

"That case ain't officially closed yet, is it?" Jeremiah said. "Ain't no statute of limitations on murder, right? I suppose if I did talk, I could get in trouble, too, for, what do you call it, accessorizing after the fact. But, you know, I've done time before. I could do it again." He leaned closer. "Do you think Julie could?"

Boggs stood up, feeling even dizzier. People other than Smith were watching him, first on account of his shouts and now due to his spastic motions, the horror in his eyes.

He pointed at Jeremiah and said, "Stay away from her," his voice robbed of its former power, his heart robbed of its illusions. He grabbed his cap, then stumbled past Smith and out into the darkness.

47

Dale was very distracted indeed as he ate dinner with his family. Sue Ellen chided him for having his head in the clouds. He smiled and tried to joke with the kids, but his world was spinning.

He hadn't wanted to believe Rake—who, after all, had *assaulted* him a few hours ago. But the more he considered what Rake had told him about Coyle, the more sense it made. He'd heard Coyle rant about the Klan many a time, which Dale had figured for a misplaced, territorial thing—clannishness, no pun intended, one group jealous of another. Now he understood, burning with shame at how easily he'd been manipulated.

They had just finished supper when Dale got a phone call. A voice he did not recognize asked, "Is Mr. Ayak in?"

Klan Kode, *Ayak* being an acronym for *Are you a Klansman?*

Dale found himself staring at his two boys as he responded, "No, but there's a Mr. Akai." Meaning, *A Klansman am I.*

"Good. A car is going to pull up at the corner of Spruce and Myrtle in exactly ten minutes. Please be there."

Ten minutes later, Dale stood at the intersection a short walk away, almost dizzy with fear. He'd manufactured an excuse for Sue Ellen, claiming he needed to run an errand. He had kissed each boy on the top of their heads, the kids barely noticing, as he hadn't wanted to overplay things, afraid of broadcasting to his wife his suspicion that he was about to walk a plank.

If they were coming for him, they wouldn't call first, right? Surely they just wanted to talk.

A small black Ford pulled up at the opposite corner. The sun had set and the neighborhood was quiet but for the occasional dog. The driver rolled down his window as Dale approached, wary but relieved it was only one man. And an old one at that, white hair and pocked cheeks, some survivor of smallpox from long ago.

"I have a friend in Rockdale," the man said in code. Another car was approaching from the opposite side, so Dale drew closer to the man, getting out of its way.

"Yeah, yeah, I've been meaning to ask about him. What can I do for you?"

"Well," the man said slowly, as if speech hurt, "you could stand there just a moment longer."

He hadn't quite noticed the footsteps but he felt hands at his shoulders and then darkness shrouded him. Something was covering his face. He reached for it but someone reached under his armpits and lifted him. Someone else punched him in the stomach, and he squealed because his abdomen still ached from Rake's blows only a few hours ago. He heard a man whisper "Careful" even as his forehead banged into something, then a hand pressed his head down and someone pushed him from behind and he heard metal sounds and then the world itself shifted violently beneath him.

"Get the hell off me!" he yelled.

He reached again for whatever was on his head. This time he pulled it off, and he saw that he was in the backseat of a large sedan. Flanking him were two people, and in the front seat were two more, and they all wore the hoods and robes.

"What the hell's going on? I'm *with* you boys."

"Shut up." That voice seemed to come from the man in the passenger seat, but honestly it was hard to tell. "We don't want that much noise out of you, so if you can't hush yourself up, we'll do it for you."

"What's this about?"

"You know damn well."

Oh hell. Were they just going to wait him out? Or start beating it out of him? "I'm sorry, fellas, I don't."

"We want to know why you were part of that group in Coventry that beat up Letcher. And we want to know how it all happened."

"I didn't do any such thing."

Their silence implied they found this answer unacceptable and not worth arguing.

He hadn't recognized anyone's voices yet. He looked from one side to the other, hoping to get a glimpse inside their masks, but it was too dark. Driving in a hood was usually not advised, and the tip of the driver's hood was bent down sideways by the roof of the car, like a nightcap.

"Blind the son of a bitch," someone in front said.

One of the men beside him moved to put the sack over his head again, and Dale blocked his arms. Then something hard pressed into his side.

"Blindfold or bullet?" a man asked. Dale chose one darkness over the other.

Twenty minutes later, the last two of which were very curvy and bouncy indeed, they shut the car off and pushed him out. They told him he could take off the sack now, and when he did he saw he was being marched down a dirt path toward a creek. He couldn't even be sure which creek it was; given the length of the drive there were plenty they could have taken him to, and all he could see was woods.

He felt very, very far from anyone or anything.

"Now, look, fellas, this is all a big misunder—"

This time they hit him in the face. Twice, and then he was on the ground. He pulled himself to his knees, muddy from the dirt by the creek bed.

"Don't say a word unless it's to answer our questions."

They encircled him. Some were taller than others but basically they were as indistinguishable as ghosts. Except for when they hit him.

He started to stand, but one said, "You try and get up, we'll only knock you down again."

He tasted blood. "Fellas, please. I'm a Kard-carrying member, for crissake."

"You are part of a conspiracy to bring disgrace on the Brotherhood."

He heard the unmistakable sound of a chamber being loaded into an automatic pistol. Some of the men's sleeves were quite long and he couldn't even tell which of them held the gun.

"Ah, Jesus, I swear it, I don't know what y'all are talking about!"

"Confess. And explain yourself, or we leave your body here to rot before the devil's creatures."

"Look, I . . ." He was crying, his voice thick. He could feel the memory of his hand on his boys' heads, feel the knots in their ever-mussed hair. "Please. I got kids. I just, I didn't want to get in trouble with the law, all right?"

"The law ain't something you have to worry about. We *are* the law. In every possible way."

Oh Jesus, they were right. He realized too late that he'd been thinking about this all wrong. He'd been afraid from the start that he'd be arrested for Irons's murder, but in truth, he'd never had to fear the local cops; they were nearly synonymous with the Klan.

It turns out the Klansman on Dale's right was the one with the pistol, which he now aimed at Dale's head.

Dale shouted, "It was my brother-in-law!"

The gun didn't move. "Keep going."

"He's a cop, too. Denny Rakestraw. He . . . He told me he needed to borrow my car, all right? Wouldn't tell me why, just said he had to do a favor for someone. Then late that night he comes back with it and he's all panicked and he tells me I need to get the fender changed because there were bullets in it, like evidence. And he tells me Irons got killed."

"What else did he say?"

Think. What else? Jesus, it was sheer brilliance that Dale had even managed to say this much. A complete heat-of-the-moment gamble, but one worth making, as he knew they would have killed him if he'd told the truth. Of course, it was possible that one of these men was Rake's damned partner or best friend or something, and now they'd kill him for the lie. But maybe, just maybe, this was genius.

"He told me I couldn't tell nobody, that's why I didn't say anything at my Klavern. Said he was supposed to beat a white man up there, some banker, a relative of Delmar Coyle, one of the Columbians. Said they were doing it together, to stop the banker from turning Hanford Park into a black neighborhood like they did in some other part of town. But things went sour and Irons got shot."

Silence for longer than Dale would have thought possible.

One of them said, "That's crazy." Another said, "Bullshit." A third noted, "Hell, it explains a lot."

"He said they had to do it secret-like because the Klan wasn't doing nothing to help Hanford Park," Dale said. "Said they had to take the law into their own hands, and the Columbians knew how to take care of business."

"Rakestraw and a Columbian?" one of them said, disbelieving.

"One thing they have in common," another said, "is they both hate us."

"Son of a bitch."

"He told me I couldn't say nothing," Dale ranted on, "and he's my brother-in-law and a cop so I tried to protect him, even though I know I shoulda turned him in to you boys sooner. I mean, how do you turn in a cop? And family besides?"

One of the Klansmen leaned toward another, whispering. Another nodded.

"We know who your brother-in-law is, Dale. He's no friend of ours." This speaker, whoever he was, spoke in a rasp, as if to disguise his voice. This wasn't a *one-hand-washes-the-other* arrangement—these boys were local, come to clean up a mess that had a great deal of personal interest for them. They were his neighbors, men from his own Klavern, maybe even cops. They were lit fuses, and Dale's mouth was spewing kerosene.

Then he saw that one of them had taken a leather strap out of his pocket, and another held a length of rope.

48

Rake realized he'd made a terrible mistake shortly after he finished dinner. The chicken casserole seemed to fester in his stomach, as if he'd consumed it raw. All through the meal Cassie had told him about this neighbor who'd spoken to a Realtor and decided to sell, and that neighbor who was going to call a Realtor first thing tomorrow. Apparently the arrest of the Greers had not allayed anyone's fears; it justified them, proved that Negroes were lawless and that their presence in Hanford Park had rendered the area toxic.

Coyle was being proven correct.

Rake wanted to tell Cassie about all he'd been doing to preserve the neighborhood, but how could he tell her without explaining the Dale problem and so much else that reflected poorly on him? He felt it like a glass wall sitting between them.

"We need to call a Realtor, Denny," Cassie insisted.

"I know things look bad right now. I just . . . don't want to do anything rash."

"I think waiting any longer would be rash."

He told her to wait until morning and see if the panic had faded, and she rolled her eyes.

After dinner, he placed a call to Dale. Only hours ago, telling Dale about Coyle had seemed a good idea. He would set the two against each other, see who won, and then deal with what was left. Now it didn't seem so wise. He might have a body on his hands. And as much as he loathed his brother-in-law, he didn't want him dead. If Dale came at Coyle late at night, there was a strong chance Coyle would be expecting it, and have accomplices lying in wait. Had he sent Dale to his death?

His sister answered the phone. "Dale's not here."

"Do you know when he'll be back?"

"No. He doesn't like it when I ask him too many questions, so I let it go."

Imagining the day-to-day aspects of that marriage pained him. "Okay, well, just ask him to call me when he gets back."

"He left his car. I just noticed that. I don't know, maybe he just needed to take a walk and blow off some steam or something."

"Yeah, that sounds like Dale," he said, trying to make sense of this. "How are the boys?"

"Yelling at each other."

He let her go, then told Cassie he had to run an errand of his own. Giving his own wife an equally vague explanation, he realized.

⁂

Dale wouldn't have been able to walk to Coyle's house, so surely he hadn't set off to confront the Columbian. Unless he'd hit the local watering hole to get a buzz going first, work up the courage. Rake checked the two taverns that were within walking distance, but no Dale. Then he drove out to Coyle's neighborhood again, killed his lights, and rolled slowly down the street until he was in front of the shack. The place looked empty, no lights emanating from it. No signs of a recent struggle.

Where the hell was Dale?

⁂

Later, he drove by Dale's place again, but the fact that Dale's car was in the driveway wasn't helpful if Dale was on foot. He parked a few doors down, then knocked on the door, knowing that he would only alarm his sister.

She looked haggard, another tough night getting the kids to bed. "What's wrong?" she asked.

"Have you heard from him?"

"He doesn't always check in, Denny. He'll probably stumble into bed smelling like booze in a few hours."

Maybe he'd gone to one of his friends', Rake hoped. Drinking there rather than at a bar. He didn't believe it.

"You're scaring me, Denny. What's going on?"

"I just wanted to talk to him about the neighborhood stuff, that's all."

"Yeah. We're thinking about selling."

"Jesus, you, too?"

"I don't like it, either, but this has gone too far. A burglary like that, and half the neighborhood running around at night ready to lynch those Negroes?"

"That wouldn't happen here." Wishing he believed himself.

"Denny." She sighed. "I know you don't much like Dale."

"That's not tr—"

"And I know he says some things about Negroes he shouldn't. He's a good man, and he loves those little boys to death. He just . . . was brought up different than us. The way he expends himself might not be right, but his heart is in the right place. If we wait too long, and enough Negroes do move in, then, no matter what's in *their* hearts, the value of our house will be less than our mortgage. *And* we'll be stuck living next to them. I know you don't want that, either."

"Sue Ellen . . . We're gonna find a way to keep things the way they've been."

She rolled her eyes. "Sure, you men and your plans. First it's trying to buy their houses back, then God knows what. Men in hoods will be next, right?"

"*I* would never do that. I can't speak for Dale."

She looked hurt. "I just mean that maybe the better idea, instead of drawing up whatever strategy you want to talk to Dale about, or whatever it is he and his friends are probably talking about right now, maybe the right thing to do here is listen to the wives who have to spend almost every waking minute here. Maybe you should listen to what we're telling you."

He sighed. "Cassie wants to sell, too."

"You married a smart gal."

He was walking down the short walkway in Dale's front yard when someone approached from the sidewalk. A very large someone.

"Dale Simpkins?" the man asked in a thick country drawl.

" 'Fraid not. Can I help you with something?"

"Bullshit," the man said, and Rake picked up on the movement behind him too late, as something hard hit him in the back of the skull.

He went numb and fell to one of his knees, barely catching himself with his hands. The yard was unlit and for a moment his vision grew even yet darker, his head fuzzy. He took a breath and things were slowly, slowly returning to their usual clarity, but with pain attached, when he heard the hammer of a gun being pulled back and saw two very large men looming over him.

49

Boggs could have used a smoke, but lighting it would have given him and Smith away. They stood in position, standing in the first floor of an abandoned house in Summerhill. He heard scurrying somewhere behind him, rodent squeaks, and he prayed that they not venture near him while he waited.

The only thing worse than a dull stakeout was a dull stakeout at a time when you desperately did not want to think about something. Yet he couldn't banish it from his mind: *Julie* had killed Isaiah Tanner. He wanted to believe that what Jeremiah told him was a lie tossed there to distract him. But it made too much sense: *this* was why Julie had never told him the truth about Jeremiah, *this* explained her defensiveness and raw pain whenever he asked about her past. Lord God, she had been raped by her boyfriend's older brother, and she had shot him dead. Her boyfriend had helped her evade the law by moving the body, and they'd worked out a story they could tell. Jeremiah had kept the secret for her, but now he was back, and unpredictable, and envious of Boggs. He was a walking potential death sentence for Julie.

What was Boggs to do? He had been ready to cast Julie aside, but now he saw that she was just a victim of things he could barely fathom. What she'd done was probably self-defense. A Southern jury wouldn't see it that way, but the Lord would.

Wouldn't He?

If Boggs stayed with her, if he helped her keep that secret, he needed to do something about Jeremiah.

Boggs wasn't sure how much Smith had overheard, and how much he'd understood. After leaving the diner together, they had been silent for a charged minute, then Smith had asked, "Are you sure you can still do this tonight?"

"Of course I can. Why couldn't I?"

"I just want to make sure your head's in the right place."

Smith had studied his expression then, as if daring Boggs to explain what had just happened. Boggs hadn't asked if Smith had understood the conversation, terrified of the sheer possibility that yet another man might know the truth about Julie.

As planned, they had made their way to the vacant Summerhill storefront that, according to Malcolm, was used as a transfer point by Feck's smugglers. A few miles away, a freight train would be pulling into the yards, and men disguised as janitors would be showing up here in about an hour, handing tight little bundles of marijuana to Quentin Neale.

So they waited. Just like they had two weeks ago, outside the telephone factory, stumbling into a mess that had grown more personal than they ever would have expected. What a small town this still was. Despite the new buildings and legions of strangers, despite all the changes the last decade had wrought, Atlanta was still a town where you couldn't even arrest someone without possibly implicating your own family.

While Boggs and Smith waited in this abandoned building, Dewey and Champ stood in an alley that cut alongside the store, watching its side door. One block away, in a dirt lot behind a vacant bungalow, McInnis sat in his squad car.

Had white cops been handling this, they no doubt would have had more than five men. But McInnis couldn't send his entire precinct to one spot, and he'd wanted to keep quiet, lest word reach Slater. So they would go with five and hope it was enough.

At a quarter 'til midnight, a yellow Chevrolet convertible with its top up parked in front of the store. It made a point of backing into the space, all the better for a quick getaway. A man in a brown fedora got out, looked down the street both ways, then keyed into the front door.

"That's Neale," Smith whispered.

Flattened cardboard boxes had been taped inside the store's windows, but they could tell from the faint glow that Neale had turned the lights on.

Another thirty minutes ticked slowly past. Smith relieved himself against the back wall. Boggs's feet were sore but he didn't want to sit on the layers of grime.

At half past midnight a tan GMC pickup with a canvas top drove past the store. The street had almost no traffic at this hour. Five minutes later the same truck drove up again, this time backing into the spot beside the Chevy.

"Here we go," Smith said just as Boggs felt his heart rate quicken.

Smith gently swung open the door they'd earlier broken into, careful not to let it bang. Knees bent in a crouch, they quickly ran across the street as two men in janitor's uniforms left the GMC and carried metal trash barrels toward the store, where Neale stood in the open doorway.

"Police, freeze!" Smith hollered. They could hear footsteps coming from the alley. They heard the roar of an engine—McInnis, hopefully, having spotted the truck driving past twice.

The two janitors froze as commanded. Then one of them dropped his trash barrel and ran, darting behind his accomplice.

Boggs saw that the second janitor was Jeremiah.

Then gunshots called his attention elsewhere.

Neale had retreated back inside but poked his gun out, firing blind. Smith and Boggs both dropped, Smith hiding behind the front of the truck and Boggs crouching beside the dropped trash barrel. A third shot, fourth, fifth.

When Boggs looked up, Jeremiah, too, had dropped his barrel and was running behind his accomplice. Boggs stepped forward, the truck now blocking him from any more bullets that Neale might fire, and aimed his weapon at the two retreating "janitors." The one who wasn't Jeremiah turned at that moment, aiming a weapon at Boggs—not aiming so much as pointing randomly, about to fire.

Boggs pulled his trigger. Aiming more purposefully than his adversary. Two shots, and the man dropped from thirty feet away.

More shots, other weapons. Something happening inside the store. Shouting now, the voices of Dewey and Champ, "Police!" and a cry of pain.

McInnis's car pulled up behind them as Jeremiah turned an alley corner and vanished. The sergeant kicked open his door and leaped out, hollering, "Get after him!"

They ran down the alley, Boggs carefully holding the pistol facing up as he ran, then stopping just before the alley corner and aiming it forward again, then glancing around the corner quickly. A body disappearing around yet another corner.

Running again, Smith right beside him, splashing through a puddle of God knows what, shoes wet now, don't slip, the alley's brick floor slick and uneven. The silhouette of a cat vanished as suddenly as it had appeared.

How had Jeremiah let this happen?

As he ran and the blood in his head pounded and his chest ached, he realized that he was doomed, he had been doomed all along and somehow had convinced himself this wasn't so.

Boggs's confronting him in the diner earlier—that had been his last chance, and he hadn't realized it. Boggs had given him the opportunity to walk away, to flee this life that only seemed to punish him. Instead of taking the advice, he'd all but spat in the man's face. The thought of that confident, enragingly superior *Officer* Boggs banishing Jeremiah so that he could keep Julie all to himself, that had been too much, so with malicious pleasure Jeremiah had shattered the man's illusions. He had smiled at the sight of Boggs staggering away from the table, realizing that the girl he worshipped was not as pure as the preacher's son had wished.

Now Jeremiah was the one staggering.

They'd already shot Cyrus, he'd seen it happen, heard the bullets, at least one of them whizzing past Jeremiah's head like a hornet but another making Cyrus's body contort, the front of his shirt exploding.

He'd only fired a gun once before, target practice against some bottles under the watchful eye of his brother, years ago.

He ran down the alley, hoping and praying as he ran. *Please, God. Please don't let it end this way. I know I've let you down this past week and I haven't treated my freedom as I should have. I tried to do right. I tried to . . .*

To what? And does trying even matter?

He had allowed the devil to chase him all his life, let it get too close, and now it was right behind him, gaining fast.

He turned right, and slipped, got back up and ran, and found himself facing a brick wall.

Boggs pointed his gun around the next corner, poked his head around it, and saw Jeremiah's back. The ex-convict stood, shoulders heaving, not fifteen feet away.

Smith stepped out past Boggs, aiming his gun as well.

"Police!" Smith hollered. "Drop your weapon!"

Jeremiah, his gun pointed at the ground, turned slowly to face them. Boggs felt the enormity of the fact that he could shoot Jeremiah right then, shoot him for not having already dropped the gun, for turning, for breathing, for doing anything but obeying.

Smith and Boggs both stepped forward.

Jeremiah stared at them for a second, what seemed like the longest second imaginable. His eyes wide.

Boggs was pointing his gun at Jeremiah's chest. One tiny twitch of the finger was all it would take.

Jeremiah lowered his right shoulder a bit. He bent down and dropped the gun.

Held out his hands.

"I said, drop your weapon!" Smith hollered.

Jeremiah's face wrinkled. Confusion, fear. Then understanding, terror.

Boggs kept his body still but turned his head to look at his partner. Both their guns still pointing at the defenseless subject.

"Drop it now!" Smith yelled.

Jeremiah opened his mouth to explain that he already had in fact dropped it. Boggs opened his mouth to tell Smith *No, don't do this,* but he didn't do it fast enough, and what good is mouthing, what good is even talking right then, when your partner won't even look at you.

Smith pulled the trigger, twice.

Boggs didn't even see Jeremiah fall—Jeremiah was there one moment, flat the next. Blood on the wall behind him, flecks of brick and mortar from where at least one of the bullets had passed clean through him.

Smith stepped forward, still holding his gun in position. Then much faster steps until he was able to kick Jeremiah's pistol away, his gun pointed down at Jeremiah's face, etched now and forever in permanent puzzlement at this world that had been too much for him.

Boggs walked slowly toward them, the muscles in his arms taut but somehow weightless, as if that gun were the only thing tethering his body to this earth, and maybe if he let go of it he would float up into the sky, reach the heavens. But no, he was here, he was grounded, and it was someone else's soul that had been set free.

Footsteps running toward them. Boggs felt dizzy as he turned around, aimed his weapon behind him, and then saw the white man and familiar uniform. He lowered his gun so he wasn't pointing it at McInnis, who lowered his, too, like a mirror on a delay. McInnis walked toward them, his uniform still a mirror but his face a negative of theirs, and even as he stepped closer to them Boggs felt himself being pushed farther away.

"I tried not to, Sergeant," Smith said to McInnis. He was panting—they all were—and his words came out in short bursts, like gunfire. "He wouldn't listen. Thought he was in a movie, maybe."

The smell of cordite in the air, the sound of local dogs asking each other what happened. An engine starting, probably unrelated, a resident fleeing the sounds of violence, a guilty conscience escaping.

"I know," McInnis said. With his right forearm he wiped sweat from his forehead. "I heard it."

McInnis crept closer to check on the body, and Boggs stared at his partner, took a step in front of him, eyes wide. Smith returned the stare, eyes hard, then looked down at Jeremiah.

"I'll be damned," McInnis said. "That's Jeremiah Tanner."

Boggs could only nod, stunned silent.

McInnis's eyes seemed to soften at the realization that here was the same man whose brother may have been killed by McInnis's former partner years ago. Now dead in an alley, at another cop's hand.

Smith offered, "Maybe . . . Maybe I should have—"

"No," McInnis said. "You did the right thing. Better him than you. Remember that, always." He moved his eyes from one of his officers to the other, as if he could press the point into their foreheads, brand them with it. "Better him than you."

It took far, far too long for Boggs to get Smith alone. First there were the bodies to process—Jeremiah and Cyrus and Quentin Neale, who had run into the store to hide from Smith and Boggs, only to see Dewey and Champ storm in. Neale had dropped his empty pistol and tried to draw a second from behind his belt when Dewey fired three rounds. White cops showed up in force, Vice and Homicide detectives among them, but no Slater, so perhaps McInnis was right and the son of a bitch would back slowly away from the mess.

Jeremy Toon from the *Atlanta Daily News* had shown up as well, tipped off somehow, anxious to record for posterity this major scoop: the first time Atlanta's Negro officers had taken lives. Officially.

More than an hour had passed when Boggs and Smith were alone together, in one of the alleys they had run through earlier. No other cops in earshot, Boggs leaned forward and asked simply, "Why?"

"Because I knew you couldn't."

"I never asked you to—"

"And you wouldn't have asked. But that little thug would've held you in his pocket forever. Him and your girl, and that little boy."

So Smith had heard and understood everything at the diner. Boggs struggled with this, still unable to reconcile his image of his partner and their jobs with what Smith had just done, the decision he'd made, the line he'd crossed. One Boggs believed he himself could never cross. Because he'd had that opportunity. He could have done it, but had chosen not to.

He wanted to hit Smith, wanted to scream, wanted to run past his partner and apologize to the man who would never hear him or anything else again. "That doesn't mean I wanted—"

"What? You gonna judge me again? The words you're looking for are *thank you.*"

Then Smith walked away, as if he could leave the weight on his partner's shoulders.

50

Rake felt dizzy when one of the men who'd knocked him down said to the other, "Check his wallet to be sure."

A hand removed his wallet from his back pocket. Rake tried to remind his muscles how to flex, wondered when he would be able to stand again, or at least look into the face of the big man in front of him. He managed that last part, saw the gun in his hand.

"I'm not Dale. I'm a *cop*."

"Shit," the one behind him said, dropping Rake's wallet on the ground. "It ain't him."

Then more light, which Rake at first took for his body reacting to some new pain but then he realized it was headlights, from a Hudson driving unusually slowly down the road.

"Well goddamn," the man with the gun said. His thick drawl matched the others, South Georgia or Alabama. "Looks like we've hit the jackpot."

Rake saw it then, a long blue Hudson, pulling over on the other side of the street. Packed inside it was a veritable posse of Klansmen, their white robes and hoods almost glowing from the streetlamps. A back door popped open but the engine was still running.

"That's Dale in there, ain't it?" one of the big men asked Rake.

He didn't reply. Something slammed into Rake's ribs, the second man's foot kicking him away, maybe. He looked across the street and saw Dale, not wearing a shirt, stagger out of the Hudson's backseat.

"Dale Simpkins?" one of the men demanded.

"Oh Lord, what now?" Dale pleaded.

Rake heard the sound of a shotgun being pumped, inches away.

"Come on outta there, you damn clowns," one of the big strangers yelled, "and get what's coming to ya!"

The driver's door opened and one of the Klansmen held out his palms. "Hold up, there! This is a misunderstanding, fellas! Lower that weapon!"

"Y'all are the ones that went up there with him, ain't you?" one of the big men called out. Rake remembered then that he'd spoken days ago to the coroner about Walter Irons, asking if any family had identified the body, and the mortician had described two very large brothers from Alabama. Jesus, it was them.

He pulled himself to his knees, trying to make the dizziness subside. He needed to tackle the big fellow with the shotgun, who was a step in front of him now, but his legs had gone leaden. The other one held a pistol, both of them aiming at the surreal scene: Dale standing topless beside a Klansman and in front of a car filled with three other Klansmen, more white laundry than on a Monday-morning clothesline.

One of the other Klansmen emerged from the far side of the backseat, pointing a pistol at Rake and the Irons brothers, using the car as a shield.

"Lower your weapons!" the Klansman yelled in a deep, officious voice Rake recognized somehow. "We're the police!"

"The hell you are!" one of the brothers replied as a second Klansman brandished a pistol, the standoff growing more volatile by the second.

"I am a police officer!" the Klansman insisted.

The other brother called out, "Maybe you're Sheriff Marone, right? You sonsabitches drove our brother to his grave and now you're covering it up!"

"I am an Atlanta police officer and I'm ordering you to lower your weapons, now!"

Rake began lifting himself up, one palm pressed to the earth, knees unbending, just as he realized this was the worst possible moment to be anything but flat on the ground.

One of the brothers started to holler something but it was obliterated by the concussive sound of a shotgun.

Gunfire, everywhere. And screaming. Many people screaming. One of them, from behind walls, his sister.

Splinters from the house ricocheted into the air and hit his shoulder. Or at least he hoped that's all it was. One of the giants in front of him fell, silently. Rake pulled a revolver from his ankle holster and staggered to his left, toward some hedges. He saw the other brother drop his shotgun, having fired it twice already, and pull a pistol from his pocket. Rake fired at him but the man's giant frame managed to escape behind an oak tree.

More gunshots, coming from the Hudson or thereabouts. Meaning toward the house, with his sister and nephews. Irons fired back. Rake looked out at the road, where a halo of lamplight around the Hudson was filled with exploded glass, shreds of upholstery, blood. The car lurched forward, only a bit, like a body in spasm. The open rear door was half dislodged from the car itself. Inside the Hudson nothing but white clothing and blood.

Rake lay flat beneath azaleas, gun forward, a position he hadn't employed since the war.

"Police!" he screamed, not realizing until later how ridiculous it sounded to be issuing the same command as one of the shooters on the other side. "Drop your weapons!"

The Hudson drifted forward again, like it was in drive but no one was alive to press the brake. The driver's-side door was pockmarked from buckshot and a body was slumped so far to the left that the pointy top of its Klan hood pointed directly at Rake. Then it fell off, the dead man's sweaty blond hair visible.

More gunfire, from Rake's right, and perhaps on the other side of the street. One of the Klansmen, maybe, having escaped from the Hudson. Then two more shots, from the brother hiding behind the oak.

"Reece! You killed Reece, you bastards!"

Rake heard footsteps, quick and frantic, but fading. One of the Kluxers running away.

Two more shots and glass broke behind him. He heard his nephews screaming, his sister. *Jesus Christ.* Whatever the hell this was, he needed to stop it.

Another shot, from this side of the street again, as he saw the flash from the muzzle. He crept, keeping as low as he could, hoping he wouldn't step on a branch or fallen leaves, hoping the shooter across the street wouldn't fire again, since Rake was exposed. Finally the near figure took shape in the darkness, and then it twitched and that was all the confirmation Rake needed. He fired twice, chest high.

He heard a grunt. Heard wood splinter. He stepped closer now and saw the big man slip away from his hiding place behind the oak and fall, landing on his back. He held a pistol in his right hand. Rake ran, and the man's arm was moving, though not quickly, the gun raised now, and Rake kicked it away before it got high enough to aim. Rake pointed his gun down at the man's face.

"Roll over on your stomach, now!"

The last Irons brother gritted his teeth, grunting in pain, and as he rolled over Rake saw that his huge shoulder was soaked red. Rake remembered he had no handcuffs with him, yet having Irons on his chest with his hands laced behind his head made Rake feel a bit safer. Then there were two more gunshots.

Rake leaned against the same tree Irons had been using for cover. One of the Klansmen across the street was firing as he fled. Rake hid for another moment and thought he heard footsteps, but his ears were ringing and that might have been the blood echoing in his ears. He aimed around the tree and glanced down the block, seeing two parked cars that the shooter had used for shelter, one of them with windows shot out, but no shooter. He waited, then he dared to emerge from behind the tree and step out into the street and the haze of gun smoke, eerie memories of Europe flooding him, but he was home now, this was his neighborhood, two irreconcilable worlds imposed on each other, making him even dizzier.

He heard sirens. Shrill dogs, deeply alarmed. Nothing else but the ringing in his ears.

He was about to call out to Sue Ellen, tell her to get the boys into the dining room, at the rear of the house, when the world spun on him. The previous blow to the back of his head was reminding him it was still there, a badly timed attack of vertigo dropping him to one knee again. *No no no.* He had to stand back up but his body was taking the moment off, uninterested in heeding his brain's commands.

Woozy, he fell on the ground, lying on his back. He heard footsteps.

Irons, the one he'd shot in the shoulder. He'd found his pistol and was standing over Rake. *Why?* Rake tried to ask, but all he could do was breathe.

"Killed Reece, you son of a bitch. I'm the last one."

He was huge, a damned monster, his pomaded hair askew, strange unnatural shapes almost like he was horned, and *BOOM* the loudest sound Rake had ever heard.

Too loud for a pistol.

Rake opened his eyes and the monster before him looked more terrifying than before, shiny and newly colored. Then it fell beside him.

Slowly across the street moved a new shooter, and from Rake's vantage he could only see her upper half, no legs or feet, like some ghost hovering above ground. Her hair was shorn very short and unevenly, like she'd done it herself blindfolded. She wore a fierce expression and held the smoking rifle before her as if in search of her next target.

Her predator's eyes considered Rake, judged him unworthy, and she eased her grip on the rifle, its muzzle now pointed at the heavens.

This time his voice worked: "Who are you?"

"Hortense Bleedhorn. Those sonsabitches nearly killed my cook. Who are you?"

"Officer Denny Rakestraw, Atlanta Police Department."

"That'd sound more impressive if you weren't laying on the ground there."

"I'm going to get up now."

"Don't let me stop you."

He rose to his feet, slowly, and stared at his odd savior. "Thank you."

"They had it coming. I been looking for them for days." She spat on the nearest corpse. "Finally figured out where they were staying and followed 'em here. I saw 'em get the drop on you and was about to do something about it when that clown car pulled up and all hell broke loose."

Hell may have stopped breaking loose, but it had left its mark everywhere. Pistol still in hand, Rake scanned the street for a sign of the other shooters. The Hudson, lights aglow and engine purring, had rolled into the back of a parked car and sat there, waiting for someone to put it out of its misery.

"I need you to hand me that gun, ma'am."

She gave him a cold look. "You got a badge on you?"

"Not on me, ma'am, no." He repeated his name and rank and advised her that in less than a minute quite a few uniformed officers would be here, itching to fire at anyone holding a weapon. She gave him the rifle.

He walked toward the Hudson, its windows reduced to jagged shards covered in blood. He could see the dead, robed driver but wasn't sure if there was another body inside. Halfway there he stopped and looked at two more bodies. The Klan robes on one were so covered in blood it almost looked like he'd dyed the whole getup crimson, promoted himself to some Klan officer position. Rake removed the hood and found himself staring at Barnwell, Helton's young partner.

Dale lay a few feet closer to the house, as if he'd been seeking refuge where he had so many times, believing it would protect him as he had tried so hard to protect it. He wore no shirt, only some gray pants that Rake recalled Cassie giving him for Christmas last year. The shotgun had opened his chest, spreading blood as high as his chin. He lay on his side and appeared to have fresh welts on his bare back.

"Jesus Christ."

He couldn't hear his sister screaming anymore, couldn't hear the boys. Had they been hit?

The sirens were almost there and he staggered to the house, but the door was locked. She'd locked it, as if that would help. Every light was out. Two windows were shattered, including one in the boys' bedrooms.

He knocked, called out her name. Told her it was over, it was safe, he needed to see her.

Squad cars pulled up, their lights dancing on the front of the house. Cops would yell at him to put his hands up in a moment. She opened the door, eyes wide, the skin pulled so taut over her skull it was like he could see through to the bones.

"Are the boys okay?" he asked her.

She nodded, quickly, like she wanted to hurry up so she could run back and hide.

"Sue Ellen, Dale's . . ." Three times already his job had compelled him to inform stunned relatives that a loved one was dead. He could intimately describe all of them, had memorized their names, those people he'd never seen before in his life until that one, raw moment. And this was his sister, his longtime babysitter, his former source for all female-related advice, his fraught ally when they needed to gang up on their elder brother, God rest his soul.

"Dale." He held her shoulders but his own voice shook. "Dale's been shot."

"*. . . What?*"

"I'm so sorry. He was shot. He's . . . He's dead."

She stared, a certain veil closing her eyes off to the rest of the world forever. Then she tried to look over his shoulders, walk past him.

"No, you need to stay here." He couldn't let her see. "You need to go back inside."

"Let me by!" She tried to knock him away but he held firm. She took a step and slid into him, his hands moving from her shoulders to her back, embracing her, and she screamed into his chest and he held her there, feeling her whole body heave.

Confused cops were yelling at them to put their hands up and turn around. But if he obeyed, she would be free of his grasp and would slide past him, run toward Dale, inspire their terrified fingers to twitch. He held her as they yelled, and he called out his name to them, hoping they could hear him over the sirens, over his sister's screams, because no matter what they said he would not raise his hands and release her.

51

Julie was dreaming she could fly again, an old schoolgirl fantasy she still had now and again, floating through the skies and looking down at the maplike world passing below, when the cannons started firing. Loud bangs, and she turned to see where they were coming from, tried to dodge them, who would be shooting at her? And then she thrashed so hard that she woke up, and that's when she realized it wasn't a cannon but knuckles rapping on her window.

She rose from bed, the autumn floor cold beneath her feet, and pulled at the thin curtain. Just enough light outside for her to see Lucius's face. He motioned to the door.

She checked to make sure Sage was still asleep in the bed next to hers, but the child could sleep through the most intense of thunderstorms and was undisturbed. He lay nearly sideways in his bed, so she adjusted him, then made her way toward the door. She lit a small lamp and glanced at the clock, saw that it was past three in the morning.

"Are you all right?" she asked Lucius when she opened the door.

He nodded. He looked shocked, but maybe it was her. She felt jittery, her body off, this hour so very unnatural.

"I'm sorry, I . . . had to talk to you. It couldn't wait."

She told him to come in. They would have to whisper, as the apartment was so small. They could hear her father snoring from here, so at least her parents hadn't woken. Lucius stepped inside and kissed her on the lips. They hadn't kissed in so long—she hadn't even seen him in days. But his face looked ashen. If this had been at a normal hour she would have feared he was here to break off the engagement officially. He sank onto the sofa and she sat beside him.

"Tonight, we busted some moonshine and marijuana smugglers. It got rough and . . . some folks were killed." He had been staring ahead of him as he said this, but now he faced her. "One of the men was Jeremiah. I'm . . . I'm sorry. He didn't make it."

She looked at her hands, folded together in her lap. She tried to understand this, Jeremiah being dead. Was this another dream? Where were the cannons that would wake her this time?

"I didn't want for this to happen," Lucius said.

The jitteriness faded and she felt a deep calm, like something had placed its hands on her, pinning her there. She realized her silence was worrying him but she wasn't sure what to say.

Jeremiah is dead. She tried to understand.

"I hadn't even realized he was involved with the group we were after," he said.

"It's not your fault. He . . . shouldn't have been mixed up in that. Like he shouldn't have been the last time."

He was dead to me before, she thought. *And now he's actually dead.* She knew her heart was only beginning to grasp how profound was the difference.

Her father stopped snoring in the other room, and they heard weight shift, then snoring again. The parlor clock seemed to tick more slowly than usual, exhausted.

"There's something else," he said. He reached out to take her hand. Their earlier kiss had been so quick, this touch felt significant, the warmth of his hand, his stillness.

"I spoke to him earlier," Lucius said. "And he told me the truth. About what happened to Isaiah."

She realized she wasn't breathing. And she couldn't withstand the way he was looking at her. She tried to move away, but he put another hand on hers, holding her down.

"I wanted you to know that I know," he said, and she felt pressure at her temples, like something was trying to shrink her, compress her, and she would need to start breathing soon. "Julie. I love you. But . . ."

That word should never follow those other three, and his silence hung there so long she thought she'd burst.

". . . But I need to hear it from you. I need to know for sure."

The hands holding hers were sweaty and large, his fingers so much thicker than one would guess given his delicate features. She saw redness at the edges of his eyes, eyes that were wide and staring into hers, like he so desperately needed to hear what she was about to say, needed to commit it all to memory.

Did he want details? Did he want it wrapped up in a tidy story? Did he simply want her to confirm or deny? Did he want it under oath, as a plea deal? Did he want her to start crying? Because already her eyes were burning, her throat knotted.

"What do you want me to say?" So difficult for her to speak, trying to keep herself from breaking apart. "Do you have . . . *any* idea . . . what that was like?"

"No. I don't. But you need to trust me."

She shook her head, the tears falling now. "His brother . . . was a son of a bitch. And after what he did . . . to me . . ." She finally tore her hand away from his, and she wrapped her arms around herself, suddenly very cold, shivering, gooseflesh everywhere even though it wasn't that cold, just the memory of it sending chills down her neck. She shook her head and the tears were everywhere and she knew that she must have looked a fright, but she said, "I do not regret what I did. I regret that it happened, but after what he did . . . I do not regret that at all."

Some mercy finally took hold of him, and he reached for her, wrapping her in his arms, and finally she could let it all go. He told her he was sorry three or four times, or however many it took, however long they sat there, him rocking her slightly.

"It's all right. It's over now. It's gone."

She nodded, her head on his chest.

"Does anyone else know? Anyone else at all?"

"No."

"Not even your parents, or his? Anyone in the world?"

"No one. He helped me . . . get rid of the gun. And he moved Isaiah's body to some car they used. But we knew not to say a thing, ever, to anyone."

Jeremiah had helped her, and had kept her secret for so long, and for that she would forever be in his debt. Despite this, gratefulness had not been the emotion that flooded her when she saw him freed from prison a few days ago. Even she had been amazed at the anger that had swelled, and the fear. As the months and years had passed, she realized how much she blamed Jeremiah for what his brother had done to her. If only Jeremiah had resisted getting involved with Isaiah's schemes from the beginning, if only he had followed her advice and walked a different path than the one Isaiah had chosen, things might have turned out differently. She would not have been attacked, and Jeremiah would not have been jailed, and Sage would have had a father from the start. She didn't know any of that for sure. All she knew was that, when Jeremiah tried to return to her these many years later, the pain she'd finally dammed up had overwhelmed her. She wanted a new life now—she *had* a new life now, and she would not give it up. She would not be reduced to Jeremiah's past mistakes, even if he must be.

Lucius told her, "No one else ever will know."

She looked up. "Thank you."

"I've missed you," he said.

"Missed you, too."

They sat there a long while.

"I know I've . . . pretty much disappeared the last couple weeks. There were some things going on with my partner's family, and . . . I think I just needed time to get my head right about this."

"How about your heart?"

"My heart's crazy about you, girl." He smiled, nearly laughed. "Sometimes my head tries to tell me something else, but I'll stop listening to it. It isn't as smart as it thinks it is."

"I know this must have been confusing for you, but . . . I didn't know any other way."

"I understand now."

"But you can't keep doing this to me, Lucius. Can't pinwheel back and forth all the time. When that preacher says 'til death do us part, that's serious business."

"I know that. And I still plan on saying 'I do.' If you'll have me."

It was as if she realized she'd been breathing shallowly all week, and only now did her lungs expand and her shoulders rise. She took his face in her hands, held it there for a moment, then kissed his lips.

"Yes, I'll still have you."

They kissed again, longer this time, long enough that she feared her parents might get up for a glass of water and find them like this.

When they stopped, she said, "*I'll* have you, but you're gonna have to sweet-talk Sage some. He's sore you haven't come by in a while."

"I'll make it right with him. And with you."

Despite the hour, they talked longer, about Sage, about Lucius's parents, about Smith's family troubles in Hanford Park. The sorts of things they hadn't been able to talk about, that had been eclipsed by her past, which hopefully now was receding again to where it belonged, like a distant planet, ancient and cold.

Then she had another thought about Jeremiah, and though she probably should have let the subject stay closed, she said, "You asked me once why Jeremiah wasn't killed when those other men were. I don't know. I never knew. But I know what he would've said: it was because he's been chosen."

"What?"

"Chosen by God. For something great. He said that sometimes." The memory of it made her smile wistfully. It also made her almost start crying again. "Said the Lord was going to do something amazing with him. He always believed that. And I did, too, for a time."

She felt something in her chest that she needed to press down, forever.

"But he was wrong," she said. "He was just another boy who got into trouble. God didn't want nothing to do with him."

Shuffling feet, tiny ones. She looked up just as Sage walked into the parlor. "Mama?"

Lucius was even faster than she was, walking toward the boy and bending down on one knee.

"You all right, son?"

"I had a nightmare."

She felt guilty for not having been in her bed when he woke looking for her. On the other hand, this was a drill she'd performed so many times now, so she stayed on the sofa and watched as Lucius lifted Sage into his arms.

"It wasn't real. Let's get you back in bed."

Eyes half-mast, Sage briefly looked at her, no more confused by Lucius's presence here than he was by the sudden absence of whatever monsters or demons he'd been dreaming of. He let his head droop onto Lucius's shoulder as he carried him through the doorway and into a place where those demons would not catch him.

Word spread quickly through Hanford Park: the neighborhood association had come to a new understanding with the Negro community, and borders were being redrawn. Magnolia Street would now serve as the dividing line. Three square blocks that had been all-white for years—until two months ago—would soon be acceptable for Negro homeowners. Which meant three square blocks of white people would need to sell their homes, immediately.

Those who found themselves on the wrong side of a line someone else had drawn were outraged, as were plenty of others, livid that white people's property rights could be forfeited like that. And by whom? Not by elected officials but by a few self-important men who'd sat at a table *with Negroes*. Yet once the deal was announced, it was like a stampede broke loose as people moved to sell, imbuing a mere gentlemen's agreement with all the force of ratified law.

The desire to torch those three Negro houses became all the more intense. But that only would have cast a darker shadow on the neighborhood, driving home values further down. It was now in the white residents' best interests to keep the peace so they could get out for as much money as possible. A few more bricks were tossed through some Negroes' windows, and some garbage barrels were emptied onto their lawns, but no more blood was shed. For Sale signs sprouted like autumn-blooming goldenrod on every front yard, and the Negro realtists descended without fear this time, no need for Cassie Rakestraw or anyone else to document license numbers.

The Klan shoot-out had horrified not just Hanford Park but far beyond. The violence in an otherwise idyllic area generated headlines nationwide, even in some Northern papers that liked to look down their noses at those backward Confederates, even though housing-related violence was occurring in Chicago, Detroit, and other cities where people couldn't buy a decent biscuit or enjoy a warm November afternoon. The death of a policeman who'd been clad in Klan attire made the story unprintable for some publications; others ran the story but omitted that detail. The pertinent facts were that four men had been shot to death, and despite the racial tensions in Hanford Park, every victim and shooter had been white. Salacious as the event was, a certain shame about this one-sided bloodbath led residents to avoid the subject after the first days of shock. They seemed to understand that something terrible had occurred, something no one condoned but no one had stopped, and for many this only underscored the fact that Hanford Park just wasn't what it had once been, and the time had come to leave.

Within the doomed three-block zone marked as transitional stood the Rakestraw residence, a mere block from the new border separating it from acceptability and the abyss. Denny Jr. would never learn how to ride a bike in Hanford Park, Cassie realized. Maggie wouldn't chalk hopscotch patterns on the sidewalk. The family would never host another cookout here or carry a Christmas tree through that front door. The bulbs she had just planted would yield orange and white tulips next spring to delight an altogether different kind of family.

Among the first homeowners to sell were the Thameses. They sold so quickly that they had, in fact, disappeared.

No one had seen them since the night Denny had demanded that the plumber confess to staging the burglary. The next day, after Rake had made his reports and spoken to all the investigators and tried without success to console his sister, who refused to let him come near her now, he had collapsed in bed. Fourteen hours later he woke up, and then, taking a drive to clear his mind, he saw the Sold sign in their front yard.

No car in the driveway, the lights off. The rooms viewed through the break in the curtains looked hastily emptied. Furniture remained, but pictures had been removed from the walls, white rectangles of unfaded wallpaper glaring at Rake like the soulless eyes of some villain he couldn't lay hands on.

The next day, Rake learned that Thames had sold to a Realtor the day before. And Thames was a no-show at a deposition into the theft of the CAHP money. Without the city's one witness, the Greers' lawyer petitioned the judge to drop the case. Seeing that the community was already moving on from the crime—most of them were moving, quite literally—the judge agreed. The case dropped, Malcolm and Hannah walked out of jail and returned to their home, sweeping up the broken glass.

In ten days, Hannah would go into early labor from the stress. Her small but healthy baby girl would be the first Negro born on that block in fifty years, yet by the time she mouthed her first words, the local playground would be busy with colored children.

⤙

Sue Ellen and her boys left Atlanta.

Their house, too, was within the newly Negroes-allowed area, so she had to sell. They moved to Macon, where two of Dale's sisters were raising families. Rake felt terrible when he remembered how calculating he'd once been, back when he'd imagined what might happen if Dale were jailed and Sue Ellen and the boys moved in with him. That had seemed like a horrible fate, yet now he wished he could have it. Anything would have been better than the crushing guilt he felt.

He had failed to protect Dale from himself, from Dale's delusions of power, from Dale's cloying need to cast himself as the hero against Negro marauders. Rake had failed to protect his family from the changes happening around them, failed to keep the neighborhood's anger from degenerating into violence, failed to win the support of any of his fellow officers. He likely would always be a pariah within the Department. First his former partner, Dunlow, disappears, and now two years later a white cop in a Klan getup is gunned down in a shoot-out in which Rake fired several shots. Would any officer ever trust him again? Who would promote someone with ties to two alarming incidents like that?

And who had the other Klansmen been, the ones who'd escaped into the night? Were they cops as well? Cops he worked with? He feared he would always be surrounded by enemies who pretended to be friends, smiling to his face while planning the best time to slip a knife in his back. He would need to keep his guard up forever.

He avoided discipline, though not suspicion, by leaving a few facts out of his official story. He explained that, after the GBI agents had spoken with him about Dale's suspected involvement in the Coventry attack, he'd talked to Dale to ask if it was true. Rake lied and said that Dale had denied it, which had seemed good enough to Rake, but that the next night he'd decided to drop by his brother-in-law's and ask a few follow-up questions. That's when the Irons brothers had shown up, and the Klansmen, and Mrs. Bleedhorn, leading to the violent culmination of at least two different blood feuds.

When Cassie asked Rake what had really happened with Dale, he told her the truth, making her vow never to tell another soul, certainly not Sue Ellen.

"You did the right thing," Cassie consoled him. "You put your family first. Anyone would have." She'd kissed him on the lips, something he hadn't felt he deserved or even wanted right then. "You do the right thing and you protect your family, then you're right with God. What He does from there, no one can predict."

He couldn't tell if such simplicity was naïveté or wisdom. Yet he clung to it.

Some good news: Delmar Coyle was under arrest for conspiracy to assault his cousin, Martin Letcher. Rake had finally managed to track down the man claiming to be "Whitehouse"—witnesses at the bar where he and Dale had met that night described him, and it turned out he, too, was a cousin of Coyle's and had felt their mutual relation, Letcher, needed to be taught a lesson. Rake wasn't confident those charges against Coyle would stick—with Dale dead, they lacked key testimony—but once arrested the Columbians had quickly informed on each other for various other assaults and crimes. Anxious to avoid doing more time, Coyle did try to tempt investigators with a story about how Rake had been more involved in that Coventry Klan beating than they realized, but the investigators didn't buy it. Or so Rake hoped.

The mysterious phone caller to Rake, claiming he'd seen Klansmen beating Malcolm, had been a ruse, called in by one of the Columbians to throw Rake on the Klan's trail. When Rake relayed this information to Smith, slightly apologetic for never solving the mystery of Malcolm's assault, Smith had thanked him hurriedly and hung up. It made Rake wonder if Smith actually knew more about Malcolm's beating than he let on, but at that point, Rake was past caring.

One thing was certain: if Boggs, Smith, or any other Negro officer ever asked another favor of him, he would decline. He wouldn't spit in their faces, no, but neither would he take a single risk for their cause ever again. He had his own battles to fight, and he couldn't afford to weaken himself by associating with the troubles that shadowed their every step.

The next shift for Boggs and Smith was very awkward indeed.

Boggs at first couldn't even bring himself to talk to his partner. Eventually he spoke, but only when necessary, avoiding the kind of chatter that usually made their shifts bearable. Smith had committed a grave sin in Boggs's eyes—no, the Lord's eyes, *anyone's* eyes—and just because it happened to be a sin that benefited Boggs greatly, that shouldn't matter.

Their case against Feckless, meanwhile, was as dead as Jeremiah and Quentin Neale. Too many dead men, who couldn't testify against Feckless. Malcolm only knew so much; the information he'd fed Boggs and Smith had been enough to lead them to the smuggling location and the shoot-out, but it wasn't enough to get a judge to sign a warrant for them to search Feck's bar or house. They and McInnis kept Malcolm's identity as their source secret, lest he face retribution. Feck had lost a lot of his men, and the former smuggling point at the rail yards was being watched carefully, so at least they'd hindered his operation for now. They would have to hope his many losses would convince him to walk away from smuggling again.

Malcolm had followed through on his promise to Smith, taking a construction job for one of Clancy Darden's new Negro housing developments and staying away from the Rook, so far.

Martin Letcher himself, though still recovering physically, was making out quite well financially. Agents backed by his real estate venture were happily buying homes from white families anxious to flee to the right side of the new color line. The agents would then, no doubt, resell those properties—at a significant markup—to Negro families who were even more desperate to leave the overcrowded, crime-ridden, run-down neighborhoods to which they'd previously been consigned.

Rake soon saw that he and Cassie had no option but to sell. He managed to work through a different Realtor, at least; he could not bring himself to talk to anyone associated with Letcher, anyone associated with the case. Yet in a way, he understood now, everyone was associated with it.

Their new home in Kirkwood, on the east side of the city, was not the disaster they'd feared. A retiring cop was moving to Savannah and wanted to unload his place quickly, no haggling. The front and backyards were smaller than their Hanford Park place, and the three-bedroom home needed more work, but it had an unfinished basement they might expand upon. The trees here weren't as tall, and the lack of an oak canopy would be especially disappointing in the summer heat. But that gave them a better view of the lavender sunsets, and they were still close to downtown. The neighbors seemed friendly so far, the lack of tension almost surreal.

"I might even like this place *better*," Cassie said the first night, when they sat in the backyard, listening to the new sounds: the different traffic patterns, the louder owls, the occasional train whistle.

"Me, too," Rake lied. Because as promising as the house was, living here felt like failure, and he feared it always would.

Boggs realized he was supposed to be happy now, yet he felt consumed with self-loathing.

He had Julie now, but at what cost? He had killed once before, in self-defense, yet this time, even though *he* hadn't been the one to pull the trigger on Jeremiah, guilt overpowered him. It was as though his selfish thoughts had been made flesh, compelling his partner to become a killer. Smith had killed in the war, many times, but surely this was different. Boggs's pride and jealousy and fear had allowed him to be morally compromised. He needed to put an end to it.

Two years earlier he had come close to resigning from his position. He'd had second thoughts after a near-death experience, deciding to stay on after all. But this time trauma was leading him in the opposite direction. He'd made too many mistakes, of the kind that weighed heavily on his soul. He couldn't possibly show Sage how to be a good man while being party to murder. Or maybe he just couldn't stand the thought of what Smith had done, couldn't bear to work with him any longer.

He remembered how, in his rookie days, McInnis had chastised him for writing overly professorial arrest reports laden with the fruits of a Morehouse education. So he used simple words and short declarative sentences in the resignation letter that he left on McInnis's desk one perfect late-October morning.

Smith couldn't sleep.

It wasn't the loud neighbors and it wasn't the sun rising too early after his night shift. It wasn't the booze he'd been drinking at night, alone, in his dingy apartment. It was the realization that he wasn't keeping pace with who he'd expected to be.

His own partner could barely look at him. Treated him like a moral leper. Which only made Smith angrier, wanting to justify himself. And as he lay awake in bed, he feared he *couldn't* justify himself, and that his sudden hatred of Boggs was fire that should be directed elsewhere.

What had he been thinking? His blood had been flowing and the adrenaline had clouded his judgment, he'd nearly been shot and beside him had stood his partner, a man he deeply respected, but who was still too naïve to realize how in danger he and his girl were. Smith had found himself pointing a gun at the source of all Boggs's problems, so why not? Why not?

He had crossed another line.

And lines are only ideas people dream up, to govern what should be possible, to keep you from moving toward the forbidden. Tommy Smith had gotten this far by ignoring lines, crossing them whenever he needed to take a next step, or talk to the right lady, or show people that he was not afraid.

But because he'd crossed that line, now he *was* afraid.

They found Thames on Tybee Island, hundreds of miles away. A man missed a stop sign that had been completely obscured by tropical shrubbery, and his Ford slammed into the side of Thames's Chevy. Thames tried to leave before filing a report, but a cop took down the drivers' info, learning that Thames was wanted for questioning in Atlanta, and what had happened to that five thousand dollars?

To Rake's surprise, Cassie's obsessively compiled log of the comings and goings of Negroes and all other suspicious traffic in Hanford Park had come in handy. One of the cars she had made note of turned out to match the description one neighbor had given of the getaway car from the Thames "robbery." Cassie had taken down the tag number when she'd spotted it on the previous day, stopping at that same house; the car was owned by one of Thames's friends, a man who, coincidentally, had bought himself a fine new car just two weeks later.

Rake wasn't sure whether Thames had been planning all along to use the neighborhood collection as a ruse for his own enrichment, or if he simply had proven unable to resist temptation, especially with the neighborhood going to hell.

Six in the evening, dark had fallen and Boggs was not walking the streets.

It felt so odd. He'd only had one night off a week for the past two years, with two weeks' vacation, but still, this was different. Right then Smith and the others were walking without him. He felt guilt not just for his decision but for the fact that he hadn't told them yet, hadn't done them that courtesy, which he realized was because of his all-consuming anger at Smith. He would need to drop by tomorrow, say a proper farewell.

He sat in a rocking chair on his parents' porch. Crickets revved their engines, and he wondered if they sensed they would all be dead in another week or two.

His mother, sister-in-law, fiancée, and future mother-in-law sat inside, sipping iced tea (no wine from Mrs. Boggs, no sir) and discussing the upcoming nuptials. Reginald's wife, Florence, had brokered the meeting, which Reverend and Mrs. Boggs had no doubt hoped would never occur, and Lucius and Julie had been afraid to propose. After an icy start, though, the ladies had gotten to talking (the reverend and Reginald, as usual, were running late). As the conversation ran to wedding colors and favorite Bible passages on love, Boggs had felt that his presence was less than necessary, so he'd stepped outside for a smoke, glad to see that they seemed to be treating Julie with respect.

He'd smoked most of the cigarette when a squad car pulled up in front of the house.

"Enjoying your freedom, Boggs?" Out stepped McInnis, skin ghostly in the streetlight. He walked up to the porch, glancing into the windows, perhaps impressed by the Boggs family estate but not one to comment on it.

"It's a lovely evening. What brings you out here—shouldn't you be at the precinct?"

"So should you." He gestured to the rocking chairs, Boggs nodded, and they both sat down. "I'm here to inform you that I've considered your resignation, and, after giving it careful thought, I've decided to reject it."

"You've— Excuse me?"

"You're still a police officer, and I'll expect you at the precinct tomorrow. Enjoy this night off. Have a nice dinner, clear your head, and I'll see you at tomorrow's roll call."

"Sir, I was serious. I am serious."

"So am I. And it so happens that at about the same time you turned in your notice, so did Officer Smith."

"*What?*"

"That's right, two resignation letters on the same day, expressing many similar sentiments. How you both feel you can't continue to work with one hand tied behind your backs, how you don't have proper institutional backing to do your jobs the way they need to be done. And how you've both made some mistakes you're having a hard time living with."

Boggs was stunned. "*Tommy* wrote that?"

"Yes. And let's just say that I found his letter much more believable than yours."

"But . . . why?"

"I know how desperately you want to be a good cop, Boggs. I see it in everything you do, the way you polish those buttons in the morning. The way you crumple up a report and start over if you hit the wrong key halfway through. I see it in the way you talk to the people we police, even when they drive you crazy. *Especially* when they drive you crazy."

He wasn't used to being complimented. By his sergeant, or his father. Or anyone but Julie.

"And guess what: you *are* a good cop. You will do more good, far more good, by continuing to serve in that uniform than you will if you walk away."

"I just . . . I've made some mistakes, and I—"

"Yeah, you wrote that. We've all made some mistakes. Welcome to life. I've made mine, too, as you know."

"What else did Smith write in his note?"

"I won't go into it all. But he felt his actions did not reflect well on the police department, and that it was best for him to step aside. I'm inclined to agree."

Boggs thought for a moment about the vastness of the responsibilities he himself had walked away from. Or tried to walk away from. "What about Slater?"

"He seems to have gotten our message. He lost his link to one operation when we busted Thunder Malley, and he can see that it's too much trouble to pick up where he left off."

"You think he's just going to go straight?"

"I don't know what he's going to do. But I think he realizes now that causing trouble in our precinct would be extremely foolhardy. You should feel good about that."

"It's hard to feel good with a man like that walking free. And wearing a badge."

McInnis rocked in his chair, hesitantly, like he'd never used one before and didn't entirely trust it. "That burns me up, too. But there will always be cops like him, and you're going to have to get used to it. That's why it's so important to hang on to as many good cops as I can find." He gazed out at the night. "You can't rid the world of snakes, Boggs. But you can do everything possible to make your property inhospitable to them."

Even though he didn't like everything McInnis was saying, it felt good to talk about this, to strategize, to make plans. To imagine a better city than the one he'd inherited.

McInnis said, "I'll camp out on this porch until you change your mind. You've always been hard on yourself, and I like that, but this time you're wrong. What you had to do out there was difficult, I know. Your head might not be right for a while. But we've got work to do yet, and walking away doesn't become you."

The front door opened and out walked Mrs. Boggs. "Lucius, stop hiding out here and . . . oh, I'm sorry." She looked flustered, only for a moment, as that was not the way she normally presented herself. Her dress and hair perfect as always, her jewelry sparkling from the light over her head. "I didn't know we had a guest."

Boggs himself was flustered—he hadn't yet told his parents about his resignation. With the wedding itself such a touchy subject, unemployment would have sent them over the edge. Julie he'd told, and she'd sounded supportive, but only because she'd thought it was what he wanted. When he was honest with himself, he realized she'd been disappointed in him.

"Sergeant Joe McInnis, ma'am," the uniformed officer said, removing his cap and nodding to her as he stood. "I work with your son. Sorry to intrude, I just needed to tell him something that couldn't wait."

"Felicia Boggs," she introduced herself. "I'll be out of your way, then."

"Not at all, we're finished," McInnis said, smiling. Boggs had rarely seen him so polite.

"Can I offer you some dinner while you're here? We're still waiting on my husband, but there's plenty."

Oh Lord. It was not unheard of to entertain white people at the Boggs residence, but he couldn't imagine McInnis at that table, getting a glimpse inside his private world. *Please say no.*

"Thank you, but I should be at work right now." He shot Boggs a look that said, *and you should, too.* "Good meeting you, ma'am. You've raised a fine young man, and you should be proud. Officer Boggs, I'll see you tomorrow."

No question mark on the end of that sentence. Yet he stood there an extra moment, awaiting Boggs's response.

"Yes, sir. I'll see you then."

To walk through the hallways of the *Atlanta Daily Times* was to court disaster. Stacks of newspapers rose knee-high in some spots, shoulder-high in others, allowing such narrow passage that Tommy Smith had to scoot sideways as he sought out Jeremy Toon's office. Some of the papers were new, ready to be sent out by newsboys to local subscribers and stores, or shipped to Terminal Station, where vendors would hawk them on the trains. Those copies would circulate across the country, but especially throughout the South. Porters, after reading every page, would leave them behind at small stations in South Carolina and Mississippi and Arkansas, like long-ago subversives scattering literature across the vast tundra of tsarist Russia, flickers of knowledge that might one day start a bonfire, ignite the masses, and smoke out their overlords.

Judging from the yellow borders, many of these papers were weeks or even months past. The *Daily Times* lacked the staff to clean up, so the papers accumulated like striations of some vast canyon, where future historians might plot the slow death of Jim Crow by excavating the layers: a story of a falsely accused young man here, a lynching there, a law passed here, a labor strike there, until finally at the top, please, Lord, flowers of a better day might grow.

"Officer Smith," Toon said, surprised. He sat in a tiny office in which two desks unhappily coexisted. He looked like he wanted to stand and greet Smith but was pinned in place by stacks of his past reporting.

Smith didn't bother correcting him on the "Officer." It was only the day before that he'd left his resignation letter on McInnis's desk, not standing around long enough to realize Boggs had already laid one there.

"To what do I owe—?"

"Your paper is terrible."

"Excuse me?" Toon favored tweed jackets, which with his tortoise-shell glasses made him appear like an academic, which he perhaps would have been if professorships for Negroes hadn't been as rare as six-toed bobcats.

Smith grabbed a copy off the nearest stack.

"You get some good stuff from the wires, and you're solid on Washington developments, I'll give you that. Got some smart people in the other Southern capitals, too. But here in town, where you should be cleaning up? C'mon. White papers get better info from city hall and the police station than you ever will. And don't get me started on your crime beat, Jeremy. You write about crime like a man who's never sinned in his life."

Toon stared for a silence that lasted a good five seconds, likely longer than he'd ever needed to respond to a professor's question.

"So you came in here today just to tell me this to my face?"

"I've come to offer you a bit of news. I resigned yesterday. And it seems to me, you could use another reporter. One who isn't afraid to put himself in tough spots."

Toon shook his head, slow to catch up. "You . . . what?"

"I need a job, and you need a reporter with some spine. So let's talk."

Five weeks after the shoot-out, Hanford Park had transformed.

South of Magnolia, every white resident had left. A mere two doors down from the Rakestraws' old place, in a house where Rake and Cassie had once been dinner guests, Boggs and Julie gave a tour of their new home to his parents. They walked through the front yard on a gorgeous November morning, the air cool but the sun kissing their skin, the gentle breeze whispering promises. A maple in the front yard had turned deep red, the ground beneath it littered with confetti of burgundy and scarlet. Down the block, redbuds had gone yellow, and the orange crape myrtles and mustard oaks glowed golden in the sunlight.

Reverend Boggs managed to mask his disappointment that Lucius hadn't bought a place in Sweet Auburn, asking if this meant they'd start attending another church. Lucius assured him that it was strictly a financial decision—the only homes anywhere near Auburn that he could afford sat on unappealing blocks.

But then again, these days no financial decision lacked politics, or history.

"It needs work, but not as much as my first place did, I can tell you that," the reverend said. "Wasn't a day I didn't spend a few hours hammering something, tearing out and putting in."

"That's not my strong suit."

"Next week I can help you with that sink, if you'd like."

Boggs knew he needed to buy tools, likely from the nearby hardware store, owned by Mr. Gilmore of the neighborhood association. He wondered what that experience would be like, if Gilmore would recognize him. The store sat on the new official border, but would the border stay there long? Would the store?

The government had declined to offer Boggs a low-interest GI Bill loan, as south Hanford Park was now a Negro area and thus deemed high-risk. As Reginald had predicted, the house cost more than he'd wanted to spend. Simple market economics: many Negroes wanting to buy a respectable home in a safe area, few such houses available to them. Nothing unfair or prejudiced about it, other than the fact that thousands of houses remained off limits to the Boggses due to their skin color and dislike of bombs thrown through windows.

The wedding was two months away. It was hard to figure how he might afford a mortgage payment *and* a car, but hopefully he could swing something.

"I like it more each time," Julie said, taking his hand as the reverend circled the house, inspecting the soffits and eaves.

Boggs asked Sage what color he'd like his room to be. Sage was still adjusting to the idea that he wouldn't share a room with his mother.

Sage said, "Purple."

"Purple, wow." He would have to ask him again later, keep asking until he received an acceptable reply.

Oak leaves lay scattered across the lot, as well as some pods from a massive magnolia next door. He mentally added *rake* to his apparently endless shopping list. The sheer magnitude of this endeavor seemed overwhelming, so he reminded himself to break it into discrete tasks, one at a time. He could do this.

A jet streaked overhead, lower than usual, and Sage pointed at its contrails, mouth open in silent awe. Lucius picked him up so the boy would be that much closer to it, his free hand shielding his eyes from the sun as Sage's tiny finger traced that line in the heavens.

ACKNOWLEDGEMENTS

Thank you to everyone I thanked on this page of *Darktown* (has it really only been a year?). Especially my family, from Mullen to Strickland, Comeau to Quant, Ruiz to Koenig, Menon to Newman; my editor, Dawn Davis, who did some especially heavy lifting with these pages; Judith Curr, David Brown, Yona Deshommes, and everyone else at 37 Ink and Atria; Susan Golomb and Rich Green for making this all possible; the many readers who have reached out to me and shared their stories and opinions over the last year; Atlanta police officers current and retired who have spoken with me about their experiences; booksellers everywhere; and Jenny.

Several books and articles were helpful in my research, too many to list, but I should point out in particular my debt to Kevin Kruse's *White Flight*.

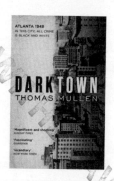

Atlanta, 1948. In this city, all crime is black and white.

On one side of the tracks are the rich, white neighbourhoods; on the other, Darktown, the African-American area guarded by the city's first black police force of only eight men. These cops are kept near-powerless by the authorities: they can't arrest white suspects; they can't drive a squad car; they must operate out of a dingy basement.

When a poor black woman is killed in Darktown having been last seen in a car with a rich white man, no one seems to care except for Boggs and Smith, two black cops from vastly different backgrounds. Pressured from all sides, they will risk their jobs, the trust of their community and even their own lives to investigate her death.

Their efforts bring them up against a brutal old-school cop, Dunlow, who has long run Darktown as his own turf – but Dunlow's idealistic young partner, Rakestraw, is a young progressive who may be willing to make allies across colour lines . . .

Soon to be a major TV series from Jamie Foxx and Sony Pictures Television.

A brilliant blending of crime, mystery, and American history. Terrific entertainment'
Stephen King

'Magnificent and shocking'
Sunday Times